Praise for *Kookaburra*

'Linnell's lightness of touch and straig[ht]... this delightful rural romance.' Better Reading

'*Kookaburra Cottage* sucked me in and held me captive, it was skilfully written, beautifully evocative of the setting and heartbreaking in its conflicts.' Mic Loves Books

Praise for *Paperbark Hill*

'A wonderfully rich, feel-good read. I just loved it and I know you will too.' Jodi Gibson, Books & Bakes blog

'Full of warmth, humour and genuine heart, just like eating scones fresh from the oven.' ABC Wide Bay

Praise for *Magpie's Bend*

'Immersing yourself in the country characters and spirit of Bridgefield is a delight.' CWA *Ruth* Magazine, Qld

'So many moments throughout the book that I caught myself smiling, it definitely was a story that had all the feels and left me with a full heart!' @KateTheBookLover

Praise for *Bottlebrush Creek*

'Loved this book ... such a delight from beginning to end.' Emma Babbington, *New Idea*

'Charming and enjoyable ... fans of Maya's first novel will keenly enjoy this latest outing.' *Canberra Weekly*

Praise for *Wildflower Ridge*

'*Wildflower Ridge* is a really wonderful place to start your Australian rural romance journey . . . told with plenty of heart and lashings of authenticity.' Mrs B's Book Reviews

'Five stars—a great addition to the rural family fiction with a dash of romance, a sophisticated plot, very convincing characters . . . a book you can't pass up.' Happy Valley Books

Bestselling rural fiction author Maya Linnell gathers inspiration from her rural upbringing and the small communities she has always lived in and loved. *Wallaby Lane* is her sixth novel, following *Kookaburra Cottage*, *Paperbark Hill*, *Magpie's Bend*, *Bottlebrush Creek* and *Wildflower Ridge*. A former country journalist and radio host, Maya also blogs for Romance Writers Australia, loves baking up a storm, tending to her rambling garden and raising three young bookworms. She writes to a soundtrack of magpies and chickens on a small property in country Victoria, where she lives with her family, their menagerie of farm animals and the odd tiger snake or two. For a regular slice of country living, follow Maya on social media or sign up to her monthly newsletter at mayalinnell.com.

@maya.linnell.writes

MAYA LINNELL

Wallaby Lane

ALLEN&UNWIN
SYDNEY·MELBOURNE·AUCKLAND·LONDON

First published in 2024

Allen & Unwin
Cammeraygal Country
83 Alexander Street
Crows Nest NSW 2065
Australia
Phone: (61 2) 8425 0100
Email: info@allenandunwin.com
Web: www.allenandunwin.com

*Allen & Unwin acknowledges the Traditional Owners of the Country on which we
live and work. We pay our respects to all Aboriginal and Torres Strait Islander
Elders, past and present.*

A catalogue record for this
book is available from the
National Library of Australia

ISBN 978 1 76106 961 1

Internal design by Bookhouse, Sydney
Set in 12.1/16.6 pt Sabon LT Pro by Bookhouse, Sydney
Printed and bound in Australia by the Opus Group

10 9 8 7 6 5 4 3 2

The paper in this book is FSC® certified.
FSC® promotes environmentally responsible,
socially beneficial and economically viable
management of the world's forests.

Dedicated to the tireless volunteers who keep country communities alive, especially the gems behind the scenes at the Tyrendarra show.

1

The radio station's production switchboard had been lit up like a Christmas tree all morning and Lauren Bickford was desperate for a double-shot latte and fresh air to blast away the 4.30am-alarm fatigue.

She bustled out of the studio and nearly bumped into a colleague in the hall. 'Woah, George, you right with that?'

The long-serving breakfast presenter, George Whitehead, peered over an armful of perilously stacked items: newspapers, coffee cups and his laptop. 'Absolutely,' he insisted, his emphatic nod making the mugs clink together. 'Only a fool would stand in the way of a producer and her caffeine fix.'

Lauren laughed, swooping in before the towering pile crashed to the ground. 'I'm going to miss your sweet-talking, George. Caravan all packed and ready?'

'Ready as we'll ever be. My wife's even vacuumed the curtains,' he said, attempting to open the staffroom door with his elbow. 'And how about you, Blondie?' He lowered his voice. 'Is your suit dry cleaned and ready to go?'

'I've never seen you wear a suit to work, George,' Lauren said, grinning and opening the door for him, 'nor any of the other presenters. But if it's good news tomorrow, perhaps I'll dust off the iron.'

'Dress for the job you want,' George replied. 'Those wrinkly shirts might be okay for the producer's box, but you'll want to look the part when you accept this new gig. As I told the HR team, you're the right lady to host the brekky show.'

'Fingers crossed,' Lauren said, donning a jacket and dashing outside into the crisp autumn air. Gold and ochre leaves crunched under her boots and puddles reflected the overcast sky, a timely reminder to pack her fingerless gloves for tomorrow's outside broadcast.

The barista, Jean Dellacourte, waved from the mobile coffee van. 'Lauren, you're late! I almost left.'

'Sorry, the listeners kept calling in. They're missing George already.' Lauren handed over her reusable cups, a twinge of anxiety running down her spine: excitement that she might finally step into the radio host's seat or nerves that she'd put herself out there with no guarantee of success? Probably both.

'It wasn't just George, everyone loved today's topics too. You've got a nose for good stories,' Jean said, lowering the radio volume and raising her voice over the grinding coffee beans. 'Everyone's got an opinion on the cost of firewood, especially when the temperature drops and folks are scrambling for a trailer-load of red gum.'

Lauren's topic suggestion had attracted calls from across the district, listeners sharing fond memories of family wood-chopping days and stories of snakes in wood piles and close chainsaw incidents. 'I'll be dreaming of a wood fire and lap rug tomorrow when we're broadcasting from Lacewing Estate. Fancy making a morning coffee run?'

'For a hardworking girl like you, I'll make an exception,' Jean said, promising she'd set up her coffee van bright and early.

The morning flew past and despite another coffee and the last of her Easter egg stash, Lauren was dead on her feet by 1pm. Yawning, she returned to her desk for another few hours, checked her running sheet one last time then lugged the recording equipment to the work car.

Heavy footsteps thumped behind her.

'Great show today,' said the station editor, Paul Wanganeen. 'Now go home and get some rest, all this overtime is going to kill my budget. Boss's orders, especially seeing George left hours ago.'

George is retiring, not hoping for a promotion.

'A couple more things to tick off the list, then I'll sleep easier,' Lauren said, resisting the temptation to ask her boss about the job announcement.

Less than twenty-four hours and you'll know one way or another, she told herself.

Satisfied they were packed for tomorrow's show, Lauren drove out of the radio station, leaving Mount Gambier for the vineyards, quaint shopfronts and houses of Penwarra. Instead of turning into Petticoat Lane and crawling into bed, Lauren continued through town to Lacewing Estate, where volunteers ran back and forth from the winery car park to the barrel room, arms laden with baking.

'Perfect timing,' called a familiar voice. Lauren's best friend, April Lacey, appeared with shopping bags over each arm, a smile on her face and the most sumptuous platter of sweets.

'It's busier than Rundle Mall in here,' Lauren marvelled, tucking her fair hair behind her ears and admiring the mini lemon tarts, homemade lamingtons and chunky chocolate chip biscuits on April's platter. 'It looks like you're hosting a wedding, not an art festival opening.'

April laughed, passing Lauren the platter. 'Our committee takes their art almost as seriously as their wine. I won't knock back the help, but it's almost eight o'clock. Shouldn't you be sleeping?'

'Dotting my i's and crossing my t's. I want tomorrow's live broadcast to go off without a hitch for George's last day.'

'Speaking of big days, when do they announce your job?'

'It's not *my* job.' Lauren looked at her watch, 'But we'll know in seventeen hours and fifty-two minutes. Whoever gets the gig has big shoes to fill.'

'What do you mean "whoever"?' April swatted Lauren's arm. 'You're a shoo-in. You know the region inside and out, and you've paid your dues in the producer's chair.'

Lauren wasn't so sure. 'If the outside broadcast runs smoothly, I'll feel better about my chances,' she said, waving as Geraldine Corcoran—resident cooking instructor, chef and the star of tomorrow's radio show—tore into the parking lot.

'I've been thinking about tomorrow, Lauren,' Geraldine said after she joined them. She cast a fraught look at Lauren. 'I can't do it. You don't want me tripping over my tongue. April's a far better choice!'

Lauren heard the older lady's voice falter. Geraldine barely batted an eyelid when faced with a classroom of incompetent cooks, she swam in the ocean without a wetsuit year round and regularly plated up for a hundred or more diners at the Penwarra Golf Course, but tonight she looked like she'd rather face a firing squad than a microphone.

'Nerves are okay, Geraldine.' Lauren offered a reassuring look. 'But that's why I'm here, we'll run through the questions and you'll be good to go tomorrow.'

And even though it was already an hour past her bedtime, and the alarm would hit like a tonne of bricks at 4 am, Lauren talked Geraldine through the interview, role playing the questions several times until Geraldine was comfortable.

She fell asleep with her fingers still crossed the moment she crawled into bed.

Jack Crossley pulled a seatbelt over his shoulder, gripped the steering wheel with two hands and looked in the rear-view mirror.

'Got your lunch box?'

His niece, Harriet, nodded, her glossy braids swinging.

'Drink bottle and hat?'

She pulled her thumb from her mouth, gave another nod, then fixed Jack with a look. 'I'll be fine, Uncle Jack. Do we have *your* lunch box, hat and drink bottle?'

Jack returned his eyes to the road, amused by the sass in his niece's reply. 'Roger that,' he said, as the rusty property sign for Sunny Cross Farm faded from view. The sign had been rustic when he'd first arrived in Penwarra as a teenager. Two and a half decades later, it was positively ancient.

'Now, you remember what your mum says?' Jack said as they pulled up at the school gate a little while later.

'Use my manners, smile when I say hello and wash my hands. But why do *I* have to smile when I don't want to, Uncle Jack? You don't always.'

'Ouch.' Jack cast a mock-wounded look over his shoulder. 'That's a bit rough, kiddo.'

'But it's true!'

'We'll swap notes over dinner tonight to see how we both scored on that front.'

Harriet crossed her arms and peered out the car window, the spitting image of her mother, Clem—all bluff and bluster, especially when she was nervous.

'What if no one else goes for Port Power, Uncle Jack?' She tugged at the neckline of the football guernsey they'd bought for the first themed dress-up day of the year.

Jack scanned the car park. 'I can see a bunch of Adelaide Crows supporters, a handful of interstate teams and some that forgot about footy day altogether, but there's a good spread of Port Adelaide fans too. You'll be right, Harri.'

She turned to Jack, her tiny hand on the car door handle. 'Do you think Mum will be okay?'

Jack unbuckled his seatbelt. Had she picked up on Clem's mood too? 'It's just a cold, she'll be fine,' he said, placing a bucket hat on Harriet's head, hoping his optimism sounded genuine to her little ears. It wasn't the coughing or sneezing he was worried about. 'Now let's get you signed in.'

The car park was swarming with students in their team colours, so Jack moved fast. He snapped the pre-requisite photo outside the classroom, sent it to the family group chat and wrapped his niece in a hug.

'Don't forget to be awesome,' he said.

'You too, Uncle Jack.'

Cars wheeled out of the school car park, but Jack pulled away slowly, using the short drive to the Penwarra Police Station to work out exactly when his sister Clem's morning had taken a nosedive. The farmhouse had been silent when he'd left for the pool at 5 am, and she'd seemed fine, albeit sleepy and a little sniffly when he returned from his swim to find her with Harriet eating breakfast.

The football-day fuss, that's what did it.

Clem had still been in her pyjamas at 8.45 am, the oven humming with muffins that hadn't been ready in time. Like with a lot of things, Clem's heart had been in the right place, but her determination to give Harriet the best footy-themed day hadn't gone to plan. It wasn't the football-shaped pancakes or the fishtail braids with black, white and teal ribbons that sabotaged the morning, nope, it was Clem's vision for a lunch box with all the bells and whistles, even though she was under the weather. A basic melt-and-mix muffin recipe might have worked, but after she'd coloured the cake batter, mixed up teal and white buttercream icing and shaped fondant into Port Power lightning strikes, it had been too late.

Jack's phone flickered on the dashboard as the brown brick police station came into view. He parked underneath a towering gum tree and checked his messages.

His grandfather, Arthur, had sent through a text with a string of emojis.

> Snazzy Port Power colours, Harriet! Hope your footy day is tops. When are we scheduling in another game of Scrabble, Jacko? I've got a ripper ready for the next triple-word score 🖊️🚗⚡

Jack replied, then pocketed the phone. Returning to Penwarra hadn't been easy, especially seeing as it was his first country posting, but it wasn't about him.

Clem will be fine, Jack told himself. He locked the ute and started for the station, wondering how long his promise to Harriet would last. Hand washing was a cinch and manners were pretty much automatic, but when it came to unnecessary smiling, he had a feeling his niece's scorecard would be better than his on that one.

Lauren pulled into the Rural AM radio station car park the following day, savouring the last post-program debrief with her friend and mentor George.

'You've done it, Blondie,' George told her, unbuckling his seatbelt. 'One of the best outside broadcasts I've heard, and a full complement of magnificent guests to boot. Wasn't sure you'd be able to coax Geraldine back to the mike after her first fluff-up, but you did well,' he said, adjusting his flat cap.

A bunch of helium balloons was tied to the station front door and the words 'Congratulations' beamed at them from the biggest silver balloon.

George grinned, nudging Lauren with his elbow and opening the passenger door. 'You got the job!'

Lauren shrieked with joy, almost tripping over her feet in her hurry to get out of the car and confirm her selection as the new breakfast show host.

'Didn't I tell you?' George, who was one step ahead, batted the big balloon away and opened the door. 'Bravo, Blondie, bravo!'

Colourful streamers crisscrossed the station staff room and every ounce of ill will towards the pernickety senior producer, Patrice O'Neill, evaporated when she rushed out of the staff kitchenette with a bunch of flowers in her arms.

'You're late,' Patrice said, frowning over her shoulder at Lauren. 'The sausage rolls will be dry as chips, they've been in the oven so long. Hold these, would you?'

Lauren froze as Patrice shoved the flowers into her hands, adjusted the ribbon, then reclaimed the bouquet.

'Congratulations on a brilliant final show,' Patrice said, passing the posy to George.

'Oh—' Lauren felt her cheeks flush scarlet, realising at the same time as George that the festivities were for him, not her. She whirled around, glimpsing the awkwardness on George's face, and marched down the corridor, so intent on reaching the bathroom she nearly collided with the station editor, Paul.

'Ah, Lauren. You got a minute?'

The tiny hope Lauren had been holding onto fizzled out as Paul walked with her to his office, sat on the edge of his desk and steepled his fingers.

'Look, it's never easy—'

Lauren slumped into a chair. 'They passed me over again?'

Paul's grim nod was confirmation enough.

A knock at the door and Patrice's voice carried through the thin wall. 'Any time you're ready, then. We've got speeches to get through.'

'Thanks, Patsy, we'll be there in five.'

Patrice's indignant 'hmppfft' was like petrol on a bonfire for Lauren.

'This is bulldust,' Lauren said, shooting out of the seat. 'I interviewed perfectly. The HR lady loved me, *you* encouraged me to go for it and George gave me a glowing reference.'

'I'm sorry, Lauren. My hands were tied.' Paul shifted on the desk, sending papers fluttering to the floor.

'Did they listen to the material I uploaded?' Lauren blew out a breath, pushing her hair away from her flaming cheeks. 'Nobody knows the district like me, Patrice doesn't want the job and the fill-in guy is worse than a sensor light, only works when someone walks past.'

Paul shook his head. 'I can see you're upset.'

'Really? What did they say, though? They can't fob me off without feedback. Maybe I can change their minds,' she said, a pleading note in her voice. 'Do they want more references?'

'You've made great progress with your delivery and with sourcing news,' Paul said, 'but management didn't think you were ready yet.'

'Ready? I've done the graveyard shift for four years, darn it.'

'I like your spunk, Lauren, and you're right; you know the lay of the land better than any outsider. But you're working for the national broadcaster, not a dinky independent station or community radio. Freezing on air is only okay when you're a junior. They want to see more public speaking experience, more time in the presenter's chair without any hiccups.'

'But how can I get better at managing my on-air nerves without more on-air opportunities?'

Another knock came at the door, then Patrice tapped on the office window, pointing to her watch. 'Chop chop! The party pies are going cold.'

Her footsteps disappeared down the corridor at a brisk pace.

'I think we're done here,' Paul said gently, opening his office door. 'Come have a sausage roll. I've got bubbly in the fridge and we really do need to toast George's farewell before his missus hooks up the caravan and heads off without him. You're a fine producer, Lauren, and one day we'll make a presenter out of you.'

Lauren slowly re-rolled the cuffs of her blazer so the striped satin lining was on display and pictured her mum's response.

Hold your head high, especially in the face of defeat. Gabrielle Bickford would be bitterly disappointed about the job, but she'd be equally horrified if one of her girls dissolved into tears at work. *Chin up, keep powering on.*

Lauren swiped at her smarting eyes, straightened her spine and headed for the staff room, searching for positives within the disappointment.

Clem Crossley's battered jeep was in the driveway when Jack pulled into Sunny Cross Farm that afternoon. He parked, grabbed a cloth from the shed and dampened it before polishing the bugs from the front bumper of his 4 x 4. The cloth didn't clean off every splatter, but his evening habit kept the vehicle looking smart between weekend washes. He moved to Clem's car, scrubbing at the headlights and the grille, but the bugs didn't budge.

'Uncle Jack!' Harriet stood by the laundry door, her dark hair swirling around her face and flour smeared across her cheeks. 'We're making a passionfruit log and Mum's rolling it up in a tea towel!'

Jack stepped out of his boots and followed her into the kitchen.

'Don't even look at the mess,' Clem warned, glancing up from the rectangular sheet of sponge cake as he assessed the sprawl of bowls, trays, wire racks, measuring tools and ingredients. 'We're in the middle of our pièce de résistance.'

'Chocolate sponge with passionfruit?'

Harriet beamed. 'That was my idea. So it looks like a real log!'

He wasn't sure how the combination would taste, but if their smiling faces were the benchmark for a successful afternoon's baking, it was already a winner in his books.

'Hope you don't have plans for dinner,' Clem said, carrying the tea towel roll to the dining table. 'But no stress if you do,' she hurried to add. 'We can save you some.'

'No plans apart from a quick bike ride before it's dark and grilling Harri about her day,' Jack said. 'Dinner sounds good, thanks.'

The coat rack by the door was laden with quilted jackets and vests but he found a spot for his duffle jacket and picked his way past tubs of their grandparent's knick-knacks, piles of crockery and partially sorted bed linens. Sentimentality had hampered Clem's best efforts at decluttering the rest of the house in the months since they'd arrived, and the spare room resembled an auction storeroom, especially with Clem and Harriet's unpacked belongings.

'The second-hand store will take the antiques,' Jack reminded his sister. 'And I can help shift them on the weekend.'

Clem shot him a pained look. 'It'd be easier if we didn't know the stories behind every piece. The record player Pop bought Nan for her fortieth. The matching armchairs she recovered five or six times. Pop's recliners, the drinks trolley, the little side table you made in high school.'

Jack laughed. 'That wobbly side table's the opposite of an antique.'

'Is it just me, or is it weird living here without Nan and Pop?' Clem asked, looking around the house Arthur and Shirley Crossley had built as newlyweds.

'Strange as,' Jack agreed, setting the table. 'I keep expecting Nan to wander out of the laundry with our school shirts in one hand and the ironing board in the other.'

'Or Pop to amble in from the sunflower paddocks, dust in every crease of his clothing and those faded bucket hats he liked. I can hardly bear to toss his old work clothes in the bin.'

'He doesn't need much at the retirement village, and don't hang onto anything on my behalf. There's enough in my storage unit to fill the station house once it's ready.'

'But we like you living with us,' Harriet said, bringing water glasses to the table. 'Can't you stay forever?'

'Not sure it's Uncle Jack's dream setup, but he does own half the house, so it's his as much as it is ours. Stay as long as you want, Jack.'

Clem was kinda right. If someone had told him eighteen months ago he'd be sharing a house with his sister, he would've frisked their pockets for drugs. But the gift of their grandparents' farmhouse, combined with the Penwarra policing position and Clem's redundancy, had felt like three ducks had waddled into their lives and lined up in a millimetre-perfect row.

'You'll be sick of me after a few months,' Jack said. 'And the station house is part of the job. My door's always open for you two. Especially if you bring desserts like this.'

He'd eaten more sweets in the last five months than the last five years, but the pride in Harriet's smile and boost in Clem's confidence as she plated up each delicacy, were worth every calorie.

2

'Sorry again for the misunderstanding, Blondie,' George said, tipping the brim of his flat cap towards Lauren. 'I've felt wretched all day. I really thought the fuss was in your honour. You're a plucky thing, though, it took mettle to soldier on in there.'

'Wouldn't miss it for the world, George.' Lauren wound a scarf around her neck. She'd gritted her teeth and smiled through the cake and speeches, turned her phone to silent as the impatient texts flooded in from her mum, sister and best friend, and resigned herself to giving George the farewell he deserved instead of retreating to lick her wounds.

She collected her car keys, studying the Moroccan carved camel keyring, the plastic Eiffel Tower and the porcelain babushka doll. The wanderlust she'd had while bouncing between radio and newspaper jobs, high on the thrill of European adventures, provided her with the answer she needed, just a moment before George asked, 'Am I right in thinking you already have a Plan B simmering away?'

'The start of a very loose plan,' Lauren admitted, smiling properly for the first time since lunch. 'I'll chase a short-term secondment to another radio station, one that'll offer airtime to get the experience I need.'

'Atta girl,' George said, bracing her shoulders with his hands and giving an almost fatherly squeeze. Her dad had been a fit and healthy forty-something when they'd lost him, and while George was years older, she'd always appreciated his paternal warmth. 'I knew they wouldn't keep you down for long,' he said, hugging her goodbye.

The phone reception between Mount Gambier and Penwarra was notoriously patchy, and Lauren waited until she was past the sawmills and the small towns that had once thrived in the peak of the forestry industry before dialling April's number.

'Cancel the celebration dinner,' she said, getting in quickly before her best friend's hopeful question.

'You're kidding me? You were a dead cert.'

'Apparently not,' Lauren said, giving April the abridged version of the day. April's loyal indignation, outrage and assurances that the radio station had made a monumental mistake soothed Lauren's wounded pride.

'Did your mum lose her mind?'

'We'll find out in about five minutes.'

'Need me to come by and referee? You can put Gabrielle on speakerphone and we can play Bickford Bingo. Five bucks says she'll try to convince you to move back to the city again.'

Lauren parked outside her pretty pink cottage on Petticoat Lane. 'You're on. Ten bucks says she'll mention Tahnee's pre-tax income and remind me that I should aim higher.'

They both laughed. Gabrielle Bickford *wouldn't* take the news in her stride. Nor would Lauren's big sister, Tahnee.

Lauren took a moment to appreciate the late afternoon light and the way it transformed the soft weatherboards of her house to king-protea pink. The feminine facade was a daily reminder that strength and stability come in all shapes and sizes.

The screeching started the moment Lauren unlocked the heavy front door.

'Cool bananas! You're flamin' mad! Give us a beer then!'

'I'm sorry, Gaz,' Lauren crooned. She unlatched the large aviary and put her hand inside, but instead of climbing onto her wrist and allowing himself to be petted, Gary—a pink and grey galah—hopped from one perch to another, squeezed into his nesting box and sulked.

'I'll get you some sunflower heads and cuttlefish on the weekend,' she said, topping up his seed bowl and adding an Iced VoVo biscuit as a peace offering. She took a second biscuit for herself, poured a gin and tonic and braced herself for the phone call ahead.

'We've had the champagne on ice for hours, darling. Were you out celebrating?' Gabrielle said when she answered.

Lauren sank onto the couch and kicked off the lace-up boots that were a fraction too snug across her toes. 'I didn't get the job, Mum.'

The line was silent for two sips of G&T and Lauren was just raising the glass to her lips for a third time, when Gary burst out of his nesting box with one of his favourite phrases. 'Piss off, Curly! Piss off, Curly!'

Lauren startled and the mulberry-flavoured gin and tonic slopped down her knit blouse. She uttered a few salty words of her own as she mopped up the spill.

Gabrielle sighed. 'I wish you'd rehome that infuriating bird. What happens when your editor calls after hours? She must have quite the sense of humour.'

'He,' Lauren corrected. 'Not she. And if Paul needs me after hours, he's more of a texter, not a caller.'

'Your sister's phone rings all hours of the night, you know. Meetings with Japan, powwows with the Danish clients, updates from the Florida team. Tahnee dropped in for dinner yesterday and that phone barely stopped buzzing the whole time. But at least she gets paid accordingly.'

Strike one for Bickford Bingo. Lauren fixed herself another gin, stronger this time, and tried not to compare her mid-level radio job to her sister Tahnee's executive role at a prestigious law firm. *We both work hard. Success looks different for everyone.*

'Your sister will be furious when we tell her you were overlooked. Furious!' Gabrielle's ire set off a round of barking in her Unley Park townhouse. 'We are not happy about this, are we, Bruno? No, no, no.' Gabrielle's tone momentarily softened to the baby voice she reserved for her daschund, but once her attention was back on Lauren, she was all business. 'I'm sure it's against some HR protocol. Tahnee can help me find a legal loophole.'

Lauren managed a laugh. 'It's not high school, Mum. You can't send in letters appealing my grades.'

'We're gutted for you, sweetheart, really we are. If you were in Adelaide we could recap the interview, examine their feedback and work out where you went wrong.'

'Not that again, Mum. I'm not planning on moping around. I'm already working on Plan B.' *Poking sticks into my eye would be better than an interview post-mortem with my mother.*

'That's the spirit! I'm glad you've come to your senses. That tiny country town was always just a stepping stone. Stuff the lot of them!'

'I'm not leaving for good, Mum. Just a short secondment to iron out a few kinks and nail the job next time it comes up.'

While the thought of another panel interview made Lauren shudder, it was better than waiting for luck to find her—or worse, letting her family shoehorn her into a corporate career she didn't want.

After investigating a suspected break-in that turned out to be the homeowner's daughter 'borrowing' her parents' holiday house, and a welfare check on an elderly resident, Jack arrived back at the police station later that week to find the calendar on the wall had half-a-dozen new entries.

Sammi Altschwager, the station receptionist, bounced into the office, her ability to text and talk while walking despite barely looking at the phone in her hand making him feel even older than his forty-two years.

'Just in time, boss,' she said. 'You're due at a ribbon cutting in fifteen minutes.'

He frowned at the calendar. 'You sure I need to attend this luncheon?'

Sammi tossed him the patrol ute keys. 'If it were me, the lure of cake would make it a no-brainer, but it's not the same for a health-nut like you, is it?'

'I'm not a health—'

'Ahem?' Sammi cut him off mid-protest, with a pointed look at the carbon-frame bicycle, helmet and cycling shoes beside Jack's desk.

Jack shrugged. There were worse habits than lunchbreak workouts. Short of police emergencies, Mondays and Fridays were for cycling, Tuesdays and Thursdays for jogging and Wednesdays were for weights, plus the morning laps at the town pool.

'And don't get me started on your boring lunch box, either. I'd take a CWA catered luncheon any day of the week over those pitiful leftovers in the fridge.'

Biting back a smile, Jack pocketed the keys. 'Just saying, I'd get more bang for the taxpayer buck with an hour on highway patrol or dropping into the local businesses and saying g'day than swanning around at the Wildlife Sanctuary, watching them cut a ribbon for a bunch of new enclosures.'

Nevertheless, Jack put his hat on, then adjusted his belt. Unlike in Adelaide, he wasn't carrying the full quota of weapons and he suspected it would take some time to get used to the lighter load. He grabbed a water bottle from the fridge, wiped down each surface of the kitchen, then applied 50+ sunscreen.

Sammi followed him to the door. 'Try to have fun.'

Jack drove past the award-winning wineries, down a series of back roads and eventually along a limestone track until he reached a succession of homemade welcome signs. Judging from the cars lining the driveway and flowing out onto the dusty laneway, the wildlife shelter was a much-loved community facility.

Colourful flags flanked the entrance and the low hum of conversation, plus the unmistakable sounds of country music, came from the far end of the property. An older lady waved him over to the food table.

'Good to see you've settled into town, Mr Crossley, though it's a shame they couldn't have your accommodation ready in time,' she said with a 'tsk'. 'Fancy that, offering you a job in January and not having the station house renovations completed five months later. Lucky that old farmhouse is plenty big enough.'

'Sure is,' Jack replied, trying to conjure her name from the wealth of residents he'd met in the last few months. He mightn't know many faces yet, but Penwarra knew him, alright.

'I'm ruddy glad they didn't send us a fresh-faced young whippersnapper from the city. Least you've had a little life experience.' Her sharp gaze went from the smattering of silver at Jack's temples to his belt. 'You look like you could do with a good feed though.'

Despite Jack's protests, the woman piled his plate high with sandwiches, quiches and savouries, adding three more items after he'd assured her there was plenty. 'Don't forget the condiments,' she said, gesturing to the smorgasbord of jam jars and chunky chutneys. 'Not a patch on your nan's preserves but better than any of that store-bought rot.'

'Thank you,' Jack said, spooning sticky chilli jam onto a devilled egg and calculating the extra cardio he needed to do that evening to counteract the sumptuous lunch.

The woman pointed to the chalkboard by the steaming urn. 'They're running guided tours on the hour—you'll just catch them. Don't forget to swing past afterwards, the sweets will be out by then.'

And while Jack wasn't sure he'd manage such an enormous lunch, let alone sweets, he thanked her and went in search of the tour group.

Jack was impressed with the facilities for injured and orphaned native animals, especially the quirky possum shed, which had been fashioned from recycled materials to resemble an old miner's hut.

'Possums might look cute, but as a protected species, they can be tricky to evict from your roof and garden,' said wildlife carer and today's tour guide, Sean Dainty.

'Not wrong there,' said the lady next to Jack with a frustrated sigh. 'When they're not stealing fruit and veggies from my garden, they're munching on my rosebuds just before blooming! Barely had a rose left by the time the brushtail possums had their fill.'

Jack's phone rang and he let the tour group walk ahead. 'All good, Pop? Is Clem okay?'

'No need to sound so worried, Jacko.' Arthur Crossley's rusty laugh came down the line. 'And your sister's probably relishing the peace and quiet. I was just calling to see how you're faring. Out and about, from the sounds of it?'

Jack leaned against the rustic possum hut and told his grandfather about the open day.

'Harriet would love that. What do they have?'

'Fruit bats, possums, a wedge-tailed eagle, wombats, wallabies, kangaroos, potoroos, flying foxes, turtles,' Jack recounted the animals he'd seen. Just thinking about the feeding and cage-cleaning schedule and the kilos of food and milk powder the centre used every day made his head spin. 'What *don't* they accept?'

It caught Jack off guard when somebody other than his grandfather answered.

'Domestic animals,' said the flat voice.

Jack whirled around, not seeing anyone. It wasn't until he lifted his sunglasses and peered far into the possum enclosure that he spotted a figure inside.

'I'll call you back, Pop,' he said, then pocketed the phone and frowned at the near-invisible eavesdropper. After two decades in the force, Jack was normally much more alert, automatically aware of each and every person in the room, suspicious until he had reason not to be.

'Why on earth are you hiding in there?' The question came out sharper than Jack had intended.

Stepping out of the shadows, the teenager dipped a hand into the front of a baggy T-shirt and Jack couldn't help automatically reaching for his holster.

'Hey, hands where I can see them.'

'Shh,' the boy growled. 'Keep your voice down.' He pulled a small possum from the neckline of his shirt. It was clearly not in favour of leaving its warm, dark, human cocoon and by the time the boy had carefully extracted the creature and returned it to a fabric pouch, his neck was covered in fine scratches.

This is a country kid, Jack reminded himself, *not a wannabe gang member.*

The boy locked the enclosure behind him. When he stepped out into the light, Jack surmised he was about sixteen or seventeen. Like the tour guide Sean, this kid wore a khaki shirt with the sanctuary logo on it. But unlike the adults with their matching baseball caps, the boy wore a flat cap backwards. A curtain of greasy hair hung over his ears. His arms were criss-crossed with faded ink designs, waves, intricate mandalas and little animals, all the way up to his biceps.

'You a volunteer?'

'Sebastian Dainty,' the teenager said. 'Which is why I'm here instead of smiling for the cameras. And as I was saying before, my parents only take natives. No cats, dogs, turkeys, sheep, goats,' he added with a sigh, intent on his dusty shoes. 'Especially not goats.'

'Can't save them all.'

'Not that it stops people dropping off strays on a regular basis. Just yesterday someone left a sack of kittens by the gate with no water or nothing.' He gave a snort of disgust. 'Scum.'

Jack agreed with him. Unfortunately, he'd seen kids in the city subjected to similar levels of neglect.

'They're cutting the ribbon soon,' Jack offered, looking at his watch. 'Shouldn't be too long before everyone clears out and leaves you guys in peace.' He pointed to the penmanship on the teen's forearms. 'Nice drawings.'

Sebastian folded his arms and the biro-drawings disappeared from view before Jack could comment any further.

A woman bustled up to them, peered at Jack's name tag and gave a sharp nod. 'Art and Shirley's grandson, right?'

Jack didn't blame the teenager for shrinking into the shade. There was something schoolmarmish about the woman's bossy tone and pointed finger.

'How can I help?'

'Well for starters, you can go home via Victor Jenkins' disgraceful property,' she said, tapping Jack's arm as if he were personally responsible for the issue. 'Car bodies, grass up to your ears ... You can barely drive past his boundary without spotting a tiger snake or a copperhead. It's a stone's throw from your grandfather's old sunflower farm. Someone needs to do something about it—'

Jack nodded, lifting his hand to interrupt but the woman shook her head and waved her finger at him.

'And then there's my chickens. Someone keeps breaking into the hen house. Three chickens I've had stolen this year, and some days there's barely an egg in the nesting boxes. That's a lot of empty egg cartons, Constable Crossley.'

'Foxes, perhaps?' he ventured.

She bristled as Sebastian let out a snicker of laughter.

'This isn't a joke, young man. Foxes leave feathers and mess, and I'm yet to hear of an egg-eating fox. Mark my words, there's something fishy afoot, now it's chickens and eggs, next they'll be stealing pumps from water tanks and pinching hot water services from new house builds. At least mark Victor Jenkins' property into your official complaints register. I'm not the only one who's fed up.'

Jack promised to note down both matters.

Once she was gone, Sebastian stepped out of the shadows. 'Vic used to help with some of our overflow,' he said. 'When Mum and Dad had too many wallabies and roos, Vic would raise the odd joey, sometimes the runts that needed the extra attention. Oldies like her—' he glared at the woman heading for the exit, '—they might toss a bit of cash around, make themselves feel better about the cause, but Vic does his bit too.'

The teen paused and Jack had the sense he wanted to say more.

'If you see Vic, can you tell him I said hi? I haven't visited in ages and I could use his help with an ... um ... overflow issue.'

'Isn't today all about new extensions and extra space for more animals?'

'Well, don't go out of your way if it's a big deal,' Sebastian huffed, eyes flashing.

'It's not a problem,' Jack said. 'I can pass on the message. What do you want me to tell him? That you've got a joey?'

Sebastian's eyed darted back to the possum enclosure he'd been perched in and if it hadn't been for Jack's police training, he may not have noticed.

'Something other than a joey?'

Sebastian kicked the dirt with his boots.

Boy, he'd be easy to fleece in a game of cards. Jack waited, curious to see if the boy would trust him with whatever it was.

'It's a kid goat,' Sebastian blurted out eventually. 'And Dad can't stand goats. I mean, he, like, really, really hates goats.' His words came out in a rush, coinciding with a round of polite applause from the audience. 'I was gonna keep it here for a week or two, just until it was stronger, then give it to someone like Vic or surrender it to the pound. I'll be grounded all holidays if Mum and Dad find out.'

Jack chewed his lip. He didn't owe this kid anything, and it probably wasn't wise to get caught in the middle of a family tiff, but there was something about the edge to Sebastian's voice.

'Can't you give it back to whoever dropped it off?'

Sebastian shook his head. 'My mate was supposed to dong it on the head when it was born, because it's only got one eye. Not a good look for a stud breeder. Mum and Dad have been so busy getting this place ready for today, they haven't noticed.' He sighed. 'Yet.'

'And now it's in the possum house?'

'Vic's is too far to ride my bicycle with a goat in a backpack.'

Jack couldn't help it, his lips twitched at the mental image of a teenager cycling along the road with a goat in a backpack.

Sebastian scowled at him. 'Go on then, have a laugh. Hardy-bloody-har. Or you could help me out and drop it to Vic on your way back.' He scratched at his ear and shot Jack another grudging look. 'Please?'

By the time the speeches were over and the crowd had started to disperse, the goat was stowed in a dog carrier in the back of the ute, along with half a bag of milk powder.

Jack opened the passenger door, trying to avoid eye contact with the pitiful, one-eyed animal. He'd go direct to Victor's house, and then back along Wallaby Lane to Sunny Cross Farm. No way he wanted to risk Clem and Harriet falling in love with the darn thing.

※

'Too early to light the fire?' Lauren asked Gary, offering the galah a sheet of newspaper, which he promptly shredded. Even though it wasn't particularly icy outside, she was in the mood for carbs, comfort food and a cosy wood fire.

Clouds scudded across the sky while Lauren collected an armful of kindling from outside, and the soft patter of rain settled on the roof as she scrunched up the sports section to light the fire. Soon the fire was roaring, Heinz spaghetti was bubbling away in a pan on the top of the wood burner and she was settled on the couch with her laptop.

Just a quick look at the job ads, she promised herself.

The broadcasting intranet was a rabbit warren of information, but she soon found what she was looking for. And while the bureau over the border in Warrnambool didn't have any backfill openings for presenters, there was a short-term journo's position up for grabs. Her bottom lip caught between her teeth, Lauren tapped out a quick email.

'Three months in South West Victoria, Gaz. Reckon we can handle that?'

The galah hopped along the floor towards her and used his beak and claws to climb up to her shoulder. Lauren smoothed his rosy chest, traced the delicate curve of his silver wing and tickled the sweet spot beside his ear that made him coo.

She ate dinner at the dining table, determined not to refresh her email for at least an hour, but she had barely finished the washing up when the laptop dinged. 'Bloody heck, bloody heck,' sang Gary, bopping up and down with his feathered crest fanned out.

Lauren hurried to the laptop, then grinned at the bird. 'Get your whale-watching binoculars ready, Gaz, looks like we're daytripping to Warrnambool for a meet and greet this weekend.'

The sun was spreading its golden tendrils towards the horizon when Jack pulled up outside Victor Jenkins' property that evening. The old lady at the wildlife sanctuary luncheon was right about one thing: the place *was* a pig sty.

Many years ago, when the paddocks at Sunny Cross Farm had bloomed with sunflowers, Jack had been able to glimpse the beginnings of Victor's car collection from his grandparents' back porch. The sunflowers were long gone, but the shelter belts of native trees had since grown, blocking their view of what now looked like a car cemetery, not the collection of an enthusiast.

A 'private property' sign hung from Victor's gate, but even that was tired, with rust peeling the corners and the print faded by the sun. A tortoiseshell cat was perched on the gate post, a tabby sunned itself on the brick path, a pair of ginger kittens scampered out from under a decaying car body and an enormous fluffy white cat groomed itself on the front doormat. All but the fluffy cat fled when Jack shut the car door and opened the gate.

After knocking on the door and receiving a 'you want me to move?' look from the snowy cat, Jack surveyed the property. It was even worse up close.

Victor answered the door after several knocks, and while he wasn't much younger than Arthur, age hadn't treated him well.

Victor squinted at the uniform, then the plastic crate Jack held. 'Another cat hater, huh? Join the queue,' he snorted and made to shut the door.

Jack shook his head, put his boot inside the door and removed his cap.

'I'm Jack Crossley. Shirley and Art's grandson. And I'm not here to collect anything.' He lifted the carrier. The goat wobbled on its spindly legs. 'Sebastian hoped you'd save this fellow from the gallows.'

Victor folded his arms over his chest. 'So this isn't about the cats?'

Jack shook his head and set the carrier on the ground.

'Or the cars?'

Jack shook his head again. *Not today.* 'The goat's got a birth defect, so the breeders planned to destroy it. Sebastian thought you'd take it, but it doesn't have to be your problem.'

'I'll see about that,' said Victor, his arm shaking under the weight of the carrier.

'Sebastian sent along milk powder too. Where shall I put it?'

'Gate's fine,' Victor said brusquely and, with a click of the door, Jack was dismissed.

3

The final weeks of autumn disappeared as quickly as the mild weather, and before Lauren knew it, it was time to dig out the winter woollies, prepare the cottage for a few months without her and decide which essentials deserved a spot in her luggage.

Lauren dumped the second basket of washing in the hallway, the tower of wet towels and bed linen higher than the bags she'd packed for the Warrnambool secondment.

Her rickety clothes hoist struggled to manage one load, let alone two, and with a weekend of rain to come, there was bugger all chance of the washing drying on the line. 'Think we should outsource it, Gaz?' she asked, squashing the king-sized sheets back into the basket.

Gary trilled from his perch on the lampshade.

'I'll take that as a yes,' she said, enticing the bird back into his cage with a handful of damp milk thistles from the front garden and a dusty paperback, which he'd delight in shredding in her absence.

Lauren arrived at the laundromat with her brimming washing baskets, a small cushion and a bag of snacks. The laundromat was toasty warm as the industrial-strength washers

27

and dryers worked their magic. She loaded coins and the contents of her baskets into two dryers and retreated to the hard plastic seats with her cushion.

'Looks like you came prepared,' said a deep voice. A man came through the doorway cradling a laden washing basket. 'Those plastic chair are like granite. You'd think they could spring for comfier seats.'

'Not wrong there.' She grinned, pleased she'd remembered her cushion. Although the man was vaguely familiar, and a little older than her, she adjusted her age estimate when she noticed flecks of silver in his closely cropped dark hair.

He loaded the dryer with pinks, sunny yellows and lilacs. Definitely not his wardrobe, judging by his monochrome jeans, jumper and baseball cap. Where had she seen him before? One of the town's new footy coaches or teachers? Or was he the new manager sent to sort out the swimming pool's sticky-fingered staffing issue?

He set the first machine running and headed for the door, abruptly turning on his heel.

Startled at being caught gawking, Lauren said the first thing that came to mind. 'You're braver than me, I worry someone's going to pinch my good linen if I drop and run.'

He smiled, a grin that went as quickly as it came, then hooked a thumb over his shoulder. 'Nah, just getting the next load. Harriet would have my head if I let someone steal her Bluey pyjamas.'

She smiled back, factoring a small child named Harriet into the equation but still coming up blank. *Was he in the young professionals group with April, maybe?*

It wasn't until he'd returned with the second load of washing and his phone rang while he was filling the dryer that it clicked.

'Sorry, Aunty Jean, I haven't had a chance to call back,' he said, wedging the phone between his ear as he kept loading the clothes.

Jean! Penwarra's beloved mobile barista had mentioned her great-nephew returning several times.

'I think we met at Beachport over summer,' Lauren said once he'd ended the call and settled on a plastic chair. She introduced herself, pleased to finally have all the facts in order when he introduced himself in return.

'No hiding away in a small country town, right?'

Lauren gave a sheepish shrug. 'I work at a radio station, it's my business to know everyone else's business. And even if I didn't, your aunt makes it her mission to spread the word.'

Jean was also the town Cupid, with a dogged determination to match up every singleton in town, but Lauren knew *that* wasn't a smart rainy day laundromat conversation topic. At least not with a handsome stranger.

'Harriet's your little girl?'

Jack followed her glance towards the blur of pink and purple in the dryer. 'My niece,' he corrected, flipping open a newspaper.

He didn't look up as she rifled through the free library beside the vending machine, but as she flicked through the pages of a hard-cover literary novel, trying to decide between it and a romcom she'd already read, he said, 'That novel's even harder going than these seats.' He met her eyes briefly. 'You'll need tissues.'

If he thinks I'm the type of girl who sobs over a book in a laundromat, then he's got another thing coming. Keeping a tight rein on her emotions had been as important in the Bickford household as table manners and the nightly homework routine.

Lauren offered him some corn chips, unsurprised when he declined. Then, after reading the lengthy prologue of the brick-sized novel, she passed the time making a few assumptions of her own.

The only thing Jack was wearing that wasn't black were the white soles of his sneakers. The shoes were either brand new or he was the type of guy to clean them each time he veered off the footpath. And those toned arms weren't a happy accident, it took discipline or hard labour for a physique like that.

She returned to the novel. Apart from the whirring of the machines and the rain pounding the footpath outside, Lauren and Jack read in silence.

Lauren put the book down when the first dryer stopped, smothering a yawn. For all his awards, the author had spent an awfully long time describing the maudlin setting.

'Enjoying the book?'

'You were right, it's heavy going,' she said, watching him pair up pink and purple socks. His hands were massive in comparison to the socks and she couldn't help wondering if those same hands also tied shoelaces, untangled knotty hair and turned the pages of picture books at bedtime. The images were as enchanting as they were confusing. Hadn't she and her last boyfriend, Fergus Abernathy broken up because he was already imagining hordes of children, while her thoughts were on her career?

'So you live with your sister or your brother?'

'My sister, but just for a spell,' Jack said. 'The police house was mid-reno when I accepted the position, and the builders don't seem to be in a hurry.' He rattled off the list of tasks required on the small house.

Lauren folded her towels beside him, in no hurry to brave the downpour. 'I hate to say it,' she said, 'but Neilson Builders don't have the best reputation. My friend April was waiting on them for months before they pulled the pin on reroofing her winery. Hope it's cosy at your sister's house?'

'Most of the house is warm and weatherproof,' Jack said, 'but I'm staying in my nan's old sewing room. I get the feeling the drip bucket and extra blankets are going to be there for a while yet. Better than commuting from the Mount, though.'

An idea formed as Lauren added more coins to the dryer but she quickly dismissed it. It would be more trouble than it was worth to have a tenant or house-sitter while she was away. And besides, his sister probably appreciated having his help around the house.

By the time her final load of washing was dry, Lauren was another two chapters down and although she hadn't been actively stickybeaking, she'd deduced Jack was a briefs rather than boxers man. All of his socks, t-shirts and jocks were black. And he owned an exorbitant amount of exercise gear.

'You liked that book then?' Jack asked as she put both novels into her handbag.

'I'll give it a few more pages,' she said. 'And if the story doesn't pick up, I'm sure I'll find someone who'll enjoy it.' He didn't need to know it would likely end up in Gary's aviary. 'Good luck settling into town.'

Jack opened the door for her and as she stepped under his arm, she caught the scent of laundry liquid and peppermint. Clean sheets and toothpaste were different from the understated aftershave she'd suspected he'd wear.

As Lauren reversed out of the car park, the outline of Jack folding pink bed sheets just visible through the foggy windows, she was disappointed she wouldn't be on the producer's desk when they invited him into the radio station for a 'getting to know you' interview.

With the laundry sorted, Jack headed for Arthur's retirement village.

'You're just in time for afternoon tea, Jacko,' said Arthur, brightening at the sight of his grandson. 'Cream buns today, and a date scone if you're lucky. And how was Vic the other day? Still a grouchy old bugger or has he mellowed with age?'

'Mellow as a puffer fish.' Jack placed the pile of library books on Arthur's bedside table and handed over the drawings Harriet had sent. 'I'd planned on staying for a cuppa, Pop, but I've had a call-out, sorry.'

And although he grinned as he tried to guess the reason for the call-out, Jack could tell Arthur was disappointed the visit was being cut short.

'Wildlife collision,' Jack explained, 'and the driver's having trouble clearing the road. Those books should keep you busy until I'm in next.'

'Give the girls a hug from me,' Arthur said, making a shooing motion. 'And don't be a stranger, Jack. It's good having you home.'

It was only a short drive to the accident site and when Jack arrived, the driver was huddled in her car, hazard lights flashing through the heavy rain.

'I slowed down when I saw them on the shoulder. A whole mob of them!' she said, dodging the puddles to his patrol car. 'But these two came out of nowhere. I just couldn't miss them.'

'At least there wasn't oncoming traffic,' he said, pulling supplies from his ute and checking his notebook. 'Miss Walker, right?'

She nodded. 'That's me, but call me Sarah. And you're Jack? Jean said to keep an eye out for you at the gym, I didn't expect to meet you on the job.'

Again, Jack was struck with the lack of anonymity. Did his great-aunt have a flyer stuck to the side of her coffee van or had she placed an advert in the newspaper?

Sarah grinned at his expression. 'She was at the Beachport Markets yesterday, singing your praises to anyone who'd listen!'

Jack wasn't sure he liked being the centre of so many discussions. Would it work in his favour or against him, when he started investigating crimes and doing the dreaded doorknocks?

He noticed the logo on Sarah's car bonnet. 'You're with Rural AM? I met one of your colleagues, Lauren, a few hours ago.'

'Lauren's a sweetheart. I'm going to miss her and Gary. She's a lot easier to deal with than the other producer but you can't stand in the way of a girl and her career right?'

Gary? Lauren's washing pile hadn't contained any men's apparel. He filed the detail away and turned his attention back to the wallabies.

'I'll check for signs of life, if you can get the spray paint from the box in the back seat?'

'The what?' Sarah stared at Jack like he'd grown another head.

'Spray paint to mark the carcasses,' he explained. 'So other motorists know the pouches have been checked. You've never seen a cross sprayed on a dead wallaby before?'

The pair of wallabies were still warm to touch and while neither had survived the collision, once Jack had moved them a few metres off the roadside, a quick check revealed a joey. It had been years since he'd dated the vet nurse with a soft spot for injured fauna, but the basics she'd taught him were still fresh in his mind.

Warmth, quiet and fluids.

Sarah yelped as she peered into the pouch. 'It's tiny. And I've just murdered its mother.'

'Unfortunately, there's not much we can do now,' Jack said, 'But the wildlife sanctuary will take it.'

He retrieved the joey, nestled it in a faded towel from his roadside rescue box and, remembering Sebastian's trick from earlier that week, tucked the bundle inside his shirt. Then he left a message on the wildlife shelter answering service and expected it would be them when the phone rang shortly after.

But instead of Sean Dainty or his son Sebastian, Clem's cough carried down the line.

'Sorry, Jack, I know you're busy, but I've just run out of cold and flu medicine. Do you have any in your bathroom cabinet? I didn't want to fossick through your stuff without checking.'

'Go for it,' he said, farewelling Sarah. 'And if there's none, I'll grab a box in town and come home. I was just leaving.'

'Oh, here's an old bottle of Demazin. Dusty, but better than nothing.'

Jack did a U-turn and headed back towards town. 'Toss it out, I'll get a new one.'

'You're a superstar, Jack.' Clem hung up the phone with a sneeze.

Was that why she'd been out of sorts this week? Could it really be that simple? He sure hoped so.

Jack placed the joey in an insulated shopping bag while he went into the shops, dashing back into the rainy twilight with cold and flu tablets, plus Soothers and cough medicine. The tiny wallaby stayed in the snug towel-filled shopping bag for the drive home.

Harriet was huddled over a bag of Scrabble tiles when he went inside, while Clem was almost buried under a pile of mittens, blankets and booties.

'Look at these itty-bitty baby things,' Clem said and sniffed, holding up a purple onesie. 'Can you believe Harriet fitted this once? Oh, and look at this darling blue cable-knit beanie. Nan was knitting with a brood of great-grandkids in mind.'

'Well, at least she's not around to give us grief about it,' Jack said, putting the hat back into the tub. 'Donation pile?'

Clem pulled the tub back, retrieved the knitted beanie and set it to the side. 'It's too sweet to donate. You never know when it'll come in handy,' she said.

'O-kaaay?' he said, wondering whether she'd ignored his advice about taking the old cough medicine. She almost sounded clucky, which didn't make sense, because he was sure his sister had sworn off childbirth after the ordeal she'd had last time.

'Can we visit the little goat next door, Uncle Jack?' Harriet said, her words bookended with a sniff. 'You promised!'

'Not tonight, Harri. It's too wet and wild out there for little girls with sniffles, you need to stay rugged up. But I've got a surprise in the car. Wait here.' He loaded the fire with more wood, then headed outside, where the stars twinkled between the clouds, to retrieve the joey.

Lauren looked around the living room of her cottage, savouring the colourful prints, the mismatch of checks and florals, textures and fabrics that she'd so carefully chosen to make her house a home. It had been a rough night, tossing and turning before waking with a start and a pounding headache when the alarm went off at 4.55am. Was she doing the right thing, heading across to another bureau in the hope she'd gain more of the experience she needed and wanted? Or was it a knee-jerk reaction to hide her wounded pride, an attempt to prove that even if her local radio didn't want to promote her, another station would appreciate her for the short term?

Lauren headed for the shower, dodging suitcases and bags in the hallway. *No pain, no gain. Whether it's the right decision or not, it's too late now.*

She dressed quickly after her shower, then checked the driveway. No sign of her mum, Gabrielle, or her Volvo. She grabbed her phone.

'Hey, Mum,' Lauren said, loading crumpets into the toaster. 'I thought you'd be here by now? Did you have car trouble?'

A high-pitched bark carried down the phone line. Wasn't Tahnee supposed to be dog sitting? Lauren suppressed a groan. The last thing they needed today was a randy sausage dog trying to hump their legs while they carted boxes around.

'I'm sorry, honey, change of plans. Tahnee's had a last-minute work thing, and you know how Bruno hates those rotten kennels. I'll come next weekend instead.'

Lauren plunged her knife into the butter. It wasn't like she'd asked for her mum's help, nor were there many bags to shift, but she'd been touched by Gabrielle's suggestion of a mother–daughter interstate road trip.

'I start at the radio station on Monday, Mum!'

'I'm sorry, Lauren,' said Gabrielle. 'You'll only be gone a few months—surely there isn't that much to move?'

Lauren surveyed the luggage, determined not to be disappointed by her mother's no-show or think how it would have played out if Tahnee were the one moving house. Gabrielle Bickford loved both her girls, Lauren had never doubted that, but Tahnee was older by three years, and after a lengthy childhood illness, she'd become the apple of their dad's eye. Her mum had taken that admiration up a notch after his death and over time, Lauren had got used to being second-best.

'I'll be fine, don't give it another thought.'

'Call me when you arrive,' Gabrielle insisted.

Lauren dashed to the supermarket to stock up on road-trip supplies and grabbed a selection of Cadbury's on the way out. A familiar ginger-haired hunk joined the checkout queue. *Really? Today of all days?*

It wasn't that she had a problem with bumping into Fergus Abernathy, her ex-boyfriend, but a little bit of notice, perhaps some make-up and a better outfit would have been nice for meeting his new girlfriend.

'Hey ya, Lauren! Great to see you!' Fergus's Scottish accent was every bit as hot as it had been when they'd dated a few years back. Fergus's new girlfriend, Clarissa, gave her a bright smile.

'We've just moved in together,' Fergus explained after introducing them. He added a vegan cake mix to the checkout counter, along with an array of distinctly feminine groceries. Gone were the tins of MightyMan Beef Pie in a Can, frozen pizzas and bulk sausages. *So Clarissa had not only moved in, but she was hoping to turn Fergus into a vegan.* 'Chocolates, I see?'

'They're not all mine,' Lauren protested. 'The boys next door are keeping an eye on the place while I'm interstate, I've just got this little bag of Caramellos and a measly packet of Maltesers. And everyone knows they're hardly even chocolate.'

'The Lauren I knew would have one box of Favourites for the neighbours and two for the road.' Fergus grinned, looking over her shoulder to see if she was hiding a second box behind her back.

Clarissa's laugh was a little strained, and Lauren rushed to put her at ease. 'I'll crack out the chocolate when I've arrived in Port Fairview and unloaded the car. I've still got to shift Gary's aviary next door yet.'

The bungalow she was renting in Port Fairview had a strict no-pet policy. And with a bit of luck, the chocolates and five dollars a week pet-sitting fee would help make up for the bird's noisy outbursts.

'Aye,' Fergus said. 'I'd have offered to have Gaz at the golf course, but we've just got a kitten. A wee little thing it is.'

Moving in together, baking cutesy vegan cupcakes *and* getting a kitten. How long before an engagement party invitation arrived in her mailbox?

Lauren tried not to think about Fergus and Clarissa as she returned to her pink cottage, and it took all her might not to feel guilty as she gave Gary a final pat and returned him to his aviary, before loading it onto a sack trolley and wheeling it next door. Gary carried on the whole way.

'This is *not* a good impression, Gaz,' Lauren said, shushing the bird and apologising as soon as her neighbour, Val, opened the door.

Val chuckled. 'It's never quiet around here anyway. The bird will make a change from the boys' bickering and music practice.'

Gary flew about the cage, squawking and flapping. He was still making a ruckus when Lauren left, apologising as she went.

Rubbing at the knot in her midriff, she put the final suitcase in her car and locked her cottage. *It's not defeat, it's taking the bull by the horns.*

As she drove out of Penwarra and towards the Victorian border, she repeated the mantra again and again, hoping that saying it enough times would make it true.

4

The seaside town of Port Fairview was a similar climate to Penwarra, but the north-west-facing windows in Lauren's rental harnessed the late afternoon sun. With a glass of chardonnay in one hand and a bag of Caramello Koalas in the other, Lauren sank into the wicker chair and tipped her face up to the golden warmth.

She snapped a quick selfie in her new digs and sent it to her mum and April. A flurry of replies came through, multiple messages from Gabrielle apologising for the last-minute change of plans, and then a FaceTime call from April.

'Turn the around and give me the grand tour of that gorgeous granny flat!' Ever since April had renovated the old stables in her family vineyard, she'd been addicted to architecture TV shows. 'Ocean views and rammed earth? My God, you lucked out there. I'll come visit soon so I can admire it myself.'

'I'd love that,' Lauren said, settling in as April updated her on the B & B bookings, the events planned for Lacewing Estate's cellar door and the winemaker her British boyfriend, Connor Jamison, was mentoring. The mention of April's boyfriend, who was firm friends with Fergus, reminded Lauren of this morning's supermarket visit.

'Guess who I bumped into today,' Lauren said. 'You didn't tell me he was moving in with Clarissa.'

'They've got a kitten too, I hear. There'll be baby showers and gender reveals before we know it. Lovely guy, but you dodged a bullet there.'

Lauren snapped the head off a chocolate koala and agreed.

'I bet you'll miss your cottage,' April added.

It had been almost a year since Lauren had bought the cosy nook in town, with its pretty little garden and postage-stamp backyard. She should have known better than to factor a promotion into her budget. *All the more reason to ace this secondment*. Despite the sunny aspect, Lauren shivered as she considered the enormity of the challenge in front of her.

'You're doing the right thing, Loz,' April said, reading her silence in the way only old friends can.

'Well, I'm not sitting at home moping. I'll be producing the brekky show tomorrow and hopefully talking my way into some on-air opportunities.'

'You deserve it.' April wrestled a stick from the jaws of her golden retriever Mishka, held it like a microphone and put on a faux newsreader voice. 'You're tuned into breakfast with Lauren Bickford, live from Lacewing Estate, the Limestone Coast's most beloved boutique winery.' April grinned, gesturing to the bed and breakfast she'd recently opened. 'And I must say, listeners, there's some fabulous accommodation in these parts to match the wine, I'd better book another night at Kookaburra Cottage before it's completely overrun with high-paying guests.'

Lauren nearly fell off her chair laughing. 'Well, you'd be out on your ear before the first show finished, wouldn't you?

No business promotions, no brand names, and definitely no drinking on the job.'

April grinned, tossing the stick back to the dog and retrieving her wine glass from the outdoor table. 'I'll stick to the B & B and the horticulture and leave you to slay the media circus then. You'll ace this role and when you come home, you can put pain-in-the-arse Patrice back in her box.'

Lauren swirled her wine, trying to ease the stiffness between her shoulder blades that occurred whenever Patrice, the senior producer, came up in conversation. 'She'll need to be on her deathbed before she loosens the reins.'

April walked with the phone back inside and topped up her glass. 'I thought that about my dad too, but he's mellowing with old age. He's letting me name the vintage again next year, and we're designing new labels to match.'

Lauren signed off with a promise to update April on the radio station's vibe as soon as possible, tugged on a jacket and headed out to explore her new town before dinner.

The limestone road was riddled with potholes and the white, powdery splatter coated Jack's ute as he and Harriet drove to the wildlife sanctuary before school the next morning.

Even though he'd called ahead and left another message, it took several knocks before Sebastian answered the door.

Jack raised an eyebrow at the boy's gruff greeting, noting his sleep-mussed hair, the rumpled hoodie that quite possibly doubled for pyjamas and the way his glare suggested it was an ungodly visiting hour instead of a perfectly reasonable 8 am.

Didn't he have a school bus to catch?

'I left a few messages, but I didn't hear back.'

'Mmmm,' Sebastian mumbled through a yawn. 'Answering machine's busted. The olds are in town now, getting a new one.'

Harriet bustled up to the door in her green school uniform and pulled her thumb from her mouth to wave hello.

'We've got a joey for you,' she said.

Harriet's words unlocked something in the teenager and despite his brusque manner with Jack, Sebastian rewarded Harriet with a smile. He assessed the pink, hairless orphan. 'I'd say it's a swamp wallaby, can't be more than three months old. You didn't feed it cow's milk did you?'

Jack shook his head. Lactose intolerance in macropods was one of the first things he'd learned from the vet nurse with the wild curls and extensive native animal collection.

'Leave it with me,' Sebastian said, transferring the joey into a fabric pouch, hanging it on a free-standing hook inside the house. He returned the insulated shopping bag and towel to Harriet.

'You want a lift to school?' Jack asked, starting the car. 'I'm driving right past.'

The boy shrugged. 'I'll head in after I get this guy settled. The other pinkies are on three-hourly feeds too, so it'll take me a bit.'

Jack backed out slowly, wondering how often the teenager skipped class. Sebastian jogged across to meet him at the gate.

'Was Vic cool about taking the kid goat?'

Jack leaned a forearm on the car window frame, his skin still smelling like chlorine from his morning laps. 'Cool wasn't the word I'd use, but he took it in.'

Sebastian nodded, then looked across the paddock. 'You're not going to mention it to the olds are you?'

'Don't see any reason to, unless you want me to.'

'Nah,' Sebastian answered. 'Thanks.'

On the way back to town, Jack was amused to hear the radio presenter inviting callers to share their wildlife traffic incidents and narrow misses they'd had on the road. Wasn't that what Lauren had said in the laundromat when they were folding their washing? That one small incident or community event could fuel a whole hour of radio content? Was she producing this show too, or had she already left for her interstate posting?

He dropped Harriet at school and checked his phone messages at the police station.

The first was from Neilson Builders, reporting a delay in the supplies for the police house renovations and the window repair at Sunny Cross Farm.

'Bugger it,' Jack said.

The next message was from the golf club president, Barney Anderson.

'Three incidents in two months,' Barney told Jack, returning the call. 'I can see why the golfers are getting concerned. Burnouts on the fairway are bad enough, but messing around with the club's watering system and tossing equipment onto the course is wearing thin.'

'Sounds like bored kids to me,' Jack said, pulling his police kit on and checking his water bottle was full.

Jack thought of Sebastian. Did the teenager have anything to do with the trouble? Was he tired from late nights minding their menagerie of wildlife or was he out all hours making mischief?

The message machine was blinking when Jack hung up the call.

'Not urgent,' the caller said with a nervous laugh, 'just a missing bicycle. Well, I think it's missing. Unless, of course, my boys left it somewhere and didn't want to admit it. But, um, give me a—' A shriek in the background of the recording made Jack flinch.

'Sorry, we're pet sitting a very vocal galah. Give me a call if you can. Thanks!'

Jack noted down the details and headed off, sparing a look at the small police property partially covered with building tarp, a safety fence and a sign for Neilson Builders. Vacant

houses and stores were an open invitation to thieves and
teenagers with spare time on their hands, and while the proximity to the police station should likely deter most would-be
offenders, he didn't like tempting trouble. It was time to get
to the bottom of this.

Lauren arrived early to the new radio station, pulling up
between a no-nonsense Kia and a sleek little Mazda 6. She was
two steps from the door when a wave of panic engulfed her.

*What if they're all like Patrice? How long before I mess
up? Will this really help me get a presenter's role, or am I in
for months of pain with no gain?*

She rested a hand on the Kia's warm bonnet and sucked
in big gulps of air until she'd quashed the urge to turn tail
and run.

You've got this. Best foot forward.

With a trembling hand, Lauren rapped on the back door,
ninety-nine per cent ready for whatever lay ahead.

She met her new colleague with a bright smile. 'Lauren
Bickford, reporting for duty.'

'So great to meet you,' said the woman who welcomed
Lauren inside. 'Carli Hamilton, I do the brekky show. Miriam
was telling me about your background. Radio in London,
magazines in Vancouver, presenting in Adelaide and producing
in Mount Gambier too. We hit the jackpot scoring you!'

Lauren liked Carli instantly. 'Gosh, you make it sound
good.' It was an effort to clamp her mouth shut before she
blurted out her on-air stuff-ups and explained her overseas
roles were more a means to keep travelling, rather than a
deliberate effort to acquire international experience.

'I just love telling stories,' Lauren said instead, 'and I'm
hoping this post gives me more airtime.'

'I'm sure we can make that happen, can't we, Miriam?'

Lauren turned to see her new chief-of-staff striding down the corridor with two steaming mugs of coffee.

'Welcome to the station,' Miriam said, handing across a mug.

Lauren accepted it, taking in Carli's leopard-print dress and Miriam's warm welcome. Poles apart from the senior staff at her local bureau.

'You might have trouble getting rid of me at this rate,' Lauren said, already wondering what Patrice—a fan of muted pastels, shapeless dresses and clear hierarchy—would say.

The station had its own quirks, but the programming and her role were almost identical to her position at the South East bureau and the morning whizzed past. With the breakfast show finished, Carli and Miriam carried their lunches into the staffroom. Lauren took a seat beside them.

'No need to ease in slowly, hit us up with your story suggestions and pitch ideas for any segments you'd like to run. I'll also schedule a one-on-one review midway through your stay, so we can chat about maximising this opportunity,' Miriam said.

'A review?' Anxiety pulsed through Lauren's blood. Much like dead air and job interviews, staff reviews made her stomach churn.

'Nothing to worry about,' Miriam said, passing Lauren a cloth and gesturing to the coffee she'd just slopped down her shirt. 'I like to touch base with my team regularly, set goals and make sure we're working in the right direction. It's just a professional chat, not a grilling. If your editor doesn't do them, then you're missing out on valuable feedback.'

Lauren pencilled in the date Miriam suggested. *No pain, no gain.*

'Righto,' Miriam said, closing her diary and turning to Carli. 'What are we working on this week?'

Lauren took notes as Carli outlined her plans and the talent she'd already lined up, and earned an impressed nod from Miriam when she suggested several topics.

'Community projects always score well on the feel-good factor back home, so I assume it's the same here. The local show for example,' Lauren said. 'It's a treasure trove of human-interest stories, and from my research, you guys have a spring show, only a few months away? I can gather some early leads?'

'Love it,' said Miriam.

Although it was only day one, Lauren had a feeling the secondment was a step in the right direction.

'Port Fairview's just lovely over winter,' Carli said, walking her to the car park that afternoon. 'There's a gym, running club, all the usual suspects like squash, netball and footy, or if you're brave you could join "The Strokes" for an ocean dip each Saturday morning?'

'A heated pool's more my style.'

But even as Carli gave directions to the aquatic centre, Lauren found herself fancying the idea of joining an ocean swimming group. And if she hated it and only went the once, at least nobody in Port Fairview knew her well enough to give her grief about it.

Lauren found the aquatic centre easily. The pool water was warmer than Penwarra's, and while there were only a couple of designated lap lanes, at two o'clock in the afternoon, Lauren had the water all to herself.

A couple of messages awaited her when she finished showering.

'Hey Val,' she said, returning her neighbour's call while tossing her swimming gear into the car. 'Everything okay? Has Gary settled in?'

Val's quick laugh made her nervous. 'Yes and no. I mean he's stopped yelling blue murder each time we enter the kitchen, but he's taken to biting the boys when they feed him.'

'Biting?' Lauren combed her chlorine-damp hair with her fingers. 'He hasn't done that in ages, I'm so sorry.' Gary had only ever bitten her once, but she still remembered his sharp beak and the blood that followed.

'The boys won't go near him now,' Val confessed. 'But I'll give it a shot and see if Gary's better behaved for me. And I don't want to alarm you, but was that lovely terracotta pot on your front verandah broken when you left?'

Lauren sat up straighter in the car seat. 'Broken? The one with the standard rose?' It had been a housewarming present from April and was most certainly in good condition when she'd left town a few days earlier. She told Val as much.

'That's what I thought,' Val said, apology in her tone. 'The pot's on its side, the rose half hanging out. You might want to mention it to the new cop. He was here yesterday about a missing bike, said to keep him posted if anything else was amiss.'

Lauren assured Val she would and after apologising again for Gary's biting, she searched for the Penwarra Police Station number. If there was mischief afoot in town, she didn't want anyone thinking her pretty pink cottage was fair game.

'They're in here somewhere, Harri,' Jack said, shining the torch into the deep corners of his grandfather's old toolshed, past the mass of garden implements, rusted bike carcasses and sacks filled with empty bottles and cans. The topic of welding and creating sunflowers from scrap steel had somehow captured the five-year-old's imagination and Harriet had asked so many questions about Jack's old hobby that he'd promised to dig out the recycled sunflower sculptures.

'Wow,' Harriet said, admiring the chain Jack had coiled up for the centre of the first sunflower, then reaching for the old car bonnet he'd cut and shaped, hammered and folded until there were enough petals to go around. Dust and rust flaked off at her touch.

A low whistle came from Clem in the doorway. 'Here's a blast from the past,' she said. 'It's hard to believe, Harriet, but your uncle was once thinking of ditching high school to become an artist. Maybe there's still a sculptor there under the uniform, just waiting to bust a move?'

Jack arched an eyebrow. 'Not likely. These things would barely pass an OH&S muster. They're probably more dangerous than those old chemicals drums.' He wiggled one of the petals, remembering the hours of work he'd put into each piece, channelling his teenage fury into something productive. The petal dropped to the ground.

'What's under there?' Harriet asked, pulling aside a hessian sack to reveal a dusty blue box.

'My old welder,' Jack said, peering at the leads and knobs that had once felt like an extension of his body, before steering Harriet back to her mum. 'But I'd say my welding skills are even rustier than that sculpture.' He covered the welder again and carted the metal sculptures outside, thinking of the paddocks of sunflowers from his teenage years, the way their golden heads followed the sun when they were all in bloom, as tall and proud as the man who had planted them.

He was still thinking about sunflowers when he returned to the police station shortly after.

'Penwarra Station, Senior Constable Crossley speaking.'

'Jack, I'm glad I caught you. I don't know if you remember me, but we were chatting at the laundromat. I'm Lauren.'

How could he forget someone who brought her own cushion to the laundromat and alternated handfuls of corn chips with M&Ms?

'How can I help?'

'My house is vacant while I'm away for work and there've been a few incidents. A broken pot plant yesterday, and someone's pulled a flyscreen off around the side of the cottage today. Ordinarily, I wouldn't be too concerned, and I wasn't going to bother you about the broken pot but my neighbour said a bike went missing from their yard too.'

'Sure, I'll take a look,' Jack said, recalling the lady who'd called about the bicycle. Missing or stolen, she hadn't been sure, but in the face of further issues next door, he suspected it might be the latter. 'Petticoat Lane, right?'

'Yep.' She paused. 'Are you still waiting on those building renovations at the police house? No pressure, but if you are, I've got a house-sitting arrangement you might like.'

A house-sitting police officer . . . Was that kosher?

The station receptionist Sammi walked in the station's back door and propped it open with a brick as Jack noted down Lauren's details. A flash of movement crossed his vision and he hung up the phone to see Sammi dragging a whiteboard down the corridor. What on earth was she doing?

'You're just in time,' Sammi said, wiping her forehead with her sleeve, 'this thing weighs a tonne. I wasn't sure how I'd get it into my car, but it'll be easier with your brute strength.'

'We don't need it anymore?' he asked, lifting the whiteboard into Sammi's car, beside a large canvas bag he'd seen in the staff room just the day before.

'Oh, we do, but I'm just borrowing them for the weekend. The netty team's getting thrashed week in, week out and I'm going to write a game plan out for all the players to see, just like they do in professional games.'

'And that bag?'

Sammi nodded. 'Ah, the marquee. That's heading to the showgrounds for the annual working bee on Sunday. It's supposed to be bucketing down, so this should keep the worst of the winter weather off our heads.'

She studied his confused expression. 'Everything will be back in the staffroom Monday morning. If any of the top brass complain—which they won't—then we can explain it's a community branding exercise.'

Six months in and he was getting a sense that country policing had a different code to metro.

Jack arrived at Lauren's cottage at the same time as her neighbour, Val, was pulling out of her driveway.

'Lauren just called to tell me you're moving in,' she said, pressing a set of spare keys into his hands before he'd even shut the patrol car door—or decided to move in.

'I've got to collect a sick kid from a sleepover, but have a look around. It's the cosiest little cottage. I'd love to move in there myself sometimes, especially when my kids are driving me nuts.' Val laughed. Then, with a quick wave, she was gone, leaving him holding the keys for a cottage that looked like it belonged in a fairytale.

5

The radio station phones ran hot all morning, with listeners weighing in on the state of the roads after the recent rain, flagging dangerous potholes and slippery shoulders.

'Talk about throwing a cat amongst the pigeons. Do you get that type of response every time you feature the roads and transport chap on your station back home, Lauren?' Carli asked when the show was done and they were planning the following week's topics and talent.

'It's one of our most popular segments,' Lauren confirmed. 'As long as the callers remain polite, and I remember to keep my finger on the dump button for those who arc up, then it's a win for everyone.'

She closed her laptop, wondering if Jack had found anything amiss when he'd arrived at the cottage last night. She excused herself and slipped outside to return his call.

The day was grey and gloomy, with a bone-chilling wind whistling between the buildings.

'Thanks, Jack, that's a weight off my mind,' she said after Jack had filled her in. 'But I don't like the sound of the garbage bin propped against the side of the house. Had anyone been inside?'

Jack cleared his throat. 'I thought the master bedroom had been ransacked at first, but maybe it's just well lived in.'

Lauren burned with embarrassment. 'I was planning on tidying next time I came home. Please tell me the rest of the house is liveable? The spare bed should be good to go.'

Jack assured her it was, and even though she barely knew him, Lauren felt better knowing her cottage wouldn't be sitting vacant, a beacon for whatever mischief was brewing in the neighbourhood. 'Keep those keys,' she said, 'and sing out if you can't find anything. I'll message you the wifi password. Treat the pantry and fridge like your own, there should be ample firewood and please, Jack, don't hesitate to make your-self at home.' She found it hard to picture his big frame clad in all black clothing or the navy-blue uniform amongst her pink walls and bright colours.

'Are you sure your friend Gary doesn't want to house-sit? Val was saying something about him as she left, but I didn't catch it.'

Lauren laughed. 'He'd chew every power cord and end up either electrocuting himself or burning down the house if I left him unattended.'

When Jack didn't respond, Lauren added, 'You realise Gary's a galah, right?'

It was Jack's turn to laugh and when she hung up a few minutes later, Lauren had a good feeling about her unexpected house guest.

She returned to work and called April with an update when she got home later that afternoon.

'You only met him once! What if he rifles through your bathroom cabinet and underwear drawer? Takes random girls home with him and does the wild thing on your bed? Running the B & B has opened my eyes, and it's the ones who turn up in the nicest cars, wearing the swankiest clothes and jewellery that treat the place the worst. At least I'm getting paid to put up with strangers. Have you met Jack's family or anything?'

Lauren pulled on her bathers and tossed a beach towel and goggles into her bag, ready for an afternoon swim. 'Anyone who takes on the laundry for his sister and niece and lives out of a suitcase in his nanna's sewing room, surrounded by quilting supplies, Janomes and overlockers, can't be a mass murderer. And he's a police officer, for God's sake.'

'Point taken,' April laughed. 'How's the radio station?'

Lauren searched for her swimming cap, finding it between a box of books and a tub of toiletries. 'Really good,' she said. 'My story ideas have gone down a treat, they've let me record a few pieces for the digital media channels and promised I'll get some live airtime next week. Cross your fingers there's no dead air, no tripping over my tongue and absolutely, under no circumstances, no stammering.'

'Consider it done,' April said. 'Now, I promised Fran I'd quiz you on a project she's considering for the Penwarra show.'

'The last show's just been,' Lauren said. 'Tell me Fran's not in a tizz about next year's baking contest already?'

'She's not in *full* show mode yet, but she's thinking of compiling a recipe book for the show's one-hundredth anniversary. A hundred recipes for a hundred years. God only knows how she'll find time to round up all the entries, test them and compile the darn thing, but she wanted your thoughts.'

Lauren was touched. Fran had always been like a second mum to her. Where Fran baked, her own mum, Gabrielle, had the Thai restaurant on speed dial. Where Fran held her tongue and led with praise, Gabrielle's encouragement often looked, sounded and felt a lot like criticism. Where Fran recycled the wrapping paper and only took the occasional weekend away, Gabrielle spared no expense with gifts or holidays.

As much as Lauren loved her mum, she had a special spot in her heart for April's stepmother.

'Tell Fran it sounds fabulous. Not sure I'll be much help while I'm over here—this kitchen has a Barbie doll–sized oven—but I'm happy to be a sounding board and I can pump it up the minute I'm back at the local bureau in spring.' *Am I putting the cart before the horse, planning content and hoping I'll have any sway when I return?*

'It's just an idea,' April said. 'And Franny's trying to limit the recipes to just Penwarra residents, or former locals, so she probably doesn't want to cast too wide a net at this stage.'

'Still . . .' Lauren's journalist's brain was already whirring with ideas. She couldn't directly promote the cookbook with 'pre-order now' suggestions or blatant advertising, but there were plenty of other ways to spread the word about community initiatives like this. 'If Fran's in charge, it will be brilliant, I can already tell.'

'You're lucky your great-nan isn't here, Miss Harriet. You'd never have got away with rollerskates at *her* dinner table,' Jean said.

'Uncle Jack gave them to me,' Harriet chirped. 'He said I can keep them on until I get sore feet, but I've been wearing them all day long and they're fine.' Harriet beamed, flashing a toothy grin in her great-great-aunt's direction. 'I might even sleep with them on!'

'We'll see, Harriet.' Clem laughed wearily, but Jack could tell the effort of having them all over for dinner and dodging Harriet's speedy laps around the kitchen, had tuckered her out.

He surveyed the kitchen, breathing a little easier when he saw a cobweb in the corner of the doorway and a Harriet-sized handprint on the window. Clem kept a tidy household, but when the line between neat and spotlessly immaculate became blurred, he knew his sister was heading into overwhelm territory.

Arthur ambled in with his walking frame and settled himself at the head of the table.

'How's the new place, Jack?' he asked, pouring drinks for the table. 'Took me months to settle into the retirement village with all the different noises, the cars, and staff coming and going all hours of the night.'

Jack had been in Lauren's cottage for a week now, sleeping soundly for the first time since he'd returned to Penwarra and starting his days without a chill in his bones, but he didn't want to offend either his grandfather, who had gifted him and Clem the house, or his sister and niece.

'It's quieter,' Jack admitted. 'But it might not be for too much longer. The neighbour minding Lauren's galah said his language was too salty for her household, so he's heading my way.'

'Ah, yes, Gary's an acquired taste,' Jean said. 'A cray fisherman from Beachport raised him from a chick, but he scored a job on the oil rigs, and obviously that's not a pet-friendly workplace. Lauren's one of my regulars,' she added.

Regular for coffee or matchmaking? Jack wasn't sure he wanted to know the answer.

'Poor lass must have been lonely to adopt a galah,' said Arthur. 'Beats me that you haven't found the right bloke for her yet, Jean. Isn't that your specialty?'

'Not from lack of trying, Art, believe you me,' Jean said.

Sensing his great-aunt was about to launch into a lengthy spiel on the subject of matchmaking, with quite possibly himself and Clem in the firing line, Jack hastened to change the subject, asking Harriet how school was going.

Harriet happily regaled them with stories from her classroom and the moment she'd finished dinner, she tottered outside to continue testing out her new skates.

Jack started washing up, smiling at the whooping and clapping as Harriet flashed past the window, followed by Clem. Even at the speed they were going, their smiles were unmistakable.

'Looks like she's got the hang of it,' said Arthur. He and Jack headed outside in time to see Harriet looping around the driveway.

'A whole lap around the house and not a single gutser. I knew you could do it, honey,' said Clem, twirling the little girl around. With matching jet-black hair and identical smiles, Harriet was Clementine all over. Jack only hoped the little girl didn't have to fight the same demons that had cursed the Crossley family the last two generations.

'Returning to Penwarra was a good idea,' Jean murmured to Jack while nodding at Arthur, who was gazing out to the paddocks that had once been filled with sunflowers, the sheds full of forgotten treasures, and the pine forests that stood between them and the small township of Penwarra. 'You lot returning has given Art a real boost. And I think it'll be good for Clem. That rough patch really knocked her confidence, didn't it?'

Jack watched his sister beaming as Harriet rounded the corner, hair streaming behind her as she skated into her mum's open arms. An outsider wouldn't know how hard Clem had found early motherhood, and perhaps they wouldn't notice her subsequent bouts of depression, but having seen it firsthand, her family knew the toll it had taken.

'Sure did,' he said. 'And as much as I'd like to say those days are behind her, I don't think it's that straightforward.'

Arthur clapped with gusto and shuffled across to them. 'A house is more of a home when there's little people around, your nan always said. She was right, of course.'

Lauren's cottage was quiet when Jack returned from dropping Arthur at the retirement village. He knocked on the neighbour's door.

'I hope you've got ear muffs,' Val said, leading Jack to the aviary in the corner of the kitchen. 'We didn't see eye to eye, did we, Gary?'

The bird bobbed up and down on his perch, making a shrill noise, but it was nothing on the noise coming from the lounge room. Saxophone practice with a side of quarrelling, Jack guessed.

'Least he'll be in familiar surroundings. Any more missing bicycles or unexpected visitors?' He slipped on his welding gloves, glad Val had given him a heads-up about the biting. The aviary was light but cumbersome and he nearly took the skin off his elbow angling it through the front door.

Val closed the door behind her to keep the heat inside and stepped onto her front porch. 'Not a whisper. Hopefully they've been scared off by the police presence.'

'Keep the place locked when you're away, Val. I haven't seen anything amiss since I moved in, but these things don't generally stop of their own accord.'

'You bloody turd,' cried the galah, his light-pink crest standing to attention as he bobbed on the spot.

Laughing, Jack carried the cage inside Lauren's house. 'If nothing else, you'll give any would-be burglars the fright of their life, Gaz.'

He removed the welding gloves and snapped a quick photo of the bird in its rightful spot and sent the picture to Lauren. He hoped he'd have better luck with Gary than the neighbours.

Lauren wrote back instantly.

Jack! You're a deadset legend. Many thanks! Lauren

Returning to Penwarra was a good idea. Jean's words repeated in his head that night.

Jack moved through the colourful cottage, with its clash of patterns, travel mementos on shelves and mismatched artworks hanging on most of the walls. Everything in Lauren's cottage was colourful, from the frames and bright paintings to the crockery dresser and the antique tea chest that served as a coffee table in the lounge room, but instead of being cluttered, the house had personality.

He stopped at the colour-ordered bookshelves. Romance novels outnumbered all the other genres and he pulled one out at random, wondering what drew Lauren to them. They were all cheesy clichés with formulaic storylines, weren't they?

But as he settled on the couch with one of Lauren's books, Jack found himself laughing at the witty banter between the two main characters. *Maybe there's something to be said about assumptions,* he thought, turning the page.

Three chapters later, Jack set the book aside and made a belated start on his evening routine. After years of pre-preparing his packed lunches, he had the process down to a fine art. Within forty-five minutes, the benchtop was covered with containers of brown rice, steamed greens and grilled chicken.

He fetched the mail, spread it out on Lauren's bench and sent her another photo, this time of the envelopes, postcard and catalogues so she could discern whether they needed attention now or if they'd keep until her return.

Gary shrieked from the lounge room, promenading from one side of the perch to the other until Jack strode over.

'Missing your girl, hey?' Jack asked. Pausing, the bird cocked its head, fixing Jack with one beady brown eye. 'Do I need these gloves, or are you going to let me change your water without ripping my finger off?'

A stray feather floated to the ground as Gary stretched one silver wing and leg, giving Jack a 'who, me?' look.

Leaving the gloves on the table, and keeping one eye on the bird, Jack slowly opened the cage and removed the water. Gary stayed put, allowing Jack to change the water without incident but the moment Jack's phone started ringing, and he stepped away from the cage to answer it, the bird was through the unlatched aviary door like a shot.

'Seriously, Gary?'

He looked from the phone screen to the bird flapping around the room. Would Lauren freak out or was he a regular escape artist on her watch too?

'Hey, Jack, how's things?'

'I'd love to say everything's under control, but we've got a slight situation—'

'Shit a brick! Shit a brick!' called the bird, landing on the coffee table and promptly tearing into the paperback novel.

'That good, huh?' Lauren burst into laughter.

'How do I get him back in?'

With Lauren on speakerphone, and an Iced VoVo biscuit, Jack eventually coaxed Gary back into the aviary. He double-checked the latch before scooping up the phone and assessing the novel.

'Looks like Gary and I owe you a new book.'

'Oh, he's a devil for paperbacks. Was it a good one?'

'It was a rural romance,' Jack admitted. 'I only just started it, but I was pretty invested before Gaz tore the last chapter out. Now I won't get to see how it ends.'

Lauren laughed, sounding pleased he'd started one of her books. 'I'll give you a *Reader's Digest* version,' she said and as he sat on the arm of the couch, she told him how it ended.

'Thanks for the photo of my mail. And who's the postcard from?'

Jack went to the bench and flipped over the card. 'Fellow called George, old school cursive.'

'Can you read it to me?'

'Sure,' he said, clearing his throat. Sleeping in someone's spare bed, rearranging their spice drawer and weeding their garden . . . Was it really that much of a stretch to read their postcards to them?

While he hadn't spent more than one hour in person with Lauren Bickford, Jack was learning more about her every day. He knew Lauren was a beloved neighbour to Val and had been nicknamed 'Blondie' by her retired colleague George, who was enjoying his caravan trip but missing her cheery nature, and he knew she loved books about strong country women and the rocky road to romance. He knew she liked cooking but hated cleaning, and even though she said she wasn't particularly green-thumbed, the garden that surrounded her cottage suggested otherwise.

'You're a gem, Jack, thanks heaps. Have a good night,' she said, signing off with a smile in her voice.

6

After a month at the Victorian bureau, Lauren felt like part of the team.

'Another whale! Look, over there,' said Miriam, handing Lauren the binoculars. 'That's two this morning.'

Lauren grinned. 'Not a bad day in the office.' She scanned the ocean until a plume of water and a black tail flashed into view, then watched a moment longer before returning the binoculars to Miriam.

'It's whale central out there, folks,' Carli said into the microphone, gesturing to Lauren, then the spare microphone and seat opposite her. 'And we're about to speak with another avid whale watcher at Warrnambool's main beach on this brisk morning.'

Lauren turned, but their boss was still staring out at the ocean. Lauren pointed to herself and then the mike to make sure Carli meant her and not another whale watcher.

Carli nodded.

Lauren found herself rooted to the spot. *Me?* Her breath hitched in her chest. *We haven't discussed this in advance!* All of a sudden, her mouth was dry and the words fell completely out of her head.

With an impatient shake of her head, Carli cued up the song Lauren had chosen instead.

'That chat's coming up next folks, and to get you in the mood, here's an oldie but a goodie from the fifties' film *Twenty Thousand Leagues Under the Sea*. See if you can remember which Hollywood actor sang this ditty.'

With a grimace, Lauren hit the mute button and rushed to Carli's side. 'Sorry, you caught me on the hop. I thought we were going to do it *after* the news if there wasn't any talent amongst the crowd.'

Carli cocked her head and took a swig of tea from the travel cup. The aroma of lemon and ginger did little to ease Lauren's hammering heart. 'No stress, we don't have to do it now, unless you'd prefer to get it over and done with.'

Am I really that transparent? Lauren rubbed her hands together. *Had the wind chill just picked up?* Lauren glanced back at Miriam again. Had she noticed Lauren's nervous energy too? In the headphones and on the airwaves, Kirk Douglas sang about having a whale of a time, the complete opposite to how Lauren felt.

'I really do want to do this,' Lauren said, lowering her voice. 'I just need more warning before jumping behind the mike. Breathing exercises, you know?'

Carli and Lauren both leaned across to check how long the song had left.

'Aren't you after the presenter's gig back at your old station?' Carli said. 'You *do* realise that means going on air and speaking off the cuff every single day, right?' She laughed, clearly perplexed.

'I do, I do. But when I'm not fully prepped with my notes in front of me and my lines rehearsed, I have a habit of freezing.'

'Interesting.' Carli's eyes flicked back to the monitor. 'Does Miriam know about this?'

Lauren shook her head quickly. There wasn't enough time before the song finished to unpack the situation or tell Carli it was the reason she'd been passed over for the promotion at her home bureau. She reached for her notepad instead. It was hard to do the deep-breathing exercises while she was furiously scribbling down notes, but she didn't want this to stymie her.

'Throw in a couple of promos or rave about the Port Fairview Winter Warmers, and I'll get myself sorted,' Lauren said, determined now.

'Good to go in less than a minute?'

'Absolutely.'

After back-announcing the song and promoting the local winter tourism campaign, Carli introduced Lauren.

In through the nose, out through the mouth. Lauren adjusted the microphone and forced a smile into her voice.

'That's right, Carli, we're having a whale of a time with flippers and tails bobbing up through the waves, keen whale watchers lining up to see these majestic so—sou—' Lauren consulted her notes, relieved to see they were indeed southern rights and not blue whales as she'd feared the moment the word left her lips. 'Southern rights frolicking not far from the shore.'

Carli gave her a quick thumbs-up and Lauren returned the gesture.

'And Lauren, you're only new to the district. Can you describe for all our listeners what it's like seeing a whale for the first time?'

Lauren nodded. This was an easy one. 'Gosh, they're amazing. I've holidayed in Beachport and Robe many times and I've never seen them cavorting in the ocean like this.'

Carli made a rolling hands gesture.

Does she want me to elaborate or hurry up? Lauren's mouth opened and closed like a Murray cod. *Speak, darn it!!*

'That's only a few hundred kilometres away, isn't it?' Carli said. 'Lovely part of the world, they've got the wineries and we've got the whales. Perhaps tell us a little about the other spectators here today, Lauren. Are they mostly locals or inter-state visitors like yourself?'

'A good mix.' Lauren nodded, so relieved that she'd finally found her tongue she nearly tripped over her words. 'I hear the high school science classes came down yesterday, when the whale and her calf were first spotted; there's also a busload of Melbourne visitors on their way and we'll speak with a Port Fairview resident in a moment who is involved in the um—' Lauren consulted her notes, trying to remember which festival the lady was involved in. Her notes were messy with lines and arrows, towns and names. 'Her, um, her daughter Claudia was in one of the enormous whale puppets that walked down the, um, town's main street during the parade, I've got the details here somewhere.' She flicked through the notepad, alarm rising. *Somebody just shoot me now and put me out of my misery.*

'Sounds like the Upwelling Festival,' Carli offered. 'I haven't yet been but I've heard great things. We'll get back to you with all the details of that fabulous community event after the break. And wherever you're tuning in from, stick around because we'll be speaking to more whale watchers and a marine biologist after the news.'

Carli threw to another song just as Lauren found what she was looking for. 'I knew it was here,' Lauren groaned, turning the notepad to Carli. 'The Bonney Upwelling Festival.'

Although she waved away the apology, Lauren could tell Carli was disappointed. She grabbed her notebook and hurried off to find the talent, glad she was not only easy to spot with her curly ginger hair, but that she was still happy to chat on the radio.

Lauren settled the guest in the seat, and after they crossed back from the news, Carli introduced her.

'We're here today with Angie McIntyre, a Port Fairview local, who's also involved in the Bonney Upwelling Festival. I hear you're a regular whale watcher?'

Angie nodded. 'I can't resist coming to watch. My daughter, Claudia, loves marching in the Upwelling parade and this year her little brother, Ted, will be part of the daycare float too. It's a great day out for the whole family.'

Lauren gave her a thumbs-up, but inside she recognised an unpleasant burn of envy that this lady could talk on air, without notes, without stumbles or stutters, at two minutes' notice.

Miriam came back, carrying a tray of takeaway cups from the nearby bakery and a brown paper bag. Lauren perked up as she sipped the coffee, realising that in the chaos of live broadcast prep, she'd forgotten her 9 am coffee and neglected to transfer a chocolate bar or two from her desk drawer into her laptop case. *So that's why I'm off kilter today!*

She drained the coffee and tore into the chocolate muffin, and while neither were in the same league as Jean's double-shot lattes or her own home-cooked treats, after today's on-air hiccups, they tasted like the answer to her prayers.

Jack could smell trouble the moment he walked into the Sunny Cross farmhouse that afternoon. Double-strength eucalyptus cleaning product–scented trouble, to be exact.

Harriet sniffed the air. 'Mum's tidying *again*?' She hadn't seemed too perturbed to have been left waiting at the school gate long after pickup, but the phone call from the principal, explaining Clem had been uncontactable, had sent chills down

Jack's spine. Maybe he was supposed to pick Harriet up, and *he'd* been the one who'd forgotten? She dumped her school bag and rushed to replace her school shoes with rollerskates.

'Good idea, Harri. I'll see if Mum needs a hand.'

Jack slipped off his work boots, knowing paddock mud traipsed across a gleaming floor wouldn't be the best start to this conversation, and followed the trail of cleaning products to the master bathroom. He found his sister standing in the bathtub, a bandana over her dark hair, cleaning cloth in one hand and rubber gloves almost up to her elbows, stomping with such vigour that the soapy water crashed over the side of the bath and onto the tiles.

Jack closed his eyes briefly, trying to remember the last time Clem had worked herself into such a state.

'Hey,' he said, knocking on the doorframe. 'You ready for a break?'

Clem shook her head, wiping her hands on the oversized t-shirt that came halfway down her thighs and covered a set of ragged running shorts. 'Mice! I caught one climbing the curtains this morning, so they all need a wash,' she said, not letting up her pace on the curtain-stomping mission. 'This fabric is disgusting, by the way, and you should see the grime behind the curtain pelmets. Who knows how long since Nan cleaned them? These tiles are ghastly too.'

Jack glanced around. The place had been spotless when he'd last visited, and even though the bathroom floor was now flooded with curtain-washing water and the bathtub a grimy haze of fabric and dusty muck, he couldn't imagine anything in the household being 'disgustingly' dirty.

He waded into the bathroom, his socks drenched from the first step, feeling the energy radiating off his sister like a forcefield. 'C'mon, Clem. You need to stop now.'

She paused, pulled the bathtub plug, then returned to stomping the curtains. 'I've found mice, didn't you hear me? And if I don't get rid of them quickly, they'll start breeding up and we'll be inundated.'

Jack took a breath to steady himself. Obsessive cleaning had always been one of Clem's tell-tale signs that she wasn't coping and it hurt seeing her like this. 'I bet it's that dicky window in the sewing room. I'll see if Pop has some steel wool in his shed to fill the gap.'

He quickly checked on Harriet, who was delighted with the offer of a juice box and a bag of chips for afternoon tea.

She grinned, ripping the packet open gleefully. 'Mum only lets me take them for school.' She rolled quickly across the driveway before he changed his mind. 'What's she cleaning today? I already helped scrub the kitchen yesterday.'

'Curtains,' Jack said, giving his niece a gentle smile and cursing himself for not checking in more often since he'd taken on the house-sitting role.

He returned inside, but a quick walk around the house didn't fill him with confidence. Every wardrobe had been emptied onto the bedroom floors, the contents of the ensuite and laundry cabinets were spread across the tiled floors, and the small sewing room he'd stayed in last month had a distinctly mousy smell.

Jack called his grandfather.

'Jacko, what's shaking in your neck of the woods?' Arthur said.

'Looks like the mice have set up shop in Nan's sewing cabinet.' He crouched down beside the timber-veneer cabinet and when he opened the door, a nest of shredded paper, fabric scraps and stinky mouse poo tumbled onto the carpet along with a handful of bobbins and a dangerous-looking pincushion.

'What does Clem think of the unexpected guests? Mouse traps on every surface like Shirley? Your nan could kill a snake with one swift flick of the spade, but put a mouse in the house and she'd scream blue murder.'

Jack sat by the sewing table with its neatly folded stacks of fat quarters, cotton spool holder and quilted wall hangings, remembering his nan chasing a mouse around the kitchen in her chenille dressing gown. 'Clem's not thrilled,' he said. He hoped his sister's overreaction to the mice was more of a hereditary reflex than a reflection of her mental state.

After speaking with his grandfather, Jack plugged a hole in the wall near the damaged window frame with steel wool and cleared the mouse-nest from the sewing cabinet.

He found Clem wringing the curtains out, flakes of perished block-out backing crumbling off with every twist. 'Might be easier to buy new ones.'

'Nan sewed these.' Clem glared as if he'd suggested they light the curtains on fire and drape them over Shirley's gravestone.

'And she did an awesome job, but they're past their prime now. From the look of Nan's sewing room, we've got more pressing things to worry about.'

Suddenly, Clem's eyes widened and she clamped a hand over her mouth, dropping the curtains. 'What time is it?'

'It's okay, I picked Harriet up from school,' Jack said softly. He settled Clem in the kitchen with a cup of tea, relieved to find ANZAC biscuits in the pantry. Sugar, tea and sympathy weren't a bad combo when his sister was in this kind of state. Jack finished wringing the curtains, then draped them over the clothes line and pulled together a quick pot of pumpkin soup.

'Are you sure you're alright?' he asked Clem. 'I can stay here and feed the galah on the way home from work instead of house-sitting, if you need.'

'It was just an overreaction,' she assured him. 'Those bloody mice! I feel terrible for forgetting school pickup, but we'll be fine, honestly.'

Jack returned to the pink cottage reluctantly, adding mice to the list of known triggers that sent his sister into a tailspin.

This is why you're here, he reminded himself, pausing at Lauren's door. He hadn't been there for the darkest days after Harriet's birth, but he was here now.

7

Although it had only been three months, the send-off Miriam and Carli had planned for Lauren seemed more deserving of a long-term colleague, not a fill-in producer.

'You really don't have to do this,' she said, watching the waves crash onto Port Fairview's East Beach.

'Nonsense!' shouted Miriam over the roaring ocean. 'We never miss an opportunity to celebrate around here, and if it involves a champagne breakfast, even better.'

'You sure there's no sharks?' asked Carli, dropping her towel on the sand and rubbing her arms.

Lauren studied the swimmers striding into the water, confident in their Saturday morning routine, while a handful of newcomers dawdled at the shore. She lifted a finger to her lips and shushed Carli. 'They said the number one rule of ocean swimming is not to mention the "S" word unless it's an emergency.'

'Let's do it,' Miriam said, and with a war cry, she led the way into the water.

The September water temperature took Lauren's breath away, but when they emerged from the surf fifteen minutes later, she felt more alive than she had in weeks. Months, perhaps.

'Holy heck, that's good for the soul,' Carli said, towelling off. 'And you're dead right, Miriam, it's almost like the rush of live radio.'

Miriam grinned, uncorking the sparkling wine. 'Here's cheers to good workmates, new experiences and staring fear in the face. You've come along in leaps and bounds, Lauren. We've loved having you at the South West bureau. If you ever want a change of scenery, come back over the border.'

Lauren brushed the sand off her plastic champagne flute and took a sip. 'Thanks for being so patient with me.' And if she hadn't been dripping wet, and the wind hadn't whipped up at that moment, sending gusts of sand across the beach and onto their damp legs, Lauren was pretty sure she would have embarrassed herself by hugging them both.

They retreated to the change rooms, and with salty skin and wet, windswept ponytails, went out for a farewell brunch.

'Don't you let them push you around back home,' Carli said. 'You're an awesome producer and you're good on the mike. If that grouchy Patrice gives you stick, just remember she's only as powerful as you allow her to be.'

Lauren pressed her fingertips into her palms, hating how the mere mention of Patrice made her nerves skitter.

Patrice is only as powerful as I allow her to be, Lauren repeated to herself as she farewelled Carli and Miriam after brunch. She'd miss their patient guidance and regular on-air opportunities, knowing their help had been pivotal in finally getting her nerves under control. *With this secondment up my sleeve, there's no reason I can't ace the next six months and be the preferred candidate when the presenter's role opens up again. I just need to back myself, keep my head down and work hard.*

She drove into Penwarra with her eyes darting this way and that, cataloguing changes that had taken place in the time she'd been away. The grapevines had sprung to life after their winter snooze, tulips and poppies waved in front yards and signs for spring shindigs, markets and open gardens fluttered from the tall streetlights.

Her little pink cottage was in better shape than she'd left it, neat, clean and smelling like fresh flowers. She went straight to Gary's aviary.

'Did you miss me, Gaz?' she asked, his soft feathers tickling her as he snuggled into her cheek.

'Salty as a sea dog, salty as a sea dog,' he sang, nibbling her silver earrings.

Propped beside a vase of ranunculus on the kitchen bench was a card with a picture of a galah wearing a party hat. Jack's handwriting was nothing like she'd expected. Where his house-keeping, laundry folding and, from the look of that pantry, cupboard-sorting skills were immaculate, his penmanship was distinctly—delightfully, even—messy. There were capital letters in the middle of words, small gaps between some letters and big gaps between others and the ink was smudged, as if he'd written the note in haste, then shoved it into the envelope. For some reason, Lauren liked this new insight more than the immaculate carpet and precisely folded linen in the cupboard.

Lauren and Gary, thanks for your hospitality, happy to house-sit or pet sit whenever you need. Jack. PS Hope you can still find everything OK. And you were right about the RuRo books.

Lauren went around the house, checking the door locks, topping up Gary's food and pulling the cover over his cage, growing even more excited for the first day back at the Mount Gambier bureau. She fell asleep with a smile on her face.

'Dark grey carpet, soft grey walls and charcoal cabinetry,' Clem said, setting a box on Jack's dining table. 'I'm sensing a theme here.'

Jack pushed aside a curtain, but the overcast day and view of the brick police station entrance didn't much improve the appeal of his new home. He opened a window, hoping it might dispel the scent of fresh paint and rubbery carpet underlay, and went for another armload of boxes.

A car tooted as it drove by and Jack lifted an arm to wave.

'Neat and tidy with a hint of prison cell,' Clem continued, passing him with a storage box. 'Or maybe a tomb. It wouldn't be so bad if your furniture wasn't all black and grey too. Maybe we can find some timber side tables and colourful cushions to break things up a bit. We get a family discount at Fiona's store.'

While Jean had cornered the market with her mobile coffee van, her daughter Fiona had a loyal following at her second-hand shop. As well as taking the excess farmhouse furniture, she'd also offered Clem a part-time job.

'No cushions,' Jack grunted, lowering a filing cabinet in the room that would be his home office. 'And my furniture's fine.'

But as he tidied the small house that night, after Harriet and Clem had left and it was just him and a pile of boxes, he couldn't deny it was drab. Especially in comparison to Lauren's kaleidoscope of colour. Maybe he'd humour Clem and add a few house plants.

The cotton sheets were cool on Jack's skin when he slid into bed that night, and again his mind went to the linen he'd been sleeping on for the last three months. Maybe he could invest in some French linen sheets too. Not bright pink like Lauren's, but something, *anything*, other than grey would be a start.

Jack headed to Sunny Cross Farm before his shift the following day to transfer the last of his packing boxes from the garage. Harriet jogged alongside him as he worked.

'I saw three little kittens outside Vic's house, Uncle Jack. Mum won't let me get one, though,' she said and harrumphed. 'Or a goat. Or a joey!'

'Maybe later, Harri, when she's not still settling into her new job at the second-hand shop and you're into a routine with school.'

She wasn't impressed with his answer but brightened when he told her about an article he'd read in yesterday's *Penwarra Pennant*.

'As well as show rides, horse events and the scarecrow competition, they're planning a mini petting zoo at next year's show,' he said. 'And apparently there's heaps of things for kids to enter.'

Harriet, strapped into her car seat, was full of questions. 'Is there really a bouncy castle? Dodgem cars? Tell me about the baking competition again! Can we cook everything?'

He laughed and answered the best he could. 'It's been twenty-something years since I went to the show, Harri, and this year I'll be working for much of it, but I'm sure we can sort something out.'

He dropped Harriet at the school gates with a promise to track down a show program, then unloaded the last of his boxes and clocked on for the day.

Lauren slept solidly, waking only slightly disorientated in her own bed. She rushed through a shower before heading to work.

The station parking lot was empty and Lauren was surprised to find the office equally dark and vacant. She used her keys to let herself in. First stop was the lights, then the coffee machine. With the milk heating in one hand, she read the staff whiteboard on the kitchen wall.

As well as Patrice's efficient cursive, the newsreader Sarah's loopy scrawl and Paul's favoured all caps, there was unfamiliar handwriting that could only belong to Nigel Hewitt, the chap who had pipped her at the post and taken the six-month temporary breakfast program position. *Nigel obviously hadn't altered things.* The same familiar guests were pencilled in for updates from community organisations and interest areas, like the gardening club and resident foodies.

Same old, same old. If I was in the hot seat, I'd shake things up a little and put my own stamp on the program.

With her coffee made, Lauren took a photo of the board so she could start creating an alternative talent list in readiness for the job interviews. She was scrolling through her contacts in the production studio, working out who her first substitution would be, when her phone rang.

'Hey, Nigel,' Lauren said, glancing at the time. 'You're cutting it fine.'

A moan came down the phone line. 'I'm crook. Someone else has to do the show or else cross to the Renmark bureau. You don't want me chundering on air. Patrice is on her way and—' Another groan came down the line, followed by a gagging noise.

Lauren pulled the phone away from her ear, screwing up her face. Her guts twisted in sympathy. 'We'll sort it,' she assured him, striding across the production studio. Hadn't Miriam encouraged Lauren to reframe the live-radio experience as exhilarating rather than fear inducing? And now was no time for self-doubt; they were going live in less than an hour. *I can do this.*

With trembling legs, Lauren lowered herself into the presenter's chair and adjusted the mike. She kicked off her heels and grounded her stockinged feet, gently shuffling them on the carpet. *I deserve to be here.*

'Do you *really* think that's a good idea?'

She snapped out of her zone as Patrice rushed in, pencilled eyebrows arched and a condescending smile on her lips.

Lauren held onto the radio presenter's padded swivel chair, willing herself to sit tight in the face of Patrice's scepticism.

'I really don't see many other options,' she said. 'George and his wife can't possibly tow the caravan back in time, and Paul only wanted us to fall back on the Renmark station as a last resort. I'm game if you are?'

Patrice pressed her lips into an even thinner line and crossed her arms before disappearing into the production suite.

Lauren's fingers flew across the keyboard, making notes for herself. After throwing a sneaky look at Patrice, who was busy on the other side of the glass, she closed her eyes and recalled Miriam's advice.

Ground yourself.

Remember it's exhilaration, not fear.

Repeat the mantras.

I can do this.

I deserve to be here.

'On air in ten minutes,' said Patrice over the intercom. 'You sure you want to host? I can only do so much to keep the ball rolling if you freeze on air or let your tongue run away with you.' Patrice gave Lauren another of her patronising smiles, watching as her words hit their mark.

Lauren slipped off her headphones and bolted to the bathroom.

'It's just nerves, it's just nerves,' she reassured herself, assessing her mirrored reflection as she wiped her face with a hand towel, erasing all evidence of the upset stomach. She slicked on a coat of shimmery peach lip gloss. If she looked the part, she'd be more likely to sound the part too.

With one last look in the mirror, Lauren marched towards the studio and settled into the presenter's chair. *This is the start of the beginning.*

Fifteen minutes, two on-air stumbles and one town name mispronunciation later, and Lauren was sweating bullets. Patrice queued a forty-five-second promo and the moment the recording came on, Lauren buried her head in her hands.

'This is a disaster!' she wailed. 'I said the community meeting was at Tantanoola instead of Tarpeena and did you hear the way the weather update came out? Do you think anyone noticed when I read the grazier's warning twice?'

'Only those with ears.' Patrice's disdain travelled from the production room. 'But you didn't want my opinion before, so no use asking for it now. One minute to go, pull yourself together and stop making such a fuss.'

Lauren gulped down the last of her cold coffee and bargained with herself. *Make it through the next half-hour and the rest of the show will be smooth sailing.*

'And you're on again in ten seconds,' Patrice chirped.

When Sarah arrived for the first news bulletin, Lauren's linen blazer was lying crumpled on the studio floor, her shirt was sweaty under the armpits and she'd chewed her nails to the quick.

'You did it,' said Sarah a couple of hours later when they crossed to the statewide morning show.

'I'm knackered,' Lauren said, fanning her face.

'First time filling in for an entire show! You should be celebrating.'

'It wasn't pretty,' Patrice said, appearing in the doorway, 'but at least it's over now. I've noted the worst blunders. I'll email them across.'

Patrice caught Sarah's sympathetic wince.

'Don't look like that,' Patrice said. 'You need skin like leather for this gig, and if she's not ready for a little constructive criticism, she's definitely not ready for the presenter's chair.'

Gabrielle Bickford's version of constructive criticism was hard enough, but always softened by the knowledge that she wanted Lauren and Tahnee to succeed, whereas Patrice seemed more invested in seeing Lauren fail.

'Bold plan to go on air this morning,' said Paul when he came into the station. Was he annoyed, impressed or amused? Perhaps all three?

'Um . . . I wasn't sure what to do. Nigel was crook and you always avoid throwing to the other bureau unless the situation is dire. I should have—'

'It's okay, Lauren,' Paul said. 'These things happen and I'm sorry I wasn't there today to help sort it all out. But well done, I look forward to debriefing tomorrow.'

Lauren had a spring in her step as she logged her timesheet, left the station and started on her list of after-work errands. She entered the garden and giftware shop to find Fergus's new girlfriend Clarissa behind the till.

'Here's our local celebrity,' said Clarissa with a broad smile. 'I nearly choked on my Weet-Bix when you came onto the radio this morning. Fergus was so proud, said you've always dreamed of the presenter's gig.'

Lauren was touched. It had been a sticking point between them—her career drive chafed against his urge to settle down and start a family. 'Tell him thanks from me, but I was only filling in today. The new job isn't up for grabs for a few months yet.'

'Hopefully you're in with a good shot,' Clarissa said, retrieving the dahlias Lauren had ordered for her mum's birthday. 'They're great tubers. Grown just over yonder near the Grampians by a lovely lass called Diana,' she continued, sprinkling sawdust over the plants and wrapping the cardboard box.

It wasn't until Lauren was in the car park that she realised Clarissa had started adopting Fergus's expressions. *Lovely lass . . . Over yonder.* No doubt about it, they were on a fast track to romancelandia, and unlike the run-in at the supermarket all those months ago, she didn't feel one bit envious.

Lauren was just about to drive off when Clarissa tapped on her window.

'I almost forgot, we're throwing a Labour Day bash at the Ten Mile beach and we'd love you to join us. April and Connor are coming. You could catch a ride or if you've got a four wheel–driving friend, pitch it to them.'

And before Lauren could ask whether they'd all be eating vegan sausages and barbecuing plant-based burgers, Clarissa rushed off to greet another customer.

Wonder how Senior Constable Jack Crossley feels about sand in his four-wheel drive?

After a late night spent fielding complaints from residents who'd had rocks thrown on their roofs, Jack was relieved to hang up his hat and walk from the police station to his air-conditioned house. The smell of fresh paint and the spongy feel of brand-new carpet still lingered and although he was unpacked, it didn't yet feel like home. He climbed into bed. *Perhaps it would feel more like a home if there were someone or something waiting for him at the end of the day.*

He considered the cats swanning around Victor Jenkins' property, dismissing the idea as quickly as it came, entertained the idea of a budgie or cockatiel for a moment longer and considered a dog. He rolled over, trying to clear his head. He'd buried Clem and Harriet's cocker spaniel Oreo after a snake bite eighteen months earlier, and he wasn't going down that path until the memory of their heartbroken faces faded.

After a restless night, the alarm hit hard on Friday morning and when Jack walked across to the station, he found there'd been plenty of mischief overnight.

'Mr Davidson from Whitfield Drive called to say the roadside speed signs on the western and northern town entries have been changed from 60 to 69, Monica from the post office found not one but five pobblebonk frogs in the red post box this morning and some little bugger thought it would be fun to redecorate one of the primary school classrooms.'

'Not again,' Jack groaned. 'Toilet paper?'

Sammi shook her head. 'Eggs. They hosed it down, but apparently the putrid smell remains. They've got the security footage ready and waiting.'

Nuisance acts were one thing, but egging a classroom and graffitiing road signs . . .

'I told you my uncle Jack would investigate,' Jack heard Harriet tell her friends when he arrived at the school. She led the way towards the principal's office. 'He'll find out who took your garden gnomes too.'

'It's not just the gnomes,' her school friend said. 'We haven't seen Taj the Turtle either. Dad says it's the boys from Morley-Morley Road.'

Jack left the girls to their recess rollerskating session.

'See? There,' said the principal, showing him the footage. Even with their caps pulled low, there was no mistaking the two figures. 'Cohen Moriarty was a good kid in primary school. I don't know what's got under his skin since he started high school. And Sebby . . .' She toyed with the glasses on the chain around her neck. 'Loyal to a fault, that one.'

Jack thanked her for a copy of the footage. 'I'd appreciate you keeping this matter to yourself while I follow it up.'

'I'd recognise Cohen's rat's tail anywhere,' she said, tapping the computer screen. 'I'm not telling you anything the whole town doesn't already think. But that footage will stay between you and me, Jack, you have my word. I don't want to press charges if we can avoid it, but I don't want them getting off scot-free either.'

Jack fielded several more calls during the day from indignant residents.

'It's those kids, the ones that wear their pants halfway down their thighs and keep their hoods over their heads, even when it's not raining,' said one caller. 'One was loitering around Mick and Mandy's house, bold as brass. Their blue heeler was going off its chops, but this kid just leaned over the fence and helped himself to the mandarins like it was his garden.'

'And some wretched teenager keeps peeling the "G" and the "L" off my road sign,' said Jan, owner of Jan's Fine Glass.

Jack stared at his lace-up boots, trying not to laugh. That roadside sign had been amended to 'Jan's Fine Ass' many times before this spate of mischief. 'Let's not jump to conclusions,' he said, promising to continue his enquiries.

He headed to the post office next, relieved to see the book he'd ordered for Harriet's birthday had arrived, and was on his way back with the gift, a roll of purple wrapping paper and a card when footsteps rang out behind him.

'Mate, can I've a word?' A young man fell into step with Jack. 'I've heard about the trouble in the neighbourhood and it made me think about the centenary show celebrations. I'm the poultry convenor.' He explained he'd been tasked with repairing the poultry pavilion before the big day. 'I've picked up extra work at the library and my chickens, ducks and bantams take up more time than you'd imagine. I could use a helping hand and I suspect that when you find the kids responsible, you'll be looking for community projects.'

'You're not wrong there,' Jack said, unlocking the station house. 'I'll be in touch.'

Jack hurried through his lunchbreak set of squats, lunges and weights, and had just enough time after showering and eating to wrap Harriet's birthday gift. The gold foil on the book cover gleamed in the spring sunshine, and as he cut the paper to size, he hoped one day she'd read about the March sisters in *Little Women* and love them as much as Clem had. He taped the paper, folded the corners until they were just right, and curled the ribbon with scissors. It was the sixth illustrated classic he'd bought her, and though he snuck in extra gifts throughout the year, he liked to think the hardcover novels would be treasured long after she'd outgrown the rollerskates, doll houses and Lego.

He added the book to the brimming gift bag and carried it through the back door, catching sight of his reflection in the station's door. The image in the hazy glass stopped Jack in his tracks.

He shook his head to banish the memory of his father handing out gift bags on that very last Christmas, all those years ago. Before the bank had come calling. Before Jack and Clem had become too much to handle. Before the depression had swallowed him whole and he'd quit on his family.

Inside the police station, Sammi waved at him, then gestured to her wrist. Jack yanked the door open, shoved the giftbag under his desk and grabbed the patrol car keys.

Sammi was right; as the town's sole police officer, he had work to do. There wasn't time to waste on the ghosts of the past.

Jack drove to the wildlife shelter with a heavy heart. He'd got pretty good at compartmentalising, but the irony of his father's image appearing out of the blue, just before he told two families their sons were responsible for the trouble in town, wasn't lost on him.

Sebastian's parents had previously taken in troubled youths and allowed them to do their penance by cleaning out cages and stalls, prepping food and caring for the injured and orphaned animals at their wildlife sanctuary; how would they handle the news that their son was now on the other side of the coin? Would it change the course of their futures, too?

'You're joking me,' Christine Dainty said. 'Those Moriartys have been nothing but trouble since they switched to goats. Bad debts, bad decisions and now their kid is ploughing off the tracks with ours in tow. I'll ground Sebby for a month! A year! Dammit, I'll take away his phone and if he thinks he's getting his L-plates any time soon, he can ruddy well think again.'

'Chrissy! Do we know for sure it's our Seb?' Sean Dainty's expression was optimistic. 'Plenty of kids around here are his age and height. He was probably tucked up in his room watching a movie.'

Christine slammed the lid of a feed bin. The row of aviaries erupted with shrieks and squawks and the joeys hovering by the bins in anticipation of an early lunch scattered. 'Those bloody Marvel movies with all the fighting. What did I say about comic books and video games? I'll throw the Xbox on the bonfire, you watch me.'

And with a bang of the door, Christine charged across the lawn.

Sean gave Jack an apologetic smile. 'Chrissy's always been a fiery one, but she'll calm down. And she likes the peace and quiet way too much to throw Sebby's Xbox out. So what now? Obviously we'll read him the riot act when he's home from school but will he be charged?'

Jack felt for the bloke. He explained Sebastian's options, starting with an official visit to the station this afternoon so he could issue a formal caution and draft up a community service plan.

Jack was halfway down the Moriartys' driveway, a kilometre and a half from the wildlife sanctuary, when three kelpies rushed at the car, barking and snapping at the wheels. He began to suspect Cohen's family wasn't going to be as receptive as the Daintys.

A tank of a man with a ripped flannel shirt emerged from a large shed. 'Didn't you read the sign on the gate?'

'Senior Constable Jack Crossley. I'm here about Cohen.'

'I don't care if you're the Queen of Sheba, this is private property. And unless you've got a warrant or an invitation, you can phone ahead for a suitable time.'

Jack gritted his teeth. There were plenty of reasons people didn't want police on their property unannounced, but none of them were good.

'Are you Shane Moriarty? I need to speak with you and Cohen about a series of incidents in town,' Jack said, pulling out his notebook and pencil to write down the station number.

The man muttered something Jack couldn't hear.

'I'm not looking for trouble,' Jack said, 'but if you don't make a time to discuss this at the station, perhaps I *will* get a warrant and have a look around when I return. Your choice.'

The bloke wasn't chummy, but he listened as Jack explained the family conference. 'It's about the youth admitting to the offence, taking responsibility and agreeing to an undertaking to make amends.'

Shane Moriarty looked out across the paddocks. 'I don't want him going to juvie.'

'Agreed,' Jack said. 'I take it personally when my community doesn't feel safe, and right now, Cohen and his offsider are tipping the scales in the wrong direction. It's a family meeting with the youth justice team or it's court.'

'I'll be away but my missus, Jody, will drag Cohen in by his ear if needs be. Give him a tour of the cells while you're there. Even better, lock him in for a few hours, or book him in for a guided tour of the Mount prison, that should do the trick.'

'We don't want to traumatise him,' Jack said. 'But we *do* need to correct this behaviour and if a hundred hours or so of community service keeps them out of the juvenile justice system, then it'll be time well spent.'

8

There was something so satisfying about cooking for friends, Lauren decided as she scooped up a spoonful of white sauce, blew on it and lifted it to her lips. Rich and silky, with a pop of lemon and the gentlest hint of Lacewing Estate chardonnay, the sauce would pair beautifully with the crayfish she'd collected from Southend that morning. Along with a cheesy topping, a quick brown under the grill and a garden salad, the meal would have all the hallmarks of a perfect night. 'Don't go to too much effort,' April had insisted when they'd spoken and Lauren had laughed her off, telling her that was exactly the point. After months away from her own kitchen, she *felt* like making something fancy.

With dinner sorted and dessert chilling in the fridge, Lauren let Gary out to stretch his wings and stepped onto the front porch. Two new matching pots sat either side of the verandah posts, annuals replacing the potted roses that had been there, and she clipped a few marigold stems before running the sprinklers. She wasn't sure what magic Jack had worked on the garden, but the purple bearded irises and the pink David Austin roses hadn't stopped blooming since she'd returned from

Port Fairview. It was a crime that he'd put in so much effort and didn't get to enjoy it. She snapped a photo on her phone.

> Hey Jack, What's the name of the stuff you put on the garden? And BTW do you know where the fine mesh strainer is? I can't find it anywhere!

She sent the photo and message, impressed to see the ellipses pop up right away as Jack responded. They hovered, then disappeared, and she was still standing there, flowers in one hand, phone in the other, when she heard her name.

'Hi Lauren, I think . . . up in the—'

She whirled around to see Jack's patrol car. 'Were you just driving around, chasing criminals and looking for damsels in distress? I'm impressed with your turnaround time, Senior Constable Crossley.'

Jack cut the engine and got out. As he strode around the car towards her, she saw he was growing a moustache. Was he making an early start on Movember perhaps? With his uniform and sharp haircut, there was a sexy Top Gun–vibe about him.

'Just in the neighbourhood, following up a lead on more minor incidents. Someone's been playing silly buggers with mailboxes,' he said. 'But if it makes you feel better, then let's go with me sitting a street or two away, on standby for answering gardening questions and locating missing kitchen implements.'

They laughed.

'If you're not in a hurry,' she said, 'and you like seafood, there's a spare seat at the dinner table. Locate that strainer and there'll be lemon tart with a dusting of icing sugar, mint and strawberries too.'

Gary gave Jack a hero's welcome, whistling and bopping as Jack showed Lauren the hanging hooks he'd installed during his stay.

'Sorry, I should have mentioned it earlier. The sieves and strainers were always clogging up the small utensils drawer, so this spot inside the cupboard seemed a better idea.'

Lauren was as impressed with his suggestion as his rapport with Gary. The bird leaned up against the cage and allowed Jack to scratch his head and then threw himself upside down on the perch in protest when Jack nipped back to the police-station house to change.

Lauren thought about Jack as she folded the crayfish meat through the white sauce and spooned the mix into the hollowed-out shells. He knew a lot about her, but it was high time she found out more about him.

April and Connor arrived just as she was layering flakes of parmesan cheese over the creamy filling.

'Happy birthday, gorgeous,' April said, handing over a gift bag and a basket of fresh produce from her garden.

'I told you not to fuss,' Lauren scolded, admiring the veggies, then unwrapping a bottle of Marc Jacobs perfume and a box of Lindt balls. She spritzed on the scent before hugging her friend. 'But thank you, it smells amazing.'

'I knew it'd suit you. And you're cooking us dinner, it should be the other way around, birthday girl.'

Lauren laughed. 'That's what Mum said, too, but she knows I love whipping up a feast.' She showed April and Connor the French casserole dish Gabrielle had sent down for her birthday, and the matching cast-iron ramekins Tahnee had ordered.

'Blimey, it weighs a tonne,' April said, lifting the hefty lid. 'The eggplant colour is magnificent though.'

'My thoughts exactly,' said Lauren, moving the cray tails to the fridge before the blowflies could sniff them out.

'I think I've died and landed in seafood heaven,' Connor said, slipping an arm around April's waist. 'Stuff the cookware, did you see there's crayfish?'

'Ooh la la, you *were* in the mood for fancy, Loz! And who's joining us? I thought it was just us three? Don't tell me you've taken a leaf from your mum's book and started setting a plate for Gary at the table, like Gabrielle does for that horrid sausage dog?'

Lauren laughed and shuddered at the same time. 'Not a chance. Jack's coming too.'

'Is he now?' April exchanged a look with Connor, the winemaker who had stolen her heart. 'Do I mention the fact that you've called the spare room "Jack's room" at least twice since you've been back? And I bet my cheesy-crayfish tail that bed's still made up with the good linen sheets.'

With a cheeky grin, April headed towards the spare bedroom but was interrupted by a rap on the door.

Lauren saw Jack's outline on the other side of the flyscreen. *How much had he heard?*

Thanks, April. Lauren gave her best friend a stiff side-eye.

Connor, who had one of those complexions that flushed bright red at the hint of embarrassment, could have doubled as an emergency beacon. His British awkwardness as he welcomed Jack reminded her of Hugh Grant's earlier acting days.

Jack had changed into dark denim shorts and a black linen shirt ironed to crisp perfection. He carried a bottle of local wine.

'Just in time.' Lauren gestured to the table set with cloth napkins, white entrée plates nestled on local-fired pottery dinner plates, wine glasses and flute upon flute of roses from her garden, before introducing them. 'April's a horticulturalist by trade, she was asking about the stuff you used on the roses,' Lauren said, fibbing to cover up her embarrassment. She pulled out the chairs, encouraging them to sit.

And while Connor fetched the cheese platter and Jack fell into a deep discussion with April about the gardening brilliance of seaweed extract, Lauren grilled the cray tails.

The conversation flowed over dinner and the subject turned to wine and then cooking when Lauren retrieved the lemon tart from the fridge.

'Divine,' April said. 'Did you submit this to Fran for the show society cookbook?'

'Nope, it's straight from the chef's kitchen at Costin & Jankowski Wines,' Lauren said.

'Ah, that explains this dessert wine pairing,' Connor said, filling their glasses with the sweet, acidic wine. 'You know they use botrytis, the mould that grows on the grapes, to make this riesling?'

Lauren caught April watching her boyfriend, noticing the love and pride on her face as he explained the process. Just like the lemon tart and riesling, Connor and April were a great fit. She was just about to serve up generous wedges of tart when April interrupted.

'Wait!' April shouted, almost making Lauren drop the dessert plates. 'You can't cut it yet. We haven't sung happy birthday.' She launched into song, harmonising with Connor. Jack joined in, and after the singing was finished and the tart was dished up, he turned to Lauren.

'You didn't mention the occasion. I would've brought more than a bottle of wine if I'd known it was your birthday.'

Lauren shrugged. 'Nah, I'm not too fussed on birthdays. Good food, good friends . . . that's my idea of the perfect present.'

'Plus perfume and chocolate,' April grinned. 'Fran wanted to send you an advance copy of the show cookbook, but the printing was slightly delayed. It's on the printing presses as we speak, though, so the first copies should arrive any day now.'

'She's a sweetheart,' Lauren said. 'But I'm more than happy to buy a copy, it's for a good cause.'

'I heard you contributed a recipe too, Lauren,' Connor said. 'Can't fathom why she didn't ask April and me to submit anything.' He turned his sheepish grin to Jack. 'Smart move, really. A food-poisoning lawsuit would put quite a dent in the show's fundraising kitty.'

'It's a fundraiser?' Jack asked. 'Doesn't everyone find recipes online these days?'

April leaned in, warming to the subject. 'That's true, but there's good dough to be made with community cookbooks, pardon the pun. It's not just the contributors who'll get a kick out of seeing their recipes in print, everyone who's pre-ordered the book is banking on the familiar names and their tried-and-true recipes. Audrey Cartwright's jelly slice is pure click-bait for anyone who's ever sampled her slices at a clearing sale or CWA luncheon.'

'So it's just sweets?' Jack asked.

'The full gamut from soups and salads, cakes and casseroles, to puddings and preserves, mains and mulled wine,' April told him. 'A hundred recipes to commemorate the hundredth Penwarra show, including a Bickford family fav from our lovely host, who also rallied the sponsors to subsidise the printing costs.'

Lauren clinked her glass against April's. She'd deliberated between her trusty chicken and corn soup, and several of her winning tomato chutney blends, before eventually submitting the chocolate rock cakes recipe that had been in her father's family for years.

'You and Fran did all the hard yards,' Lauren said. 'Drafting a few sponsorship letters, sending in a recipe and ghost writing a few media releases took no time at all, it was the least I could do to help out.'

While Fran had gone hammer and tongs to compile the book over winter, Lauren knew April had spent countless hours on the project too, creating spreadsheets to coordinate the submissions, researching printing companies and creating an online pre-sales platform.

'The committee must be thrilled to have a new income stream to fund their baking pavilion refurb,' Lauren said, 'Have they decided how they'll spend the money?'

Connor laughed. 'They're only just rolling off the printing presses, they might want to wait to see how the cookbooks sell first.'

'Don't be such a Negative Nancy,' April said, giving Connor a good-natured elbow in the ribs. 'Fran's already pre-sold a bunch through the school newsletter and local Facebook page; they should go like hotcakes at the Christmas markets.'

'Sounds like I'd better grab a copy before they sell out,' Jack said, accepting a second helping of lemon tart.

Lauren brushed Jack's arm as she placed the dessert onto his plate. And while the movement was unintentional, there was no denying the subsequent zing that ran through her veins.

'Thanks,' Jack murmured and for one outrageous moment, Lauren imagined them alone in the cottage as she spoon-fed him the tart and then kissed the icing sugar from his lips.

Woah! Where on earth had that come from?

She took a sharp breath. Was crayfish an aphrodisiac or was that just oysters? And while she'd had maybe one or two sneaky thoughts about the hot, buttoned-up Senior Constable Crossley, most of them had involved him reorganising her wardrobes and her office the way he'd reordered the kitchen pantry, rather than explicitly sexy daydreams.

Under the pretence of pouring them all another glass of water, she snuck another look at him. Was it the moustache? Or was it just the wine, the warm night and the joy of feeding her friends?

'How are you at four-wheel driving, Jack?'

Lauren explained about the Labour Day beach bash Clarissa and Fergus had planned.

'Con and I will be there too,' April said, nodding encouragingly.

'Sounds good, let me know what I can bring,' Jack said.

Lauren felt a new awareness of Jack as she walked him to the door at the end of the night. Not as a random person to make small talk with in the laundromat, or the convenient houseguest guarding her place from mischievous teenagers, but as a red-blooded, downright hot and single man.

The outdoor light flickered on, bathing the front yard in a soft glow. She shut the door behind them.

'I'm glad you're coming to the Labour Day barbie, Jack,' she said, swatting away the bugs drawn by the light. 'Tonight was nice.'

'It'll be hard to beat crayfish, and a lemon tart,' he said. He ran his fingertips along his burgeoning moustache, the first time she'd seen him even the tiniest bit self-conscious. 'Am I wearing half my dinner in this moustache? It's for a great charity but, boy, is it a crumb magnet.'

'Just a little icing sugar.' She grinned and looked away before she spent more time than necessary examining the soft curve of his lips.

She was thinking of a reason not to move closer when a noise came from next door.

The noise came again, closer this time. It sounded like hail.

'Huh?' Lauren said. *Why was it hailing on a mild September night?*

Jack's hand caught hers, pulling her closer as he stepped in front of her. *Can he hear my heart hammering?*

'Who's there?' Jack called, no hint of the playful low tone from moments earlier.

A pitter patter, just like hailstones, sounded across the road and like a Mexican wave, windows lit up and sensor lights flashed along Petticoat Lane.

Jack swore softly under his breath, patting his pockets for his keys. 'I'd better look into that,' he said, loping off down the path. 'Thanks again for dinner and happy birthday.'

Lauren hugged her arms around herself and smiled as she watched him go.

The family conference with the Daintys was first, then later that week, Jack discovered scowling was the default setting for the Moriarty clan. Jody Moriarty was every bit as stand-offish as her husband Shane and their son Cohen.

'Nice shoes,' Jack said as the youth justice worker ushered Cohen and his mother into the interview room. The joggers had a cult-like following amongst teen boys in the city areas where he'd been stationed, but were less common on Penwarra farm kids, where daily contact with paddock mud and animal poo was more of an issue. And while the school principal had recognised Cohen's hair in the video with the school vandalism, the tipping point for Jack had been the incongruous shoes.

'That could have been anyone,' Cohen Moriarty said, squinting at the laptop footage.

'We went through this in the car,' Jody said. 'You're on camera with a gnome in one hand, a carton of eggs in the other and Air Jordans that cost twice as much as your work boots. Suck it up, Cohen. Your dad thinks you should have a tour of the cells if you're so hell-bent on a life of crime.'

She rifled through her handbag, pulled out a lawyer's business card and waved it at her son. 'Do you know how much it costs to get a lawyer? Your fancy shoes would barely cover thirty seconds of expert legal advice. As well as paying people back for the damage and writing them an apology letter, like Senior Constable Crossley here said, you've got a lot of ground to make up.'

Cohen squirmed in his seat, his chin tucked into his chest. 'You can't pin it all on me.'

'I was at one of the houses that had rocks thrown at their roof earlier this week,' Jack said. 'And just like in that video, a set of size 13 Air Jordans prints in the garden bed were enough to tell me you were probably involved in that incident too. This has to stop.' Without Arthur's and Shirley's guiding hands, Jack knew it could just as easily have been him stealing garden gnomes, defacing signs and smashing rotten eggs against public property. If he didn't steer these kids onto the right path, then who would?

Just like he had with Sebastian and his family, Jack ran the Moriartys through a few options for community service. 'Repairs to the poultry pavilion; volunteering at the inaugural Men's Shed meeting; helping on show day. We'll find more as we go, but that will be a start.'

'I don't care what you say, I'm not volunteering at a stupid Men's Shed. They might be paedos,' Cohen spluttered. 'It's slave labour. It's so lame I'll die of boredom. It's not even fair. Making me go to school is bad enough. I'm nearly sixteen, you can't force me to do nothing.'

'Life's not fair, Cohen, you should've cottoned on to that already.' Jody Moriarty zipped up her handbag, leaned back in her chair and nodded to Jack. 'Cuff him, then. Take him to juvie in the paddy wagon, save me the drive.'

Cohen gawped at his mother. Jody tipped her chin, looking away. But underneath her feigned nonchalance, Jack noticed her brimming tears and her shaky breath.

Jack turned back to Cohen. 'I've seen inside those places and worked with kids both before and after they've been through the juvenile justice system,' he said quietly. 'And I can promise you, a few apology letters and a stint of community service will be a darn better option.'

Jody wiped her eyes. 'And what happens if he takes the piss?'

Jack looked between Jody Moriarty and her son, but the youth justice worker answered first.

'Then it'll go to court.'

'You're looking mighty perky for quarter past six on a Friday morning,' Jean said, pre-empting Lauren's order by pulling out a coffee cup.

'The fruit trees are blossoming, the birds are singing and spring is in the air, Jean,' Lauren said, tossing her chewing gum in the bin and rubbing her hands together. 'Who wouldn't be happy to be alive on a day like this?'

Jean lifted an eyebrow. 'You obviously haven't woken in the middle of the night to little hooligans knocking on the windows, tossing rocks on the roof or leaving a steaming bag of dog turd in your mailbox lately?' She thumped the coffee down on the counter and Lauren stepped back to avoid the foamy splatter.

'I had rocks on my roof, though I didn't know about the dog poo. That's gross,' Lauren said. 'But I'm sure Jack will be onto it.'

'Did you hear the community cookbooks are almost ready?' Jean asked.

'Any day now.' Lauren nodded. 'April was telling me last night that Fran's sure there'll be a second print run. Must be your special scone recipe.'

Behind the coffee machine, Jean preened. 'They're just my standard scones. Anyone who's ever cooked for a shed full of shearers will already have a version of that recipe in their repertoire.'

'Well, I look forward to giving them a whirl this weekend,' Lauren said. 'Sultanas and nutmeg, jam and cream. I already know I'm going to like them.'

'The nutmeg's only a recent addition, I must admit. That was Clem's idea. She'd make a right little chef, that niece of mine. Should be running her own cafe or catering business instead of daydreaming about sunflowers and working at Fiona's shop.'

Jean's daughter, Fiona, sold a mix of antiques and pre-loved household items, and while it was a great spot for browsing, Lauren wasn't sure she'd want to work there.

But running a cafe or catering . . . From what Jack had said about his sister, a food-themed business sounded like a better fit for Clem's interests. Lauren thought of Geraldine Corcoran, who had carved a niche with her catering business, cooking classes and weekends feeding hungry golfers at the Nineteenth Hole. Was there room for two catering businesses in a town as small as Penwarra, or another cafe?

The morning passed swiftly, and soon Lauren was ushering Fran Lacey into the studio and introducing her to the fill-in presenter, Nigel. Moments later, Fran was miked up and ready for her interview.

'We have one of the Penwarra Show's tireless volunteers in the studio this morning. Fran, I hear the excitement about the cookbook has inspired a new twist. Tell us about this recipe book cook-along.'

Lauren's ears pricked up as she consulted her notes. A cook-along? Why was this the first she'd heard of it?

'It's not fully nailed down,' Fran said, 'and I only thought of it in the wee hours of the morning, so I might be getting ahead of myself, but what if we took the recipe book one step further and made everything in the cookbook before show day?'

'Sounds good to me, Fran, we love getting the inside scoop here on Rural AM Radio. So how would it work? Would people pay to make the dish, or would they enter them into the baking contest on show day?'

Fran laughed. 'Gosh, no. We don't have a section for entrées, main courses and puddings in the Penwarra show, Nigel, nor do we have room in the baking pavilion to add extra categories. This little community challenge could run in the lead-up to the show, generate a bit of buzz about the cookbook and hopefully, in turn, attract more media attention for the big occasion. Folks can pledge money towards the overall cook-along, or they can pay for the honour of cooking a category.'

Nigel scratched his head and Lauren could almost hear him thinking.

She tapped out a message and sent it to Nigel's screen. If he was confused, then it was probably just as confounding to the listeners at home. She needed to help him spell it out.

And have a stern word with Fran afterwards about going off topic on live radio without prior warning.

'So, kind of like the MS Read-a-thon they used to do for Multiple Sclerosis, Fran?' Nigel asked, giving Lauren a thumbs-up from the presenter's desk.

'Exactly, no flies on you, young man. There's one hundred recipes, and we've got several months until D-Day. Loads of time to get the job done.'

'And who would the money go to? And the finished dishes?' He shot Lauren another grateful look as he read her questions verbatim.

Fran explained how different parts of the cookbook would be allocated to various community members. 'One person could be on entrées, another could cook all the mains and so on, until all one hundred recipes have been cooked and enjoyed. Money raised from the book and a cook-along would help tart up the show hall.'

She paused, her mouth twisting as she considered the technicalities.

'I'm not sure about the finished dishes, though. In a perfect world, we could ask all the home chefs to gift their cooked items to a worthy cause, but there's red tape galore when it comes to food donations. That might be tomorrow's 2 am problem-solving session.'

'If they need taste testers, I'm sure our listeners can help,' Nigel said. 'Sounds like another prime example of Penwarra pulling together to get the job done.'

Lauren caught up with Fran on the way out.

'A cookbook and now a cook-along? Are you sure you'll have time, Fran?'

'Once I've nutted it all out, I'll be fine. It'd be a crying shame not to capitalise on this cookbook's popularity, and you know how hard it's been raising money to fix up the baking pavilion.' Fran fiddled with her wedding rings. 'I probably should have run it past the show society first, but if I've learned one thing from my time on committees: it's better to beg for forgiveness than ask permission with that lot. I hope you didn't mind me diverting the interview like that, pet?'

'Course not, Franny,' Lauren said with an understanding sigh. She'd heard many a tale over a Lacewing Estate shiraz about the committee relegating Fran's enthusiastic ideas to the 'too hard' basket. 'Actually, I'm pitching a Penwarra show series to my boss this morning. If Paul gives me the green light, we can throw a spotlight on your new cook-along, as well as the cookbook and the show regulars who always put in a good effort for show day: Archie with his giant pumpkins; Simon and his scarecrows; the chap that runs the poultry pavilion.'

'You're a treasure, Lauren. I'll get the names of our cook-along crew to you as soon as I've locked them in. What are you going to call it? Spotlight on Penwarra? The centenary series?'

Lauren rocked back on her heels, steepling her fingers. 'How about the 'Best in Show' series?'

'That's got a good ring to it,' Fran agreed.

When Lauren raised the idea at the planning meeting, Paul was just as keen about the series as she'd hoped. He wrote it down on the whiteboard. 'Love it, this is exactly the stuff George's listeners loved. You're happy for Nigel to run this?'

'I'd hoped to record it myself,' Lauren said, 'like the series I did on the Port Fairview Show for the South West Vic bureau. I know the locals involved and I'll have it all prerecorded, of course, so they'll air during the brekky show.'

Patrice set her elbows on the table, lacing her fingers under her chin, then said to Paul, 'Really, it sounds a bit advanced. I understand you delegating that to a *senior* producer, but isn't Lauren's time better spent producing, not confusing listeners by packaging up something the presenters would normally record?' She wore a concerned smile, but Lauren felt the burn.

She doesn't think I can do it.

'I'd just hate for her to get all flustered again and stress out over nothing. Everything's always such a drama with you, Lauren, isn't it?'

A familiar *thunk-thunk-thunk* pounded in Lauren's chest. Her breath quickened.

'Let's revisit the idea tomorrow, after everyone's had some time to think on it,' Paul said.

'I don't need to think about it,' Lauren said firmly. 'I'm ready and willing to run the series myself.'

Lauren took the recording equipment home with her that weekend, more determined than ever to start on the series, and instead of spending Sunday afternoon prepping for the beach barbecue, she drove to Lacewing Estate.

'Are you sure you need me for this?' Fran fidgeted with her lapel microphone. 'The locals who contributed the recipes are the ones you should focus on, Lauren. I'm just the lackey, I shouldn't monopolise the airwaves.'

Lauren laughed, checking the audio levels on her laptop. 'You're the engine room behind the show's whole baking section, Franny. Without you, there wouldn't be a baking pavilion at the Penwarra Show. I'm recording now, before you can try to talk your way out of this.'

She pressed the record button.

'We have Fran Lacey on the radio today, kicking off our new Best in Show series, celebrating one hundred years of the Penwarra Show. Can you tell us how you segued from show baking and winning all those ribbons to taking on a stewarding role, Fran?'

Lauren made notes, and encouraged and prompted Fran until her guest relaxed. They covered the annual rush to fill the competition tables, the cookbook and the new cook-along venture.

'Is the cook-along garnering the response you were hoping for, Fran? Can you tell us who's cooking what?'

Fran's chest puffed out as she told Lauren about the community response. 'It's been very well received. The preserves section was the first to be allocated, then Michelle from Elliot's Newsagency took charge of the chapter on salads, a new Penwarra lass put her hand up for the cakes, biscuits and main meals this morning, and dear Ruby McInnes is on desserts and puddings. Just the soups, dips, breads and nibbles to go, but I've got my feelers out and imagine they'll be snapped up soon.'

'And you reckon they'll rise to the challenge and tick everything off the list before mid-March?'

'I sure hope so,' Fran laughed, 'especially now I've announced it on national radio and people are pledging money if all one-hundred recipes are made before the deadline.'

Somewhere between the introduction and sharing her tips for first-time show bakers, Fran seemed to have forgotten there was a microphone between them.

'See, that wasn't half as bad as you expected, was it?' Lauren asked after they'd finished. 'You did a wonderful job.'

Fran groaned and shook her head. 'I rabbited on for twice as long as I needed to. You'll have a hell of a job editing that down to five minutes.'

'I'd rather be looking at it than looking for it, Fran. Now, tell me who else I should be interviewing about this baking fundraiser?'

9

It had been years since Jack had needed to put his ute into anything other than two-wheel drive, but as he rattled along the rutted track in Canunda National Park, he decided it was long overdue.

'Nice coastline,' he said, following Lauren's gaze out the window, where the azure ocean sparkled. 'Is it good swimming or just good for fishing?'

'As long as you watch the rips and stay away from where they've rigged the fishing lines, it's pretty good. I'm not sure what Clarissa will make of it, though.'

'And she's the one going out with the Scottish guy, right? Connor's friend?'

Lauren nodded. 'It's an odd pairing, but Fergus seems happy. It'll be interesting to see what happens when it's time to fillet the fish and serve up the barbecue. April said Clarissa's officially pescatarian with a vegan-curious bent.'

'I'm not sure if you're still speaking English, but that made no sense to me,' Jack said, making Lauren grin.

When they arrived at the beach, and the rods came off the car and were sorted into rod holders, Jack could see Fergus was torn in his loyalties.

'I'm going to hook up the squids. Clarissa, maybe you don't want to watch this part.'

Jack watched Lauren engage the quiet woman in conversation about their new kitten and when the lines were baited and in the water, Fergus asked for his help pulling a second barbecue off the back of April's Hilux.

'How much are you planning to catch?' Jack asked, giving the tall and cheerful Scotsman a hand. 'There's only six of us.'

Fergus nodded, swiping a shock of ginger hair from his eyes. 'Aye, but Clarissa's plant-based patties and chicken-esque kebabs can't go on there with the regular snags and fish. Trust me.' He gave a good-natured smile. 'How are you settling in at the Penwarra cop shop? You're well off to have found Lauren. She's a great lass, isn't she?'

'Yeah, she is, and settling in well, thanks,' he said, wondering if the conversation was as awkward for Fergus as it was for him. Lauren had already told him they used to be an item.

'Aye,' Fergus said. 'A real good egg. Have you met her mum and sister yet?'

Jack shook his head, setting meat and barbecue utensils onto the fold-out table.

'Well, you wouldna pick the Bickford ladies in a line-up.' Fergus shot him another broad smile. 'They're pretty hard on Lauren. And just so you know, the Christmas trip is always a challenge.'

Before Jack had a chance to question him further, their conversation was cut short by the arrival of a boisterous golden retriever intent on inspecting the lunch supplies.

'Oh no, you don't, Mishka,' Fergus said, catching the dog by the collar and hauling her away from the eskies.

Lauren joined Jack with the deckchairs. 'You enjoying yourself?'

Jack nodded, offering her a piece of the jam and coconut slice Harriet had helped make. 'They're a nice crew. You guys do this every public holiday?'

Lauren smiled, running a hand through her still-damp hair and pulling it into a ponytail. 'We've had a few beach fishing trips, sometimes camped overnight, but this is the first time we've done Labour Day here.'

Jack applied more sunscreen, wary of the sunny spring day. 'Sounds like you're onto a good thing. Perfect day for the beach.'

'Glorious, isn't it?' April said, joining them with Clarissa and Connor. 'If only I could order weather like this for Christmas Day. We're catering for our biggest Chrissy function yet— they're even arranging a band to play in the vineyards so the guests can have dinner in the cellar and dessert between the vines. I'm going to need plan B, C and D if the weather's horrid.'

'Clem's hoping for an outdoor lunch too,' Jack said.

'Us too,' chimed in Clarissa.

'I'll be in WA,' Lauren said. 'Rottnest Island. It should be great.'

Her bright smile was at odds with her weary tone and Jack recalled Fergus's comment.

'Sounds terrible,' he deadpanned. 'All those quokkas, sunshine and white sandy beaches.'

'Which reminds me,' Lauren said, ignoring his teasing. 'Any chance you'd mind house-sitting again over Christmas? I know you only just finished the last gig.'

'Sure, count me in,' he said. 'Though I think we've got to bottom of the neighbourhood nuisance acts, so if that's what you're worried about, you can rest easy.'

Lauren leaned in closer. 'Really? That's great news. Was it the teenagers?'

'I can't say,' Jack said, remembering the long list of regulations he'd agreed to honour and uphold when he'd graduated from the academy. If there was a leak in the system, it wasn't coming from him.

'My lips are sealed, it's not like it's on the record,' Lauren said.

April studied him. 'What about when you're old and married, would you maintain the cone of silence even then?'

Jack made a zipping gesture across his lips. 'Duty bound,' he said with a shrug. 'When I make an oath, I take it seriously.'

On the topic of oaths . . . It was an odd time for Jack's former best friend, colleague and brother-in-law, Adam Dunkirk to gatecrash his subconscious, given the social setting and the lighthearted conversation, but Jack couldn't stop the memory of them standing shoulder to shoulder on two occasions making vows. He and Dunkirk both in full police dress uniform reading an oath to uphold the law, and then six months later, in tuxedos, when Dunkirk made an oath to love and protect Clementine. His sister and his best mate had made a striking pair at their wedding, and they'd both welcomed the pregnancy news. It was *after* Harriet's birth that things had fallen dangerously apart.

A man's only as good as his word.

When Jack arrived at the Mechanic's Institute a fortnight later, there was a good turnout for the first meeting of the newly opened Men's Shed. He stood in the back corner beside a table of power tools, keeping an eye on the door for Sebastian and Cohen.

'I couldn't believe it when I heard ladies were welcome,' a woman told him, delight written on her face. 'Better late than never, I always say.' She introduced herself as Geraldine Corcoran. 'I'm friends with Lauren and April. And do you like birds too?' She pointed to her 'Save our Red-Tailed Black Cockatoo' t-shirt. 'The cocky count isn't an exact science, but we're on the ground, counting nests, inspecting hollows and tracking our results year in, year out. You should come—'

Geraldine broke off as there was movement at the front of the institute and the organiser gave a short welcome before introducing Mayor Jillian Dangerfield.

After the speeches, the mayor sought Jack out.

'So you're the one strong-arming those louts into joining the Men's Shed program?'

'I wouldn't say "strong-arming",' Jack said, 'and they should be here soon.'

'Perhaps when you've finished making wooden chopping boards with the retirees, you might want to focus your attention on graffiti,' the mayor said, pulling her phone from her pocket and thrusting it in his face. 'Look what they did.'

'It's quite artistic,' Jack offered, zooming in on the photo. Although it wasn't flattering, the artwork was unmistakable, right down to Jillian's pearl earrings and the formal mayoral robes she must wear for official ceremonies.

'Good? It's horrid. I don't even like cats,' Jillian said, her eyes flashing. There had to be a dozen cats in the graffiti portrait, some on her lap, others playing with a ball of wool, one on her shoulder. It looked like something a cartoonist would put in the *Advertiser*.

'Are you pressing charges?'

'I don't have a scrap of evidence, but instead of playing Bob the Builder with the oldies at the Mechanic's Institute, I think you should be putting these hoons to work, teaching them that bad behaviour has bad consequences.'

Geraldine, still by Jack's side, didn't hide the fact she'd been listening in on the conversation.

'Great idea, Jillian, hard labour always works,' Geraldine said. 'We should get them hoeing up paddocks of scotch thistles. Shifting old railway sleepers and ripping up the unused train tracks. Maybe a few months repairing dry stone walls?'

Jack coughed to cover his amusement at Geraldine's deadpan manner.

'This isn't a laughing matter, Mr Crossley. I expect you to take a firm line. Is it the kids from Morley-Morley Road? What are their parents doing about it?'

'I'm afraid I can't discuss individual cases,' Jack told her.

'Well, if you don't do something, someone else will. Perhaps a neighbourhood watch group could catch them at their own game,' Jillian said. A car pulled up outside and she raised her voice over the engine. 'Those boys need to be held accountable for terrorising residents. We don't want louts and troublemakers in our town.'

A movement at the door caught Jack's eye. His heart sank when he spotted Cohen and Sebastian in the doorway. They'd clearly heard what Jillian had said.

'Told you this was going to be a waste of time,' Cohen muttered. 'We don't want to be here and they sure as hell don't want us either. I'm outta here.'

Ruby McInnes was waiting at the door when Lauren arrived for the interview, looking nothing like the frail 98-year-old Lauren had been expecting.

Ruby laughed at the expression on Lauren's face. 'Just because I'm almost as old as the Penwarra Show doesn't mean I need mollycoddling.'

She led Lauren through to the kitchen where they'd be recording the interview for Lauren's Best in Show series.

'It's like an American diner,' Lauren said, marvelling at the furnishings. Everything from the black-and-white chequered tiles to the retro fridge reflected the theme. 'This is a story in itself,' she continued. 'I know I'm here to talk about the show, but I have to take this in first. Is that a real working jukebox?'

Ruby was amused by her delight. 'Sure is. Had it shipped over from our diner in Massachusetts years ago.'

The older lady explained she was one of the last war brides in the type of matter-of-fact tone one might use to say they were an Aquarius or fond of chocolate.

'You married a Yankee sailor?'

'Oh, that's just the tip of the iceberg, Lauren. We ran a diner for twenty years—boy, could I tell you some tales—but you don't have all day to humour an old lady.'

It was a herculean effort to focus on the show series. Lauren set up her equipment at a vinyl-wrapped table and sat on a stool straight from an American fifties sitcom set. A sky-high jelly-topped dessert sitting on the table wobbled lusciously each time Ruby laughed, and the hour flew by as she spoke about show baking and why she'd pledged to cook the hot puddings and dessert recipes in the community cook-along.

'Keeps my mind sharp, little challenges like this,' Ruby said. 'Just like the journals I kept on the voyage to the States.'

'I can't imagine you as anything other than sharp,' Lauren said. 'And I can't believe your life story hasn't been turned into a Hollywood blockbuster, or a Netflix series at the very least!'

Ruby laughed. 'And what would we call this masterpiece? "From Pavlovas to Popcorn"?'

'You think of a title and I'll think of a way to start getting it down.' Lauren wasn't sure if she could do Ruby's story justice, or what form it would take, but she was keen to at least try. And while Ruby was spritely for her age, they both knew time wasn't on their side.

Cohen and Sebastian were silent on the way home from the Mechanic's Institute, glued to their phones or staring out the window. Jack berated himself as he drove. *Should've stopped Jillian Dangerfield the moment she began ranting.*

'It'll be better next time. Not everyone thinks like her,' Jack said as he turned into the Moriartys' driveway.

'Next time? You're nuts.' Cohen dragged his hood over his head and instead of opening the gate for Jack to drive through, vaulted over the fence post and loped down the driveway without a backwards glance. Jack suspected he had a better chance of talking sense into Sebastian, especially without Cohen's presence.

'You've agreed to one-hundred hours of community service,' Jack reminded the boy. 'You can't shop around and refuse the options until you find the perfect match. It's not Tinder.'

'You heard the old duck: they didn't want us there and we didn't want to be there. It's punishing everyone, not just us, especially when the whole town's trying to pin all the trouble on us.'

'So tell me who else is up to no good, Sebastian. You know I can't do anything if you stay quiet.'

But Sebastian had gone mute.

'Nice artwork.' Jack gestured to Seb's arm, changing the subject. 'Don't s'pose you know anything about the mayor's front fence?'

The boy tugged his sleeve, slouching lower in his seat before shrugging again and shaking his head, still not meeting Jack's eye.

Jack dropped him at the wildlife sanctuary, then made his way through Penwarra, determined to persist with the boys until he'd exhausted all the options.

He returned to the station to find Sammi on the phone and a tower of cookbooks on the front counter beside the missing persons photos.

'Yep.' She nodded, beaming at Jack. 'Yep, count me in, Fran.' She shook her head and leafed through one of the cookbooks. 'The boss has just walked in. I'll tell him.'

Jack paused halfway through removing his kit vest. Sammi had already signed him up for a school visit and a guided tour of the police station for the Year Six class this week, what was she dobbing him in for now?

She hung up and handed him two cookbooks. 'This one's yours, and this one's Clem's. You owe me fifteen dollars.'

'Bargain.' Jack studied the front cover.

'Apparently your awesome sister's volunteering for the cook-along, so her copy's free.' Sammi laughed and nudged him with an elbow. 'I can see by your smile you're already daydreaming about a whole lotta cakes, biscuits and slices coming your way soon.'

Jack flicked through the cookbook. A project was good. A baking project, a sewing project, heck, even planting out a paddock of sunflower seeds would be a good project. Because if there was one thing he knew about Clementine Crossley, it was that a project—any type of project—gave her a focus and helped her stay on top of things. The part-time work at Fiona's shop was helping Clem's budget, and getting her out of the house several times a week, but the cook-along would tick a few extra boxes in the mental wellbeing department: connection and a sense of giving back to the community.

A toot came from outside and Jack turned to see a motor-cycle pull into the car park. The rider waved a leather-clad arm in their direction. Sammi waved back cheerfully, a goofy smile crossing her lips.

Young love. The bubbly young receptionist was his only colleague at this single-officer station and Jack hoped she'd be focused enough to help him hold the fort.

She caught Jack watching. 'Don't look so worried, Jack, it might never happen! Come and meet my new boyfriend, Logan.'

The bloke clearly doted on Sammi, and had an easy-going manner that seemed more suited to a surf instructor than a council ranger.

'Yell out if you need a hand, whether it's a police matter, a council matter or somewhere in between. Or even if you're just after some company on a Saturday night. I don't need much of an excuse for a bonfire or a few coldies at the pub,' Logan said.

'He does an awesome campfire roast,' Sammi said, smiling and reaching for Logan's hand.

Logan grinned right back. 'Not as good as your cinnamon scrolls or that pumpkin and ginger soup. I've gotta pull my weight to keep up with you, Sammi.'

Keen to extract himself before they started whispering sweet nothings, Jack gave them a nod. 'Nice to meet you, Logan.'

'You too, buddy. We look out for one another around here, so don't hesitate to call.'

Jack thanked him for the offer and left the two love birds canoodling in the car park. After finishing up the paperwork and locking the station, he changed into his welding gear, collected Arthur from the retirement village and headed for Sunny Cross Farm.

'You said I could choose the music today, Uncle Jack!' Harriet rolled around the side of the house on her skates and followed him into the three-bay garage. She did a circuit around the shed's smooth concrete slab and climbed onto a stool at the workbench, reaching for the portable speaker.

'How about rock today, Harri? Not sure I can handle Taylor Swift two afternoons in a row.'

'Go on, give the kid a shot at choosing the music,' Arthur called.

Jack turned to see his grandfather emerge from the house, a tray of glasses and iced water rattling precariously on the seat of his walking frame as he shuffled down the ramp.

'Pop!' Jack dropped the pair of sawhorses and strode across to collect the tray. 'Weren't you happy in the air conditioning, watching the cricket?'

Arthur grinned, intent on his favourite spot under the shady tea tree. 'Too nice a day to sit inside, I can do that back at the lodge. Vic called about a scrap metal pile he's sorting. Old washer or something for the tip, if you don't mind carting it away.'

One electrical appliance wouldn't touch the sides, but at least it would be a start.

'Tell him I'll call around soon. How's Clem going?'

'You know your sister, she's in a flap with this radio interview prep. It's safer out here with you two.'

Jack glanced at the house, then his watch. Lauren wasn't due for another hour at least, and when he'd arrived, the place had already been spotless. What was Clem doing now?

'I'll go see—'

Arthur held up a hand. 'Leave her be, she's baking a batch of nutties. Once she's spent a bit of time mixing and measuring, she'll be much easier to deal with.'

Jack cast his grandfather a dubious look. There it was again; that little surge of worry. 'Do you think the cook-along's too much? I could ask Lauren to reschedule the radio interview.'

'Trust me, son,' Arthur said, his hand cool on Jack's forearm. 'Maybe it's women's troubles or she's just tuckered out from running the second-hand shop while Fiona's on holidays, but I don't think it's more than a passing thing. She was excited about the radio gig when she dropped into the retirement village yesterday, and the cooking challenge is right in her wheelhouse. Don't go storming in there all guns blazing because she's having an off day.'

It wasn't easy to go against the impulse to check on his sister, to see with his own eyes that she was tracking okay, but Jack trusted his grandfather to know the difference between Clem feeling overwhelmed and the dangerous tendrils of her depression.

Arthur raised his voice. 'Now if little missy's in control of the music in there, I think we need something to sing along to. And it'll have to be loud if we want to hear it over the tools.'

The opening strains of Taylor Swift's first pop hit blared out of the portable speaker and Arthur grinned.

Jack bit back a groan. 'Not this again?'

Harriet rolled onto the bitumen driveway, singing and holding a pretend microphone out for Arthur, who somehow knew all the words.

Jack carted his sawhorses a little further away from the speaker and set to work cleaning the metal sunflowers he'd retrieved from the tractor shed.

There were only a few small welds that needed fixing, and he knew it would take longer to clean the sculptures than tack on the fallen petals, but after the disastrous Men's Shed meeting, Jack wanted Sebastian and Cohen to trust him when he pitched the poultry pavilion project.

Teaching Sebastian and Cohen to weld would be a soft start, before they moved onto fixing the chook cages at the show-grounds, but first he needed to brush up his skills. The slightest hint that his welding was subpar, and the game would be up before it had even begun.

He peered at the sunflowers. The recycled metal looked even older in full sunlight, a thick coating of dust hiding the intricate details and rough welds he'd used to fix the pieces in place. Layers of grime and mouse droppings came off with a blast from the pressure washer, then the air compressor made light work of the rest.

And while Arthur and Harriet sang along to Taylor Swift's chart-topping tunes, Jack tacked the sunflower petals back on and reinforced the welds that connected the sunflower stem to the brake drum he'd used as a weighted base.

Harriet and Arthur were singing 'Shake It Off' at the top of their lungs when Lauren arrived.

'Are you Lauren from the radio?' Harriet's elbow pads and knee pads were a blur of green as she hurried in their visitor's direction.

'Yep, I'm here to interview your mum.'

Arthur eased himself up from his walking frame seat and stuck out a hand. 'Art Crossley's my name. Clem said someone was coming from the radio this afternoon, but I wasn't expecting a young thing like you. Thought it'd be crusty old Patrice, she seems to like knowing what everyone's up to.'

Lauren let out a snort of laughter, then clapped a hand over her mouth. 'Oh, I shouldn't laugh. You must be so pleased to have Jack and Clem back in town.'

'Sure am, not many young 'uns would be interested in an old place like this, but these two were never run-of-the-mill teenagers either.'

And just when Jack was wondering what story his grandfather would pull out from his mental archives, Arthur launched into a story about Jack's first and only entry in the Penwarra Show craft competition.

'Did you know our Jack was a champion knitter?'

'Pop—' Jack groaned. 'Lauren doesn't need to hear this.'

'She sure does.' Lauren grinned, nudging Jack with an elbow. 'Go on, Art.'

It was all the encouragement Arthur needed. 'My wife, Shirley, bless her cotton socks, taught Jack and Clem to knit over a wet summer holiday stay when he was about ten. The kids section at the show wasn't well patronised, but our Jack was a champion knitter.'

Jack hovered between embarrassment and apprehension. Even though he'd lived in Lauren's house for months, washed her sheets and knew colour-ordered bookshelves floated her boat, they hadn't broached the unusual dynamics of his family yet.

'He knitted in front of the telly watching the cricket, in the car when we drove anywhere, at the dinner table when he'd finished his dinner. Never dropped a stitch.'

Widening his eyes, Jack threw his grandfather a silent message.

Arthur nodded, still beaming. 'So Shirley entered his scarf and matching slippers in the show, he won a sash and a voucher for the craft shop. Had his picture in the paper and every-thing, clever lad.'

Lauren clapped.

Harriet whooped. 'You didn't tell me that, Uncle Jack!'

'Many hidden depths,' Jack managed, his smile tight. He'd never told his grandparents that the photo of his gap-toothed smile and show knitting had returned to haunt him when he'd started at Penwarra High in Year Nine. It hadn't been their fault that the newspaper had reprinted the photos in their pre-show promotions, or that the schoolyard yobbos had considered his hobby a new and novel way to ostracise him.

'Well, I look forward to hearing more,' Lauren said, 'but first, I need to know everything about these gorgeous sunflowers. Are they your work, Art?'

Arthur stood to go over to the sculptures, slightly wobbly on his feet.

Oh no, you don't. Jack quickly retrieved the walking frame. And while Arthur gave him a 'gee, thanks' look, and reluctantly took the handles, his grandfather's pace was steadier with the extra support.

Harriet zipped past them, her speed a stark contrast to Arthur's considered shuffle. 'My Uncle Jack made them. He's going to make little ones just for me.'

'You're the artist?'

It was Jack's turn to laugh, enjoying the look of surprise on Lauren's face. 'Hack welder, more like it. Don't look too closely.'

A few more sunflowers will get my head back in the welding game, he thought, packing away his equipment.

They went inside the house to find the warm air heavy with baking smells. A batch of scones sat in the middle of the table, alongside a pot of fluffy whipped cream and jam made from the blackberry bushes that ran up and down the roadside.

'What a spread,' Lauren said. 'I should have brought the video camera, not just the voice recorder.' She pulled equipment from her backpack and set it on the scrubbed pine table, then caught Jack's eye and smiled.

'Are you involved in the cook-along too, Jack? Art?'

'We're just the lucky ones who get to enjoy the spoils,' said Arthur with a wink. 'Clem's been baking since she was knee-high to a grasshopper. Learned her numbers multiplying recipes and measuring ingredients.'

'Baking's always been my thing,' Clem said. 'It calms me when everything else feels like chaos. And moving house, looking for a new job, this one starting a new school—' She shrugged. 'It's been a big year.'

A fierce loyalty surged within Jack. Clem had been better since she'd started seeing a new doctor in Mount Gambier, but phrased like that, she *did* have a lot on her plate.

'I always thought I'd be baking for a big brood of kids, you see,' Clem continued. 'But things didn't work out like that. At least in Penwarra, I get to cook for Jack and Pop too.'

She makes it sound like Art and I are doing her a favour, not the other way around. And what's with the 'brood of kids' comment?

'Is your day job in the food industry?'

'Restaurant hours aren't exactly day-care friendly, and as a single mum in the Adelaide 'burbs, it wasn't ideal. It'll be easier now Harriet's in school. My cousin Fiona offered me a few shifts at her second-hand shop, so I'm working around school hours until something else pops up.'

'She'd do well with a farm-gate cafe,' Arthur said, heaping jam onto a scone. 'That's what my Shirley always said.'

Clem traced a pine knot on the tabletop. 'Anyone can make a few cakes and scones, but I don't have a head for business. Sorry, Lauren, we've gone totally off topic. Please,' Clem glanced at her, 'don't put that in, it's just pie-in-the-sky talk.'

She beckoned Harriet over, and the little girl gave the show recipe book to Lauren. 'I helped Mummy with this one,' she said, pointing to the sweet and sour meatballs. 'See, we've written an H for Harriet next to that one and a C for Clementine. And we made this one. And this one.'

Lauren flicked through the pages of the booklet and her face lit up when she got to the sweets. 'Oh, you made the choccy rock cakes too. H and J.'

Harriet stuck her tongue out and shook her head. 'They were gross! Yuck, yuck, yuck. Uncle Jack said the recipe was bad.'

It wasn't a lie, Jack thought. *They'd had been a disaster.* The mini cakes had barely held together on the tray and even after they were cooked, the consistency was off. Despite the recipe review coming from a cute-as-pie six-year-old who looked like butter wouldn't melt in her mouth, he could tell it was a blow all the same, as Lauren's face fell.

'Harriet!' Clem scolded. 'That's not very nice. They were just a bit dry, that's all.'

'Oh, um, that's not good. It's my recipe, actually. They're usually foolproof.'

Lauren studied the recipe, running her finger over the text and frowning at the page.

10

Embarrassment burned at Lauren's neck and cheeks. *One recipe! That was all Franny asked me to provide, and I couldn't even manage to do that right. And of all the home bakers in Penwarra, I had to discover my mistake in front of the Crossleys.*

She cleared her throat, trying to pull together a professional face. Paul had praised the first show series episodes and was planning to air them next week, so it was essential to keep these interviews humming along. She had another in an hour and then two recordings to edit and talent to line up for tomorrow's show before a brisk thirty laps at the pool. Whatever was wrong with this recipe, she'd have to put it aside and sort out later.

She gulped down her panic with a mouthful of tea. 'I must've transcribed it wrong—I'll get you the correct version ASAP.'

The promise satisfied Harriet, who passed around the basket of warm scones while Clem poured tea from the cosy-covered teapot.

As Lauren interviewed Clem, Harriet climbed into Jack's lap and stretched her arms behind her to loop around his neck. She looked up at him like a sunflower turning to the sun.

Jack whispered to his niece, holding a finger to his mouth to indicate silence. Lauren couldn't hear what he said, but Harriet's stifled giggle and Jack's murmured response were so wholesome, it made her heart swell.

Clem posed for a photo with her cooking equipment and Harriet rolled into the tableau wearing the tiniest apron Lauren had ever seen. *So stinking cute.*

The Crossley family were on Lauren's mind long after she'd finished the following two interviews. 'I'm not sure what this guy is doing to me,' she told April later that afternoon, holding the phone with one hand and juicing a lemon with the other. 'But I feel like I've been teleported to a parallel universe. I thought FaceTiming when he was house-sitting to see him rearranging my pantry in his cop uniform was the hottest thing I'd seen all year, but I think my ovaries almost exploded today when I saw him with his niece and pictured him as a little boy, knitting in front of the Boxing Day test. Before I knew it, I'd invited him for dinner again. Tonight! Who even am I?'

April laughed. 'A slight variation on the Lauren Bickford I know and love, but a good version all the same. What are you cooking?'

Lauren poured the fresh lemon juice into the blender, plucked two hairy anchovies from a jar and added them to the garlic, Worcestershire sauce and olive oil. 'Chicken caesar salad.'

'Your poor mum won't be happy about you being distracted by a mere man. She told me she's holding a spot in the pool room for your Walkley journalism award. Does she still think your career will go to the dogs if you get married?'

Lauren grimaced at Gary, who was preening himself on the windowsill, as she grated the parmesan. She kept half for the salad, gave a sliver to Gary and used the rest in the dressing.

'Don't joke. Tahnee's framed post-grad certificates already outnumber my piddly little bachelor's degree. I don't dare mention Jack's name in conversation yet, or Mum will be down here in a flash, reminding me of everything she sacrificed for my education. Remember what she was like when I started dating Fergus? She dredged up Dad's dying wishes about Tahnee and me excelling in our chosen fields, then guilt tripped me about returning to Penwarra so many years after she'd moved away. I'm already nervous about Christmas—you know what she's like.'

'It's your life, Loz,' April said gently. 'You get to choose what you prioritise.'

Lauren tucked a strand of blonde hair behind her ears, catching sight of Jack's ute pulling up outside.

'Oh my, I take back everything I said about the sexiest version of Jack Crossley. That boy's outdone himself. He's walking through my front gate with an armful of sunflowers as we speak.'

'You're smitten, my friend. Smitten.'

Lauren shook her head, untying her apron. 'This is me we're talking about, April. I don't do smitten.'

April was still laughing as she ended the call.

Lauren whipped off the apron and answered the door.

'Hey,' she said, hoping he couldn't hear the thumping of her pulse as he leaned in to peck her cheek. It should be criminal to smell that good and look that fit in a round neck t-shirt and faded black jean cut-offs.

'Smells great in here,' Jack said, handing over the sunflowers. 'Can I do anything to help?'

Lauren directed him to a seat at the bench and passed him the wine glasses. 'Nope, everything's sorted. And I've revised the choccy rock cakes recipe for Harriet. I transcribed it incorrectly. God knows how Fran's going to send the correct version to everyone who's already bought the cookbook.'

Jack opened the wine he'd brought and poured her a glass. 'She'll work something out. Maybe she can have print-outs at the baking registration table on show day?'

Impressed with the suggestion, Lauren handed him the amended recipe. 'That'd be a start. I hope Harriet forgives me.'

'She will, she's a soft touch, that one.'

His eyes crinkled in the sweetest way when he spoke about his niece but the moment Lauren stepped back, and her fluttery sleeve slipped over her shoulder, the vibe between them went from acquaintance-level comfortable to charged.

So he's human after all, she mused, watching Jack drag his eyes away from her lace bra strap as she pulled her sleeve back in place.

He recovered quickly, and as they sat down to dinner, Jack had her in stitches with a story involving a 'wanted' poster Harriet had made for her friend's stuffed toy turtle.

'I'm not sure the description "green, cuddly and sometimes smells like the inside of a belly-button" is going to help bring Taj the Turtle home, but she's stuck them up outside the bakery.'

'Such a little character,' Lauren said, serving up the salad. 'She's lucky to have an uncle like you.'

'I'm the lucky one,' Jack said. 'How about you? Were you a wild kid growing up?'

Lauren told him about her childhood, how her family had lived in Penwarra for several years, and how losing her father had made her mum determined to raise smart, independent and driven daughters in his honour. 'She's like a bull terrier.' Lauren tried to make it sound like a joke, but underneath the table, her legs twitched restlessly. 'Still works twelve-hour days and expects us to be just as devoted to our careers.'

If Jack's expression was anything to go by, she'd painted a pretty harsh picture of her mum.

Ugh! This is not *how you set the scene for an intimate meal.*

Lauren hastened to soften the description. 'I mean, she loves us, really, but she's also our harshest critic. Tahnee's the golden child, but that's a whole other story, for a whole other night. More wine?'

She refilled their glasses, pleased when Jack pushed his chair back and gathered the empty plates. Together they took no time to do the dishes, and she liked the way he moved around her kitchen with an easy familiarity, opening the right drawers and finding a home for the platter in the corner cupboard he'd reorganised during his stay.

Lauren leaned against the doorframe, noticing the way his jeans moulded his butt when he scooped a pink feather from the floor. Jack straightened, lips twitching as he caught her watching.

'Imagine a pillow made with feathers this soft,' he murmured, tracing the feather along the underside of his arm.

Lauren gulped, unable to draw her eyes away from the smooth skin between his wrist and his elbow. Did he have any idea what that simple gesture and those eight words did to her insides? She was sure he hadn't intended it to be a cheesy come-on, but her skin itched to be caressed so gently, to have his fingers, his lips, an errant feather even, sweep over her body.

'I can, but I'm not sure Gary would appreciate being plucked,' she joked, holding out a hand for the feather. Their fingers brushed but instead of placing it in her palm, as she'd intended, Jack tickled her wrist with the feather.

'Hey, cut it out,' she giggled, catching the golden glimmer in his eyes.

'Or what?'

His teasing tone amplified the undercurrent of chemistry that had rippled in the background during dinner, and Lauren wasn't sure who was more surprised when she returned the tickling, digging her fingertips into his side. 'Or I'll tickle you back until you beg for mercy,' she grinned, dancing her fingertips up and down his ribs.

Jack squirmed, collapsing onto the couch in an attempt to escape her attack, hooting with a giddy laugh she hadn't heard before. She jumped down beside him, poking her fingers into his armpits, then his neck. It was a delight to find that beneath the muscles and tough exterior, he was as ticklish as a little kid. He huddled against the onslaught.

'Mercy!' He choked out. In the nearby aviary, Gary burst into a fit of shrieking.

'Pluck a duck! Pluck a duck!'

The bird's random comment sent them into breathless stitches of laughter and Lauren fell onto the couch beside Jack. She tipped her chin to meet his gaze, finding him pink faced, hair all mussed and one hundred per cent kissable.

How long had they skirted around the edges of their attraction? Weeks? Months? Either way it felt like way too long, especially when she could read the hunger in his expression, a satisfying reflection of her own, despite the protests from the nearby aviary.

Lauren's pulse skidded in her chest as she leaned in closer.

Kiss him or tickle him? She bit her lip.

'Hey, no sneak attacks,' he grinned, squirming and accidentally clipping the floor lamp, which pitched sideways. The globe shattered on impact, spraying fine shards in every direction.

'Bugger.'

'I'll get it,' Lauren groaned.

Jack shook his head, smelling like peppermint and fresh cotton as he leapt from the couch. 'You've got bare feet, and I'm the one who broke it. I'll sort it.'

There was nothing more to do but tuck her feet up and curse the bad timing as Jack carted the Dyson across, setting off an even louder round of shrieking from inside the aviary.

'Gary isn't having a bar of this, is he?' Jack chuckled wistfully.

'Piss off, Jack! Piss off, Jack!' Gary continued, revelling in their attention.

'He'll be sleeping outside at this rate,' Lauren said darkly.

Jack leaned in and placed a gentle kiss on her cheek before gathering his keys and phone from the bench. 'He's right, I should probably get going. Can we do this again, though? Soon?'

And while she nodded reluctantly and watched him walk into the fading light, another part of Lauren was tempted to tickle Senior Constable Jack Crossley into submission, and nail down his definition of 'soon'.

Jack was helping Harriet make gingerbread men and the farm-house kitchen smelled better than a Christmas candle.

'Can I have another taste, Uncle Jack?'

Jack pulled his niece's wooden spoon from the bowl and halved the gingerbread dough on the end before allowing her to cram the rest of it into her mouth.

'Officially fantabulous,' Harriet said, passing him the rolling pin. They worked as a team, him rolling, her pressing the cookie cutter into the dough and Jack lifting the shapes onto the trays.

Soon the gingerbread men were in the oven beside a slab of crunchy oat slice and the almost-cooked fruit cake made with their nan's recipe. Clem had been soaking the mixed fruit in brandy for the last fortnight and Jack had the bottle on standby, ready for drizzling over the cake when it was done.

'Let's clean this up and we'll work on the icing, Harri.' He looked across to see a dripping spoonful of golden syrup on the way to her mouth. 'Oi! That's like eating a spoonful of pure sugar.'

She gave him an indignant look, but returned the spoon to the tub. 'Will they all be cooked when Mum gets home?'

'Sure hope so, short stuff,' Jack said, showing her the selfie from earlier. He and Harriet had flour on their cheeks and Harriet's hands swam in the oversized oven mitts. 'She's got a few jobs to do in the Mount and by the time she's done at the hairdressers, it'll almost be dark. Shall we send her this photo, remind her not to hurry back?'

'Yep, and tell her we crossed gingerbread biscuits and slice off the cook-along recipe list,' Harriet said proudly. 'Oh! And send the photo to Lauren too, she'll love it!'

Jack grinned. Nothing came close to the self-belief of a confident six-year-old. He'd spent much of the day thinking of Lauren and was happy with the excuse to text her.

His phone rang and Jack listened as Sammi explained a situation with kids lurking around the tip. 'They might be gone by the time you get there, but an official warning won't go astray, especially now school's out for summer. Logan's meeting you there with the keys.'

Jack nodded. 'Roger that.' Jack took down the address, then took the gingerbread men and slice from the oven and switched it off. Taking Harriet on a call-out didn't sit especially well, but it was after-hours and with Clem out, what option did he have?

Jack was backing down the driveway when he remembered the dryer Victor had asked him to help shift. *Two birds, one stone.*

The ute tray was already loaded with steel for the forthcoming welding lessons, so with a bit of elbow grease, Jack manoeuvred the dryer onto the back seat.

'You'd better put a seatbelt on it,' Harriet said.

Jack studied the old dryer, knowing it would be easier to humour her than waste time explaining the dryer didn't need a seatbelt.

They arrived at the tip to find an old chair pushed against the gates. Something darted between the recyclables and the e-waste sections.

'Wait here, Harri,' Jack said, leaving her in the car with the windows down. He used the rickety chair to vault over the fence in much the same way he expected the kids had gained entry, wincing as the stink of rubbish intensified. It wasn't as bad as decomposing bodies, but on a warm mid-December day, it wasn't pleasant either. Then he caught a whiff of aerosol cans and fresh paint.

'This is not a place for mucking around,' Jack called out. 'You're not in any trouble, but I'd like a word.'

His voice echoed off the steel carcasses of ovens and rusty 44-gallon drums, tin from dismantled sheds and panels of glass from long-removed windows. A kookaburra called from the gums and Jack found the start of another graffiti piece on the side of a skip bin. He took in the dark, military-style hair and the navy blues and realised he was looking at a caricature of himself.

And even though he couldn't condone vandalism and the picture was as unflattering for him as it had been for Mayor Dangerfield—instead of cats, he was surrounded by round, pink pigs and sported the moustache he'd grown for Movember and since shaved off—Jack could appreciate the crude attempt at humour and the raw talent in the artwork. Lips twitching into a smile, he took a photograph, as much to show Lauren as for his own evidence, and picked up a nearby spray can.

Navy paint came away on his fingertips. Still wet. A quick scout around the perimeter revealed no further clues about the unexpected visitors.

'Any luck?' Logan asked when he arrived with the keys a few minutes later.

Jack shook his head. All signs pointed to Sebastian and Cohen, and Jack could have kicked himself for not actioning a new community service plan yet.

When he opened the ute door, Harriet looked up from her picture book. 'Phew-eeee!'

'Did you see anyone, Harri?'

She shook her head and pointed to the book she'd brought with her. 'Nope, I'm busy reading my book. This one's about mummies and babies. Look, I can spell baby. B-A-B-Y. I'm asking Santa for a sister this year, Uncle Jack.'

Another movement caught his eye—inside the car this time—and all of a sudden, graffiti and his niece's sudden interest in babies were the least of his worries.

'Harriet,' Jack said stiffly, his fingers feeling like thumbs as he took the book and unbuckled her seatbelt. 'I want you to stay really, really still, and I'm going to lift you out of the car.'

'What's—' Logan peered over his shoulder, confused, then jumped back when he saw a flash of brown and gold scales disappear under the dryer.

'Shit a brick!' Logan gasped. 'We need to get her out of there, man.'

'I'm trying,' Jack said, time slowing as he scooped Harriet out of her car seat.

Only when her feet were on the ground and the door was shut behind them was he able to breathe again.

Harriet giggled. 'He said the S-word.'

She could have been bitten by a tiger snake in the back seat of the patrol car.

She could have been sitting there in the goddamn car seat, venom seeping through her veins while I was ten metres away worrying about graffiti.

She could have died.

Harriet, oblivious to the danger she'd been in, tugged at the car's door handle.

'Oh no, you don't,' Jack said, catching her hand and steering her towards Logan's ute. Until he'd evicted the snake, nobody was jumping back in there. 'We're going to leave the ute here and catch a ride back with Logan, Harri. I'll get the dryer out later. You can show Logan the gingerbread men and check the cake.'

Logan, who had gone whiter than a freshly shorn sheep, nodded. 'Biscuits. Mmm. G–good,' he stuttered. The guy was a dab hand with a snake hook, but evidently, the proximity of the snake and child had thrown him for a six too.

'You want me to come back later with you, Jack, to get rid of the . . .' Logan turned his wide-eyed gaze back to the patrol ute, 'The, um . . . dryer?'

Jack shook his head. 'I'll ride out here later, take care of it myself.'

Snakes had been as common on the sunflower farm as bush rats and possums, and while Jack's early curiosity had turned into a cautious respect for the venomous creatures, Clem bolted in the opposite direction at the briefest sighting.

'What about my car seat, Uncle Jack? Mum will be grumpy!'

Not as grumpy as she would be if she knew you'd been sitting beside a tiger snake.

He didn't know what time Clem would be home tonight, but as they locked the patrol ute and climbed into Logan's, he hoped Clem stayed out just that little bit longer—until he'd thought of a way to tell her about the close call.

11

'I can only speak for myself,' Gabrielle said, her green-and-red earrings sparkling in the West Australian sunshine, 'but I'd go easy on the buffet if I were you, girls. Just because it's included in the resort package, doesn't mean you need to go nuts.'

Lauren looked at the plate she was carrying through the resort courtyard. An almond croissant, chocolate muffin and Nutella-smothered pancakes might have been a bit overboard, but it was Christmas, right? She glanced at Tahnee, who had already separated the egg yolks from the whites and relegated the unwanted orange orbs to the side of her plate. *It's only our third day of holidays*, Lauren reminded herself, *just smile*.

'These muffins are almost as chocolatey as mine,' she told Gabrielle when there were only crumbs left. 'The trick is using choc chips and choc buttons, so you've got different sized chunks. Perhaps I should have submitted that recipe for Fran's cookbook.'

Gabrielle threw her a perplexed smile over the newspaper. 'You and your baking. Fine for now when you're so young and fit, but you'll have to curb that habit when your metabolism slows down in your forties, darling. Tahnee, what's the name of your Cross-Fit trainer? You should see if they've got any contacts in the Limestone Coast. Or have you thought of taking up tennis again, Lauren? Bunny says—'

Tahnee gave Lauren a 'here we go again' look and said, 'Swimming's more Lauren's thing, isn't it?'

Relieved by her sister's comment, Lauren sliced a strawberry and added it to the fork with a wedge of pancake. 'Thirty laps, three times a week works for me.'

'It was *just* a question,' Gabrielle said. 'Why do you always assume it's a criticism?'

'Not everyone likes team sports, Mum, and Lauren's not exactly Teletubby proportions.'

Thanks for the vote of confidence, Tahnee.

Gabrielle folded her newspaper, miffed. 'I'm just saying, you've got your father's sweet tooth. Even if your arteries hold up better, all that baking can be hard on one's waistline. I only want the best for you both and if pushing you to be your finest makes me a bad mother, then it's a cross I'm willing to bear.'

Lauren put a hand over her mum's, knowing exactly how this conversation would end if it wasn't nipped in the bud. 'We're not saying that, Mum. I'm just saying it's Christmas, and a few extra calories aren't going to kill anyone. What's on the schedule today?'

Tahnee pulled out the typed itinerary, a slight variation on the week-long spreadsheet used for Bickford family Christmases for almost a decade. How had Tahnee described it last night? Relaxing and pampering with a side serve of motherly haranguing.

With her ruffled feathers smoothed, Gabrielle gave them a bright smile. 'Excellent, girls, I'll see you at the sun loungers directly.' She pulled a rewrapped gift from her bag—a gift Lauren had spent ages choosing. 'And Lauren, you have this back. Those light and fluffy beach novels aren't my thing, darling, but you might enjoy it. If I'm going to read, I want something I can sink my teeth into.'

Like the non-fiction tome Tahnee had chosen?

Rising from the table, Tahnee shot Lauren an almost-apologetic wince before falling into step with Gabrielle, leaving Lauren with her half-eaten pancakes and wounded feelings.

Her phone buzzed in her pocket and she opened the message to see April, Connor and Mishka posing with Lloyd and Fran Lacey outside Lacewing Estate, all wearing matching ugly Christmas sweaters. She couldn't imagine Lloyd or Fran chastising April on her choice of reading material, breakfast and hobbies before noon on Christmas Day.

A second text came through, this time with a pic of Gary perched on top of the pine Christmas tree.

> Happy Christmas from your star galah! All's well here, hope you're having a good one in Rotto.

Jack's sweet text and photo made her smile, and as she packed up her cutlery and thanked the waiter on her way out, Lauren wondered whether his Christmas was smooth sailing, rocky with a chance of insults or somewhere in between.

Although the forecast for Christmas Day was overcast, the Penwarra skies were clear and the temperature was already creeping into the high teens by the time Jack and Arthur arrived at Sunny Cross farm.

After they ate and opened the presents, Harriet grabbed the packet of waterbombs Santa had left in her Christmas stocking. She raced through the back door, intent on the hose.

'Shut the door behind you, Harriet, we don't want any snakes sliding inside,' Clem called.

Jack froze, bracing himself for Clem's wrath, as she scooped up the wrapping paper. Did she know about the snake at the tip? Had Harriet seen it after all? 'Snakes?'

'One of the school mums got a tree from the Christmas-tree farm and it was only after they'd decorated it and were hanging the tinsel that they spotted the snake wrapped around the trunk. Can you even imagine?'

Jack studied Clem, then dismissed the idea that she knew of Harriet's close call. They wouldn't be sitting here unpacking Christmas stockings and chatting about other people's close encounters if Clem knew about the tiger snake, which must have been coiled around the dryer motor when he'd driven to the tip, likely the same place it had happily lived before being carted across town. And while the reptile was now long gone, the close call had gnawed at him ever since. He'd gone back and forth, changing his mind with every toss and turn. Telling Clem would only freak her out, he reasoned, and he didn't want Harriet to have a life-long fear of snakes.

'Funny story that,' he said. 'The other day I had this call-out—'

Clem held up her hands and squeezed her eyes shut. 'Ugh, don't tell me. If it's about snakes, I really don't want to know.'

Not telling them was the right thing to do, Jack thought as he started clearing the brunch things and setting the table for lunch.

'Not sure Nan would approve,' Clem said, handing him crackers to add to the settings. 'Only a light lunch, no hot pudding with flaming brandy sauce.'

'No broken teeth when someone bites the lucky penny,' Jack countered.

At lunchtime, Arthur sat at the head of the table, his knife and fork already in hand. 'Looks pretty darn festive to me,' he said, eyeing the array of salads and crayfish. 'And Nan would've been pleased just to see you lot happy. Family gathered around the table was always the important bit for us. Still is.' Arthur gave Jack a wink. If his grandfather felt the absence of his son—Jack and Clem's father—he didn't mention it.

Clem gestured with a crayfish claw. 'How's the house-sitting going? Are you sure Lauren doesn't mind Harriet joining you for a sleepover next week? You can stay here, if that's easier?'

'No way, Mum,' Harriet said, 'I want to see Gaz! And Lauren's streets are even smoother than Uncle Jack's, great for rollerskating.'

Jack cracked another crayfish leg and handed it to Harriet, who sucked out the soft white flesh. 'Lauren doesn't mind at all. We'll be fine, won't we, Harri?'

Harriet nodded, eyeing off another crayfish leg.

'You've got a taste for the good stuff, missy,' said Arthur, cracking a claw with the handle of his butter knife. 'Can barely believe Vic turned this feast down. He doesn't know what he's missing.'

'Doesn't surprise me,' Jack said. 'Vic barely answers the door, so he's hardly going to roll up here as the only plus one on Christmas Day.'

'You'd be surprised,' Arthur said. 'Before his wife left and his son took off, Vic was as sociable as the next guy. They came here for Christmas once or twice; the odd party.'

'So why'd Kev Jenkins disappear?' Clem asked. 'Jail?'

'Fell onto the wrong side of the law. After he went off the rails in high school, everyone started pinning the misdemeanours on him. Unofficially, of course, but there's one thing you've got to remember about a small town. Once your reputation's tarnished, it's easier pushing you-know-what uphill than changing everyone's opinion of you. Vic gave him an ultimatum, and Kev walked away and never came back.'

'Harsh,' Clem said. 'And that's why you and Nan played it so cool when this hooligan started giving you grief?'

Arthur gave Jack a fond smile. 'Partly,' he said. 'We'd already lost so much. Which reminds me, Vic's had another letter from the council. Apparently the police will be involved if he doesn't act on those notices or pay his fines. Are you really going to evict him?'

'It's a tricky one, Pop,' Jack said. 'If council takes him to court over his property as a health and safety matter, and Vic fails to comply, then I'll get roped in to assist.'

'Gah, can't a man be allowed to sit in his mess a little? We're his nearest neighbours and we can live with it. He's not well, Jacko, he's been strapped for cash for as long as I've known him and look at the way he's fostered so many animals over the years. He's got a big heart.'

'And a big, big mess,' Harriet piped up from her side of the table, making them all laugh.

'But enough of that old guff, it's Christmas,' said Arthur, leaning back in his chair, the Christmas hat on his thick thatch of snowy hair askew. 'If I were a younger man, I'd have a nap and then go back for seconds. These days, with a belly this full, I'd get into bed and not be able to get myself out of it. Tell you the truth, Jacko,' he said, as Clem got up from the table to transfer the last of the spidery crayfish legs into a Tupperware container, 'I'd have thought you'd be Christmassing with your new lady friend, not us.'

Jack caught the cheeky grin that passed between his sister and his grandfather.

'Maybe she just wants him for his house-sitting skills,' Clem said with a wink, filling another container with salad and a serve of potatoes. 'Not everyone's cut out for living with a talkative galah.'

'Mock me all you like,' Jack said, 'but even if Lauren'd asked, and even if we *were* officially dating, there's no way I'd tag along on her Christmas holiday. Rottnest Island is a pretty small place to spend a week with a family I'm yet to meet. From what Lauren's said, her sister and mum are pretty intense.'

'Look before you leap, that's my logic,' Arthur said. 'And why wouldn't they want a strapping young lad like you in their family? You like her, she likes you . . . they might have to get used to it.'

Jack raised an eyebrow.

His grandfather tapped his knees and then his ears. 'My joints might be past their prime, but my hearing and eyesight are just fine. Life's for living, right, Clem?'

'You're the one telling the story, Pop. Not sure I'm a shining example.'

'Bulldust! You've just got to back yourself, Clemmy. Go after what you want with two hands. Harriet's a bundle of sunshine, and I can't wait to see you make your mark in Penwarra . . . A farm-gate cafe, an orchard, resurrect the old sunflower farm or have a whole gaggle of kids. Go out on a limb while you're young enough to brave it!'

Jack arched an eyebrow, meeting Clem's gaze.

She laughed. 'Has someone slipped you a few pre-lunch sherries, Pop? I'm too busy keeping my head above water. Jack's your guy when it comes to high achievers. He'll have this town shipshape in no time, just you wait and see.'

Jack helped clean up, then swapped his sneakers for boots and headed down Wallaby Lane to Victor's property, a takeaway container of Christmas lunch in one hand, a wedge of mulberry pie in the other.

'Merry Christmas, Vic. Pop said you got another letter?'

'Where do I even start, that's what I want to know,' said Victor, peering at Jack through the flyscreen. 'You might think it's all rubbish, but I've got a lot of special memories in those cars.' He cracked the screen door and pointed to the trio of Falcon utes. 'Those were the first cars Kevin brought home. He knew a good vehicle when he saw it.'

A good car? Maybe thirty years ago. 'How about the others, Vic?'

'I can't get rid of them. What if Kev finally comes back to claim them and they're all gone? He'd probably walk right out the gate again and I wouldn't see him for another thirty years.'

Jack wracked his brains for a response, but before he could ask more about Victor's son, the tiny goat appeared at Jack's ankles, staring at him with its one eye.

Victor tutted. 'This thing is a right royal pain in the arse. Got an eye for trouble. Tell Sebastian it won't last if it keeps nosing around snake holes.'

Jack helped herd the goat back into its pen.

'You could tell Sebastian yourself,' Jack said. 'The Men's Shed didn't work out, and until they fix the concrete slab at the showgrounds, the boys can't start on the poultry pavilion upgrades. You could use a helping hand and they need something to do over the summer holidays.'

'Heard they were repainting the rotunda and mowing the roadsides for the glassblower with the fine arse. That'd be punishment enough for anyone.'

'It's your choice,' Jack said, knowing if he pushed too hard, he'd lose Victor faster than a sunflower seed in a chook pen. 'But they've agreed to a hundred hours of community service and the work they've done so far's barely dented the tally. A friendly face would mean a lot to Seb.'

Victor snorted.

'A *familiar* face,' Jack clarified, receiving the merest suggestion of a smile.

'Can't afford to pay them.'

'You wouldn't need to. Can you at least think about it?'

After making his farewell, Jack paused at the pair of Holden utes. 'I thought you said Kevin was a Falcon guy? Those are Holdens.'

Victor shrugged. 'They were a bargain at the time. Couldn't resist.'

Jack brightened. Maybe this could be a starting point for clearing up Victor's property.

Jack pulled up outside the main entrance of the retirement village later that afternoon and helped Arthur inside.

'Hampers for all the residents?' Jack asked, spotting a green-and-red gift basket on the side table when they got to Arthur's room.

'Only my first Christmas here, but I guess so,' Arthur said, rubbing his hands. 'Is that a novel? With a bit of luck there's a bottle of cognac and some scorched almonds inside too.'

Jack peeked inside the cellophane-wrapped basket as he passed it over. Only one person would send a bible for Christmas: his mother, Renee.

'Not a paperback.'

'Ah.' Arthur's mouth tightened and he tugged at the bristles of his white moustache. 'Clem said she got one of these too. It was addressed to you both.'

That was news to Jack. *Why was Renee sending gift hampers now? Was the church running a recruitment drive for excommunicated family members? And who had told their mother they'd returned to Penwarra?*

'She didn't hear it from me,' Arthur said, answering Jack's unspoken question.

'You want me to toss it in the bin?'

'You and Clem are peas in a pod. Seems a shame to waste a good basket, but that's exactly what Clem did too, although your sister read the card first. Surprising how many times the words "repentance" and "forgiveness" cropped up. Be my guest, unless you're light on reading material or you want to sign up?'

Jack snorted. 'Not likely. Surprised Clem didn't mention it, though.'

The cellophane rustled as the basket landed in the bin.

Arthur retrieved a box from his top drawer and passed it to Jack. Inside, there were Christmas lollies, three mini liquor bottles and mixed salted nuts. 'You know where the glasses are,' he said, unwrapping the chocolates. Jack chose two tumblers and a bowl for the snacks.

'Your sister's been out of sorts these last few months. The job at Fiona's shop pays the bills and we both know she's got her hands full with Harriet, but something else is amiss. Normally contact from your mother, even as transparent as this, would send her into a tailspin, but she barely batted an eye when she told me.'

Jack poured them a finger of Drambuie. Clem *had* been distracted, and not just today. He told his grandfather about the necklace she'd been wearing that morning and how she'd sidestepped the question when Harriet asked who it was from.

'The sunflower pendant?' Arthur tapped his glass thoughtfully. 'I commented on that too, while you were at Vic's. I thought it was a treasure from the second-hand shop, but Clem said it was a gift from a fella she'd met online. If you ask me, online dating sounds almost as dangerous as joining a fundamentalist church.'

Jack unwrapped a Santa-shaped caramel. Clem's love life was none of his business, but he couldn't quell the urge to protect her from the minefield of keyboard romeos and romance scams.

'I just hope she knows what she's doing,' he said, recalling the way she'd cooed over the box of baby clothes all those months ago. They'd sorted through the rest of the belongings, a job Arthur had been relieved to outsource, and donated most of the old clothes and excess linen, but for some reason, that box of size 000–0 clothes hadn't left the house. And then there was Harriet's sudden interest in babies. 'I'll let you know if I hear anything else.'

Gary put on his usual performance when Jack walked into Lauren's pink cottage that night, swinging upside down on the perch and screeching. Jack grinned, putting his Christmas gifts onto the hall table and unlatching the cage. The bird didn't fawn over him, like he did with Lauren, but they had formed quite the relationship in the last week.

'Keep your feathers on.'

The bird climbed beak over foot down the wire cage and shimmied through the door in a flash, launching himself into the air for a hot lap around Lauren's lounge room.

Unwinding windows and propping open the front door, so fresh air could flow through the screen door, Jack settled on the couch with a tin of Clem's gingerbread. Gary settled on his shoulder and rubbed his beak against Jack's cheek.

'You want some too, huh?'

He snapped an arm off a gingerbread man and a shower of crumbs fluttered down the front of his shirt as the galah happily nibbled away. After much of the day spent dwelling on his own family, Jack happily turned his thoughts to Lauren.

'So, you think she's still at the swim-up bar sipping eggnog martinis?'

The bird bobbed on his shoulder and cocked his head.

'Nah, you're right, I bet she's belting out Christmas carols on a karaoke machine, scaring all those quokkas back into the scrub.' Jack scratched the bird under his chin and grinned at the notion.

He hadn't been to Western Australia, but from all reports, it was a ripper of a holiday destination. So why had Lauren been reluctant to go? He glanced at the framed photograph on the side table, a candid shot of Lauren, her mum and her sister poolside, with floral leis around their necks and cocktails in coconut shells in hand. It obviously wasn't the heat she was worried about, seeing that photo was taken somewhere equally tropical. And while a schedule of massages, day spas and sightseeing wasn't his cup of tea, it didn't sound strenuous.

He looked again at the Bickfords' matching smiles and pool-slicked hair. Even as a boy, well before his dad died and his mum Renee found religion, family holidays had been something other people did. Not that he'd minded spending school holidays fending for himself and Clem, or the summers helping at the sunflower farm, but every time a kid returned to school with a Gold Coast tan, Wet'n'Wild memorabilia and the inside scoop on the best Movie World rides, Jack had felt a twinge of jealousy. Not because of the air travel or the Queensland warmth, but for the reminder that the Crossleys weren't the family-holiday type.

Moving back to Penwarra, setting up camp at his grandparents' house and looking after his family mightn't have been in his ten-year plan but there was one thing he knew for sure: if he didn't do it, nobody else was going to step up and fill the void.

The swim-up bar at the resort was playing Christmas carols and the bartender's Santa outfit looked way too hot for the

West Aussie climate. 'One pink peppermint cocktail for you, madam,' he said, sticking a candy cane into Lauren's drink. 'And a gingerbread martini for you two ladies.' He garnished Tahnee's and Gabrielle's drinks with matching gingerbread men and fanned himself with the menu.

Lauren sank back against the inflatable chair, paddling towards the shady side of the pool as Gabrielle signed the tab. The sunset was glorious, the view from the pool as pretty as the brochures had promised, and the water enticingly warm. But Lauren couldn't stop thinking of her cosy cottage. Or more specifically, the man who at this very moment was probably sprawled on the French linen sheets *inside* her cottage.

And while she wasn't sure how Jack had spent his Christmas, she was confident he hadn't been dodging questions about his work and listening to a list of 'helpful suggestions'.

'I'm just saying, darling,' Gabrielle said, floating closer in a hammock-like contraption, 'you have so much potential. You know Bunny, from tennis?'

Lauren took a deep drink. Bunny, her mother's doubles partner, was apparently a media industry expert these days.

'Well, Bunny says you don't want to be typecast as the girl next door. You need to hunt down the big scoops if you want ratings.'

'Listeners love my Best in Show series, Mum. Mount Gambier and Millicent usually hog the airwaves, it's high time we shined a spotlight on small towns doing great things. Everyone in the community gets behind the show, and the folks I'm interviewing have brilliant stories to tell, from the school kids who fill the art pavilion to the farmers who enter their fleeces and the dahlia judges that come from Adelaide specially for the event.'

'People also love sugar and lollies, but what does that get them? Cavities and diabetes, that's what! Did you see that job link I sent you? They're looking for a presenter in Townsville and also Broken Hill. It's hard to attract staff, you'd get a queen's welcome. The Silver City real estate agent says it's cheaper to buy than rent, and Bunny thinks—'

The phone chimed on Lauren's pool lounger and she was relieved to see Jack's name on her screen when she dripped her way across the warm pavers.

'I just don't know why you're so tied to that little town, my darling.'

'I've got to get this call, Mum,' said Lauren, wrapping her towel around her waist and walking towards the beach. 'Jack, you have impeccable timing. Happy Christmas!'

'Don't tell me you were being mobbed by quokkas? I've heard they're deceptively savage.'

'Not exactly, but my mum just likened my show series to diabetes-inducing lollies, so that's always fun.'

'Ergh, that's tough. What type of monster doesn't like lollies?'

She grinned, feeling better already, if not a little disloyal for her snarky dig at Gabrielle. 'So what's shaking in Petticoat Lane? No one's stealing ornaments off the town tree or making rude pictures with the fairy lights?'

He laughed again, setting off Gary in the background. 'Nothing that dire. I'm just seeing how you're faring? The weather sounds awesome.'

Lauren made her way down the resort steps until she was on the sand. 'It's magic,' she said, 'but I bet it's beautiful in Penwarra too.'

Jack laughed. 'Not half bad. You had a delivery on your doorstep this morning.'

'Oh no,' she said. 'The troublemakers didn't leave something gross?'

'Nothing like that,' Jack assured her. He switched the call to video and showed her the gift-wrapped box of produce. 'Strawberries, spring onions, cucumbers, tomatoes, squash and sweet corn.'

April knew she was away, so it could only be from young Archie Winklin. He'd left her little gifts in the past, punnets of seedlings he'd raised, fresh veggies from his garden and even a get-well card when she'd been bed bound with a nasty flu the winter before. 'Archie, what a sweetheart,' she said. 'Feel free to eat anything you like, it won't last until I'm home.'

Jack turned the camera to face him and set the phone on the coffee table. He disappeared off camera for a moment, and not only was the house spotless, but Lauren could see a bunch of sunflowers in the kitchen. When he reappeared, Gary was on his shoulder.

'Look at you go! When did that happen?'

'We've been working on it all week. Check this out.'

Slowly, Jack lifted a hand until it was level with the galah's belly. Gary stepped on without hesitation, and when Jack moved his hand until they were nose to beak, Gary bobbed up and down, then lowered his head for a scratch, tweeting softly.

Lauren watched, adding the moment to her ever-expanding mental file of Jack Crossley's soft side. Seeing him win over the cheeky galah was almost as good as tickling Jack until he squirmed, watching him lace up Harriet's rollerskates, or imagining a younger version of him with a ball of wool and his grandmother's knitting needles. She felt her heart expand just that little bit more when Jack beamed at her through the phone camera.

That smile . . . It was better than all the ocean sunsets in the west.

12

It was a week after New Year's when Lauren stuck her head out the back door of the radio station, looking for Rupert Winklin's sleek Jaguar or his young green-thumbed son, Archie. They were due for an interview, but there was no sign of either of them.

She tried Rupert's number once again, then loaded the recording equipment into her car and headed for Winklin Wines to find Archie jogging down the limestone laneway that separated his family's vineyard from Lacewing Estate. The lad was red-faced, sweaty and decidedly pleased to see her.

'Lauren! Can you give me a hand with the lambs?'

She smiled at the Doc Martens she'd chosen for work that morning. Much better sheep-herding footwear than the heels and suit Tahnee had suggested she start wearing if she wanted to be taken seriously for promotion.

They walked slowly down the laneway, clapping when the notoriously cheeky lambs paused to nibble the roadside grass, and eventually ushered the wandering pair back into their paddock.

'If I had a dollar for every time they escaped, I'd be able to buy a hothouse and one of those fancy heat mats for starting seedlings,' Archie said, latching the gate.

Lauren laughed. Most kids his age would be thinking about dirt bikes and PlayStations, not gardening supplies. 'I thought we were recording the interview today, Arch? I was waiting for you at the radio station.'

'Today?' Archie paled. 'Dad said that was tomorrow! Sorry!'

'It's fine,' Lauren said. 'We'll just record it at your house instead.'

Archie pointed to the driveway full of cars. 'Dad's got winery meetings today and I'm supposed to stay outside all arvo.'

'How about the shearing shed?' she suggested, hoping she could capture the background noise of kookaburras in the nearby gums, sheep penned up for shearing and the humming cicadas for her Best in Show series.

Lauren set up the recording equipment on the slatted wool classing table. 'Let's start with your pocket-money plan, Arch. Can you tell the audience how you first funded your hobby?'

'I sold about a gazillion bags of sheep poo,' he said, telling her about the stinging nettles he'd contended with underneath the shearing shed. 'The garden club ladies took heaps of bags!'

They spoke about his love of growing veggies, how an over-the-fence friendship with his neighbour, April, had fuelled his passion for showing his produce, and gave tips to listeners keen to show their homegrown delicacies. Archie's enthusiasm and earnest joy shone through with every laugh and anecdote, and she could just tell the episode was going to be a hit with listeners.

'And how's your giant pumpkin going, Arch? Almost ready for the big day in March?'

He nodded, holding his arms out wide. 'I've got a few to choose from, but I've named the biggest Trumpy, and I can barely fit my arms around him. April says it'll take three of us to lift him onto the ute come show day.'

Archie's happiness was infectious and Lauren found herself smiling broadly as she wrapped up the interview.

'You did a great job, Arch. The listeners are going to go nuts, just you wait.'

Archie whistled, leading her across the laneway.

'Blimey, your patch is almost as big as April's now,' Lauren continued, taking several photographs of the giant pumpkins and then of Archie working in the garden.

A car rumbled down the driveway as they finished the photos, but instead of April's Hilux, Brian Treloar and Geraldine Corcoran piled out of a gleaming ute. Lauren waved them over.

'Come see my veggies,' Archie called, busting with pride as he talked the older couple through his planting list. 'They're not all heirloom varieties like yours, Brian, but they're going well.'

'Anyone who's putting seeds in the soil and making them grow is a good 'un in my books, mate,' Brian said, ruffling Archie's hair. 'And I'm glad I've caught you here too, Lauren. I was going to ask Fran or April about the cook-along, but seeing you're doing the radio series, I expect you'll know the answer. How's the project going?'

'Fantastic,' Lauren said. 'All the home cooks I've spoken with have made a great start on their categories. Clem Crossley, who's in charge of the cakes, biscuits and mains, expects to finish her list with a month to spare.'

'Crossley . . .' Brian said, polishing his glasses. 'Now there's a name I haven't heard in a long time. Old Art used to have the sunflower farm, didn't he? I thought his daughter-in-law was mixed up in some religious sect?'

This was news to Lauren. 'Clem's Art's granddaughter. She moved back to the district with her little girl last summer. Her brother Jack's the new senior constable in town.'

At this, Geraldine clicked her fingers. 'The lad who knocked on our door last winter, asking if we'd heard those ruddy burnouts on the fairway, remember? I met him at the Men's Shed too. He was trying to get the teenagers involved but they didn't receive the warmest welcome, poor loves.'

Lauren nodded, but her brain was still snagged on Brian's information. Jack had told her all about Harriet's phobia of the tooth fairy, Clem's collection of vintage board games and his grandfather's grudging reluctance to use a walking frame, but this mention of his mother was the first she'd heard about his parents.

She was still thinking of Jack when she arrived at the outdoor pool an hour later. The facility was a hive of activity, with swimming lessons and an aqua aerobics class enjoying the late afternoon sunshine.

Lauren cut through the water, starting off with a fast freestyle for the first ten laps, then easing into a breaststroke. Did Jack's parents really belong to a cult or did Brian have his wires crossed?

Adjusting her goggles and swimming cap for one last time, Lauren ended her final set of laps with a sprint. Her lungs burned and chest heaved when her fingertips touched the pool wall.

'Mighty fine finish, there,' said the pool manager, Terri, as Lauren hauled herself from the water. 'We're down a swim squad coach too. I don't suppose you'd be keen to consider the role?'

Lauren tipped her head to the side and tugged at her ear to release the water. 'Must be hearing things, Terri. Did you just ask me about coaching the swim squad?'

Terri grinned. 'That's exactly what I said. What do you reckon?'

'I'd say it's about the last thing I expected today. You know it's been years since I swam squad at boarding school?'

'I know,' Terri said. 'But you've got the pace to impress the kids, you know the drills, and we're in with a shot at the state champs again this year if we can find a good coach. Promise me you'll think on it.'

Lauren rushed through the shower, considering Terri's random request before her thoughts returned to Clem Crossley.

Lauren opened her social media app when she got to her car, but a short skim through Jack's bare basics profile, and a longer trawl through Clem's regular posts and extensive following list, revealed little. And although Arthur had a Facebook account, there were no other Crossleys in Jack's or Clem's Facebook friends. What was the deal with the Crossley family? Jean and Arthur loomed large in their lives, but what about the rest of their family? Were Jack and Clem's parents dead or estranged or just indifferent?

She felt more than a little guilty for her online snooping when she turned into Petticoat Lane five minutes later to find Jack leaning against the picket fence, but it wasn't his razor short haircut or tall, well-built frame that caught her eye. He was cradling another bouquet, this time a posy of milk thistles, dandelions, wild rocket and sheaths of green oats.

'This might distract Gary from the sunflowers,' he said, grinning as he handed her a bouquet that was as unexpected as the lurch in her belly as she imagined coming home to him every night.

The needle-like blackberry thorns within the weed posy cut into Jack's bare forearms arms as he waited outside Lauren's ff:

house, but it was worth every scratch when she lit up at the sight of the posy.

'Wow! I've never seen weeds look so pretty.'

'It was Harriet's idea,' Jack said. 'She's besotted with your galah.'

'Gary seems to like her too,' Lauren said. 'And he'll be thrilled with this.' Her damp hair shone gold and platinum in the bright sunshine and she smelled of chlorine as well as her usual apple blossom fragrance.

He patted his pocket, checking the wedding invitation was still in there. Would she want to come on an eight-hour road trip to attend a wedding for people she didn't know? He wasn't even sure if *he* wanted to go.

Just ask her and see what she says.

'Busy day?' he asked instead, noticing the laptop and recording equipment in the back of her car.

'Hectic! More Best in Show interviews and then to the pool,' she said cheerfully, leading him inside and filling a blue jug with water before plonking the weeds in. Gary went to them the moment his aviary door was opened. 'Thirty laps, and the sunshine glinting through the water is something else. And then Terri at the leisure centre did her best to recruit me as the replacement swimming coach. She's stark raving mad if she thinks I'd measure up to their last coach.' Lauren laughed. 'He took them to state champs. His legacy would be like a noose around my neck.'

It suddenly felt warmer than usual in the small room, the sunshine flooding in through a skylight, and although he'd been looking forward to seeing Lauren all day and inviting her to be his plus one at the wedding, now Jack fought the overpowering urge to leave. He stumbled, banging into the kitchen table and nearly sending a pile of newspapers to the ground. The vase wobbled precariously, slopping water over the sides.

Lauren turned her back to mop up the spill, so she had no way of knowing how her words 'noose around my neck' had landed. He was grateful for her distraction. *It's just a stupid turn of phrase,* he told himself. He inhaled through his mouth, hearing the saxophone or trumpet being practised—badly—next door.

Lauren laughed. 'What a racket!' Carefully, without disturbing the windowsill trio of potted basil, chives and parsley, she wound the kitchen window shut. 'I wish Val had encouraged her kids to play piano or harp. It'd be a lot easier on the ears.'

The room still felt too hot and the closed window made it seem tinier. Jack found himself mumbling a hasty excuse. 'Can't stay, I've got a thing—'

He pulled out his phone, gave an apologetic wave and headed for the door, fighting the hazy memories he'd tried so hard to bury.

'Jack?'

He turned, managing a semblance of a smile, but kept walking. 'Sorry, Lauren, I'll catch you another time.'

Sooner or later, people will let you down.

Jack looked at the cottage in his rear-view mirror as he drove away. Lauren would never joke about something so serious as suicide if she knew the truth, but what would she think of him when she discovered his father had taken his own life?

It wasn't something he spoke about. *Ever.* Putting the incident in a mental vault and turning the metaphorical key kept it from leaching into his daily thoughts, but it didn't stop the rush of anger and shame when someone else raised the topic, even indirectly.

How come he hadn't visualised this scenario yet, and planned his reaction in advance?

Jack white-knuckled the steering wheel, swinging into a turn faster than usual. *Telling Lauren will ruin everything. And even if she doesn't think it's weird that our parents abandoned us, it'll only be a matter of time before she asks* the question.

The same question he'd been asking himself since his mother chose the church just months after their father's funeral: What was wrong with him and Clem? Was there a Crossley curse or were they just destined to be let down by the people they loved?

Lauren swept a silver curl away from Ruby McInnes's lapel microphone. 'Sorry, I could hear it brushing against the mike,' she said, encouraging the elderly lady to continue.

'Now, where was I up to?' Ruby folded her wrinkled, sun-dappled hands in the lap of her dress.

'You were telling me about the first day on the ship to America, and the Aussie girls struggling with the high seas.'

Lauren had already spent half an hour in Ruby's diner-themed kitchen, but it seemed like two minutes; last month's interview about the show cook-along was mundane in comparison to Ruby's experiences as a war bride. It was also a nice diversion from dwelling on Jack's hasty exit a few days earlier. And while he'd been in touch, he still hadn't explained why he'd run out, or left behind a wedding invitation.

'Oh yes, that's right, the voyage with the other wives and fiancées,' Ruby said. 'Are you sure you want all this detail? Your listeners will be bored to tears if I drone on for an hour.'

Lauren nodded. 'Absolutely. Your story is amazing, Ruby. Stuff Hollywood—it's a Netflix series waiting to happen. I want to hear everything, and once it's all on tape, we can work out how to present it. Movie, podcast, memoir . . . Maybe all three.'

The older lady didn't need much prompting to continue her story about travelling to the other side of the world for an American sailor she'd met and fallen head over heels with, the small Connecticut town where they'd raised their family, the local characters that frequented their Massachusetts diner, and the heartbreak when her children left home.

'My Frank died of a broken heart after all our kids scattered across the globe, leaving just the two of us rattling about in our big house. Customers filled the void for a while, but it wasn't the same living overseas when everyone I loved was so far away. So, after thirty years as an American citizen, I came home. It wasn't easy either, mind you. Families are funny things, aren't they?'

Lauren gave a wry smile. 'You can say that again.'

'You can be as brave as you like, bold enough to sail across the world on a ship full of war brides and set up camp in a foreign land, raise a family then watch them scamper, lose the love of your life and even after all that, it won't be enough for some people. Or, perhaps more precisely, it'll be too much. My mother, rest her soul, and I never saw eye to eye.

'I thought they were glorious adventures. She thought I was running away. And for the life of me, I could never understand why my older sister was so determined to cling to the way things were, horrified that people dare to change, furious that the world never waited for her to catch up.'

The conversation circled back to the show baking and Ruby's delight in contributing to the community cook-along project. 'I just love a challenge,' she said, pushing a plate of jelly cakes forward.

Lauren had already sampled one of the pink, coconut-covered sweets but she accepted another. The sponge was like biting into a pillow. 'Any specific advice you want to leave listeners with, Ruby?'

'We only get one life, Lauren, and it's up to us to do every-thing in our power to use it wisely, whether you're ninety-eight or thirty-two.'

Ruby's fervour and advice stayed with Lauren throughout the week, but when Friday night drinks with April rolled around, she felt flat.

'I know don't have much to complain about,' Lauren said, handing April a bowl of apricot FruChocs, 'it's just I'd expected to have a few more ducks in a row by this stage of my life.'

April studied her with a grin. 'You mean you haven't lived through a war, raised a family in a country ten thousand kilometres from home and run your own business yet? Such a slacker. I can barely believe I call you a friend.'

Lauren couldn't help laughing. 'First-world problem, I know, but just when I think I've got a handle on my on-air nerves, Patrice walks into the room and throws me completely off kilter. And I thought things were going okay with Jack, but he practically ran out of my house last week and if I didn't know any better, I'd think he was avoiding me.'

She'd already told April about the silver-and-cream wedding invitation, and while they'd deduced it must have fallen out of Jack's pocket when he delivered the weed posy, neither of them were any wiser on why he'd left without mentioning it.

'Maybe he got cold feet about the whole wedding thing. Maybe he'd planned to ask Gary to be his plus one.'

'Ha ha,' Lauren said. 'But don't you think it'd be awkward telling him I've not only seen the invite but he left it behind? If he's suddenly too busy to catch up, he's hardly likely to be planning a weekend away to some long-lost friend's wedding.'

Jack was pretty confident he could handle himself around most reptiles, but standing in his neighbour's backyard with his grandfather, listening to Victor talk so casually about the snake locked inside his bedroom, Jack felt his skin crawl.

'Back up a little, Vic. You're saying this snake was on your bed?'

'Slithering across my arm when I woke up,' Victor said grimly.

Jack looked to his grandfather for backup and found a similarly alarmed expression on Arthur's face. Emergency snake-wrangling was one thing, but inadvertently sharing a bed with a deadly brown snake . . . ? *Not happening.*

Jack gave silent thanks for the strict routines that kept his life neat, structured and predictable.

'Wasn't a case of too many nightcaps, was it, Vic?'

With a frown, Victor shook his head. 'A nip or two of port, Art, nothing out of the ordinary.'

'I hate to say it, old friend, but maybe you should tidy this place up.'

A silent conversation went on between the two men. Eventually, Victor nodded.

Abandoning his walking frame, Arthur hobbled over and clapped a hand on Victor's back. 'That's the spirit. How about we look at what you want Scrappy Joe to collect while the lad takes care of the snake.'

Jack grabbed the snake hook he'd borrowed from Logan and opened Victor's front door. The house was just as cluttered inside, with piles of newspapers, boxes, milk cartons and clothes on every surface. A couch stood on its end to free up extra floor space. *How does anyone live like this?*

Alert for rustling or slithering sounds, Jack picked a tight path through the debris and into the second room on the left, as Victor had instructed. The snake was coiled up in the corner of the room, between a stack of dusty records and what must have been hundreds of *Hot Rod* magazines.

It hissed at him, lifting its head off the carpet. 'I know, buddy, I want out of here as much as you,' Jack said, deftly hooking the snake and scooping it into the sack.

After releasing the snake on the far side of the paddock, Jack drove Arthur the short distance to the farmhouse and settled him in the lounge room as he prepared dinner.

'Removing a snake is one thing, but Vic could be smothered in his sleep by a pile of crap or fall asleep with a cigarette in his mouth and the place would go up in a puff of smoke.'

'Ah, surely it's not that bad,' said Arthur, turning so he could see the telly and chat with Jack at the same time.

'How long since you've been inside, Pop? It's a deathtrap,' Jack said, sautéing onions and garlic before adding the aromatics for his curry. The mustard seeds popped and sizzled, and the kitchen smelled like a Moroccan bazaar as he dry-fried the spices and stirred in coconut milk. 'A few days of hard yakka would make all the difference. I'm still hoping to recruit Seb and Cohen.' Jack knew, though, that while carting away Victor's rusty collection of cars would cut back on snakes and improve the place's appearance, it wouldn't fix his grief or quell the hoarding habit.

'Good lad,' Arthur said. 'They'll be able to put all that bother in town behind them, and maybe the task won't seem so overwhelming for Vic once they start chipping away at the surface. And when's Clementine back from Adelaide?' Arthur called over the volume of the cricket game. 'Ever hear anything more about that mystery chap? And is she catching any Big Bash while she's in the big smoke? The Adelaide Strikers are on fire this season; I know that's what I'd be doing if I were in the city this time of year.'

Jack was pretty sure Clem wouldn't sit through a cricket match on the television, let alone attend one in the flesh. And she hadn't breathed a word about the new beau either. Was that what she was doing in the city for the third time this month, meeting the new guy?

He'd just started rolling the garlic naan when a FaceTime call came through on Arthur's phone.

'Here's our girl! Yep, all good here, nothing to worry about,' he said, shooting Jack a wink. 'Missy, your mum's on the phone.'

Harriet rolled into the living room with a pack of Monopoly Deal cards in her hand. 'Hey, Mum, watch me skate backwards!'

'Thanks again for minding her, Jack,' Clem said. 'I'd forgotten what it was like to sleep in and stroll through the botanic gardens with just a book and no timeframe, not a snack bag, drink bottle, sunscreen or tantrum in sight.'

'Too easy,' Jack said. 'Harri and I are having a great time. Jean and Fiona took her to Robe for lunch, apparently Harriet and Fiona's girl Selina are already plotting another cousins' catch-up before school goes back. She wanted a night at the farmhouse, and tomorrow we're back at Lauren's.'

Arthur set three plates on the bench and called over his shoulder, 'You deserve it, Clem. And have fun with your friends tonight, don't get too wild.'

She laughed and shook her head. 'Wild is overrated, Pop. My friends are all in the motherhood trenches too, a late night is dinner at 7 pm instead of five, and rather than dancing, we're keen for an uninterrupted night of sleep.'

'What about that online fella? We haven't heard hide nor hair about that bloke. He an Adelaide chap, then?'

Clem looked between them. 'Pop! So much for keeping your lips sealed.'

Arthur lifted his hands in protest. 'I thought you'd have told your brother by now! This bloke must've been hit with the ugly stick if you haven't even shown us a photo. Hope he's not one of those scammers who preys on single ladies. Jack gets a few of those calls at the station, don't you, son?'

Jack nodded from across the kitchen bench. 'Say the word, sis, and I'll track him down if needs be.'

Clem groaned. 'This is why I keep my private business *private*.'

She hadn't said as much, but Jack and Arthur exchanged a look.

So she is *seeing this new guy in the city.*

Harriet returned to blow her mum goodnight kisses over the phone before they all sat down to dinner and then cards.

Harriet, who had no strategy but plenty of luck, somehow beat both Arthur and Jack at Monopoly Deal twice, and was still crowing about her card-shark skills when they dropped Arthur off at the retirement village.

Back at the farmhouse, Harriet snuggled into her pillows, a broad smile on her face as Jack read her a story about magical fairies and talking toads. Jack was still thinking about luck, fairytales and the false expectations they set as he bid her goodnight.

It was a crazy precedent, really. If life was anything like one of those beautifully illustrated books, then a knight would have galloped into Victor's yard with Kevin, his missing son, in tow. Or, at the very least, cleaning fairies would have ferried away Victor's piles of rubbish before they reached drastic proportions. If life was like the books, their father wouldn't have taken his own life and their mum would have chosen family and friends instead of sinking all her energy into religion. If life were a fairytale, Clem wouldn't have fallen so dangerously ill after Harriet's birth, then lost her husband and her self-confidence in one dizzying swoop.

Jack flicked on the kitchen light, but instead of chasing away the dark thoughts, the quiet farmhouse kitchen only enhanced his melancholy. He took a bottle of water to the outdoor table along with his laptop and opened the work notepad. Sleep

wouldn't be easy in this frame of mind, so instead he chan-
nelled his restlessness into paperwork.

Yesterday, he'd been spat on by a drunk driver resisting
arrest, which required a painful amount of paperwork, and
while the petty disturbances around town had initially stopped
after he'd spoken with Sebastian and Cohen, he'd noticed
several graffiti tags on stop signs. And then there was the
artwork at the tip. Summer holidays, bored kids and hot and
bothered locals weren't a good combo, and as the clock ticked
closer to midnight, Jack started work on a fresh community
policing plan.

After the report was drafted and saved, Jack leaned back
in his chair and looked across the paddock towards Victor
Jenkins' property. Pointing the finger at Sebastian and Cohen
for this latest round of disturbances might look like progress
on paper, but it would undoubtedly break the fragile bond of
trust he'd built, and then where would they turn?

Jack shut the computer and opened his phone. The text
from Lauren topped his messages and he smiled as he reread
her suggestion for catching up later that week. Most women he
knew would have waited until his babysitting duties were
done and dusted, but Lauren had gone out of her way to
consider a Harriet-friendly outing of hot donuts and a swim
at Beachport.

He walked around the living room, closing blinds, switching
off lights and preparing to turn in for the night, but the doubt
followed him around the silent farmhouse. Was it time to pull
his head out of the sand and be upfront with Lauren about his
failings, so his past didn't feel like an armed grenade? Or did
he just do what had always worked in the past: Keep that side
of him closed off, and for good reason?

'You still here?' Paul stuck his head around the doorway just as Lauren unplugged her headphones. 'We're not paying you enough to see this much of you. Go home, take a load off.'

Lauren was surprised when she saw the time. 'I'm almost done editing Ruby's interview. She's a natural-born storyteller.'

'We've had great feedback on this show series,' he said. 'Every second caller's raving about it.'

The unexpected compliment made Lauren flush with delight. 'Really? That's awesome.'

She was about to ask him if there was any news on the recruitment process when Paul surprised her again. 'Nigel's going in for gallstone surgery, reckon you could cover his leave?'

'Absolutely,' she said, only just stopping herself from breaking into a happy dance. 'Count me in!'

It was only after he explained the dates that she realised they were cutting it fine to secure a replacement producer. Dread washed over her. 'Will Patrice be producing the show?'

Paul nodded. 'Is that a problem?'

The radio station's newsreader, Sarah, was the only one Lauren had told about Patrice's habit of subtly freezing Lauren out of conversations and dropping her off email chains. Mentioning the older woman's knack for making Lauren feel unprepared, unprofessional or just plain inept to Paul would sound like schoolyard drama.

'I'll be fine.' Lauren ignored the tremor in her hands and went straight into planning mode. She remembered Miriam and Carli's encouragement when she'd left the South West Vic bureau and stood a little straighter. She headed for the car park with a determined stride.

Her mobile rang when the paddocks started to give way to vineyards. 'Hey, Tahnee,' she said, answering the phone on speaker. 'I'm just heading home from work. What's up?'

'I wouldn't dream of knocking off before 4 pm,' Tahnee said. 'Are you sure you should be skiving off like that?'

'You *do* realise what time my alarm's set for in the morning, right?' Lauren scanned the road for wallabies, annoyed at the teasing tone in Tahnee's voice.

'Of course, I'm usually up then myself, working out. Like Mum always says, sleep's nice when you can get it, but nobody really needs eight hours.'

Lauren pressed her lips together. They'd always been a 'go hard or go home' type of family, but it didn't matter what she did, Tahnee could do everything in half the time with her eyes closed.

'Are you still coming down for the wine tour next month?' Lauren asked. 'We can spend a night in Robe too, do a flower-arranging workshop at that new floristry shop, or a pasta-making course at the Cape Jaffa winery.'

Tahnee sighed. 'That's what I'm calling about actually. I can't make it. Work's sending me to Osaka to brief the Japanese team about a new legal policy. But I've got an opening in my calendar this weekend. Mum's keen too. We could stay at yours or see if April's little cottage is dog friendly?'

'Oh, that won't work either.' Lauren shook her head, sad that she wouldn't make the catch-up but relieved her home and April's cottage wouldn't be subjected to Bruno the sausage dog's randy antics. 'My brekky presenter Nigel is having an op and I'm filling in. Not much fun for him, but great for my resumé, especially leading into the job interviews.' Lauren braked hard as a mob of emus raced across the highway in front of her.

'I thought we decided Broken Hill was a better option?' Tahnee's surprise carried clearly across the line. 'If the local bureau isn't pushing you for this promotion, and you don't feel confident you've got it in the bag, then you need to vote with your feet.'

Lauren drove slowly. 'You and Mum might think that's the best option, but I like it here. I've got a house and friends.'

Tahnee clicked her tongue. 'You can always make new friends, just like when you were jaunting around overseas. Cute little cottages are a dime a dozen. If you're serious about your career, you'd analyse it on a practical level, not a sentimental one, and realise you're putting your eggs in the wrong basket. No pain, no gain.'

Lauren felt a surge of protective ownership as she pulled into Petticoat Lane and parked her car beside the hedge of rosemary and standard roses. 'I'm not sure it's as simple as you make it sound.'

'Oh, I meant to ask about your house-sitter,' said Tahnee. 'Did anything ever come of it or did it fizzle out like I predicted?'

Lauren hovered, one foot on the brick pavers, the other still inside the car. Part of her wanted to shock Tahnee and say she and Jack were having so much sex, the neighbours needed earplugs, but lying had never been her strong suit and they hadn't even kissed, let alone romped through her house.

'He's good,' Lauren said, hearing the smile in her words. 'We're going to the beach tomorrow with his niece.'

She could hear her sister shuddering over the phone. 'Couldn't think of anything worse. Sounds like he's already in a committed relationship. You sure he's got capacity for a girlfriend if he's always running around after his sister and her kid?'

'You let me worry about that,' Lauren said, but even as she hung up the phone, she couldn't help wondering if Tahnee had hit the nail on the head.

13

'Gotcha,' Jack said, lowering the speed camera and switching on his red and blue lights.

'That's sixty-six through a school zone, mate,' he said, approaching the driver with his notebook ready.

'I didn't realise school was back already, we haven't even packed up the Christmas tree,' the man blustered, his red cheeks and nose prompting Jack to run a breath test too. And while it was only 8 am on a Tuesday, his instincts proved correct.

'Just a nip to steady my nerves,' the man protested. 'You'd need a Bloody Mary for breakfast too if you had your mother-in-law staying all week.'

Jack took the chap back to the station, where his blood alcohol reading was even higher. While the motorist had the wrong approach to road safety, he was right about one thing: January *had* evaporated into thin air. It had been a fortnight since he'd last seen Lauren and they still hadn't rescheduled their cancelled beach date.

The excuses Jack had made throughout the busy summer— the influx of summer visitors; the hours wasted chasing wayward cattle dogs with a taste for lamb; the increase in evening shifts to cater to the holiday makers and their late night-revelling—were as weak as the drunk driver's. He pulled out his mobile before the station phone rang again.

'Clem stayed in Adelaide longer than planned and she's been back twice since,' he explained when Lauren answered. 'Pop and I suspect it's a summer fling, but she's keeping her cards close to her chest, and work's been epic. I've been thinking of you though. How's things?'

'I've been flat knack too,' she said, telling him about the radio reshuffle with a smile in her voice. He'd never heard someone so happy about a colleague's gallstone issues.

'Man, I can't believe I've missed it. I'll have to listen back.'

'Even better,' Lauren said, 'you can come into the studio later this week and give us an update on all things Penwarra policing.'

'Love to,' he said, jotting the date into his calendar. 'And if you're free, I definitely owe you dinner. I make a mean seafood pasta. Or we could go hiking?'

They settled on a date and Jack went back to his work with a smile on his face that had nothing to do with missing pets, graffitied signs or speeding tickets.

Victor Jenkins' property was the final stop for the day, and when he pulled up outside the gate with Cohen and Sebastian and saw the place through their eyes, he wondered whether maybe they'd bitten off more than they could chew.

'It's a tip,' Cohen said. 'Hope your insurance covers snake bite and tetanus.'

'It's got worse,' Sebastian said quietly as they walked to the door.

Victor looked as wary about the prospect of tidying the place up as the teens.

'We'll tackle it one step at a time,' Jack said. 'These guys will bring a little extra muscle, clear up the overgrown grass on the roadside and around the property. Cohen's good on a whipper snipper, Sebastian knows his way around a ride-on mower and I'll help them both out.'

'Yeah, awesome,' Cohen muttered, kicking the dirt with his boots. Jack wondered whether his mum had made good on her threat to sell his expensive shoes on eBay.

'Better than collecting rubbish on the highway, where everyone sees us,' Sebastian replied. 'And better than the Men's Shed with all those oldies.'

'I still don't know how a private clean-up job like this constitutes community service,' Victor said, shaking his head as he walked them to the garden shed. 'The equipment's in there. Mind the shelving units, though, there're valuables in there.'

Cohen didn't bother hiding a snigger as they loaded shovels, tree saws and hedging shears into a wheelbarrow. 'Valuables?' he said, checking the whipper snipper cord. 'Should've told him he was dreaming. Must think rust's a precious metal.'

Jack looked at him. 'They're valuable to Vic, and that's what's important here, guys. You mightn't have much respect for street signs, school buildings or garden gnome collections just yet, but there'll come a time when you have things that are special to you too, and you'll be wild when someone disrespects your stuff.'

Cohen rolled his eyes and set to work on the long grass around the house.

An hour later, and the three of them had made a decent dent on the overgrown hedges and grass. To their credit, the boys had worked solidly without complaint, and were covered in grass clippings when they clambered back into Jack's ute. He silently added vacuuming the car to his list of after-work tasks.

'Good work in there, guys, a few more sessions like that and we'll have better access to the cars.'

'Who's going to want those old rust buckets?'

'Joe's scrapyard will take them,' Jack said. 'The wreckers will pay for the rare ones. And I've got a project in mind for a few pieces.'

The quiet farmhouse shed had become a respite after a busy day, when he was too tired to be sociable, too wired to sleep and too late to catch Lauren. The front fence of Sunny Cross Farm was now decorated with the metal sunflowers he'd repaired, plus a few of the new, pint-sized prototypes of the sculptures he'd welded for Harriet. They were as rustic as they come, an amalgamation of scrap steel from the depths of Arthur's shed, but Clem and Jean called them charming, and to his surprise, Fiona wanted to stock them in her shop. And while Jack didn't have the time or inclination to sell his work, it had felt good to create again.

After Googling 'scrap metal sculptures' and marvelling at the array of blogs and images, he'd earmarked a few ideas for a mid-winter welding project, when the town was quiet and spare time was a given, not a luxury.

They were a few kilometres into the drive home when Sebastian called out from the back seat. 'There's a freshy, pull over.'

Jack looked at the kangaroo carcass on the roadside ahead. Someone had already dragged it off the highway so it wasn't a threat to motorists, but there wasn't an X on the body.

'Spray paint's in the back,' Jack said, pulling up.

Sebastian didn't need to be told twice. The three of them got out of the car and Sebastian approached the roo.

Spray paint done, Sebastian reached around and pulled a pocketknife from his belt.

'You normally carry a knife?' Jack didn't want to make a big deal of it, but he'd seen the other boy's impressed look. Last thing Cohen Moriarty needed was a weapon.

'Only when I'm working,' Sebastian replied.

Jack thought of the pocketknife he'd treasured when he was a similar age, a gift from his dad before everything had imploded. Would it still be sitting at the bottom of the dam where he'd thrown it all those years ago?

'Are you really going to stab it to death?' Cohen bounced on his toes, horror and awe in his question.

'I'm not going to stab anything, you moron,' Sebastian said. It was the sharpest Jack had ever heard him speak to Cohen. 'The mother's already dead but there's a joey in the pouch. I'm going to slice the teat off, so it's like a dummy for the joey, just until he or she settles.'

For all his bravado, Cohen's face blanched. He gulped. 'Jesus, that's brutal.'

'I'm not exactly pumped about it either,' Sebastian said, 'but it's kinder for the animal.'

Jack and Cohen watched Sebastian carry out the delicate task. The boy's sleeves slid up and Jack saw blue biro artwork on his arms. Comic book characters, from the look of things. The kid was good. Really good. Though Jack would feel a whole lot better if the style wasn't so similar to the graffiti he'd seen at the tip and on the mayor's fence.

Cohen went back to his phone when they returned to the car, but Jack noticed him glance at Sebastian more than once on the drive home. Was that the first time he'd seen his friend do something he couldn't?

The days tumbled on top of one another and soon enough, Lauren's week in the presenter's chair was almost over.

She slipped out of the studio while Sarah delivered the news, fixed herself a strong coffee in the kitchenette and ran through the rewards she'd promised herself for surviving the intense week. 'I'll have a sleep-in on Saturday, an hour's uninterrupted

reading on the couch tonight, a bar of chocolate at smoko . . .'
Keeping a list of little goals and tangible rewards was another
trick Miriam had taught her at the South West Vic bureau,
and it had proved handy more than once when Lauren had
felt anxious or overwhelmed. 'And in ten minutes, I'll see Jack.'

Checking the clock, she tugged a hairbrush through her
hair, smoothed down her shirt and hurried down the corridor
with her coffee, nearly running into him. She pressed her lips
together to stop the Cheshire Cat grin and wiped the milky
coffee spill with her sleeve. It felt like ages since she'd seen him
but judging from his smile, he was equally pleased to see her.

'On in two minutes, Lauren,' Patrice warned, striding past
them. 'Don't loiter.'

'I caught up on the last few programs,' Jack said quickly,
leaning against the studio door. 'Sounds like you're sailing
through.'

'I threw up twice,' Lauren admitted. 'But it's got easier every
day. We'd better mike up before Patrice starts breathing fire.'

She settled into her chair, thanked Sarah for the news and
lined up a song.

'Microphones are on mute,' she told Jack, 'we've got a
minute or two. When we're live, I'll quiz you on the community
policing program, the hot spots over summer and we'll see
where the conversation takes us.'

'This suits you,' Jack replied, gesturing to the desk as she
fiddled with the control panel. 'Mind if I take a photo for
Harriet? She'll be so impressed.'

Ignoring Patrice's glare from the production booth, Lauren
posed for the photo, touched by Jack's suggestion and proud
of how far she'd come.

'Our last guest today, folks, is a friend to the radio station
and the community at large. Maybe you've seen him on
the streets of Penwarra, helping old ladies cross the roads,

reminding school kids about the road safety rules or rescuing a stray sheep dog. Welcome to the breakfast show, Senior Constable Jack Crossley.'

It certainly wasn't the first time Lauren had had live guests in the studio, but the indecent thoughts about the person in the chair opposite were both new and *mighty* distracting. Her cheeks flushed as she recalled the last time they'd had dinner together, the tickling and their near-kiss. What would their date on Sunday bring? A long beach walk and then a dip in the ocean to cool off? Dinner for two with a side serve of romance? She bit her lip, trying to claw back her composure.

'Um, right, we're talking about community policing, um, yes,' she said, soldiering on and mentally trying to regroup. *Get it together!*

Lauren cleared her throat, ignoring a scorching look from Patrice. 'Some folks think police spend their days waiting for people to slip up, but that's not quite right, is it, Jack? Um, Senior Constable Crossley.'

Jack's wry laugh filled the studio, putting her at ease. 'A happy and safe community's the main goal, and sure, that involves enforcing the law on a regular basis, but we're always looking at ways to work *with* people.'

He was a good interviewee, leaving enough gaps in the conversation to keep it flowing, and Lauren learned more about the youth engagement program than she'd expected.

'Thanks for coming in,' Lauren said, walking Jack to the car park after the show was over. 'You're a natural on air.'

'Not sure about that,' Jack said. 'Nothing like you, Miss Breakfast Presenter. And I wanted to apologise again for going off grid most of January. With work and Clem away—'

Lauren held up a hand. 'I get it, honestly. Things have been crazy here too. And good luck with the poultry pavilions at the showgrounds. They're long overdue for a spruce up.'

Jack's smile turned shy, hiding those straight white teeth, and he rubbed the back of his neck. 'Speaking of long overdue, my cousin Matilda's getting married soon and I've been meaning to ask you for ages. I don't suppose you like weddings?'

'Are you kidding? What's not to love about weddings? There's always good food, nice wine, and even if the speeches go on for a little too long, there's cake. Oh, and there's always dancing. Everyone's all loved up—it's infectious.'

'We'd spend half the day driving there on Friday, then half the day driving home Sunday.'

'I know,' Lauren said. The confusion that appeared on his face was comical, and she grinned, explaining he'd left the invite at her place. 'My grandparents had a holiday house on the Fleurieu Peninsula and I *may* have googled the venue after seeing the invitation.'

'An old homestead, I think.'

'You haven't even researched it?' Lauren couldn't believe it. 'I thought you were a details man? There's the main homestead and a marquee for receptions, but there's also these amazing crumbling sandstone buildings where they hold the ceremonies, and an old woodshed that's done up like a gentleman's club with chesterfields, lamps, full bar. I've only seen photos but it sounds magnificent.' She petered off at his amused expression. 'What?'

'You do know that more than half the country's marriages end in divorce? None of these weddings, no matter how pretty the location, can insure against heartbreak.' He leaned against the patrol car.

'Such a sceptic. Of course I know that. Doesn't mean we should all stop celebrating love or force all weddings to be contained to a registry office. I don't agree with the crazy bridezilla thing, but I don't think we should cancel romance.'

'Guessing you haven't been married?'

Lauren shook her head, realising she hadn't even considered if Jack had been married. 'You?'

He gave an infuriating shrug. 'What do you think?'

She gawked at him. 'I think there might be a hell of a lot I don't know about you, Jack Crossley.'

Jack was all primed to spend Sunday with Lauren, so it felt like a bonus when he arrived at the Classic Clash Pétanque tournament on Friday morning to find her in the radio station polo she wore for outside broadcasts, lining up talent for the breakfast show. He waved, keeping one eye on Arthur's game and the other on the radio station marquee throughout the morning.

Half an hour later, Lauren emerged from the chardonnay grapevines, scanning the crowd. 'Have you seen a guy in a straw Panama hat and a floral shirt? He was supposed to be our next talent, but I can't find him. Can either of you fill in? It's only a short spiel, talking about the day and why you're here.'

'I'll do it,' Arthur said. Arthur started towards the marquee with Lauren, and Jack fell into step with them.

'Don't forget your walker, Pop. The nurses will rip me to shreds if you fall over on my watch.'

Arthur rolled his eyes but took the frame. It was a slow journey, and from the way Lauren checked her watch, it was longer than she'd expected.

When they finally reached the broadcasting tent, the presenter looked close to crying with relief.

'Just let me catch my breath a minute,' Arthur said, easing himself into a chair.

Nigel glanced at the song, which was almost finished.

'I'll do a recon,' Lauren told Nigel. Donning headphones, she sat herself down in the guest chair. Jack watched her adjust the microphone, shuffle her feet then shift in the chair.

'One of those superstitious routines like footballers before they kick a goal?' Arthur whispered to Jack, his breathing still laboured. 'Out with the mouthguard, up with their socks and a silent prayer as they toss a clump of grass over a specific shoulder?'

Jack wasn't sure, but whatever it was, the process seemed to work. By the time the song ended, Lauren had relaxed. She described the jovial rivalry between petanque contestants, the range of ages and summarised the picturesque setting for their listeners.

'Look at her go,' whispered Arthur. 'One week in the hot seat and she's running rings around that soppy presenter.'

Jack bit back a smile. It was the second time he'd met Nigel, the regular presenter, but either he hadn't completely recovered from his gallstone surgery the week before, or he was out of his depth in a non-studio setting. In contrast, Lauren looked like she thrived on the challenges presented by the outside broadcast.

'Art! You old media darling,' called a voice from across the next row of vines after Arthur had finished describing the friendly rivalry between the pétanque players and received a grateful thanks from Lauren.

Jack and Arthur turned to see Jean, Harriet and Clem heading in their direction.

'Don't know where she gets her energy from,' Arthur said, watching Jean lead the way. 'If she wasn't my sister-in-law, I'd probably think she was on uppers, or whatever it is you call those pills these days. But I've known her long enough to understand she's just wired that way.'

'I hope I've got that much go when I'm almost seventy,' Jack agreed. Harriet jogged every few steps to keep up with Jean's brisk pace, while Clem lagged a few steps behind.

'Aunty Jean said I can help with her coffee van when I'm bigger!'

'That's if your mum hasn't snaffled you into service at her cafe,' Jean replied with a wink. 'Fiona was just telling us she's found Clem the sweetest little cash register. Ornamental of course, but they don't come past her counter very often.'

'I'm not buying the cash register, Aunty Jean,' Clem said, covering a yawn as she caught up. 'I barely have enough time to sleep, let alone collect memorabilia for a farm-gate cafe that doesn't even exist.'

Art tapped his head and smiled at his granddaughter. 'It already exists up here, Clementine, and that's a great starting spot.'

Jack watched Clem smother another yawn. Was Harriet waking with growing pains again?

Clem leaned in towards him, her voice low. 'Jack, can we have a word?'

Jack nodded, and was just about to suggest a sleepover, so Clem could have a night off, when Jean clicked her fingers.

'Is that . . . what's his name?' Jean's eyes flashed between Clem and Harriet, then Jack. 'You know . . .' She raised her eyebrows, glanced at Harriet once more, then tipped her head to the team in the shiraz plot.

Jack homed in on the broad shoulders and tousled blond hair of the guy with the measuring tape.

'Who's she spotted now?' asked Arthur. 'Another Romeo from her black book? Handsome chap for our Clementine?'

'Adam Dunkirk,' Jean whispered.

Arthur straightened up. 'Here?' he growled.

Clem shook her head, folding her arms across her chest. 'You need your eyes checked, Aunty Jean.'

'Who are we looking for, Mummy?'

Jack watched as Clem gave Arthur and Jean an 'I'll handle this' look.

'Someone I used to know,' Clem replied curtly. 'C'mon, Harri, Mummy could do with a drink. Let's see if they're selling orange juice at Kookaburra Cottage.'

Someone I used to know ... Jack watched Clem march across the vineyard with Harriet in tow. It was a more generous answer than 'your deadbeat father' or 'the guy who dumped us like a hotcake when you were a newborn', but Jack couldn't dislodge the niggle that Clem had seemed peeved at *them*, instead of being angry with Adam the Dipshit Dunkirk.

'The bloke's a dead ringer,' Jean protested. Arthur nodded.

But having raced triathlons beside the guy and shared a locker room with him at the South Australia police academy in Taperoo, Jack could see the differences after a second glance. The baggy cargo shorts and messy hair should have been a giveaway; like Jack, Dunkirk was very clean cut and detested civilians wearing camouflage clothing.

'Lucky it's not,' Arthur said, adjusting his hat. 'Too nice a day to waste it chasing Dunkirk out of town. You'd better pull your finger out and match her with a nice Penwarra boy, Jean.'

Jean bristled. 'I thought she'd found a new flame in Adelaide, all those trips to the city and back. No wonder she's going to bed the same time as Harri these days, those summer flings catch up with you. And how about you, Jack? Have you got a date for Matilda's wedding yet? I'm on standby if you need one, don't forget.'

'I'm sorted, thanks, Aunty Jean, and I'm a bit parched myself,' he said. 'I'll see what other drinks April's selling.'

Jack was returning with Arthur's and Jean's drinks preferences in hand when the mayor cut across his path. Had someone painted her front fence again?

'I've a bone to pick with you, Senior Constable Crossley. I heard your radio interview. You made it sound like someone locked the doors and barred those teenagers from entering the Men's Shed.'

'I didn't mention any names, Jillian, only that the path wasn't always smooth sailing. Our collaborations with the youth justice team, disengaged teens and the community can only move forward if everyone's on the same page.'

'Well, what are you doing with them now? And what's the latest on Vic Jenkins?'

'The Jenkins property isn't a criminal matter, and I'm afraid community service plans are confidential.' But Jack suspected he wasn't going to have the right answer, no matter what he said. The last thing he needed was Mayor Dangerfield rocking up at the poultry pavilion on Sunday and giving Sebastian and Cohen a piece of her mind.

The mayor followed his gaze to the radio marquee. 'We need to make a stand, tell the community we take these matters seriously. I've made it a discussion topic for the next council meeting. Maybe we can double the fines? Extra revenue is always a good thing and when the media come calling, I want to say we're on the front foot.'

Jack watched her walk away. Would she really make an example of Victor? And what was going on with Clem? Why was she falling asleep at 7 pm and storming off in a huff when Jean got her wires crossed?

The sound of clinking metal balls and hoots of laughter carried across the vineyard, and Lauren listened through her headphones, loving how the outside broadcasting equipment was picking up the soundbites from the tournament.

Another OB in the bag, she thought and grinned, welcoming the final guest of the show. She tapped notes into the computer system, reminding Nigel of the guest's name and story angle. He didn't normally need spoonfeeding, but he was off-kilter today and she was feeding him lines left, right and centre.

Nigel looked at the computer screen, gave Lauren a grateful nod and used her questions verbatim.

'As you can hear in the background, listeners,' Nigel said, 'we're on location this morning, smack bang in the heart of the Limestone Coast's premier wine-growing region, pondering pétanque with Harris O'Brien, the local vigneron who brought the Classic Clash to the region several years earlier.'

'I call it the lazy sportsman's version of lawn bowls,' Harris said, beaming. 'But it's a lot of fun and interest is growing every year.'

'And who wouldn't want to spend a day between the vines, enjoying this glorious weather and sampling local produce?' Nigel said. 'Tell us about the set-up, are people playing for sheep stations?'

Harris chuckled, explaining that a few players were ultra-competitive, but on the whole people were there for the company and socialising, not line honours. Later, as they pulled the marquee down and packed up the broadcasting equipment, Lauren realised that for the first time in a long time she'd felt completely in control of her nerves, her voice and her cadence.

George had always treated outside broadcasts like an extreme sport, the high risk and high adrenaline brought out the best in him, but as she'd discovered this morning, the makeshift outdoor office had taken Nigel out of his comfort zone. This morning had been the first time Lauren had seen him flustered. *Perhaps he'd returned too early from his surgery?*

'I hope it's a bloody long time before we have to do another,' Nigel said, wincing, when they returned to the studio after the show. 'I prefer the station shows a thousand-fold.'

Lauren laughed. 'They're an acquired taste but they get better the more you do. George loved them and I'm quite partial to an outside broadcast. Today went pretty well.'

Patrice emerged from the kitchenette. 'Well, you would say that wouldn't you, Lauren? Any time you're not tripping over your tongue and freezing on air is a win in your books.' She laughed, nudging Lauren with an elbow as if they were chummy. 'Your bar isn't exactly sky high.'

Lauren whirled around before Patrice could see the hurt she'd caused.

Nigel paused, uncertainty written across his face. 'I was white knuckling it there, Patsy, and without Lauren's help, the whole show would've fallen over.'

Patrice chuckled. 'It's a joke, Nigel. Lauren knows I was just kidding.'

'Right!' Nigel gave a nervous laugh. 'You almost had me for a minute.'

How dare she? Lauren gritted her teeth and managed a tight-lipped smile, determined not to let the barb ruin her day.

'What's up her nose?' Nigel said quietly to Lauren, when it was just the two of them.

Lauren knew what Tahnee and Gabrielle would say. They'd tell her there was always someone ready to cut you down to size, if you let them. And hadn't her dad always urged her to hold her chin high?

'Nothing,' she said, feeling a nervous tremor in her traitorous body. She clasped her hands together. Giving Patrice's snarky comments more oxygen would only fuel the fire.

There was only one lane in use when Lauren arrived at the pool after work, and with the aqua aerobics class working to a soundtrack of seventies hits, her afternoon laps were interspersed with snippets from Abba, The Rolling Stones and the Bee Gees.

Lauren took the first five laps slowly, letting her body find the pace and sloughing off the work-week worries. The outside broadcast had gone smoothly, she hadn't stuttered or stuffed up on air and she'd run into Jack not once but twice. But even the lovely listener comments about her Best In Show interview series and the prospect of a Sunday with Jack hadn't shaken the niggly feeling that things were about to go downhill. Patrice's comments weighed on her mind.

You're making a mountain out of a molehill, she told herself, taking a breather at the deep end, treading water and adjusting her swimming goggles while the seniors bobbed and waved their floats in unison, some singing to the last strains of 'Stayin' Alive'. Lauren thought of the tattoo Ruby had shown her earlier that week, the crisp black ink on the elderly woman's paper-thin skin that said, 'No regrets'.

'Don't wait until your ninetieth birthday to get this down in writing,' Ruby had said as they wrapped up their fourth interview. 'You don't have to get it tattooed on your arm like me, but make sure you've got it tattooed into your mind.'

Lauren dived under the water, replaying Ruby's words over and over in her head as she resumed her laps. *Be brave. Be fearless. Say yes to adventures.*

And when she hauled herself up the steps, dripping wet and puffing from the exertion afterwards, she felt better.

14

'I'm famous, Uncle Jack,' Harriet called, rolling down the driveway and leaping into his arms the moment he emerged from the patrol ute. 'Mummy and me were on the radio today!'

Lauren had been in Jack's thoughts throughout the day, a welcome distraction from trying to trace a stolen car, researching cases on hoarding and squalor, and writing a detailed update for Sebastian and Cohen's community service plan.

'Did it sound alright? Is Mum pleased?'

Jack found Clem around the side of the house.

'Don't look so worried,' Clem said to him, teeing up the replay.

Harriet skated around the house, rolling to a halt when the radio program started. 'That's us!' She was so excited she nearly took out the row of sunflowers flanking the back door.

The hour-long interview had been condensed down to seven minutes. It was impossible to deny the upbeat tempo of Lauren's segment, the skilful way she'd mixed the audio from the kitchen into the discussion so pauses in conversation were peppered with the kettle whistling, Harriet's cheeky giggles as she whisked the eggs and the oven timer going off.

'It was brilliant, wasn't it?'

Jack looked from his sister to his niece, his eyes suddenly prickling. 'It was,' he said, giving in to Harriet's request to listen again.

On the second time around, he picked up more than the story and listened closely to Lauren's voice-over between the questions and the answers. It was cheerful and entertaining, with a light humour that was almost playful, daring the listener not to find joy in baking or smile as Harriet explained her favourite recipes. Lauren had even included the part where Harriet explained the recipe disaster and joked about her role in the typo, imploring cookbook owners to amend the butter measurement if they planned on baking her choccy rock cakes.

'Flash as,' Jack said, ruffling Harriet's hair. 'Now, what should we cook for Lauren tomorrow?'

Harriet raced to fetch the cookbook as Jack told them about his hiking plans.

'You're taking her to the Woakwine Cutting?' Clem said with a yawn. 'We went there for a high-school excursion once. Even if Lauren's a fan of made-made engineering feats, it might be an odd choice for a date . . . It's a kinda isolated spot to get to know someone.'

'She obviously isn't too worried about a Wolf Creek axe-murderer situation if she volunteered to join me on an eight-hour return car trip for Matilda's wedding,' Jack reminded her as Harriet tied her apron and opened the cookbook to a page with fruit and nut brownies. 'And she loves chocolate. Great choice, Harri.'

Clem pulled a face, as if she were somehow opposed to fruit and nut brownies, then yawned again.

'You alright?'

'Tired, that's all,' Clem said, and when Jack looked up again, she was staring out the window, a faraway smile on her lips.

At Jack's insistence, Clem ran a bath and settled in for a soak while he and Harriet melted the chocolate, chopped the nuts and stirred sultanas into the mix. Before long, the kitchen smelled like a sweet shop, Harriet was scraping out the saucepan with a teaspoon and the brownies were cooling on the bench.

'Can I take some for recess on Monday?'

Jack leaned over the warm tray, inhaling the chocolatey goodness. 'If there's any of your half left by then, Harri.'

He pulled up outside Lauren's little pink cottage at 9 am the next day to find her halfway up a ladder.

'You okay up there?'

She turned, the ladder wobbling as she tossed a handful of leaves onto the ground then waved. 'Give me a minute,' she said.

It took all Jack's willpower not to rush across and steady the ladder, or at least offer his assistance.

Triumphantly, she extracted a tennis ball and tossed it over the neighbouring fence. A cheer rose up from next door. 'Thanks, Lauren,' chorused two young voices.

After putting the ladder away, Lauren climbed into his car with a basket containing two colourful tins, a thermos and two enamel mugs. 'I can't take the credit for both tins,' she said, catching his gaze. 'I made lemon slice, but Val from next door sent the other one over, along with her kids, to apologise for the soccer ball that went through my garden shed window last week. I knew about the soccer ball, obviously, but I had no idea they'd lost a Wimbledon-worthy supply of tennis balls on my roof too.'

When they arrived at their destination, Jack transferred the tins, thermos and mugs to a rucksack that he slung over his shoulder.

'I'm embarrassed to say I've never been here before,' Lauren said, staring at the Woakwine Cutting, a kilometre-long crevasse gouged into a hill.

Jack read aloud from the information sign. 'Says here it was done in the 1950s, to drain a swamp on the property. Not bad for two guys and a D7 crawler.'

'Imagine that,' Lauren said. 'So much hard work and dedication. I wouldn't even know where to start.'

Her comment made Jack think of Victor's comment at Christmas time, and as they walked, he told her about the troubles Victor Jenkins was having, and how the expense and overwhelming emotional attachment had prevented him cleaning up. 'Seb and Cohen aren't thrilled about the task either, but slowly, surely we're getting there. The unsightliness is one thing, but minimising the snake situation is a priority.'

And while he didn't mention the incident with the dryer, he told her about the snake in Victor's bedroom.

'Just when I was beginning to relax,' Lauren said. 'I'll call you when I'm bright eyed and bushy tailed in the middle of the night, worrying about snakes, will I?'

He laughed and kept an extra close watch on the grassy path as they set out. Soon they reached the lookout, and saw the display of machinery used to make the impressive 28-metre deep cutting.

'Can you imagine hacking through the hillside and making a gorge like that,' Jack pointed from the cutting to the shed full of rusty machinery, 'with equipment like this? That's epic.'

Lauren peered into the machinery display, her lips moving and brow furrowed in concentration as she silently read the historical details.

Even in hiking gear, with sweat beading on her brow and sunscreen making her skin all shiny, she's smoking hot.

'Looks like the equipment did the trick though. And from the sounds of it, they used a fair whack of explosives to help with the task. Every little farm boy's dream, right, blowing up half a hillside and transforming a swamp into prime agricultural land? Or were you more of a cops and robbers kind of kid?'

Jack grinned, leading the way to the walking trail, and was about to explain that his childhood was more about board games than make-believe, when he saw a set of scaly grey and black stripes.

'Watch out,' he said, his arms instinctively lifting to block the path.

Lauren, who'd been walking a step behind him, stumbled into his back and he turned to steady her before they both went tumbling.

'Oh, it's just a bluey,' he said.

'You're sure it's not a snake?'

'He's definitely got legs,' Jack said, crouching to examine the lumps on the lizard's scales. 'And from the look of him, he's under attack.'

The lizard hissed.

'Yep, they're ticks.'

'Those sunflower seed–looking things?'

Jack nodded. 'I've seen blue tongues coming down from the scrub near the beach, risking the waves to try and get rid of them. The ticks will suck the life from this guy unless we help him out.'

Lauren gave him a wary look. 'He won't bite you?'

'Not if we keep him calm and support him like this.' Jack captured the lizard, resting the bulk of its body along his arm.

The return journey was slower going, and orange butterflies fluttered around them as they made their way through the scrub.

'Poor little fella,' Lauren said, glancing over her shoulder. 'Do you think he's in much pain?'

'Not sure, but if he is, it won't be for much longer. A pair of tweezers and I'll have him sorted pretty quickly. I can drop you off home first if you're squeamish?'

Lauren's laugh was as quick as her reply. 'And miss the opportunity to see you deticking a bluey? Pfft!'

What a ripper, Jack thought, returning her grin. *I could get used to this.*

Soon they were back at the car park. 'This guy should be safe in here for the trip home,' Jack said, securing the lizard in a sack and placing it gently on the floor mat behind the driver's seat.

She chuckled. 'Goats, joeys, lizards, little girls with pigtails. What *doesn't* go in the back of your car, Jack Crossley?'

The answer came to Jack within seconds, but he sure as hell wasn't going to say it out loud.

Women. Apart from Clem and Harriet, Lauren was the first woman to ride in this ute.

'Judging from that smile, *you* had a good weekend.'

Lauren turned to see Sarah standing in the studio door. She paused the audio she'd been editing and pushed her headphones back, grinning. 'If you'd asked me six months ago whether I thought my weekends would involve feeding strawberries to blue-tongue lizards and removing ticks with a pair of tweezers, I would've said you were nuts, but it was surprisingly satisfying.'

Sarah leaned against the doorway. 'Whatever you're doing, make a few notes, because that type of content is radio gold.' The newsreader shook her head in disbelief. 'Pulling ticks off blue tongues? And who said life in the country was dull?'

Lauren smiled at the memory of Jack's surgeon-like precision. She'd held the lizard as he removed more than fifteen parasites from each ear canal and a dozen larger ticks around its neck, where they'd wedged themselves between the scales. Far from being aggressive, the lizard had relaxed, almost as if it knew they were trying to help.

From the way Jack had handled the lizard, it was clear that hadn't been the first time he'd performed this task. It hadn't been the romantic date she'd imagined, but as she was coming to learn, Jack Crossley wasn't like other guys.

'Are you packaging up another Best in Show episode for the brekky show and the station's social media?' Sarah asked.

Lauren nodded, dragging her attention from Jack to the script in front of her. 'Yep, and then I'll tidy up my latest interview with Ruby.'

'It sounds like she was so gutsy.'

'She still is! You should see all the baking she's done for the cook-along. It's hard work sampling a new dish every time I drop by for an interview,' Lauren joked, 'but them's the breaks. I'm still not sure what I'll do with the recordings, but I can't think of anything else I've read or listened to recently that references the war bride era, can you?'

'It's definitely zeitgeisty,' Sarah said. 'If it gets a similar response to the show series, then it'll be a mega hit. Paul's thrilled. Did he ask you to cover Nigel's next lot of leave?'

'Yep.' Lauren grinned. 'Patrice wasn't happy.'

Sarah laughed. 'Patrice is *never* happy. You're young, bubbly and great with the talent. To grouchy old Patrice, you're a reminder of everything she's not. And even though she doesn't want the hosting gig, she knows that presenter's chair has your name on it.'

Lauren returned to editing the interview, but in the background of Ruby's amazing stories, she heard a loop of negative self-talk.

You'll stuff it up.

Imagine the ways Patrice could gaslight you when you're on air.

Filling in for half a week is nothing—you need at least another twelve months before you're good enough to do a full show for a fortnight.

The sun was still shining when Lauren left the radio station, but instead of driving straight home, she parked outside a dress boutique April had recommended. And while she'd only planned on picking out a dress for Jack's cousin's wedding in Langhorne Creek, she found herself in the changing room with several work outfits.

'What would a breakfast show host wear?' she mused, slipping on a fitted blazer and matching wide-legged slacks.

Lauren pulled out her phone and sent a picture to her mum, Tahnee and April.

Tahnee wrote back instantly with a thumbs-up.

That's more like it!

Gabrielle called a moment later.

'Make sure you don't leave without that outfit, or even better, tell me the store name and I'll call them now with my credit card. A belated birthday treat for my clever little media darling.'

'Mum!' Lauren protested. 'My birthday was months ago, and you already bought me the French cast-iron dishes. You don't have to buy me clothes, too.'

'I insist,' Gabrielle said. 'I wasn't going to say anything because I know how upset you get when I offer advice but, honestly darling, you could look so professional if you tried a little harder. Those outfits belong to a fearless storyteller, someone who chases the big issues and isn't afraid to shake things up. You need to set yourself apart from the other candidates, and as lovely as those sweet show stories are, they won't be your ticket to success.'

The shop phone chimed in the background less than a minute after her mum hung up, and Lauren heard the delighted shopkeeper taking down Gabrielle's credit card details. Could it really be as simple as that? Could a suit and a few nice dresses be the ticket to her success?

Lauren's cottage looked even more fairy-floss pink in the early golden light, and as Jack pulled up beside the picket fence to collect her for the Valentine's Day wedding, he smelled sweet peas and found them clambering over a trellis.

'Morning!' Lauren called cheerfully, wheeling a hefty suitcase onto the doormat and slipping a backpack over her shoulder. Judging from the size of the case, she'd packed for every contingency.

Jack grinned, taking the suitcase. 'You know we're only going for a weekend, right?'

'Everyone knows weddings require multiple outfits. And if a storm blows in, I'll be cosy with my spare jacket, cardigan and long-sleeved dress, while all you carry-on-only packers will be shivering in your jocks.'

His laughter sent Gary into a round of noisy farewells.

'Is Val braving the welding gloves again, or did you find a pet sitter?'

'Archie Winklin's calling in after piano practice to top up the supplies. He's wanted a pet for ages, but apart from orphaned lambs each year, he's not having much luck convincing his parents.'

With the luggage piled into the ute, they started the 350-km journey.

'Sounds like he'd get along well with Harriet. Archie's the kid with the giant pumpkins, right?'

Lauren beamed. 'You've been listening to my Best in Show series.'

'Not all of it, but I've caught a few episodes when I'm driving between call-outs, and then a few more on replay. Harri's hooked too.'

'Thanks,' Lauren said. 'How're your poultry cage renovations coming along?'

'Less than a month until the show and we're going hammer and tongs,' he said. 'It's not hard, just fiddly. I've got the boys dismantling the worst pens. Seb's good on the tools, measuring and cutting the new sheets of metal, while Cohen's better on the demolition side of things. I'm tacking the frames together for now, but a few welding lessons along the way and the boys are getting better on the welder. Once we're in the swing of it, the new pens will come together quickly.'

He looked across at Lauren, and saw she was impressed. 'I'm probably making it sound grander than it is. It's not the Taj Mahal, but it's better than the rusty old cages.'

They settled in for the drive. 'I've got lollies, biscuits, dip and crackers, grapes, fruit boxes,' Lauren said. 'Nobody's going hungry—or hangry—on my watch. She opened a packet of Fantails, unwrapped one and passed it to him. 'Ready for "Who Am I?".'

Bryan Adams played on the stereo as Lauren smoothed the wrinkles from the Fantail wrapper and Jack listened to the clues, distracted by the way her skirt had ridden up her thigh. It had happened a few minutes ago when she'd dragged the cooler bag onto her lap, leaving several inches of tanned skin exposed. *Eyes on the road, Crossley.*

After numerous games of 'Who am I?', and more nineties soft rock than he'd ever listened to in one sitting, they pulled into the country town of Keith for a coffee break.

'Look at that sweet little bookshop!' Lauren said, twisting in her seat. 'We have to check it out.'

Jack recalled the colour-coded bookshelves in her pink cottage and the RuRo series he wouldn't have chosen for himself, but had enjoyed way more than he'd expected.

It wasn't a stop he'd planned to make so early in the journey, but as they walked down the road and Lauren linked her arm through his, smelling like caramel and apple blossom shampoo, he realised that maybe a few unscheduled stops wouldn't be such a bad thing.

'According to Google Maps, we're only half an hour away,' Lauren said, looking from the dashboard clock to Jack's tight one-handed grip on the steering wheel. 'We'll be there in good time.'

His shoulders seemed to have crept higher the closer they got to Langhorne Creek, and if he kept fidgeting with the trim on the doorframe, there'd be a gouge in the leather by the time they arrived. Lauren offered him the corn chips, and even though Jack hadn't touched the cheesy manufactured snacks before, to her surprise, he grabbed a handful now. He *was* getting stressed.

'Will you know many people at the wedding?'

'Not really,' he said, staring straight ahead.

'Yet you're driving across the state for it?'

Jack reached for the chips. 'Clem and I went to live with Art and Shirley, and one summer—'

'The knitting summer?' Lauren couldn't help interrupting.

He smiled then, just as she'd hoped. 'Nope, this was when we were mid-teens. The knitting needles were well and truly shelved by then. Anyway, our cousins Matilda and Eamon came to stay one summer. She's still the only person who sends me a Christmas card without fail.'

Lauren laughed. 'I thought only smug couples with photogenic kids did that, or people my mum's age.'

'Nope, Matilda is one of those rare types who actually enjoys writing letters. Last year she sent me a copy of an old photo. I didn't realise we'd hung out as little kids too but there's a photo of me, Matilda and Eamon in a paddling pool at her property in the Adelaide Hills.'

'Aw, sounds cute.' Lauren couldn't recall the last time she'd received a handwritten Chrissy card. 'Wasn't Clem invited to the wedding? Or the rest of your family?'

It was the closest she'd come to broaching the topic, and if he was annoyed by the question, he didn't show it. 'Arthur's too frail to travel that far. Clem and Matilda fell out a few years ago—over a guy, of all things. I haven't met the bloke Matilda's marrying tomorrow, but he'll be a much better choice than Adam Dunkirk. He was a good friend once, but as a brother-in-law, he was five-fifths of useless, even worse as a dad. Ran for the hills the moment it got hard and never looked back.'

So that explains Harriet's absent father, Lauren thought, munching on a handful of corn chips. 'And your parents? Will they be there?'

She saw Jack's hand tighten on the steering wheel. 'Not a chance.'

There was something in the way he spoke that made it clear he wasn't keen to discuss it further.

The small hotel adjoining the wedding venue was bustling with guests when they arrived and Lauren hung behind as Jack checked them in. She watched him shake his head and pull out his phone, pointing to the screen.

'All good?'

He returned with a frown. 'They've overbooked, so we're looking at a double room.'

And a double bed? Lauren hadn't slept in one of those since she'd left home, and even as a teenager, it had felt tiny for one. She could barely imagine sharing such a small bed with a six-foot-two, red-blooded man.

Actually . . . Lauren pressed her lips together. The problem was more that she *could* imagine it, but the scenario her mind was conjuring, as relatives and friends reunited in the lobby all around them, didn't involve much sleeping.

'Let's take a look. Most hotels have sofa beds, right?'

Just as she'd predicted, the couch unfolded into a bed that wasn't too much smaller than the double. 'Problem solved,' she said, 'but I call first dibs on the shower.'

And while the room arrangement wasn't ideal, the water pressure in the large ensuite was divine. Afterwards, she tied her floral wrap dress at her hip, skimmed her eyelashes with mascara and twisted her hair into a low bun.

Jack turned when she opened the door. 'You look beautiful,' he murmured, his gaze sweeping from her patent leather sandals to the fluttery cap sleeves of her dress.

Heat bloomed in Lauren's body and she recalled their near kiss in her cottage. How had months passed in the interim? Her eyes locked with his, the pressure building until she looked away.

Good God, if he can turn my insides to putty from fifteen metres away, how am I going to get a wink of sleep a few metres away from him?

'What time's dinner?' she managed.

Jack grabbed his towel, breathing shakily. 'Matilda wants us there early, so we'd better get going.'

He brushed past her and, fighting the urge to follow him into the bathroom, Lauren instead tackled the explosion of shoes, beauty products and clothing in the middle of the bed. She packed most of it back into the suitcase, draped tomorrow's 'before-wedding' outfit over the bedside table, then carried her new dress to the wardrobe.

Jack had been busy while she was showering. His shoes had been shined to gleaming, his clothes were hanging inside the wardrobe and even his smalls had been tucked into a bedside drawer. A neatly folded beach towel sat on the other bedside table, topped with Speedos and goggles.

'Military precision,' she murmured. Closing the wardrobe, she smiled at the memory of discovering her baking drawer at home in a similar, perfectly ordered fashion when she'd returned from Port Fairview: cookie cutters in zip-lock bags; measuring cups and spoons stacked in ascending order; piping bags and baking trays grouped by size and usage. And from what she'd heard of his exercise schedule, he was a stickler for routine.

The ensuite door opened just as she was zipping up her suitcase.

Blimey. With his still-wet hair combed back, Jack looked like he'd just stepped off a James Bond film set. He was wearing a suit that looked like it was tailored just for him, a crisp white shirt and even cufflinks. Cufflinks! Lauren glanced from his heavy eyebrows to his lips.

'You scrub up alright yourself,' she said, feeling all kinds of butterflies, moths, mosquitos and possibly sugar gliders setting up camp in her belly. *What was it with these movie analogies?*

she asked herself. *First it was the* Top Gun*–style moustache, now it's James Bond the moment he's suited up* ...

She cast around the room to stop her brain leap-frogging to pottery wheels and *Ghost*-style love scenes. Her gaze fell on his swimming kit.

'All set for laps tomorrow, too? I didn't realise you were a swimmer—I've never seen you at the Penwarra pool.'

'And it's unlikely you ever will.' Jack dragged his eyes from her. 'I'm usually there when it opens, when you're at the radio station.'

'So what time are we swimming? Six? Seven?'

'We?' He arched an eyebrow and paused, one hand on the door. 'Six,' he said finally.

The cocktails were flowing and conversations were getting rowdy as they weaved their way between the white-clothed tables. She followed closely as he pointed out the bride-to-be, and before she knew it, she was face to face with Jack's cousin Matilda.

'So lovely to meet you, Lauren,' Matilda said, folding her into a hug after kissing Jack on the cheek.

'This is Brendan,' she said, introducing the groom-to-be, 'and I'm so, so pleased you've dragged this guy away for a night.' Matilda led them to the bar and gestured to a barman. 'Sorry about the room mix-up, it was either you or Aunt Coralie and her new "friend", Angus. She was very specific on a twin room and I wouldn't dare get her offside.'

'We'll manage,' Jack said, and Lauren flushed as Matilda grinned from ear to ear, wiggling her eyebrows.

'I'm sure you will. And that's why you're my favourite cousin. No fuss, no complaints, and you get shit done.' She leaned across Jack to grin at Lauren. 'You should see him in a karaoke club. Belts out a solid rendition of "Flame Trees".'

Karaoke? How did that line up with the guy who folded his briefs, rescued tick-ridden lizards and, from the look of the sharp pleat in his slacks, braved a hotel room iron? Lauren wasn't sure, but she sure as heck looked forward to finding out.

15

Jack waited at the bar, wallet ready, as the bartender poured their drinks. In the mirror behind the spirits, he watched Lauren on the dance floor, the wrap dress with its large green pattern flaring at the knee as she attempted a Charleston two-step. The dress hugged her curves, and judging from the admiring glances, he wasn't the only one wondering how easy it would be to untie the bow at her hip and undress her with one swift twirl.

'Now, don't take offence,' said Matilda's mum, Roberta. 'But she's nothing like your ex-wife, is she?'

Jack couldn't argue with that. Matilda had said something similar, leaving no doubt that she preferred Lauren, even though she'd only known her for an afternoon.

'She's feisty too,' Roberta mused. 'I heard her giving Eamon a serve when he made a joke about country towns. I think she's going to be a much better fit!'

By the time Jack finished speaking with Matilda's mum, Lauren had left the dance floor and was throwing her head back in laughter at something Eamon had said. Jack tamped down a surge of jealousy. He was yet to make Lauren laugh like that, but as he watched the way her back arched and the delicate skin on her neck flushed, he knew he wanted to.

'Now here's a bloke I haven't seen in yonks,' Eamon said as Jack joined him and Lauren. 'How's life in the sticks, Jacko? Change of pace from your city beat?' He laughed, clinking his beer against Jack's wine. 'Matilda invited Clem too, did she tell you?'

'She was touched.' Jack nodded as the bride-to-be joined them. 'I know things are still a bit off between you two, but she's been flat-out with a community project,' he said. He told his cousins about the recipe book and cook-along, and the way Penwarra residents had rallied around to make the one-hundredth anniversary show an epic occasion.

'How's Clemmy going these days? Her girl would be, what, in kindergarten now?' Matilda asked, empathy flooding her question.

Jack glanced at Lauren, who was watching him keenly, and deliberated on what to say. Matilda and Eamon knew Clem had struggled after Harriet's birth, but it wasn't something he'd spoken about with Lauren. 'Harriet's at school, actually. And Clem's going okay. Moving back to Penwarra and this community cooking project have been good for her, although she's been exhausted the last few weeks. Pop and Aunty Jean are trying to convince her to start a business at Pop's place.'

'Resurrecting the sunflower farm?' Eamon said. 'That's awesome but, man, you've gotta tell her to watch out for the activists. Fruit loops, the lot of them. I handled a court case for a pig farmer in Murray Bridge, idiots entering properties illegally, getting themselves injured and then trying to sue the landowners. You see much trespassing in the Limestone Coast, Jacko?'

'There's not a lot of rural crime in Penwarra,' Jack replied. 'It's more about community policing than drug busts, break-ins and organised crime. And Clem's more likely to run a farm-gate cafe than a full-scale sunflower farm.'

'She'd smash that out of the ballpark,' Matilda said. 'If Adam wasn't so anal about his fitness, I would've sworn he left me for Clem's cooking. I still can't believe we let that dickhead come between us.'

'I can attest to her cooking,' Lauren said. 'And little Harriet's not half bad either. Same with this guy.'

Lauren smiled up at him, and when she nudged him play-fully with her elbow, Jack felt his shoulders ease a little. The worries that had gnawed at him on the last stretch of driving were just that—unfounded worries—and Lauren was right: weddings were about celebrating fresh starts, not rehashing the past. Why would anyone here ask after his parents or waste their time with maudlin trips down memory lane?

The champagne flowed throughout dinner and dessert, and by the time the clock struck 10 pm, half the guests had gone to bed on unsteady legs.

'Ready to call it a night?' Jack asked during a break in the music.

'What about the karaoke?' She giggled, reaching for his arm to steady herself and giving him a tipsy grin. 'Eamon said they'll be blasting out the old tunes soon.'

Jack laughed and tucked a strand of hair behind her ear. 'You ever heard the saying "big hat, no farm"? Well, Eamon's all talk. Tomorrow, perhaps, but not now. Matilda would have his head on a plate if he ran amok tonight and everyone rolled up to the wedding hungover.' He looked around the dining room. It was mostly the groom's family, from what he could gather, and from the sweat on the bartender's brow, Brendan's brothers sure liked to party. 'But if you want to stay . . . ?'

When he turned back to Lauren, she was smiling up at him from under her long eyelashes, a broad, slightly lopsided smile directed just at him.

'Depends what else is on offer,' she whispered, hooking a finger in his belt and pulling him closer. Lust and proximity were a heady combination, and for a moment, Jack forgot about the crowded room behind him and all the reasons why he shouldn't give in to desire.

Their lips brushed but the moment evaporated in an instant when Lauren hiccuped.

Jack pulled away, swallowing hard, and shook his head. He didn't want her, not like this, not when she was drunk.

'I'm going to turn in. I'll take the sofa bed,' he said, retrieving the room keys and walking away from the first thing he'd wanted in years.

When Lauren woke the next morning it felt like a fire alarm had been hardwired to her skull. She fumbled for her phone to check the time, inadvertently sending the bedside lamp flying and a half-empty bottle of wine and a glass of water careening into her open suitcase.

Shit, shit, shit!

Feeling like a mummified cat, she fought her way out of a tangle of bedsheets to salvage the clothes. Of course it had to be the cotton dress she'd planned to wear today that bore the brunt of the spilled water and wine. *If only I'd hung everything up when we arrived.*

She glared at the empty sofa bed, knowing Jack's clothes were hanging safely in the wardrobe, then, with a wince of embarrassment, remembered how she'd made a drunken move on him. *What an idiot.*

Lauren trudged into the bathroom, washed her frock in the small sink, wrung it out between two towels and draped it over the towel rack. Then she filled her glass to wash down two Panadol, flopped onto the bed and slung an arm over her eyes. *What was I thinking?*

She knew she should be happy Jack was a gentleman, rather than take advantage of her inebriated state, but instead she felt mortified by her poor judgement and was tempted to crawl under the doona and hide there until tomorrow. If there was a God in this world, Jack wouldn't mention last night and they could pretend it never happened.

Lauren splashed cold water on her face and eyed her bathers. The idea of seeing Jack Crossley in a pair of budgie smugglers was now tainted by the fact that she might have well and truly humiliated herself, but she had three choices: order an Uber and hotfoot it outta there, hide in the room for the entire weekend or own it.

Thinking of Ruby McInnes, she tugged on her swimmers. The hallways were empty and there was only one person in the pool. As he glided through the water, she could see the strength of his shoulders and arms, the power in his efficient, concise kicking style.

Lauren set her towel beside Jack's neat pile of belongings and dived into the deep end. The icy water stripped away all traces of her hangover and she sliced through the surface, intent on catching him. The pool was long and skinny, designed for laps not lounging, and Jack executed a precise tumble turn before she could catch him, not breaking pace as he swam straight past her.

Not once in her years of lap swimming or high school swim meets had she raced anyone the morning after a big night out, but a burning need to prove herself made Lauren push harder and swim faster than her regular pool workout sessions.

After forty-five minutes of hauling himself through the water, Jack was yet to feel the satisfaction that normally came from physical exertion, nor was he any closer to straightening out his thoughts. It hadn't helped that Eamon had come up to him not even half an hour after they'd walked into the bar last night, trying to work out whether he and Lauren were friends or more. 'Because if you're not all in, then I'm willing and ready to throw my hat in the ring,' he'd said, grinning and slinging an arm around Jack's shoulders.

And as much as Jack had wanted Lauren's arms around him, her body against his, her hair falling across his chest as they slept, there was no way he'd stoop so low as to take advantage while she was drunk. He'd seen too often how blurry the line around consent could be, and unless he could be a zillion per cent sure Lauren wouldn't regret it in the morning, he didn't want to even entertain the thought.

Lauren deserved better than that.

She deserves better than you too, his conscience whispered as he surfaced for air.

Jack took the next few laps at lung-busting, arm-burning pace, his mind looping through the reasons why he wasn't good enough for Lauren, when all of a sudden he turned and there she was in the water, streaking past him.

He spluttered in shock, taking in more water than air, as the propulsion of his freestyle rocketed him forward. He took the next turn slower, curious to see her form after such a big night.

Even with a steady trail of bubbles streaming from her nose and mouth, the tinted goggles and her blonde hair slicked under a bright orange swimming cap, she was magnificent. The bathers were stock-standard black with a racer back, showcasing Lauren's curves, and Jack felt desire entwining with competitiveness as she pulled ahead.

If this is how she swims with a hangover, she must be a gun on a normal day, he thought, impressed.

It had been a long time since he'd competed and Lauren proved a worthy opponent, keeping up the pressure. They chopped and changed the lead for the next ten minutes, until he eventually pulled up.

'Thank God for that,' she said, steadying herself on the edge of the pool after completing an extra lap. 'I thought you were going to go full ironman on me.'

He grinned, taking off his goggles and slicking the water from his hair. 'I definitely don't have 3.9 kilometres in me this morning, not at that pace.'

'You know the distance of the swim leg. You've done one before?'

She was still breathing hard, her torso rising and falling with each breath, and it was an effort to focus on the question. 'An ironman event?'

She laughed. 'I'm supposed to be the hungover one here. You know, the whole swim, bike, run for outrageous distances. Someone last night said you did triathlons, so it's not hard to imagine you choosing the most painfully gruelling option.'

Jack wasn't sure what to make of that. Did he really project himself as a glutton for punishment? Did Lauren really think him incapable of enjoying things? But as he opened his mouth to object, he realised there was a prime example of his cauterising self-restraint standing right there in front of him. Even goggle rings around her eyes couldn't detract from her sexiness.

Heart beating hard in his chest, he closed the gap between them. 'You don't think I know how to have fun?'

He heard her breath catch.

'Fun? That's not exactly the opposite of pain, Jack. I'm sure you consider pushing yourself to the limit as fun as the next competitor.' Slowly, with her eyes not leaving his, she pulled the cap off her head and dipped under the surface, emerging like a shampoo model with her hair slicked to her head and flowing down her back. 'I'm talking about pleasure.' It was the sexiest thing he'd seen in a pool, her deliberate actions more tantalising than any skimpy bikini could be, and his body hardened in response.

'I've no problem with pleasure,' he answered, gripping the goggles to stop his fingers tracing the neckline of her swimsuit. 'As long as we're talking about two consenting adults, making informed decisions.'

She grinned, biting her lip, and reached out to touch him. 'Such a smooth talker. If that's your definition of talking dirty, then we really, really need to update your dictionary, Jack.'

Lauren slid her hand down his arm slowly, her touch searing each millimetre of skin.

'Not ticklish today?'

A groan escaped his lips. 'Not when you're standing there in a bathing suit, looking hot as hell.' Jack forced out the words. It was only a matter of time before someone else dragged their lazy butt out of bed for a swim and he didn't want an audience for this.

'You don't like this?' Her hand moved from his arm to the centre of his chest and then down to where the water lapped at his midriff. 'You'd rather deny yourself the pleasure than admit there's a spark here?'

Jack caught her hand before it moved beyond the waistband of his togs and pulled her towards the steps. 'I'm not sure this is the right location for this discussion anymore.' His words came out gravelly and he wrapped a blue-striped towel around his torso before handing Lauren her towel. 'But I can think of somewhere that is.'

He pressed their room key into her hand.

Lauren couldn't help sneaking glances at Jack throughout the wedding ceremony and the reception, remembering the way his body had moved with hers just hours earlier in the hotel room. For all her excitement at seeing the remarkable venue, with its gorgeous outbuildings and the open-air chapel Matilda and Brendan were married in, the venue wasn't responsible for the perpetual smile on her face this afternoon.

Jack found their place cards on the white-clothed tables after the ceremony and moved his bag of sugared almonds to Lauren's place. 'All yours,' he said, pulling out her chair.

His touch on the small of her back reminded her of the way he'd been so tender, so intent on satisfying her pleasure before his own. But rather than sit, Lauren excused herself to use the bathroom.

'Goodness gracious, my feet are throbbing,' Matilda's mother said to Lauren as they queued for the loos, after introducing herself as Roberta. 'Traipsing down a crushed limestone aisle might have looked nice and photographed well, but in these ridiculous Mother of the Bride heels, it was pure torture.'

'Ouch,' Lauren said, fossicking in her handbag for bandaids. 'You're going to need these if there's dancing on the agenda tonight.'

'You're a life saver,' Roberta said.

Matilda joined the queue in another gown, her third of the day.

'Finally, a dress that doesn't require a helper every time you go to the ladies,' Roberta said, making her daughter do a twirl to show off the short lacy number with a dipped back and cowl neckline.

'You look absolutely gorgeous today,' Lauren said. 'I can't work out which dress I like best, but this might be my favourite.'

Matilda grinned. 'I don't plan on doing this again, so I'm making the most of it. I'm glad you came with Jack, he's been alone for too long. Too much time in his own head doesn't do him any favours.'

Lauren opened her mouth to protest, to tell her they weren't a couple, but Roberta silenced her with a wave. 'Is he still punishing himself with all that training and meal-planning nonsense?'

The question threw Lauren off guard. She made a 'so, so' gesture, unsure if Jack would appreciate her sharing that type of information. 'I'm not sure what his old schedule looked like, but he rarely misses a workout, and seems pretty happy with his lunchtime staples. Is that what you mean?'

Matilda gave a wistful sigh. 'Still a fitness freak, then. We worry about him, don't we Mum?'

Roberta nodded. 'Ever since his late teens, he's always worked harder and pushed his body further than anyone else I know. Not sure he's ever believed he's good enough.'

'It's not all brown rice and grilled chicken,' Lauren protested, feeling more than a little traitorous. 'You should see the dinners he makes and the way he raves about Clem and Harriet's cooking.'

'And he's smiling these days, which is saying something, I guess,' Matilda said. 'He can be a tricky one to crack, but there's a big heart under all that armour. Go easy on him.'

When she returned, Lauren found Jack by the gift table, rearranging presents to make room for his large present. From the sharp corners and perfectly curled ribbons, she suspected he'd wrapped it himself.

'Lots of fancy gifts. I wonder how many wine glass sets they'll receive?' She pointed to a square-ish box. 'Toaster or wine glasses?'

'Toaster.' He laughed, then pointed to a wrapped cylinder. 'Antique map of Australia or a life-sized poster of the two of them?'

Like an extension of the game they'd played to pass the time while driving, their 'What Am I?' game got more outrageous as it went on.

'His and hers cufflinks or matching nipple clamps?'

'Eww,' he said, setting down the small grey box and assessing the space he'd created. 'There, ours should fit now.'

She liked that he called it 'ours', especially when she hadn't the foggiest idea what was inside.

Lauren took Jack's gift and tested its weight. 'Wait a minute.' The box was heavier than she'd expected. 'Placemats? Framed artwork? No, no, I've got it. A deluxe-edition Scrabble board with the game cabinet.'

He shook his head as she placed the gift on the table. 'It's a wooden chopping board with fancy resin on one end. She's a cheese snob, so it'll get a solid workout.'

Lauren felt her smile waver. Not only did Jack have a whole past she knew nothing about, but he could have a wedding certificate, and a whole stack of divorce papers, and she wouldn't even know. The little guessing game might have seemed like it was *their* game, especially after they'd spent the morning making love, but really, it was barely even a speck in the ocean in terms of getting to know each other.

'What's wrong?' he said, scanning her face. 'Where did you go just then?'

'Just thinking how limited my vault of Jack Crossley knowledge is. We've known one another for months now, and even after almost four hours in the car yesterday, plus a couple of stints of house-sitting, I didn't know you'd been an ironman until this morning, I had no idea that underneath your hipbone, there's a port wine birthmark, or that behind that uniform and buzz cut, you did a mean karaoke rendition of Jimmy Barnes.'

She toyed with the fabric on her teal dress, unsure how she wanted him to respond, or even why she'd raised the issue, especially after this morning. Then she locked eyes with him, feeling more vulnerable than she had in bed, completely naked and writhing beneath his touch. 'I'd like to make a go of this, but I need to know you're open to it.'

Jack studied the marquee's see-through ceiling before looking at her. 'I wouldn't have invited you if I wasn't interested in seeing where it might go.' He held out a hand. 'And I believe I owe you at least a few laps of the dance floor. I was going to hide my woeful slow-dancing skills for a little while longer, but if you insist . . . ?'

Lauren's hands felt small in his and as they headed for the dance floor, she let out the breath she didn't realise she'd been holding.

16

An eight-hour return trip could have been particularly awkward, Jack reflected as the paddock-filled countryside turned into row after row of vines, especially after the unexpectedly hot morning they'd spent together, but Lauren had been great company. She'd held her own in the hustle and bustle of the wedding, not batting an eye when a Queensland guest dropped his dacks in the middle of 'Eagle Rock'. She'd posed with Jack and the newlyweds in the fancy-dress photo booth, convinced him to sing Johnny Cash to her June Carter in a karaoke duet and even given Eamon a run for his money doing the moon walk.

He looked across, allowing himself to admire Lauren's fine features as she dozed in the passenger seat. Her head rested against the window, mouth slightly ajar, one hand still clutching her bag of sweets. Her phone lay in her lap, lighting up the folds of her skirt every now and then. She couldn't have been comfortable, not with her sandals propped up on the dashboard, the bug-speckled windscreen and sunshine casting freckles on her pale feet, but she stayed sleeping from Tintinara to Penwarra.

Lauren stirred as Jack eased off the accelerator. A sheath of golden hair fell across her face before she let out a snort and then startled awake.

He couldn't help laughing.

'Oh boy,' she said, blinking as she turned to him and un-pretzeled herself from the awkward position, 'tell me I wasn't snoring. Or sleep talking?'

He shrugged. 'A gentleman never tells. But your phone's been running hot.'

As he pulled up outside the pink picket-fenced cottage, he heard Lauren gasp.

'Everything okay?'

She nodded, then shook her head, running a shaky finger across her eyes. Black mascara smeared against her pale skin. 'Ruby, the war bride I was interviewing, passed away over the weekend. She was mid-nineties, so she'd had a good innings, but still . . .'

He cut the engine. 'Doesn't make it any easier to accept, right?' He took Lauren's hand as she struggled to collect herself.

'We hadn't finished recording the interviews yet. It's stupid to be surprised, I mean, I knew time was against us, but her stories . . . I told her we were going to make them into a podcast or a book. Now it'll be nothing close to what I promised her.'

'It's *not* stupid,' Jack said gravely, knowing exactly what it felt like to let someone down with no opportunity for recourse. 'From what I recall, you already shared a beautiful snapshot of her history in the Best in Show series and she heard that on the radio, right? She mightn't get to hear or watch or read the final product of those longer interviews, but I bet she loved reliving those moments. You did a good thing, Lauren Bickford.'

'She was so fearless. Did I tell you about her tattoo?'

Jack nodded, kissing the inside of her wrist. Why couldn't Lauren see that she was pretty darn brave herself, not just for uncarthing the untold stories and chasing her radio dream but for taking a chance on him, of all people?

'Maybe I should take a leaf out of Ruby's book,' she said, getting out of the ute and kissing him right on the mouth. She was smiling when she pulled away. 'Bugger it, we are going to make a proper go of this, Jack Crossley.'

She kissed him again after he'd pulled the suitcase along the brick footpath, past the flowers and buzzing bees, and up to her front door, and when he walked back to his car, he couldn't help smiling as she jogged back to the kerb for one last kiss before he drove away.

Clem phoned as he was pulling up outside the police station. The security lights flickered on and he yawned as he answered.

'Spill the beans, then.'

'No problems,' Jack said. 'Traffic was good. Food was good, venue was pretty snazzy, Matilda looked happy.'

'Gah, that's not what I'm talking about and you know it. How did it go with Lauren?'

Jack carried his luggage inside and started unpacking his suitcase. 'Fine.'

'Fine? Just *fine*? You're not holding back because of us, are you? Because Pop, Harriet and I all want you to be happy too. Don't go holding back on our behalf.'

Jack laughed. 'Who says I'm holding back?'

'You're dodging the question.' Clem chuckled. 'You know what, Jack? You've just got to sweat though the anxiety of being close to someone again, without pulling away, and gradually increase your tolerance to being loved. You control everything so tightly, from the job you do, what you eat and how you work out—can't you let go a bit?'

If only it was as simple as relaxing and letting someone in, Jack thought.

'There're good things to be had,' Clem continued, 'but only if you're brave enough to put yourself out there. I wouldn't have Harriet if I'd waited for the perfect time or the perfect person.'

Tiredness washed over him and Jack couldn't contain another yawn. 'I've gotta catch some sleep,' he said.

'Wait —' She sounded a lot like Harriet angling for 'just one more' bedtime book.

Keen to avoid another lecture on the wonders of love, he quickly cut over her. 'Tomorrow, Clem. I'm cactus.'

'Hey, Jack?'

He climbed into bed. 'Mmm-yeah?' It came out as half word, half yawn.

'What would you say if . . .' She sighed. 'Nah, forget about it. I just . . .' Another sigh. 'Night, that's all.'

Eyes closed, he smiled. 'Night to you too, Clementine.'

'You're texting Jack *again*?' April grinned.

'How'd you know?' Lauren asked, taking a biscuit from April's lunch box and dunking it in the coffee she'd just delivered.

'Maybe because you light up like a Christmas tree every time it buzzes? Or that gooey smile on your face.'

The day was another sunny late February stunner that made Lauren wonder why she'd ever want to live anywhere else. While Tahnee was sweltering through another 39-degree Adelaide day and Carli was shivering in South West Victoria, the Penwarra sunshine and afternoon breeze offered an enviable happy medium.

'If this weather holds for show day, they'll have record numbers through the gate,' April said.

'Fingers crossed. I'm pushing for an outside broadcast, but Paul's waiting for the forecasts before committing. Are you entering these biscuits? They're really good.'

April nodded, pleased with the praise. 'Connor's doing a few cakes and slices. Fran's counting on you too—I hope you and Senior Constable Crossley can drag yourselves out of bed for a full day to get your show entries sorted.'

Lauren tossed a biscuit at her friend, grinning as it bounced off April's arm and straight into the jaws of Mishka, who had been sitting by their feet eyeing off the afternoon tea.

'For you and Fran and the one-hundredth anniversary Penwarra Show, I'm sure we can make an exception.'

And while April may have been exaggerating, there was no denying the number of nights Jack was spending at the little pink weatherboard cottage, nor the afternoons she swung by the police station directly after work instead of catching up with April.

'Sickeningly cute, you are,' April teased. 'So what's he cooking you for dinner?'

Lauren nestled back in her chair. 'He's on an Italian bent this week. We're having gnocchi at Clem's house this weekend.'

April clapped, almost upsetting the tray of lattes. 'A wedding hook-up and now cute dinner dates with his family. I'm so pleased for you, Lauren. At this rate, you'll be inviting Tahnee and your mum around for cocktails and giving them a piece of your mind.'

Lauren snort-laughed. Being her oldest and closest friend, April was the only one allowed to make fun of the intense Bickford family dynamics. 'Steady on,' she said, sipping her coffee. 'That's not happening any time soon.'

'I bet your mum's offered a few words of wisdom about the forthcoming job interview?'

'You betcha,' Lauren said. Gabrielle had called the night before with half an hour of interview pointers.

'She can't help herself, can she? I wonder what she'd say if you bowed out now?'

That one was easy. 'Oh, she's got her tennis partner, Bunny, on the lookout for back-up jobs already. Just say the word and she'll hit send on a group email to every media recruiter in the state.'

It felt good to laugh about it, but Lauren couldn't help thinking about her mum's expectations and the ever-present pressure as she called into the shops on the way home.

The first stop was the nursery, where she stocked up on tulip bulbs before they sold out, then she headed for Fiona's second-hand shop.

'Hey, Lauren,' Clem was at the counter pricing a selection of flower vases. 'Awesome work on the show promo, everyone who comes into the shop is raving about it. You looking for anything in particular?'

'Yep. A centenary deserves a few show-stopping cakes and I want to lift my game. Any ideas?'

Clem led the way to the kitchen equipment and selected a vintage bundt tin from the collection of cooking trays. 'Whack an Earl Grey tea cake in this bad boy, drizzle a glaze over the top and you'll be right.'

'Not sure I'm game enough to try one of those,' Lauren laughed. 'Aren't they notorious for ruining perfectly good cakes?'

'They're easier than they look, as long as you grease the heck out of the bundt tin and dust it in flour. And you've got time for a few test runs between now and then. Do it for the show.'

'Alright, then,' Lauren said, hoping she could pull it off. She tucked the tin under her arm and called past Jean Dellacourte's coffee van on the way home.

'Here she is, the voice of the South East,' Jean said. 'I loved Ruby McInnes's episode about her stint as the show secretary. What timing to have it air just a few days before she passed, too. She would have been chuffed to share the interview with her family overseas. I'm so glad you started this series.'

'It's not exactly hard-hitting journalism, though, is it?' Lauren said. 'But it's warming a few hearts along the way. Ruby's family are going to play a snippet from my interviews at her funeral.'

'Things don't have to boom, crash and explode to inspire, my girl.' Jean reached for Lauren's arm, giving it a gentle squeeze. 'It's a wonderful feeling to put something good out into the world. Each time I match a couple up, I feel like I've done a good deed. There'll always be hurdles and not every pair lasts the distance, but when it works, the joy is reward enough.'

Lauren set the cake tin and tulip bulbs on the counter as she paid for the coffee.

'A bundt tin?' Jean grinned. 'Better you than me. And good luck with your job interview. Does Jack have the champagne on ice?'

'No way,' Lauren said, recalling how she'd mentally popped the cork and tasted the bubbles on her tongue last year, before the mortifying mix-up with George's farewell festivities. 'I'm not going to jinx it.' *This time.*

Gary wolf-whistled as Lauren unlocked the door to her cottage. 'Big week coming up, Gaz,' she said, feeding him an almond. She thought of Ruby again, and the honour of her family wanting to play the interview at her funeral. She couldn't imagine it, but as she unpacked the shopping, put the bundt tin in the pantry and stored the tulip bulbs in the back of the fridge, she decided that, just like dormant bulbs and baking bundt cakes, courage was something that only grew with gentle nurturing and a careful hand.

A text came through from Fran as she was crawling into bed.

Lauren, I know you've got so much on, but can you possibly cover Ruby's cook-along baking? She's already cooked
more than half the puddings on the list and I know she'd be
honoured for you to take her place.

Lauren wiped at her prickling eyes before replying.

Yep, send through the list of the remaining dishes and I'll get
baking this weekend. We can't let the cook-along challenge
slip through our fingers!

Staying busy would be a good distraction from stressing
about the upcoming job interview. Her fingers hovered over the
phone screen, then she tapped out a quick message to Jack too,
attaching a video of miniature goats in an outdoor yoga class.

Her phone lit up moments later with a reply.

Happy to help if you want an extra hand. Can BYO apron. Jack

She replied with another video and smiled as she drifted
off to sleep. She wanted him in an apron, without an apron
and everything in between.

Jack levered the first of the ANZAC biscuits off the hot tray,
tossing it between his fingers and blowing on it to speed up
the cooling process.

'Careful, Harri, it's super hot,' he said, passing his niece
the oat-studded treat.

She set the wooden spoon aside and cautiously bit into it.
'Delicious!' She wiped her hands on her apron and resumed
rolling the dough into balls, just like he'd shown her. It wasn't
the first batch of biscuits they'd made together, but it was the
first time she'd shown a little self-restraint with the uncooked

ingredients. All the cooking with Clem was obviously paying dividends.

He slid the next tray into the oven and resumed transferring the ANZACs onto a cooling rack.

'Can we listen to Lauren, Uncle Jack? I want to hear about the boy with the giant pumpkin again. And then I want to hear our interview,' she said, smiling angelically with her gap-toothed grin.

'You probably know those interviews off by heart now. Why don't we listen to the new episodes? Yesterday, Lauren spoke to a lady who knits tea cosies and a man who shampoos his cows and then uses a hairdryer to make them all pretty for show day.'

Harriet considered the suggestion, then agreed to listen to the new episodes as long as they could visit Archie Winklin's giant pumpkin at the show. Lauren's voice filled the kitchen as they finished their batch of biscuits.

Clem strolled in with the newspaper and an armful of groceries shortly afterwards.

'The kitchen's clean as a whistle. And these look delicious too,' she said, choosing a misshapen biscuit from the rack. 'Mmm.' She turned to Jack. 'Did you see a local winemaker has donated five hundred dollars to the kitty for the best rose of the show? That's a thousand smackers for *one* rose. If I'd known that, I would have given Nan's bushes a whopping great dose of fertiliser and tossed a few more buckets of water in their direction over summer.'

Jack laughed. 'Still worth entering anyway, and there's a kids' teapot-posy category for Harri.'

Harriet looked up from the local newspaper at the mention of her name. 'Awesome! I've already planned out what showbags I want, and if I win something, I can buy even more.'

'Steady on, short stuff, it's a dollar or two for first place in most categories, not enough for an extra showbag.'

'Hey,' Clem said, her voice so small that Harriet, who was busy stacking the biscuits into even piles, didn't hear. 'When you've finished there, can I've a word?'

Jack wiped his hands on the apron. 'Sure, what's up?'

'I've been meaning to tell you—' Clem paused as Harriet looked up.

Spotting them in hushed conversation, she promptly wedged herself between them. 'What are you talking about? Is it my birthday?'

'Your birthday's in September, Harriet.'

'Yeah, but I've got lots of good ideas for a party. And can I have a pet goat like the one next door? It comes to visit me sometimes.'

'Are you serious?' Clem pushed back from the bench, disbelief turning to surprise when Harriet explained.

'It used to just come to the fence for some tucker, but now it knows where the passionfruit vine is, it comes through all by itself.'

Jack glanced over the paddock. Victor's property was looking neater by the week, thanks to help from Sebastian and Cohen. And while there was still a large collection of car bodies, the long grass was gone, the surplus white goods were at the dump and the piles of rusty machinery had been culled by at least half.

Clem was out the door to inspect her passionfruit before Jack had his boots on. For someone who was so tired all the time these days, she could move fast when needed.

'That goat's decimated the vine,' she groaned. 'All the seaweed extract and sheep poo in the world won't help this poor thing. It'll be lucky to survive, let alone fruit.'

'But he likes passionfruit leaves, Mum. And you said we should share.'

'Pfft,' Clem said and, to Jack's surprise, burst into tears. 'With friends and family, not with a . . . a . . . a darn goat.'

Before he knew it, Jack had two sobbing girls on his hands. *Holy moly, there must be something in the water.*

Once he had Harriet sorted with an ANZAC biscuit and episode of *Bluey*, he carried a cup of tea and another biscuit outside for Clem.

'You want to tell me what's going on, or do you want me to find the gap in the fence and repair it first?'

Clem hiccuped and cast a filthy look in the direction of Victor's property. 'If that goat comes again, I'll . . . I'll . . .'

Jack fetched his fencing pliers from the garage and set off for Victor's.

There was not one but two huge buckets brimming with sunflowers flanking the front door of the old farmhouse when Lauren arrived, and she was so enchanted with the tall, cheerful flowers that she almost missed the purple-and-green flash zipping across the driveway.

'Yikes!' She slammed on the brakes, feeling her heartbeat kick into overdrive.

Harriet waved, rollerskating a figure eight across the widest part of the driveway, before bowing and skating across to Lauren's impromptu park.

'Hi Lauren! Didya see my skating? I'm fast, aren't I?'

'Super fast,' Lauren agreed, relieved she hadn't run the little girl over.

'Harriet Crossley, get your butt over here. Let poor Lauren get out of the car first.' Clem hurried around the side of the house, lugging a basket of clean laundry and wearing an apologetic grimace. 'No road sense, I'm afraid. I'm just thankful we're not in the city anymore with traffic coming in every which direction. She'd be as flat as a pancake.'

Lauren waved off the apology. 'All good. In fact, I was hoping for a helper.' She passed a shopping bag to Harriet and then gathered up the box on her passenger seat.

'Chocolates and marshmallows!'

'Your uncle Jack told me you have a fire pit and, technically, you can't eat marshmallows without chocolate.'

Clem led them inside and Lauren's knees went a little weak at the aroma of onion and garlic. Jack stood over the stovetop looking shower fresh and desperately handsome in dark denim shorts and a lightweight buttoned shirt. He turned the heat down and abandoned the frypan when he saw her, wiping his hands on a tea towel before resting them either side of her waist and pressing a kiss onto her cheek.

'Hey,' he said. They'd swum together twice since their trip to Langhorne Creek, and spent many nights at her cottage, but it was the first time they'd had an audience for any public displays of affection, even just a chaste kiss. His shyness made her like him all that bit more. 'How did your job interview go?'

Lauren grinned. Jack had texted her beforehand to wish her good luck and sent her a video of Gary wolf-whistling when she shared a pre-interview selfie wearing her new pants suit.

'It felt good,' she said. 'I didn't put my foot in it and with that Best in Show series, plus the secondment to the South West Vic bureau and a few fill-in stints, they said I've come a long way since the last time I applied.'

His whole face smiled, not just his lips. 'Nice work! Now you can put it out of your mind for a few weeks.'

Lauren rolled her eyes. 'It's off my shoulders, but not exactly out of my mind. This dinner smells amazing,' she said, unpacking the jars of homemade tomato passata and turning to Clem. 'I brought you some blue-ribbon chutney, relish and tomato sauce too, all from last year's stores.'

'Look at that colour,' marvelled Clem. 'You don't get that from supermarket tomatoes. Did you grow them yourself?'

Lauren accepted a glass of sparkling wine from her hostess. 'Nope, these tomatoes were grown by my best friend, April. You'll see her name plastered all over the first-prize placards on show day next week. Greenest thumbs you've ever seen. I've grown a few tomato bushes at my place this year, and even though they're April's seedlings, they're about half as tall and not even a quarter as productive as her patch.'

'We're doing artwork at school for the show and flowers,' said Harriet. 'Will there really be show rides?'

Lauren nodded. 'Definitely.' She felt at home sitting at the broad kitchen bench, telling Harriet about the forthcoming Penwarra Show and watching Jack cook. He'd slipped a tea towel into his waistband, and was in constant movement as he tasted the sauce and adjusted the seasoning, salted the gnocchi water and tore basil leaves from the cluster of plants on the windowsill. Jack's workspace was like a navy ship's galley: everything in perfect order and neat as a pin.

Clem caught her looking. 'And to think he wastes five days a week eating the exact same lunch of poached chicken, broccolini and brown rice. It's a crime.'

Jack shook his head, obviously used to the sentiment, and Lauren wondered if her relationship with Tahnee would be better if they had this type of good-natured sparring, if they understood what buttons they could press before they reached boiling point.

'How's the cooking challenge, Clem? Only a few days until the show—do you think you'll make it in time?'

Harriet dragged a chair to Jack's side and presented a spoon for tasting, while Clem updated her on the extensive recipe tally. 'If you'd asked me last week, I would have said we were pushing it, but Harriet and I only have two more recipes to do before show day and our portion is complete. I hear you've taken on Ruby's section? How's it going?'

'Let's just say I'm glad the Laceys have a big chest freezer at Lacewing Estate.'

'Do you have time for that? Jack said you've already got a lot on your plate.'

'The fundraising pledges are only good if the challenge is completed before show day. And Ruby made a solid start. It's only puddings and a few desserts anyway, I feel like I owe her that at least.'

17

'Knock, knock,' Jack called, pulling his cycling cleats off at Lauren's pink front door and leaning his bike and helmet against the verandah post. Her home smelled like the inside of a tomato soup tin, and he found her in the kitchen, ladling bubbling sauce into piping-hot bottles. After a gruelling 50-kilometre bike ride to Wrattonbully and back, the kitchen felt twice as warm as normal.

A smart guy would have ridden home, showered and waited for his body temp to regulate instead of detouring to Petticoat Lane. But, Jack thought as she greeted him with one of her glorious smiles, the lure of extra time with Lauren was hard to resist.

'Perfect timing,' she said, using the back of her hand to swipe blonde hair from her eyes. 'I'm three bottles shy and I can't reach the spare jars. If you head to the garage, you'll see a shelf above the camping gear. Short of stacking a step-ladder on a wheelie bin, it's impossible for me to reach, but it shouldn't be a problem for someone so tall.'

Jack cringed at the thought of Lauren balancing precariously on a ladder with the heavy box of jars in her arms, or worse, balancing a ladder on top of a bin. He tugged the damp cycling jersey away from his chest, located the glass jars in the messy garage and returned to the kitchen as she set a pot of water on to boil.

'I don't suppose you can wash the jars in soapy water before I sterilise them?'

He left the tap running to give her a proper hello. 'You taste like tomatoes,' he said, kissing her softly.

'Funny that.' She grinned, stepping away from the stove to kiss him. 'You smell like sweaty lycra and sunscreen. Still extremely kissable, though.'

By the time they broke apart, the bubbles were overflowing into the adjoining sink.

'That pink rose by your back door is pretty speccy.'

Lauren nodded. 'She's called Princess Alexandra of Kent. April gave her to me as a housewarming surprise when I bought this place. She's gorgeous in bud *and* full bloom.'

'Looks like a prize winner if ever I saw one.'

'Maybe,' Lauren said. 'How about Clem? Is she entering anything?'

'Anything? Try just about everything!' Jack washed and rinsed the bottles as he outlined their show plans. 'Sunflowers, obviously, roses too. There're only a few left this late in the season, but enough buds that there should be blooms for Saturday. Bikkies, scones, cakes, and I think she'll even go in for the quartet of mixed slice. And ever since you mentioned the chocolate orange pudding, Clem's been craving citrus, so she's tried at least six lemon cake recipes, searching for the perfect one.'

Lauren gestured to the Penwarra Show cookbook propped open by the pantry. 'Audrey Cartwright submitted a lemon drizzle cake for the recipe book and she always dominates the baking section. Lovely lady, but she'll talk your ear off if you give her half a chance and heaven help you if you mention using margarine instead of butter. I was stuck at her house for ninety minutes recording my Best in Show interview. If Clem's looking for a foolproof recipe, I'd put my money on Audrey's.'

Jack tried to remember that particular interview. The series was coming to an end now that the show was almost upon them, and he'd started losing track of the various guests Lauren had featured. But the name rang a bell, although it took a while to connect the dots.

'I know that name.'

Lauren nodded. 'She's also a serial complainer and petition writer, never misses an opportunity to kick up a stink. She boycotted the show a few years back. She and another show baker had a spat over a stewarding issue. April's stepmum, Fran, nearly wore herself into the ground trying to bolster the entries and fill the tables in their absence. You know April's boyfriend, Connor?'

Jack nodded.

'Connor's cooking is just as bad as April's. The show tables were full after much scraping and begging on Fran's behalf, but they sure as heck weren't pretty.'

He laughed as she told him about the entries from either end of the cooking spectrum, with their oozing insides and scorched outsides. 'Even Fergus had a go, and he was—' She broke off. 'Sorry, that's weird, isn't it?'

He used tongs to extract a glass jar from the bubbling water and set it on the draining rack. 'What's weird?'

Lauren shrugged. 'Me talking about Fergus, seeing we used to go out . . .' She waved a hand, sending a splodge of tomato sauce against the backsplash.

Jack watched how quickly she became flustered and the way the cadence of her sentences changed. He'd noticed it a few times on air, usually at the start of the show or after the break for the news, but when she was in front of him, it was easier to see that the easy-going manner sometimes had a thin veneer.

'It's not weird,' he assured her, putting the funnel into the bottle. 'We're over thirty—I'd be worried if you hadn't had any relationships. And if anyone should feel weird, it'd be the dork that dragged you to his cousin's wedding.'

She nudged him, the smile returning to her face. 'As I remember it, I pretty much invited myself, and I think we can both agree it worked out well.'

'It most certainly did,' he agreed.

Jack leaned down and kissed the tip of her nose, wishing that instead of bottling tomato sauce, he could bottle the bubble of happiness their new relationship had created.

The jars of preserves and bottles of sauce clinked in the back seat as Lauren drew to a stop outside the show hall on Friday after work. Show day eve was almost as hectic as the grand event, just a little less polished, and instead of punters and over-sugared children roaming the showgrounds, stall holders were unfolding marquee awnings, organisers were outlining areas of lawn with spray marker and entrants were unpacking armfuls of entries.

'Jean, you're certainly in the right place at the right time,' said Lauren, pausing by the small coffee caravan as she carried the first load of baking entries into the hall. 'I'll grab a latte on my way back, please.'

'With pleasure, my dear,' said Jean, picking up the milk. 'I'll even give you the family discount.'

Lauren nearly dropped her box of biscuits, muffins and jams. She spun around to see the older woman laughing.

'What? I had little Harriet on the phone last night, rabbiting on about Lauren this, Lauren that, Lauren's funny mistake with the recipe for choccy rock cakes. You've made an impact, let me tell you, and that nephew of mine is even smiling. Smiling! That deserves a fifty-cent discount in itself.'

It pleased Lauren to know that she made Jack happy and that Harriet looked forward to her visits. The photo he'd sent last night, of him and Harriet baking, was the sweetest thing she'd seen all week—heck, all month.

She found Fran at the helm of the baking section, notebook in hand, marking off entries and registering each plateful of food that arrived in front of her.

'What an incredible turnout,' Fran said, glancing adoringly at the trestle tables, already half-full. 'This radio series of yours has been a huge help, pet. It brought a lot of home bakers out of the woodwork.'

Lauren handed over her registration form and gestured to the entries, the tables jam-packed with breads, biscuits, slices and scones. 'I can't take the credit for this. Not everyone listens to the radio, Fran. It's all your hard work paying off and all that extra promo from the cook-along really added to the buzz. I know April mentioned it at every opportunity too.'

'You've just missed her and Connor. They've been helping all day, shifting trestle tables and cleaning this hall to within an inch of its life before this glorious landslide of early entries arrived. Next year, with the money we raise from the cook-along, we'll have beautiful new tables that don't wobble and maybe screened-in display cases so the rodents aren't tip-toeing over the baking aisles overnight.'

'That's brilliant, Fran, you deserve it.' Lauren stepped aside as an elderly man thumped a heavy box of sauces on the registration desk.

Lauren strode outside, collected another box of entries from her car—this one full of tomato-based sauces, chutneys and preserves—and rejoined the queue for early registrations. And as she watched April's stepmother extend the same courtesy to the region's most decorated competitive baker as she did a nervous newcomer with one or two entries, she was proud that her small role had helped Fran Lacey achieve her goal of celebrating the hundredth anniversary of the show.

With the last of the entries delivered—and a decaf latte to sip on her way home—Lauren fixed herself an easy, early dinner and turned in.

The 4.30 am alarm hit like a freight train and it wasn't until Lauren had helped set up the outside broadcast equipment and was halfway through producing the breakfast show at the showgrounds, that she realised she had her fine-wool top on inside out.

Nigel grinned. 'Were you up all night with the new fella?'

'I'm a bit more professional than that. Besides—' she gave a wink, '—all good breakfast show staff know to save the main romping for Saturday nights.'

Nigel burst out laughing and Lauren turned her attention to the interviews she had planned for the show. They'd be back on air in two short minutes and the crowd was starting to build.

'What's this I hear about romping?'

'Sounds like we arrived at just the right moment!'

Lauren knew those voices. She spun around. Gabrielle and Tahnee stood by the mixing deck with an enormous bunch of flowers.

'Surprise!'

'Lauren didn't tell me she had two beautiful sisters,' Nigel said, sitting up straighter in his chair and shooting them a winning smile.

Lauren threw her arms around her mother and sister before rushing back to her chair. 'We're back on air in two minutes, Mum, perhaps go for a walk around the showgrounds?'

With a yap, Bruno rushed forward, his beady eyes set on Lauren's ankles.

'Oh no, you don't,' said Lauren, drawing her feet off the ground so the dog couldn't nip or hump them, or attempt both simultaneously.

'Oh, Lauren.' Gabrielle swept the dog into her arms and clutched him to her chest. 'You should know better than to say the W word when Bruno's around.'

'Song finishes in one minute,' Nigel said.

Lauren glanced around. *She* should be the one counting down for the presenter, not vice versa, and Paul would be back any moment.

'Sorry, Mum. I'll be with you as soon as we're done here. If I'd known you were coming, I would've mentioned 9 am was a bad time.'

'Then it wouldn't have been a surprise, silly,' Tahnee said, handing the bouquet to Lauren.

The dachshund chose that exact moment to start barking again, right as Paul rounded the corner with the spare headphones they needed. He gestured to his watch and then Nigel, who was due on air any moment, and then to the dog.

'Mum, you have to go, we're about to go live.'

And although the yapping was barely audible by the time they returned to air, the pollen from Tahnee's bouquet sent Lauren into a sneezing fit halfway through Nigel's introduction.

🌿

Jack peeled off Wallaby Lane into Sunny Cross Farm to find Clem in the garden, assessing a bucket of blooms.

'I'm going all in, Jack. Fairytale Magic, Soul Sister and Just Joey are mighty fine roses, but as a backup, I'm also entering this beauty.' She crouched down to read the label on the rose-bush closest to the garage and grinned back at him. 'Ah yes, Summer Romance. Very fitting.'

Clem snipped two perfectly pink blooms from the bush, placed them in the bucket, then pulled off her gardening gloves. 'Should be a few winners amongst them. My money's on Soul Sister, though. That unique pink, mauve and beige colouring will be hard to beat. Which one are you punting on, Jack? Jack!'

Jack tore his thoughts away from Lauren, and the romance he hoped would outlast many summers, and considered his sister's question. 'Fairytale Magic,' he said, admiring the cupped petals and strong fragrance. 'According to Lauren and April, you'll need a magic touch to prise the champion rose title from Brian Corcoran's grasp.'

He brushed a shred of coconut off the back seat, a relic from the baking entries Clem had delivered to the showgrounds earlier that morning, and secured the bucket of roses.

'What do you think, honey?' Clem asked as Harriet bounded over with a gold-edged teapot. 'Do you think Mummy's roses can win five hundred smackers?'

'Yep,' said Harriet without a moment's hesitation. 'How many flowers do I need for my posy? These yellow ones are all I can find.' She frowned at the fluffy dandelion flowers.

'Not sure,' Jack answered, 'but Lauren said we could take what we wanted from her garden. I need to call past on the way through town anyway, she has a heap of roses I need to pick.'

'You're entering them in the show for her?' Clem pretended to swoon. 'You never cease to amaze me, big bro. Nan would be proud.'

'Yeah, yeah,' Jack tugged on his hat. 'Come on, Harri, let's see if we can't fill this teapot with something better than weeds.'

Harriet tossed the handful of dandelions back onto the farmhouse lawn and climbed into Jack's ute.

Clem was right about one thing: their nan *would* be proud, but not just of Jack, more at having them all here together. She would have loved knowing they were breathing life into the faded farmhouse, rifling through her heritage seeds and using her favourite teapot, even if it was for flowers instead of loose-leaf English breakfast tea.

'Why don't I take Harriet in early and register the entries, and you rest up, Clem? It's not like you haven't seen sideshow alley or the show stalls before.'

Clem stifled a yawn. He wondered how late she'd been up last night. 'I should come too. Make sure we support the show.'

Jack laughed. 'Says she who's already baked umpteen dishes from the show recipe book, delivered a week's worth of baking to the pavilion and looks like she's about to fall asleep. You've done your bit. Nobody will hold it against you if you're not walking through the gates the moment they open.'

'Maybe?' Clem gave him a grateful smile. 'I could crawl back into bed now and swing past at lunchtime then, if you're sure?'

Harriet chattered all the way to Lauren's house, and while Jack picked roses, Harriet told Gary about showbag alley.

'I'm going to get a Bertie Beetle one, Gaz, and you can nibble the chocolate.'

The galah bobbed on his perch. 'Stone the crows! Stone the crows!'

His niece's cheerful conversation continued all the way to the showgrounds, where she proudly carried her teapot posy into the show hall and paid the entry fees with her pocket money. Once Harriet was sorted, they entered Lauren's and Clem's flowers and headed outside.

'There's Lauren!'

Jack jogged to catch up to Harriet and scoop her into his arms before she gatecrashed the live interview. 'Shh, Harri, they're recording the radio show. We'll come back and see Lauren when she's finished work.'

Lauren waved from the marquee and after waving back, they left to explore the day's entertainment.

'Look, Uncle Jack, baby ducks and little weeny wallabies. Can I hold them?'

Jack spotted a familiar wildlife sanctuary logo on the animal nursery enclosure, and found Sebastian manning the stall. Harriet ran to Sebastian and within moments was nursing a joey in a pouch. Several more children piled into the petting zoo and Jack was impressed with the boy's patience dealing with the overenthusiastic youngsters.

'Nope, hold it gently. Don't put your finger in that cage unless you want it bitten. Pat that one on the belly—yep, just like that.'

His manner showed a different side to the sullen boy Jack had sat beside in the police station interview room in October. Over the last few months, he'd glimpsed the softer sides of Sebastian and Cohen, the candid laughter, the unguarded moments when they horsed around with fallen branches like Jedi warriors, or the playful wrestling that reminded Jack of a litter of puppies. They were just kids, really; kids with long lanky limbs, the first wisps of stubble and energy to burn.

He detoured to the closest food stall and returned with two cans of soft drink, plus two bags of potato chips. Sebastian accepted with a curt 'Thanks' and shuffled across the bench to make room for Jack too.

'You ever wear anything other than black?' Sebastian asked. 'I'd be called a goth or an emo if I dressed like you.'

Jack looked down at his dark denim shorts and the linen shirt that always needed an iron before wearing. He shrugged. 'Saves me trying to match things. How long are you running this stall?'

'All day,' Sebastian said. 'Sucks, but at least Mum's paying me. Well, more like taking it off my tally for those broken windows. And it's better than shovelling pig shit all day.'

Jack followed his gaze to the stockyards, where Cohen was clearing a pig pen.

Harriet returned the wallaby to Sebastian. 'When will the hall be open, Uncle Jack? Have I won something yet?'

Jack grinned, shaking his head. 'Not yet, Harri. Until those doors are open, nobody knows who's won what. We'll swing by the livestock first.'

The piglet stalls were as pungent as he'd suspected and even Harriet held her nose as they neared.

'This stinks!'

'You should try working here,' Cohen complained. 'Almost as bad as cleaning the portaloos.'

He brightened marginally when Jack handed him the refreshments, receiving a grudging 'thanks' in return.

'All actions have consequences, Cohen, and you rarely get to pick your punishment. Hopefully, this'll make you think twice about toilet papering the show society president's front yard.'

An older man paused by the pen, a ten-gallon cowboy hat on his head, leaning heavily on a walking stick. 'Back in my day, they had a greasy pig competition. Lubed up a piglet or two with lard, each kid paid a penny to get in the ring and the young 'un who grabbed it and held on won a prize. Animal activists wouldn't stand for it these days, but it was the highlight of the show for me and my mates. Then there was the "guess the weight of the sow" competition. Good old-fashioned fun.' He smiled at the memory, whistling a tune as he limped away.

'Can I catch a greasy pig?' Harriet asked eagerly.

'Not sure they do it anymore, Harri,' Jack said, turning back to Cohen. 'What's your next shift?'

At this, Cohen thawed a little. 'Donut van. Dunno if I'll be cooking or on the till, but it'll trump this gig.'

'Make sure you wash your hands in between,' Jack called.

Harriet dragged him to the next stall, begging for a pony ride and moments later, she was perched on a skewbald Shetland pony in a western saddle with a helmet over her pigtails.

'If I had my own pony, I could enter the show. And the jumping events,' she gushed, one hand clutching the pommel and one holding a fistful of mane. 'We could ride on the beach . . .'

The horse lady shot Jack a 'now you've done it' grin.

'Look at you, sitting up there like Lady Muck!' Clem and Arthur were waiting at the horse float beside the livestock arena when they returned from their first slow loop.

The phone in the horse lady's hand chimed and she offered Jack the lead rope. 'You mind doing a lap while I take this call?'

Jack took the rope, slowing his step to the pony's glacial pace.

'She'd make a fine cowgirl,' Arthur said.

A rumbling came behind them, and Arthur whistled as the gleaming hot rods and street cars did a lap of honour for the Show 'n' Shine display.

'So shiny you can see your reflection in their chrome work. We'll go there next.' Arthur returned his attention to Harriet. 'You really should get her a horse, Clemmy. Plenty of room at Sunny Cross.'

Jack knew Clem's answer before she shook her head.

'Not happening, Pop. Wait there, you two, I'll get a photo.' Clem lifted her phone. 'Smile!'

Before they could say cheese, a bang cut through the air. Harriet squealed. Clem screamed and ducked.

Jack automatically reached for his firearm, although common sense insisted it was a backfire, not a bullet, and he wasn't wearing his police belt anyway.

The Shetland wasn't as easily convinced, though. It whinnied, and the rope burned Jack's hand as it reared onto its hind legs and bucked. Harriet squealed again.

'Harriet!'

Back and forth the animal went, like a rocking horse on steroids. His back hooves missed Jack's kneecaps by a millimetre and Harriet pitched sideways in the saddle.

'Grab the pommel,' the horse lady yelled, dashing towards them, but the pony wheeled around, throwing Harriet off in one swift sidestep.

Clem rushed to her daughter's side. Cursing himself for letting go of the lead rope, Jack hesitated between the pony and his niece.

Cohen vaulted the pig pen, calling, 'I'll get it.'

Jack went to Harriet, pulse racing. 'Harri, you alright?'

She blinked, too winded to talk. Jack hoped the gash on her cheek looked worse than it was.

'I'm so sorry,' the owner cried. 'That pony's normally bombproof—I never thought he'd throw a rider. Can you wiggle your fingers, sweetie?'

Harriet did as she was told, and they had established there were no broken bones by the time Cohen returned the pony.

'All good?' he asked.

Clem nodded and Jack reached for his wallet.

'Mate, can you go and grab her something sugary?'

The boy set off with a five-dollar note as Jack and Clem helped Harriet up. The horse lady apologised again.

'Could've happened to anyone,' Arthur said, clapping Jack's shoulder. His grandfather would know from Jack's flat-lipped smile that Jack blamed himself for the fall.

Once the pony was secured, the horse lady carried over a large first-aid kit. With expert precision, she cleaned and dressed the wound on Harriet's cheek. 'Don't think it needs stitches, so tape will do for today and you can always see the doctor on Monday. I'm so, so sorry, sweetheart. I hope I haven't put you off ponies for good?'

'Fine by me,' Clem murmured.

Jack straightened Harriet's pigtails. 'Sorry, Harri. You might've been safer with a greasy pig.'

His niece giggled, cheering up when Cohen jogged across with fairy floss.

'The soft drink lines were a mile long,' he puffed. 'And the donuts too. But I bought this bag earlier and stashed it with my stuff in the show office.' He handed over the bag and the five-dollar note.

'It's yours,' Jack said. 'Replace your fairy floss later.'

Cohen shook his head. 'Won't be any left by the time I finish my shift. They always run out.' He pressed the money back into Jack's hand. 'I don't care, she needs it more than me. And you bought me smoko already.'

Jack hadn't seen this side of the teen before, but he sensed that once he'd made his decision, Cohen would want him to honour it.

'Okay, thanks,' Jack said.

As he'd hoped, Harriet's spunk returned along with her sugar levels. 'Can we see the flowers now? And the artwork? You should see my decorated biscuits, Pop. They're like sunflowers, with brown Smarties and yellow honey-bear petals. Come, lookit!'

Arthur winked. 'Tough like her mum.'

Outside broadcasts attracted plenty of attention, no matter where or when, and Lauren was accustomed to intercepting spectators and curious kids before they got too close to the cords and tech equipment.

She settled back at the trestle table, ensured the running sheet was still on track, and waved at two little boys, one with a ferret in his hand, the other with a kitten on a lead. *En route to the pet parade, perhaps?* She texted Jack, warning him that Gabrielle and Tahnee were gunning for an introduction, then returned to work.

Archie Winklin came over for an interview midway through the morning, and from the look on his face, his giant pumpkin had fared well in the judging. She held a finger up to her lips as he came closer, and it was almost comical watching the twelve-year-old trying to contain his excitement. Having lived next door to Archie for several years, Lauren had seen him happy plenty of times before, but today, even the tips of his ears were glowing with delight.

'I won first prize!' he said in a barely contained whisper. 'April said it was in with a good shot, but mine was six kilos heavier than the next best pumpkin! *Six kilos!*'

Nigel leaned in. 'So you're the famous kid with the green thumbs? There are a lot of people who'll be happy to hear you on the radio today!'

Paul set up the tripod and camera as Nigel interviewed Archie. 'Lauren, how do you feel about asking Archie those same questions on camera, in front of his award-winning pumpkin?' he said. 'We can cobble together a few grabs from

the next talent, film some footage of the pumpkin, the cakes
and flowers, and then, once the breakfast show's finished, you
can record a piece to camera. We'll send it to the TV news
editor in Adelaide and they can pull it together.'

The TV news! Lauren was glad she was already sitting
down. Having snippets of her Best in Show series uploaded
to the station's social media and seeing popular posts like
Archie's interview shared over and over again was one thing,
but having her content on television—wow!

'Will we be on TV?' Archie whooped loudly, then clapped a
hand over his mouth as both Nigel and the current interviewee
looked over. 'Sorry! That's just super cool! This is the best
day ever.'

Lauren couldn't help agreeing.

Once the breakfast program was finished, she recorded
the interview with Archie in front of the very large and very
orange 'Trumpy'.

'No promises, buddy, but watch the news just in case,'
Paul said.

Lauren knew what she'd be doing that night too. It took
several takes to film her short piece without tripping over
her tongue or fluffing up the words, but eventually Paul
gave her a thumbs-up.

'That's a wrap,' he said. 'You did a great job, Lauren. I'm sure
they'll snaffle that up for tonight's news. You happy with it?'

Lauren nodded.

'And so you should be. We'll take the gear back to the
station, you go find your family and enjoy yourself. Treat
yourself to a dagwood dog and a stick of fairy floss. I can't
speak outside of school, but between you and me, you've
really earned it!'

Lauren walked the two blocks back to her pink cottage,
trying not to think too hard about what Paul had said. She

was loath to jump to conclusions, especially after last time, but surely Paul wouldn't joke about something like 'really earning it' when he knew how much she wanted that job, given they were due to announce the successful candidate on Monday?

Put the job out of your mind until then.

She swapped her work polo shirt for a sunflower yellow dress she'd bought with Jack in mind and donned her Fern Akubra, feeling instantly cooler now her hair was off her neck and the sun off her face.

Her phone rang as she walked through the gates for a third time that day. 'Hey, Jack!'

The sound of the equestrian speakers blared in the background of the call. Lauren shaded her eyes, trying to spot him around the other side of the oval between the horse floats, four-wheel drives and ponies.

'Sorry I missed smoko, Harriet bit the dust on a pony ride, then somehow I got roped into helping with the horse jumps. You wouldn't believe how many rails they knock down every round.'

Lauren found him by the equestrian registration tent, near a goose-neck horse truck that looked big enough to house a stable of horses. The fabric of Jack's black shirt carried a faint aroma of horses and hay as he leaned in to greet her.

'Love the dress,' he said. 'Though after two hours watching the riders sail past in their jodhpurs and jackets, I reckon you'd look good in a set of riding gear too.'

'What about a shearing singlet and black jeans?' She gestured to the sign for the evening's entertainment. 'Or a set of wood-chopping whites?'

He grinned and kissed her again. 'You'd look good in a paper bag. Let me buy you lunch.'

Walking through the showgrounds hand in hand, they came across Connor.

'You look pleased with yourself,' Connor said when he joined them to watch the gumboot toss. 'Did your chutney win a sash or two, then?'

'We haven't got there yet.' Lauren took a bite of her battered hotdog. 'If it's a crime to grin like a loon, then I'm guilty as charged.' And even if she *had* won something in the pavilion, there was so much more to smile about today. *The successful broadcast, a possible television spot, perfect autumn weather that isn't sunburn central or pelting rain . . .*

She beamed at Jack, who had only let go of her hand momentarily to wipe tomato sauce from his chin. *One very handsome Senior Constable Jack Crossley.*

A new entrant lined up for the gumboot toss, attracting cheers and applause from the children in the audience. 'School principal,' Jack told Lauren and Connor, as the brightly dressed lady performed a series of comedic stretches before hefting the gumboot through the air. It landed a few feet short of the first-place marker, but the principal fist-pumped the air anyway and did a heel click on her way out. The crowd roared with delight.

Lauren's phone buzzed in her dress pocket. 'Hey, Mum, we're at the gumboot toss. Where are you?'

'I'd forgotten what a big day it is, darling,' Gabrielle said. 'Tahnee nearly got trampled by a Murray Grey calf, and I'm tired of swatting away flies and running into old friends whose names I can barely remember, so we've retired to a winery for a breather. I hope you don't mind?'

'Totally fine, Mum,' Lauren said. At least Gabrielle wasn't trying to hurry her out the gates and pestering her for an introduction to Jack. 'I've only just finished with the radio, so I'll be here a while yet, plus we've got the shearing and fireworks tonight. You catch your breath and we'll regroup a little later.'

She ended the call as a message came through from April.

SOS in the baking pavilion. Jack handy? Might be a blue
rinse mutiny underway!

'Yikes!' Lauren got Jack's and Connor's attention, recalling
last year's drama when the town's best bakers had boycotted
the baking contest. 'Come on, guys, April needs a hand in
the baking hall.'

'Not more nuisance issues or graffiti?'

'Worse,' she said, weaving through the crowd. 'I think
Audrey Cartwright and Eileen Mawson are about to go to war.'

18

A crowd had gathered by the time they reached the baking pavilion and from the raised voices, Jack could tell tempers were running hot. Even though he wasn't on duty until tonight, from Fran's hand-wringing and April's relieved sigh, they were in the nick of time.

'This is a packet mix cake, and if you can't see that, you need those glasses checked,' one older lady said, her chin quivering with indignation as she pointed a finger at another woman.

'Pah,' the other lady retorted. 'Packet mix, indeed. I wasn't going to mention anything, but you've forced my hand. That carrot cake isn't regulation size at all, Audrey. I followed the provided recipe to the letter and mine's only half the height. It should be *my* carrot cake going through to the regional contest like every other year, not yours.'

'Don't blame me for your lousy cooking, Eileen.'

'Once a cheater, always a cheater, Audrey.'

A titter rippled through the crowd as Eileen reached for the cake.

'Ladies,' Jack said, holding out his hands, his voice calm. 'Can we discuss this somewhere else, without hurling cakes or insults across the room?'

Lauren tapped his arm. 'The office is behind the kitchen,' she said.

Jack ushered the two ladies into the small room with Fran and Lauren hot on their heels.

'I don't suffer fools lightly, sergeant,' the stooped lady with the tartan shawl said, her chin held high. 'And I can spot a White Wings mix from fifty paces. My daughter-in-law used to palm them off as her own, you see, and I didn't let her get away with it either.'

Jack imagined Audrey triumphantly snooping through her daughter-in-law's recycling bin for incriminating evidence and felt a twinge of sympathy. And even though Eileen flushed bottlebrush red at the specificity of the claim, she wouldn't back down.

'You're just bitter because that young mum entered jam drops for the very first time and pipped you at the post.'

Jack suspected she was referring to Clem, who had not only weighed her jam drops before they went in the oven, but measured them with a ruler once they had cooled and reweighed them before she was satisfied with the uniformity.

'Fran, can you tell us something please?' Lauren asked, stepping in.

Fran nodded desperately. 'Anything, if it'll help end this argument.'

'Can you tell us how many people entered the baking category today?'

The older ladies frowned. 'What's this about?' Audrey said.

'Twenty in the fruit cake,' Fran counted, 'five in the burnt butter biscuits, the entire B-Grade footy team entered the bloke's chocolate cake category so that's another eighteen plus five extras . . .'

Lauren gave Jack a quick smile, urging him to trust her.

Go for it, he mouthed.

'Overall,' Fran said, clearing her throat. 'We had over three hundred individual entrants, across thirty-five different categories. Many people entered multiple categories, of course, and only three people, including Audrey and Eileen, entered something in every single baking category.'

Jack nodded. He knew exactly who the third person was. *Clem*.

'Right,' Lauren said. 'And that's not including the preserves or the produce, is it?'

Fran shook her head.

The two feuding women had matching furrows between their eyebrows.

'And I know it was a separate project, but out of interest, Fran, how many recipes did folks make from your fundraising cookbook for the cook-along?'

'Oh, that's easy,' Fran said, managing a weak smile. 'One-hundred recipes, you know that, Lauren. One-hundred recipes in honour of the one-hundredth Penwarra show.'

'So in rough terms, if we think about the hundred recipes that were made for the community cook-along, the three hundred people who mixed, measured, rolled and baked something for today's show, then you've engaged a quarter of the town's population as part of the show celebrations, yeah?

'And that's not including the hundreds of people wandering between those trestle tables right now, enjoying the sight of those luscious entries, wishing they'd been brave enough to enter, or perhaps being inspired, at this very minute, to choose a category, spend the next twelve months baking their recipe over and over and throwing their hat in the ring next year?'

Fran nodded again. 'Record numbers through the gate, I hear.'

Lauren reminded Jack of a lawyer preparing her closing argument in a courtroom drama, or a school principal rousing the students. 'So, of all the hundreds of people invested in this

year's show baking, let alone the ninety-nine years beforehand, do we really want to taint this celebration with a petty
disagreement? Do we want people to remember the show for
the wonderful, community-spirited event it really is or for two
bickering old ducks?'

Audrey and Eileen spluttered and for the first time that
afternoon, seemed to agree on something.

'We're not—'

'Old ducks? Excuse me—'

'What does this teach the children in that pavilion? That
we stoop to name calling and cake throwing if we don't win?
Character assassination in the pursuit of personal glory? I just
interviewed Archie Winklin, a kid who's been planning his
giant pumpkin crop since he was old enough to save up for the
seeds, and his attitude is better than both of yours combined.'

The women had the grace to accept this dressing down
and didn't even kick up too much of a stink when Fran
escorted them from the office with a warning they'd both
be disqualified from future shows if there was any more trouble.

'Thanks, you two,' Fran said when she returned to Lauren
and Jack. 'I'll check with the president, but even though Audrey
had the highest points overall, and Eileen was a very close
second, I don't think either deserves the grand champion
baking sash after that performance. I'd better get the prize
money and return to the registration desk so the place getters
can collect their winnings.'

Jack put an arm around Lauren. 'You were impressive back
there,' he said, tugging her to his chest. 'Now I can add "court
judge" to the list of outfits you'd totally nail.'

'With one of those nasty curly wigs?' Lauren bubbled with
laughter. 'You have seriously weird taste, Jack Crossley.'

'Jack!'

They both turned at the sharp tone in Fran's voice and Jack felt his chest sink when he saw her bewildered expression.

'The bag of prize money! It's gone!'

'Poor Fran. Who do they think took the money?'

April lifted a shoulder. 'Beats me, but I heard from Brian, who heard it from Geraldine, that the Moriarty boy dashed into the office mid-morning and then ran out like a flash, holding some sort of bag. She wasn't close enough to see if it was a calico bank bag, but someone must have seen something.'

Lauren winced. Jack was completely invested in Sebastian's and Cohen's rehabilitation and he thought they'd turned a corner. He'd be *devastated*.

'Stop stressing,' April said. 'Neither of us can do anything about it. As Art Crossley said before, show day comes but once a year. Let's enjoy what's left.'

Blue ribbons gleamed enticingly from the competition tables. They wandered down the trestles and discovered April had received her first ever ribbon for baking and Lauren had scored a few of her own. Then they made their way to the preserves.

'That apple and tomato chutney was brilliant—you were robbed,' said April, frowning at the red ribbon on Lauren's chutney. 'At least they knew their sauces from their sauces.' Blue ribbons were draped across three of Lauren's collection.

'Look at this masterpiece,' April said, cooing over a cake decorated like an Iced VoVo biscuit, complete with mounds of coconut-covered pink marshmallow. 'Do you think that's an actual oversized biscuit on top of there or a cake iced to look like a biscuit? That's fondant, right?'

'Spoken like someone who knows her stuff.' Lauren grinned. There had been a time, not so long ago, when April's food awareness had been limited to Lean Cuisine and ready-made meals from Foodland's freezer section. But since attending Geraldine's cooking classes, her best friend had come along in leaps and bounds. 'I still think your apple and rhubarb cake should have scored a ribbon. Taste is just as important as looks in these contests, and your practice cakes were top notch. The winning cake might be able to grace the cover of *Taste* magazine, but perhaps it tastes like styrofoam?'

April looked behind her. 'Fran will probably have the inside scoop.'

'My golly gosh, what a day,' Fran said when they tracked her down. 'The toilets by the hall are blocked again and I'm one disaster away from locking myself in the office with that chocolate mud cake and a fork.'

April slung an arm around her stepmother. 'I'll bake you one tomorrow morning, Franny. You deserve it. Any updates on the cash?'

Fran shook her head. 'Only a few false leads. We'll be the laughing-stock of the show circuit! Entrants almost coming to fisticuffs and flinging cakes and me handing out IOUs to winners. Maybe we should have quit while we were ahead.'

Lauren fossicked in her tote for a chocolate bar. 'Eat this,' she said, passing Fran a mini Toblerone. 'None of the bakers will miss a few dollars of prize money, Fran. It's a low blow to pinch the entire prize money, but individually, none of these entrants were banking on a windfall today.'

'But it's the *principle*,' Fran said, looking a little less despondent once she had chocolate in her system. 'I think you've earned yourself at least eight dollars in prize money today, Clem Crossley scored over thirty dollars, and the little kids were probably planning to spend their winnings this afternoon.'

'Then it'll be a good lesson in not counting their chickens before they hatch,' April said.

'Regardless, you both have my undying gratitude for helping today, especially with filling these tables. I know I said it before, Lauren, but I really appreciate your help.'

Fran was getting teary as she hugged them each in turn. She flapped her hands in front of her face, laughing at herself. 'I'm a blubber-puss today! Don't mind me.'

'This was a community effort,' Lauren said, but she couldn't help feeling proud to have been a small part of the larger machine that helped it come together. 'And you're allowed to be upset, it's been a tough day.'

They headed for the door, welcoming the fresh air and sunshine while Fran returned to the pavilion.

'All geared up for the speed shears tonight?' April asked as they headed to where the food stalls were doing a roaring trade.

'I think so, but I'll duck home to catch the tail end of the news,' Lauren said, telling her friend about the piece she'd recorded to camera earlier that day. 'If Archie's on, we won't want to miss it.'

'TV?' April squealed. 'How have you been sitting on that news all afternoon? Of course we'll be watching. Then we definitely need to celebrate.'

Lauren spotted Jack emerge from the photography hall. She waved him over.

'Any updates?'

'Nope,' he said grimly, 'but there's been some wild accusations flying around the showgrounds. People love jumping to conclusions.'

'I heard Cohen was in the firing line,' April said.

Jack raked a hand through his hair. 'Convenient, right? If anyone had bothered asking, instead of pointing the finger, I could have told them he had nothing to do with the missing money.'

Lauren felt even worse when he explained about Cohen's fairy-floss sacrifice after the pony-ride fiasco. *You didn't think twice before assuming he was guilty.*

'Maybe Cohen won't get wind of the gossip?'

'Too late. He overheard the mayor pinning it on him.'

'Ouch,' Lauren said. 'I can imagine how that went down.'

April shook her head. 'And how's Harriet holding up?'

'Bruised but in good spirits,' Jack said. 'Clem's taking her to the ag hall to see if their milk thistle placed in the biggest weed contest. Today's misadventure wiped ponies from her pet wish list, so one glance at the display with the pickled hydatid cyst might just put her off dogs too.'

'A hydatid cyst?' April scrunched up her face. 'Might give that one a miss.'

'The cyst was gross, like a big cream-coloured lung, but the jar of pickled tapeworm larva was something else. Let's just say, once you've seen bottled hydatids specimens, you'll never be able to unsee them,' Jack said, his lips curving into a smile. 'It'll make you think twice about letting a farm dog lick your hand or your face.'

Lauren shuddered. 'I've got to dash back to the radio station to record a voice-over for my TV script, but we're off to see Con in the poultry section first. You and the boys did a great job rebuilding the chicken cages.'

Jack waved away the compliment. 'Seb and Cohen deserve the credit, I was just the overseer.'

Lauren had heard enough about the project to know this was an understatement. *Though for all their community service, it still hadn't stopped the boys getting the blame the moment something went wrong.*

☙

Anyone could have flogged the cash and spent it on dodgem cars, showbags and steak sandwiches, Jack thought, walking through the showgrounds. He'd taken Fran Lacey's statement and spoken to several eyewitnesses, but there was still no sign of the missing prize money.

'Over here, Jacko,' Arthur said, waving from the doorway of the artwork shed. 'We've just come from the flower hall. Our Clem hit the jackpot with that funny-coloured rose, what did you call it, Clementine?'

'Soul Sister,' Clem said, raising her arms and doing an on-the-spot victory twirl.

'Get outta here? That's great,' Jack said, lifting a hand and receiving high-fives from both Clem and Harriet.

'I got a ribbon for my teapot posy,' Harriet giggled. 'Maybe there's more prizes in here too.'

Clem and Harriet slipped in ahead of Jack, while Arthur manoeuvred his walking frame through the narrow entrance.

'Any luck with the prize money, lad?'

Jack shook his head.

'Maybe the committee will lock the office door next year or keep the bag in a safe.'

'Maybe next year they won't immediately jump to the wrong conclusion if they see a teenager in the wrong spot at the wrong time,' Jack replied. 'Poor kid's getting pretty sick of being a scapegoat.'

'Forget about work for a minute,' Arthur said, leading the way inside.

The room made Lauren's colourful cottage look understated, with paintings, prints, drawings, mosaics and collages on every wall, then more covering freestanding partitions in the centre of the room.

Arthur went slowly, marvelling at the wall-to-wall artwork. 'These pictures are top notch.'

Jack soon found Harriet's work. She'd already told them about the sunflowers and he was eager to see what else she'd entered. The next piece was smack bang in the middle of the farm machinery category. A watercolour painting showed Jack in a welding helmet, tacking the chook boxes together. There were three other people in the picture—Harriet, Cohen and Sebastian—but unlike the mid-summer's day when she'd accompanied him and the boys, she'd added chickens to the picture. The sight made Jack laugh.

Arthur grinned. 'Artistic licence. Hope the poultry fanciers didn't think you welded them together with the ducks and chooks in situ.'

In the wildlife category, they found Harriet's name on the bottom of a wallaby drawn in pencil, but it was the family portrait that stopped Jack in his tracks.

There in front of him, in multicoloured Texta precision, was Arthur, with his fluffy white hair and moustache, Jack standing tall in his navy-blue uniform with short, dark hair, Harriet in her purple rollerskates, Clem in one of the poncho-like dresses she seemed to favour these days—

Jack tipped his head, trying to decide how much to read into the man she'd drawn beside Clem, with his long stick arm meeting hers. Was Harriet campaigning for a father, just like she'd begged for a pet?

He turned, searching the room for his sister. Harriet was showing her mum the class murals and Clem looked up as if she felt his gaze.

Arthur grimaced. 'From the mouth of babes.' He beckoned the girls over. 'Who's this handsome fella, then?'

Clem inhaled sharply. 'I was going—'

'That's my daddy,' Harriet said simply, speaking over her mum. 'He sent me a letter and when he comes to visit, I'm going to show him my rollerskating.'

'Like hell you are,' Arthur mumbled under his breath. He wheeled his walking frame to the window, sat heavily and fished a coin purse from his top pocket. 'Here, missy, see what takes your fancy at the craft stall,' he said, handing coins to Harriet and nodding to the table of crocheted fruit, vegetables, animals and dolls.

When she was gone, he patted the seat beside him. 'Clementine, love, I don't often stick my nose in, but this has trouble written all over it. Has Adam come crawling back? Surely you're too smart to overlook the five years when he couldn't give a stuff.'

Clem's face flushed rosella red. 'Pop!'

Arthur tried again. 'You'd tell us if he was stirring up trouble though, wouldn't you?'

'I can step in,' Jack offered. 'Just say the word.'

Clem turned to Jack, ambivalence and awkwardness fleeing across her features. 'Nothing's black and white, Jack, not when it comes to children or being a parent. I don't know what you expect me to say. It's show day, Harriet nearly broke her arm on a pony, I've got sunscreen in my eyes and every pore's gritty with dust. I'm. Just. About. *Over.* It.'

A few folks turned at Clem's raised voice and Jack gave them a tight 'nothing to see here' smile.

Clem strode across to Harriet, and whatever she'd bribed her with—show rides or sweets, Jack suspected—was enough to make the six-year-old skip outside with glee.

Arthur and Jack sighed in unison.

'I don't have a good feeling about this, son.'

Jack looked at his grandfather. 'Me neither, Pop.'

19

'How do you manage to lose your boyfriend in a town this small?' Tahnee said, laughing, when she and Gabrielle arrived back at the show an hour later. 'I'd understand if it was the city . . .' She gestured to the picnic rugs spread out in front of the flatbed truck that would soon form a stage for the evening's entertainment.

The atmosphere of the show had changed as the afternoon merged into evening, with families heading home for dinner and swathes of younger patrons coming through the gates, ready for a big night. Lauren shook out a picnic rug.

'I'm not sitting on the ground,' Gabrielle said.

'Getting down here's only going to be half your problem,' Tahnee said, rethinking her decision to recline against a hay bale. 'This stuff is itchy, and it's probably murder on my angora cardigan. Hasn't anyone in Penwarra heard of deckchairs or benches?'

Lauren caught April's eye. Tahnee was a carbon copy of Gabrielle. A suggestion that she could have brought her own chair, or perhaps given Lauren a heads-up about their visit to ensure they had the required clothes *and* seating would undoubtedly be taken the wrong way.

'It's okay,' Lauren said, pulling keys from her pocket. 'I'll fetch the other picnic rug from the car.'

Lauren returned to the gathering at the same time as Connor, who regaled them with tales of the chicken and duck breeders he'd spent the afternoon with, and Nigel, who settled in next to Tahnee. Time passed easily with the clinking of beer bottles and the local musicians warming up and soon the shearers were racing against the clock to remove the woollen fleeces.

'Honestly,' Gabrielle muttered as Nigel flirted with Tahnee, 'he's not likely to woo her with stories about venison hunting and his dreams of buying a farm, is he? Nobody can afford them these days, especially on a fill-in radio wage. Does she even look like the sheep-herding, lamb-rearing kind?'

Lauren looked at her sister's heels, angora cardigan and white jumpsuit. Nigel was definitely barking up the wrong tree there.

'Oh my, is that Fergus?' Gabrielle eased herself up for a better look as she spotted Fergus and Clarissa standing by an oak barrel with Sammi and Logan.

Lauren slouched a little lower.

Gabrielle patted her knee. 'Lovely boy, but not your type by a long stretch, darling. You need someone who's driven, who runs after success with both hands and understands the sacrifices necessary to reach the top. We'll get a good read on Jack when we lay eyes on him.' She sipped her wine and lifted an eyebrow. 'If we *ever* lay eyes on him, that is. He might be a fake boyfriend, for all we know.'

Lauren knew that was her mum's version of a joke and not intended to wound, but it still fell a little flat. There was a chance she was going to be on television tonight, the biggest

gig of her career so far, and even that wasn't enough to keep
the criticisms at bay.

Harriet was freshly scrubbed and dressed in a *Bluey* t-shirt
and leggings, immersed in a movie, when Jack arrived at the
farmhouse that evening.

'Shh,' she said, holding a finger to her lips. 'Mum's having
a long bath and she wants me to stay nice and quiet so she
can relax.'

Jack wasn't about to argue with that. From what he'd seen
this afternoon, Clem needed all the rest she could get. Stressed
Clem quickly spiralled to sick Clem and no one wanted that.
Adam Dunkirk must have sent his letter at the perfect moment,
making contact when Clem was tuckered out from show prep,
the cook-along and part-time work.

'So Mum's having a bath and you're watching a movie?'

'Mum said I can watch two!'

Jack weighed up his options. Clem only allowed back-to-
back movies when she was totally knackered, and every other
time he'd offered to babysit, she'd always been grateful for
the help.

He wrote a note and slid it under the bathroom door, so
Clem would see it when she emerged from the bath.

Taking Harri to Petticoat Lane to watch the TV news.
Lauren's done a segment about the show, just after the
sports. Will drop her back home before I start work. Rest up!
  x J

Together, Jack and Harriet tip-toed out of the house.

Lauren was waiting in the doorway when they arrived, her
curtains fluttering in the open cottage windows.

'Quick, they're just about to move onto sports,' Lauren said, as Jack wrapped her in a hug and lifted her off her toes so her lips were level with his. 'You've been a hard man to track down today.'

He nodded. 'I know, sorry.'

Lauren searched his face, then, with a look at Harriet, she kissed him once more and pulled him to her. 'Not that that's not an amazing welcome, but we need to be quick. I've just had a call from Paul to say we're up in a few minutes. Oh, and we've got guests too. Did I tell you my mum and sister came down? Brace yourself for the full Bickford interrogation.'

'Is the Penwarra Show really going to be on the news?' Harriet asked. 'Will they have my baking and my flower teapot on there?'

'Hopefully!' Lauren said, ushering them inside.

Tahnee and Gabrielle came across the room to shake Jack's outstretched hand. Harriet perched herself in the middle of the sofa, nonplussed by the sight of two strangers in Lauren's house, and grinned as Gary climbed up her arm. 'That tickles, Gary!'

Ticklishness must be a Crossley family trait, Lauren thought with a smile, recalling the moment with Jack on the couch all those months ago. 'We're going to be on TV soon,' Harriet told Lauren's sister, matter-of-factly.

'Nice to meet you,' Jack said. 'Sorry to intrude on your family catch-up.'

'Not at all, we've heard a lot about you,' Gabrielle said, taking her seat again. 'And you're a policeman, right? The local show must be one of the biggest nights of the year?'

'Sure is,' Jack agreed, taking a seat beside Harriet and looking at his watch. 'Split shifts and we've got extra manpower from the Mount Gambier station holding the fort. I'll be back on duty at nine, when the trouble apparently starts. How was it down there?'

'Great if you love itchy seating, shearers in sweaty singlets and an MC who thinks he's commentating the Melbourne Cup, not a speed-shearing contest. I'm more of a Royal Adelaide Show kinda girl,' Tahnee said, pulling a stalk of wheat from her top.

'Shh, here it is!' Harriet said.

Everyone turned to the TV as the Penwarra Showground came into view.

'It's you, Lauren! Lookit! Lookit!'

Lauren turned the volume up and when Tahnee said something quietly to Gabrielle, Jack felt like shushing them. Didn't they know how hard Lauren had worked to get this break?

He'd been so used to hearing Lauren on the radio and seeing her in person that it was an altogether strange feeling to be watching her on the TV screen. She strode towards the camera as she talked, her smile wide as she implored viewers to take a look inside the show and, for the first time all afternoon, his worries about Clem and Adam Dunkirk evaporated.

'Nailing it,' he whispered, squeezing Lauren's hand.

He looked over to see Lauren's sister making notes as the news snippet ran. Gabrielle was frowning at the television screen. Were they really sitting there taking notes and waiting for Lauren to slip up?

Who am I to judge, though? Hadn't today been a reminder that the Crossley family had their fair share of challenging dynamics too?

Jack looked at Harriet, cursing Adam Dunkirk once again. If a single letter and $1.25 stamp had been enough to secure Dunkirk's spot in Harriet's family portrait, he was pretty sure it wouldn't take much more to regain a foothold in her heart.

❦

Watching herself on TV was almost as cringey as hearing herself on radio for the first time, and Lauren winced as she watched the hand gestures Paul had insisted she use.

'You're a natural,' Jack murmured, evidently not noticing how stilted she looked on screen. No matter how many times she'd practised them in front of the mirror, her hands still looked as dorky and unnatural on the camera as they did at home and she was thankful she was only on for a moment.

Her voice-over continued, and Harriet cheered at the sight of Archie Winklin's giant pumpkin. 'There's Archie!' she yelled, getting another shushing from her uncle.

'Watch this bit carefully,' Lauren whispered to Jack, as the video cut to a slow pan of the floral section, zooming in on the champion rose, then a dainty gold-rimmed teapot with the blue ribbon beside it.

'That's— That's—' Harriet looked back at Lauren, her hand pointing to the screen and mouth opening and shutting like a goldfish. 'That's my entry! Did you see that?'

Her excitement was infectious.

'I did, Harri, well done. I think I saw your mum's prize-winning rose in there too, with the fancy sash.'

'Let's watch it again! Now!' Harriet said, the minute the segment was over.

'All these streaming services have ruined them,' Gabrielle clucked. 'Kids today have no idea what it's like to wait a week for an episode.'

After this morning's prize money finger-pointing, Lauren suspected Jack had some pretty strong opinions about the behaviour of today's adults too, but he was too polite to air them now.

'We'd best be off,' he said instead, giving them a quick smile.

Harriet jumped off the couch. 'Can we go to the hall, Uncle Jack, and see the flowers again?'

'The hall's closed tonight, it's just the adults and the music now, Harri,' Jack said, helping his niece into her boots. 'And someone's got to keep them under control. But what about Lauren's first-ever TV news report? How good was that, eh?'

Lauren had been self-conscious while she was watching, and now that all eyes were on her, she found herself holding her breath.

'You looked very pretty,' Harriet offered. 'Didn't she, Uncle Jack?'

'Absolutely,' he said, giving Lauren one of those smiles that melted her self-doubt. 'You spoke well, I liked your pumpkin pun and you snuck in a great plug for the town. Seriously, the show society will be delighted.'

'The radio station too,' added Tahnee.

'Though you might have ironed that shirt and put a little more pizzazz into your delivery, sweetheart,' Gabrielle said. 'Where was that beautiful suit I bought you?'

Lauren managed a smile, but her fingertips found the only hangnail on her left hand and tore it off, feeling the sharp sting as Gabrielle took a breath, seemingly about to list another fault.

'It was a fluke they even wanted footage from the show,' Lauren said, brushing a bead of blood from her cuticle before it could stain the couch. 'I'm just glad I didn't stutter or fall on my bum in front of the camera.'

'Darling!' Gabrielle frowned. 'Of course you did a wonderful job for your very first television appearance. A few tips, a little practice on your posture, maybe some more serious stories under your belt and you'll be unstoppable. You know I'm just trying to help.'

Lauren caught Tahnee's eye; she was nodding. Would it kill them to say something supportive for once, instead of sandwiching compliments between 'helpful' criticism?

'Thanks for having my back in there,' she said, folding into Jack's embrace after he'd buckled Harriet into the car seat.

He stepped back and cupped her cheek with a weary sigh. 'Hands down, the best five minutes of my evening.'

'Even better than the one-hundredth Penwarra Show?' she teased, trying to lighten the mood.

Instead of leaning in to kiss her as she'd expected, Jack pulled away.

'Man, what a day.' He pulled his sleeve over his wrist and buffed the side mirror until it was bug free.

'What's taking up the most bandwidth? The pony ride, the near food fight, the missing prize money or the shift ahead?'

'All four to some extent, but there's something else too,' he said, telling her about Harriet's drawing and the news that Clem's ex-husband had been in contact.

'Harriet's father? I thought he was out of the picture?'

'So did we.' Jack's eyes darkened and she could see the effort it took for him to keep his voice low. 'He's set a pretty low bar, though, so it's probably a one-off. Look, I'd better get Harri home and prep for my shift.'

'I'll keep an eye out for you at the show.'

Lauren waved him off. The cosmos and zinnias brushed against her legs as she walked back down the path. She paused outside the door.

Jack's loyalty to his family had been clear since the moment she'd seen him sorting pink laundry on that wet autumn weekend last year. Clem had welcomed her without hesitation and Harriet . . . Lauren smiled, opening her front door. Harriet was as cute as a button and the only kid Gary seemed

to tolerate. None of them deserved to be dicked about by a
fly-by-night father.

And if Jack didn't trust this Adam Dunkirk, she could
understand why his sudden reappearance in their lives, if only
by mail, made him nervous.

Even though he'd worked until 3 am, sleep didn't come easily
to Jack that night.

He'd nodded off on the couch in the police house, start-
ling awake each time he registered the ticking oven clock, the
refrigerator's rhythmic hum or the sensor light that illuminated
the police station next door.

And then, when he'd finally dragged his sorry butt into
bed, he'd lain awake thinking about the missing prize money,
the underagers smuggling cheap alcohol into the show in their
water bottles, the carnies who palmed off counterfeit notes
and the shearers who'd celebrated a little too hard and started
a brawl after the speed shears.

The incidents weren't drastically different to a city beat, it
was just that he knew the people in Penwarra: he shopped for
groceries with them; washed his car alongside theirs at the car
wash; smiled at them in the queue for the bakery.

Fergus thought back through the night. For every negative
incident, there were at least two or three good ones, like the
chap who risked his own safety to chase a dog off the dirt
bike track as the stunt rider wowed the crowd with his tricks,
and the mother of three who drove through the breathalyser
queue in her pyjamas and dressing gown, happily blowing
0.00 and explaining she'd rather get up in the middle of the
night to play taxi for her teenagers than risk them getting in
a car with a drink driver.

He'd come back to Penwarra for Clem, but somehow, when he wasn't watching, the town had wormed its way back into his heart. Would he stay if Clem hooked up with Dunkirk again and returned to Adelaide? And what would that mean for him and Lauren?

He fell asleep eventually, but his dreams turned into nightmares about Adam Dunkirk, reliving the moment his fist connected with his former friend's jaw.

Jack woke up with the sheets twisted around his sweaty torso. The swimming pool had always been a balm for his racing mind and he drove there early, when most of the town was still asleep. He struck out at a blistering pace, steaming into a tumble turn at such speed that he almost took out the lane rope. The swimmer in the next lane gave him a wide berth. He corrected course and charged down the lane.

Clem's old enough to make her own decisions. Maybe reconnecting with Adam Dunkirk will start and end with that letter.

The post-show pack-up was in full swing when Jack returned to the showgrounds later that morning. Bleary-eyed carnies with cigarettes dangling from their lips averted their eyes as he walked past, wary of his attention and even more so of the uniform. If Jack was a gambling man, he'd bet these semi-nomadic workers were likelier suspects for prize money thieves than Cohen Moriarty.

'Morning,' Jack said, finding Darren, the show president, in the site office. He pulled his notepad out and flipped to a fresh page. 'I'm running over the statements about the missing prize money—'

'Oh, funny story there,' the president said, breaking into a grin. 'Problem solved! The bag fell behind the filing cabinet and we spotted it when we were tidying this morning. You can call off the bloodhounds. Fran will be relieved.'

'It was there all along?' Jack frowned. He thought of Cohen. The teen had ignored both Jack's and Sebastian's calls and text messages yesterday afternoon, and there was no doubt the gossip would follow him around town.

'Yes! Show-day mania strikes again. No harm done, old chap.' He beamed and clapped Jack on the shoulder.

Injustice twisted Jack's guts. 'No harm?'

What about Cohen, who spent most of the day shovelling crap in the livestock stalls, only to be blamed the moment something went wrong?

'Where there's smoke, there's usually fire. It's not my fault those boys already burned a few bridges in this town. I certainly didn't ask him to redecorate my front yard with Kleenex.'

'But Cohen's making amends,' Jack said. 'When all his mates were eating dippy dogs, taking girls on dodgem cars and zipping around on the Gravitron, he was working. You don't think he was already paying penance?'

The older gentleman lifted his hands in a 'what can I say' gesture. 'If you'll excuse me, Senior Constable, I've got marquees to dismantle and officials to check on. Actually—' he smiled at Jack, '—don't suppose you feel like helping out in the equestrian ring again? With arms like those, you'll make light work of dismantling those heavy jumps.'

Seriously? Shaking his head, Jack tucked his notepad into his pocket and wished Darren luck with the tidy-up.

20

Nigel had left her a stack of notes, but when Lauren settled into the presenter's chair on Monday morning, the program came together like clockwork and she barely needed to glance at his story suggestions or backup guest list.

'Such a joy to recap all these wonderful moments, Darren,' Lauren said, peering over her microphone at the Penwarra show society president. 'It must make you so proud to hear all the feedback from our callers this morning.'

The phones had rung off the hook with listeners sharing their favourite moments from the one-hundredth Penwarra Show. The pickled hydatid cysts got several mentions, along with the pet parade, the revamped poultry pavilion and the tables brimming with flowers, baking, arts, crafts and fleeces.

'Absolutely,' said Darren. 'It takes a committee to pull together a program and arrange convenors and stewards, judges and venues, but it's up to the community to make it a success. All those cookbooks, all the people who were involved in the cook-along, from baking and sponsoring it, to Fran Lacey who cooked up two fabulous fundraisers. The baking pavilion will be better than ever next year, now there's money in the coffers for a much-needed upgrade. And I think we can agree, not just from the gate numbers, but also the entries and the feedback on the day, and now over the airwaves, that the Penwarra Show is here to stay!'

Lauren studied him across the switchboard. 'I'm glad to hear it,' she said, trying to decide whether she should broach the subject of the stoush between Eileen and Audrey or the missing prize money. Darren hadn't mentioned them, and from the rosy wrap-up he'd just delivered, it seemed he didn't want to detract from the celebrations.

Hadn't her uni degree taught her that balanced coverage was as important as remaining impartial? Could she somehow defend Cohen Moriarty's reputation by mentioning the prize money had been misplaced, not stolen, and anyone gossiping about the issue should take a long hard look at themselves?

Lauren sighed. Would it really help Cohen anyway? If he wasn't at school, then he'd be streaming music or movies, not listening to talkback radio at this time of the day.

She muted the microphone briefly and cleared her throat. A message from Patrice popped up on Lauren's screen.

Pull it together, Lauren! Throw to a song if you need to gather yourself, we can't have dead air on breakfast radio.

Lauren took a sharp, steadying breath, and refocused on Darren, who was explaining the record entries in the novelty categories, like the Lego and scarecrow competitions.

'Grass roots support is one of Penwarra's superpowers.'

Unless you're a teenager with a track record of trouble. Then it's scapegoat central.

A listener text message popped up on the computer screen.

Sending my heartfelt thanks to everyone who pulled on their
aprons for the cook-along and entered the baking category.
I'm more grateful than they'll ever know! Fran Lacey

Lauren took a deep breath. Any mention of the missing
prize money or blue rinse baking argument would reflect badly
on Fran, and after everything she had done, that was the last
thing Lauren wanted. *Now was not the time or place.*

She smiled at the show society president—*stick to the
positives*—and read Fran's text message on air. 'Fran Lacey's
probably not the only committee member who's sleeping much
easier now the show's done and dusted.'

From the corner of her eye, Lauren saw a frowning Patrice
making a 'wind it up' motion with her hands. 'Thanks for your
time, Darren, and don't go away, folks, we've got two more
guests in the studio this morning. But first, a song request from
Art Crossley, he's after an oldie but a goodie.' She smothered a
laugh as she saw the tune he'd requested and without thinking,
decided to ad lib. 'This one's for all the listeners who rely on
the bush telegraph for their news. Not always a good idea in
a small country town.'

She hit play on the song and Darren blanched as Credence
Clearwater Revival's 'I Heard It Through the Grapevine' filled
the studio. The song summed up the gist of what she'd wanted
to say, in a cryptic enough manner that wouldn't get the radio
station sued and hopefully wouldn't make Fran Lacey feel
worse about the incident than she already did.

'What the hell was that? Anyone would think you've just
stepped into a studio,' Patrice said the moment Darren left,
frowning down her nose as Lauren removed her headphones.
'Darren's microphone wasn't even switched on at first, so the
entire Limestone Coast was treated to a minute of echoey

garble at the start of the interview. Didn't you see my notes on the screen?'

It was going to be a long week working alongside the grouchy producer as she filled in for Nigel again. Lauren looked at the countdown. The song would be over in just a minute.

'*Rookie* error,' Patrice said under her breath as she marched out of the studio and back into the production room.

'Excuse me?'

While Lauren knew it was fruitless entering into a conversation like this so close to being on air, she was over Patrice treating her like an inept work experience student. Last week she'd left Lauren out of the email loop for a rostering change and now she was making a big deal about the microphone mix-up. *George made that mistake more than once too, and I never drilled him about it.*

Lauren blew out a breath, then switched into 'on-air mode' as she introduced the schools segment, reminding herself the rest of the show had been flawless. *Don't let Patrice get to you.*

Jack tried Cohen's phone number again and left a message. Officially, the boy still had twenty hours of community service left, and after the weekend they'd just had, Jack wasn't sure he'd get him back onboard to complete the final stretch.

The same snappy sheepdogs were waiting at the gate when he arrived at the Moriarty property, their warning barks sending the goats scattering across the paddock. The garage roller door slid open and a battered ute rolled towards the gate.

Shane Moriarty stuck his head out of the driver's window. 'You're looking for Cohen?'

'They found the prize money.'

'So he didn't steal it, then?'

Jack shook his head.

'Cohen's been a shit of kid since he turned sixteen, so I wouldn't have put it past him. Let me guess, one of the blue-blooded farm boys nicked it but since they used their best manners to apologise, and because of who their daddy is, they'll just get a warning?'

Jack understood why Shane was angry, but he couldn't leave without setting the record straight.

'It's my fault Cohen was in the show office yesterday,' Jack said, explaining the pony ride chaos. Shane Moriarty's scowl deepened. 'Cohen's first reaction was to help, which is something I wouldn't have expected six months ago. Cohen copped the heat for something he hadn't done, at the very moment he was helping me and sacrificing something he'd bought with his own money. Was it grossly unfair? Hell, yes. Does it also show he's growing as a person? I think so.'

'It was just a bag of fairy floss, not a gold bullion.'

Jack nodded. 'To you and me, it was just a bag of sugary junk. But Cohen went out of his way to buy that fairy floss before it sold out, he'd set it aside for later, and he then gave it up to soothe an upset little girl. There's a lot to be proud about there.'

'He's in a foul mood,' Shane conceded, looking over his shoulder.

Wonder where he gets that from? 'Rightfully so,' Jack said. 'Do you mind if I talk to him?'

'Knock yourself out.' The man put two fingers in his mouth and whistled. Jack flinched, resisting the urge to clamp his hands over his ringing ears.

The barking dogs quietened and jumped onto the tray of the ute.

Cohen wandered out of the machinery shed, a welding helmet at half-mast on his head.

'I'm right to go in?' Jack asked. Assumptions were the root of all stuff-ups, and Jack wanted a clear invitation before he set foot on the Moriartys' land.

Shane stepped out of his ute, opened the gate and waved Jack through. 'From the rate he's going through welding rods, I'll be broke if you don't hurry up.'

The shed was thick with welding fumes when Jack entered. Cohen tacked and tapped the welder, and while Jack couldn't study the sculpture while the welding was underway, he could already tell from the mutters and banging that the boy's technique needed work.

Eventually, Cohen downed tools and threw his welding gloves onto the bench. 'I already know it's shit, you don't have to tell me.'

Jack studied him. Maybe he was just a kid who'd learned to get in first before people could cut him down. A kid whose self-worth took a battering the moment he lifted his guard. In the welding helmet, with fury rolling off him in waves, Jack saw a younger version of himself.

'Pretty good. Better than the first few sculptures I ever made,' Jack said, surveying the metal bird between them. It wasn't just good, it was impressive. The body was made from the head of a spade, coiled chains and cogs, the wings were a collection of knives and scissors, and the legs and feet were formed from a series of springs and bolts. Where Jack had favoured car parts and scrap from old harvesters for his sculptures, it looked like Cohen had turned to his mother's cutlery drawer and garden shed for inspiration.

Jack told him about the missing money.

'Already said I didn't take it,' Cohen growled.

'Never doubted you for a second,' Jack replied. 'It wasn't fair that anyone thought otherwise, you didn't deserve that. Glad you found a good way to burn off steam, though.'

'Half the welds look like cocky shit and there's spatter everywhere. At this rate it'll look like an owl with acne when I go to weld the head together.'

Jack and Cohen both stared at the scrap metal sculpture. The problem certainly wasn't in the vision, it was in the execution.

'What are your amps at?'

Half an hour later, with some delicately offered tips and carefully understated praise, Jack left with a promise from Cohen to resume the community service.

He called into the wildlife sanctuary on his way out. Sebastian abandoned his wheelbarrow of fresh foliage when Jack pulled up beside the possum palace.

'He's okay,' Jack said, tipping his head to the Moriarty property. 'How'd you pull up after Saturday night?'

'Fine. Good thing Cohen didn't go to the show that night anyway. The amount of idiots gobbing off about the missing prize money—' Sebastian's mouth set in a grim line. 'He probably would've spent the night in the slammer if he'd heard them hanging shit on him.'

Jack nodded. He'd heard enough scuttlebutt around the bar to know the adults had speculated plenty too, but one thing was for certain: Cohen's decision to avoid the drama showed an extra level of perception that he hadn't displayed six months earlier. And while his growth wasn't necessarily linear, there was no doubting the boy was on a better path now.

'We're heading to Vic's this arvo, clearing out the junk shed and planting trees along the roadside. You keen?'

Sebastian nodded. 'Can you pick me up from the glass-blowing studio? After I've finished here, I'm riding my bike to Jan's. Bit of whipper-snipping should knock a few more hours off my tally.'

It pleased him that Sebastian was taking the initiative to arrange his own tasks, but just like Cohen, he knew effusive praise wasn't what the boy was after.

'Nice work,' Jack said, conveying respect and pride in a single nod.

And from the spark in the teen's eye, he knew he'd hit the mark.

After the news and weather and a guest from the Penwarra Equestrian Club, who declared the equine aspect of the weekend an enormous hit, Patrice ushered the final guest into the studio. The principal of the nearby Cockatoo Inn Area School was cheerful and chatty as she explained the importance of the annual show in their curriculum, and how the event connected the children with their community.

'It's not just about the competitions or the ribbons, the kids get to see adults having a shot at things like the gumboot throw or photography.'

Patrice had three song options lined up for the final tune, all drab and dreary ones that belonged in a funeral parlour or a doctor's waiting room at best, so Lauren threw to a Taylor Swift song to finish the show.

'If you want to produce *and* present the show yourself, just say the word,' Patrice said through gritted teeth before picking up her coffee cup and stalking out of the production booth.

Paul stuck his head into the studio, raising an eyebrow. 'Everything alright in here?'

Lauren looked at the clock then back at Patrice's empty seat. It had never helped to call out Patrice's behaviour in the past and she wasn't going to start now.

'You want me to have a word with her?' Paul asked.

Lauren shook her head, surprised by the offer.

'Her nose is probably out of joint because that seat's got your name on it.' He gave a meaningful nod. 'I shouldn't spoil the surprise, seeing the HR team was wiped out by gastro and they haven't finalised the paperwork today as planned, but I heard some inside news this morning that I think you're going to like. Congratulations.'

He was gone before Lauren could process the news. Was he telling her she'd got the job?

Don't get ahead of yourself, don't forget what happened last time.

But as she drove into Penwarra after work and turned towards the police station, the hope and excitement had worn through her resolve and she knew her thoughts had well and truly run ahead of her.

The 'closed' sign hung on the police station door, and the patrol car was in the driveway, so Lauren made for the house.

'Jack!' she called, almost tripping over the doorway as she dashed inside. 'Wait till you hear what Paul said!'

In the year she'd known Jack, his family had been his only visitors, so it came as a surprise to see someone seated at Jack's dining table, arms locked across his chest.

'Oh, hey!' She skidded to a halt and laughed because she'd been *this* close to taking a flying leap into Jack's arms, *Dirty Dancing* style. 'Sorry I didn't realise Jack had company.' She waved. 'I'm Lauren.' She turned and beamed at Jack. 'Jack?'

His jaw looked like it was welded shut and his hands were stuffed so deep into his pockets she could barely see his wristwatch.

Lauren looked between the two of them. 'Am I interrupting something?'

Jack shook his head and Lauren worked it out just as the bloke introduced himself.

'You're Adam—'

'—Dunkirk,' he finished.

Jack was glad for Lauren's company, because while he'd once done ironman races beside this guy, trained alongside him until they were both physically spent and wet the baby's head on the night Harriet came into the world, right now, Jack didn't want to be in the same town as Adam Dunkirk, let alone within swinging distance.

'Clem sounded good on the radio,' Dunkirk continued. 'And Harriet. I always thought we'd shorten it to "H" or Hatty, but I guess not.'

Jack stomped down a surge of annoyance. Dunkirk had a nerve to knock on the door, invite himself in for coffee and then talk about Clem and Harriet like they were all chums.

'There's a lot you don't know, Dunkirk.'

'I'm ready to give it another shot, the kid deserves a dad.'

Jack shook his head. Last time he'd lost his temper with this bloke, he'd nearly ruined his career in the police force. *He wasn't worth it.*

Lauren shot him a 'you alright?' look. He gave her a nod, determined to keep his cool for her sake too.

'Clem and Harriet deserve better than "another shot".'

'I'm trying to do the right thing by everyone. Clem was the one to call *me* when she was in town.'

Jack covered his surprise, mentally counting back to summer. He'd been happy to mind Harriet while Clem went to Adelaide, but he might've been less accommodating if he'd known she was rekindling her relationship with Dunkirk.

'You're about five years too late, Dunkirk.'

'It's not your call,' Adam replied. 'It's between me and Clem. I'm not going to stuff it up this time and this baby's the wake-up call I needed. A bit of summer fun has turned into something more and we're both happy about it.'

A baby? Jack swore softly. Was that what Clem had been trying to tell him? That she was pregnant? Was it intentional or an accident? Jack wasn't sure what to think, but one thing was clear: There wasn't a damn thing he could do about it.

Dunkirk drained his coffee cup and the chair scraped on the tiles as he stood up. 'I haven't messed in your life, Jack, and I'm hoping you'll do me the same courtesy.' He tapped the side of his nose—the very nose Jack had broken five years earlier—and gave a slightly smug smile before leaving.

Jack's temper flared as he watched Dunkirk drive away. *The son of a bitch.*

'I'd better warn Clem,' he said, grabbing his keys from the counter.

Lauren strode across to him. 'I might be completely wrong, but from the sounds of it, she may already know he's in town.'

It was only when he turned to Lauren, considering her quiet suggestion, that he realised her hands were visibly shaking, the mug of tea quivering in her grip.

'It's okay,' he said, taking the cup and pulling her into a hug. 'Everything's okay.'

She gave a shaky laugh, but as he pressed her to his chest, he could tell she was rattled.

'I thought he was going to challenge you to a duel or something. What an arse.'

'You're not wrong there,' Jack said, appalled that he was partly responsible for her hammering heart. He wanted to make her pulse race for all the right reasons. He wanted her heartbeat to skyrocket because he'd kissed her, or whirled her around the dance floor, or belted out a karaoke duet, not out of panic, and certainly not fear.

'I'm sorry you had to see that. I had no idea he was in town. I don't know what Clem's thinking, only that she's not thinking straight. And now she's pregnant . . .'

Even later, when Jack had fixed them coffee and cracked out Clem's blue ribbon–winning jam drops, he couldn't stop his attention wandering. Clem would call if she didn't want Dunkirk there, surely? And if he was there at her invitation, would she be introducing him to Harriet straight up or taking it cautiously?

'Will Harri be excited, or is she too young to understand?'

Jack shook his head. 'I don't know. The family portrait was the first time Harri's mentioned him in years. She deserves better—Clem too. They need safety, security, consistency and understanding, things Dunkirk's never been good at. Clem's had some big struggles in the last few years. She hasn't always made good decisions, and sometimes she—' He swallowed hard, remembering what it was like to see his sister in freefall mode and not wanting to go back there, ever again. 'She can spiral really quickly.'

In a hushed tone, Jack told her about Clem falling danger-ously ill after Harriet's birth, Dunkirk starting a fight at Harriet's first birthday party and then threatening to press charges against Jack when he retaliated, before ghosting Clem altogether.

Lauren wrapped her arms around him. 'If I was in Clem's shoes, and I had a big brother, I would have wanted him to jump to my defence,' she said softly.

'It was terrible,' Jack admitted. 'I should've been the bigger man and walked away.'

And now she was pregnant again, the perfect excuse for Adam to re-enter their lives and let her down all over again. Jack sipped the cold coffee and stared out the window.

'Moving to Penwarra was supposed to be a fresh start for her and Harriet, no mortgage stress, as much family support as possible. If Clem follows Dunkirk back to the city, I'd have to think seriously about relocating.'

'Maybe it'll all work out?'

'Mmm,' he said, leaning back in his chair. 'I wish I could share your optimism, Lauren Bickford.'

Lauren's watch illuminated the room as she took a quick peek at the time. Almost 4.30 am. She moved in fractions, careful not to wake Jack, and silenced her alarm. But instead of sliding out of the sheets, pulling on her work clothes and making for the radio station, she lingered. Moonlight and sleep softened Jack's handsome profile and she savoured the moment to study him without censure.

Over the last twelve months, she'd seen so many facets of Jack Crossley: the guy who'd do anything for his family; the bloke who baked and tidied and organised spice shelves; the constable who commanded respect in his uniform; and the lover who turned her body to molten lava between these very sheets. And at midnight, when she'd woken to find his side of the bed empty, she'd seen a new version of him: surrounded by paperwork, elbows on the table and head resting in his hands, he'd looked vulnerable.

Was Adam Dunkirk's betrayal the reason Jack put walls up, or did those wounds run deeper? And when would he trust her with his past? *All* of his past, not just the anecdotes she gleaned from Arthur and Clem? With all the people Jack cared for, all the weight he carried on those broad shoulders, who cared for him and shared his burdens in times of need?

She smiled, tracing his features with her gaze. Loving him was easy. Convincing him that he could rely on her was proving the challenging part.

Patrice was already at the radio station when Lauren arrived. Her eyebrows arched high.

'Slept in, did we? Ten minutes mightn't seem like much today, but it all adds up.'

Lauren felt that tremor again, the same one that had hijacked her composure last night when she'd sensed the tension between Jack and Adam. She pressed her fingernails into her palms and managed a smile. 'Just subtract it from all the times I've stayed late.'

She brushed past Patrice and started setting up for the morning.

When the equipment was powered up and Lauren's notebook was open with the show notes, talking points and prep she needed for the program, she fixed herself an extra strong coffee and reached for her laptop. The interviews she'd recorded with Ruby sat in a digital folder on her desktop, mostly raw and unedited, encompassing so much of her amazing, inspiring life. *I'll get to them soon*, Lauren promised herself, prepping to go live.

She caught sight of Patrice watching her from the production studio, and closed her eyes a beat, blocking her out. *Who cares what Patrice thinks? She's not the one in the hot seat, entertaining listeners for a full three and a half hours each morning.*

Lauren stretched, rubbed her feet on the ground and ran through the steps Miriam had taught her.

'Is that carry-on really necessary?'

Way to wreck the vibe, Patrice. Lauren's eyes flashed open. 'It's not like we're live streaming or anything.'

Patrice smirked. 'Thankfully. You're on in thirty seconds.'

Lauren rolled her shoulders, trying to claw back the calm she needed before going on air. *Breathe. That's it, just in and out.*

If there was ever a time to channel Ruby McInnes, now was it. Lauren set her shoulders back, willing the words to come out ungarbled and articulate.

21

'Anyone home?' Jack called, tapping on the farmhouse door-frame a second time. Clem's car was parked out front, so he was pretty sure she was there, but still there was no answer when he called a second time.

A boulder lodged in his throat as he entered the kitchen, picking up his pace. Neat, tidy, no signs of a disturbance, but he'd been in the force long enough to know that cleanliness wasn't a safeguard against trouble.

He found Clem in the sewing room, bulky headphones clamped over her ears, an iron in one hand as she adjusted a quilt cover on the ironing board.

'Hey, Clem.'

Her free hand flew to her chest. 'F . . . fruit cake, Jack.' She set the iron down and whacked him with the back of her hand. 'You scared the hell outta me.'

'I called out,' he said, relief softening his words. 'What are you listening to? Audiobook?'

'Podcast.' She switched off the iron, removed the headphones and led the way into the kitchen. 'Who knew there were hundreds of parenting shows dedicated to raising siblings with large age gaps, deciding whether to take back an ex or not and my personal favourite—' she turned to him then, fixing him with a glare, '—how to tell your big brother to stop stressing over things he can't control.'

Ouch! Jack studied his hands. It wasn't like Clem to get straight to the topic.

'Congratulations, by the way. A heads-up would have been nice.'

'I tried to tell you,' Clem said, her hand going to her stomach. 'Several times but I was always interrupted, so I chickened out.' She led the way to the kitchen. 'Cuppa?'

'No thanks,' Jack said. 'What else do these podcasters say? Because I hope there's an episode or two about looking before you leap.'

Clem heaped sugar into her mug and lifted an eyebrow. 'Just say it, Jack. Get it over and done with so we can move on.'

'Was Dunkirk the one who was sending you jewellery at Christmas time?'

Her silence was as good as an admission.

'I don't trust him, Clem. Has he apologised for being MIA for the last six years? Has he said he regretted leaving you to singlehandedly raise Harriet, that he wished he was there to shoulder the load those sleepless nights she had croup or hold her hand the time she fractured her leg falling out of a tree? Has he begged forgiveness for that stunt he pulled on her first birthday? It's your life, Clem, but that seems like the bare minimum to expect.'

'What if he's changed?' Clem said, the hope in her voice like a sledgehammer to Jack's heart. 'What if Harriet goes searching for Adam when she's an adult and he tells her he tried to make amends, tried to be a dad to her, and I blocked his path? He missed the first six years, but she's still got ten

or fifteen more years at home and he can make a big difference in that time.'

Jack nodded, trying to bury the instinct that wanted to
deadbolt the doors and lock the windows. How could he stop
Clem getting hurt all over again if it didn't work out?

'What about Harri?'

'She's met him. According to Miss Johnson, when the other
kids had finished talking about showbags and prize ribbons
at school yesterday, Harriet announced that she had a prize
ribbon, a showbag *and* a dad. Like she'd won him at sideshow alley.'

Jack imagined the bubbly young teacher had heard plenty
of rippers during class show and tell. 'Have you told Pop?'

Clem grimaced. 'I'm working up to it.'

'Bush telegraph's pretty speedy. If it's already been a show-
and-tell topic . . .'

'I'll do it before Adam comes down next.'

Jack left Clem to her podcasts and ironing, and hesitated
at the shed. He'd only planned on picking up welding rods
before heading to town, but he found himself plugging in the
welder, donning the safety equipment and getting to work.

Soon the shed was abuzz with welding sparks, noise and
fumes. He thought of Dunkirk with every blow of the hammer,
every swipe of the angle grinder and every spark that flashed
between the welding rod and the steel. An hour later, covered in
sweat and stinking of molten metal, Jack assessed the sculpture
he was making for Victor Jenkins. Even in its infancy, with
only the framework for the wingspan and a hollow body, the
piece had looked like a bird. Today's work cutting the primary
feathers and attaching them to the wings had transformed it
into a majestic wedge-tailed eagle, frozen mid-flight. He pulled
out his phone, snapped a photo and tapped out a text.

Plenty of work to do yet, but she's off to a good start.

Jack sent it to Lauren, then messaged the same photo to Sebastian and Cohen. It was good for them to see projects mid-way through, he thought, and while he wouldn't tell them about the angry snarl of thoughts that had fuelled his welding session, he knew they'd appreciate the work that went into it, and enjoy seeing the structural elements coming together. With a bit of luck, Victor would like it too.

Putting the phone away, he examined the sculpture from all angles, earmarked the steel he needed for the next layer of feathers and tidied his workspace. Welding didn't deliver the same endorphin release as exercise, but as he stepped out of his overalls, Jack knew the manual labour and creativity were a far better option than letting his frustrations simmer away under the surface.

'Look what the cat dragged in,' Arthur said when Jack arrived at the retirement village with bakery rolls and coffee later that week. 'I thought you'd drop by days ago.'

Jack sat the cheese-and-chive rolls on the bedside table. 'It's been a crazy week.'

Arthur's grin turned into a grimace as he tasted the coffee. 'What's this muck? Wasn't Jean working this arvo?'

'She wasn't parked in any of her usual spots.' He'd been glad to avoid his aunt's perceptive eye today too. He wasn't ready for her speculation about Adam Dunkirk's arrival or Clem's pregnancy yet.

'You heard from Clem?'

'Yep.' Arthur smiled, ripped the bread roll in half and took a bite. 'She's coming in this arvo, said she's got some good news. I'm tipping she's got a job offer, or maybe she's finally drawn up a business plan for that farm-gate cafe she's always wanted?' He grinned as he chewed. 'Go on, then, tell me, Jacko. I'll act surprised.'

'Not sure I'd call it good news.' Jack drained his coffee. He didn't want to steal Clem's thunder, but he knew exactly how Arthur felt about Adam Dunkirk and he didn't want his grandfather having a heart attack on the spot either. 'Dunkirk's been in town.'

Arthur's cheerful grin was replaced with a scowl. 'What's that scumbag doing in Penwarra? And don't feed me a load of rubbish about him being here for the fine wine and cellar doors.'

'He wasn't here on a winery tour,' Jack confirmed.

'Tell me she sent him packing, Jacko. Tell me that the spineless coward who dumped his sick wife and left his newborn baby with barely a backwards glance hasn't got a hope in hell of winning our Clementine back?'

Jack looked away, his gaze skimming the framed photos of Arthur and Shirley on their wedding day, him and Clem in their high-school uniforms in the middle of the sunflower paddock and Harriet's kindergarten portrait.

'Jack?' His grandfather's tone was almost pleading. 'You've got me worried, son. Please tell me she's too smart to overlook six years when he couldn't give a stuff. You remember that scene he caused at Harriet's party?' Arthur's voice was rising now. 'Thought he could turn up and everyone would fall over themselves welcoming him back into the fold. Then when Clem told him to rack off, he had the nerve to try and knock your block off.'

Jack gave a mirthless laugh. 'Not likely to forget that one, Pop. I don't want him barging in and breaking her heart any more than you do.'

Arthur thumped a fist on the arm rest of his recliner. 'Then let's tell him to bugger off.' He kicked off his ugg boots and reached for his walking frame.

'Pop,' Jack said, holding up a hand. 'It's not our decision. And as much as it kills me to say it, if Clem goes down this path, there's not much we can do.'

'Bulldust! I'm not going to sit back and pray for the best.'

At this Jack laughed, for real this time. 'I can promise there won't be any praying from my end either.'

Arthur rolled his eyes. 'For all it's worth, Renee's probably doing enough praying for all of us.' At the mention of his daughter-in-law, the wind left Arthur's sails as quickly as it had come, and as he sank back against the recliner, he looked years older.

When Clem's number appeared on his phone later that day, Jack could tell their grandfather hadn't minced his words.

'Did you tell Pop about the baby, Jack?'

'Nope,' Jack said truthfully. He put the phone on speaker and slipped it into his top pocket, putting a lid on the pan of chicken he'd been browning. 'I didn't breathe a word about your pregnancy.'

'You must have said something, because he was straight on the front foot with a whole ticker tape of Adam's stuff-ups. It was like he'd spent all morning compiling a page of notes.'

'Wouldn't have taken him all morning,' Jack said. The guy had so many faults, he could dash off a page in fifteen minutes flat, and then fill another few pages equally fast.

'Oh, you're just as pig-headed as Pop,' Clem said. 'Can't you at least try to be happy for me? You know what it was like growing up without a dad. Does it make me a bad person to want more for my kid? To hope that Adam's ready to step up and fill the void?'

Her words felt like a kick to his solar plexus. Jack knew an uncle wasn't the same as a father, just like a grandfather wasn't the same, but he'd tried his best. 'You do you, Clem. I can't make your decisions any more than I can tell Pop what he can and can't say.'

'It won't change things with us, Jack. Harriet will be around as much as you want. And you used to be best friends with Adam. If I can forgive him, can you at least consider it?'

Jack grabbed the filo pastry and slammed the fridge shut, still shaking his head long after she'd ended the call.

Sooner or later, people will let you down.

Jack stirred the diced chicken into a feta cheese and spinach mix, added more chilli than usual, then splattered spoonfuls of melted butter between layers of filo pastry, before thumping mounds of filling onto each strip of pastry. He folded them into triangles, regretting that today, of all days, he'd decided to cook with the delicate pastry. But by the time he had two oven trays filled with the savoury triangles, his breathing was almost back to normal.

And yet, his opinion of Adam Dunkirk remained unchanged. Rekindling his friendship with the bloke? Not in a million years.

'And what a great way to start our Friday. Don't you just love a story with all the feels?'

Lauren knew she was laying it on a little thick, but she'd mispronounced the first guest's name, and while the subject was heartwarming—a story about an old weatherboard house that had been shifted over the border and turned into a maker's space, offering pottery lessons, soy-candle making, art workshops, and writing residencies—Lauren had somehow mixed up her town names, telling the audience it had been trucked over from Tarpeena not Tyrendarra. She'd also messed up the timelines of the project and the guest had corrected her on air.

Nothing I can do about it now, Lauren told herself, cutting to a promo and inhaling deeply.

Two of the phone lines started flashing and Lauren juggled the calls while her leg jiggled around of its own accord, bumping against the desk. Had Paul switched the staffroom coffee to decaf? Could someone teleport Jean and her coffee van into the studio ASAP? And where the hell was Patrice?

Lauren had a minute and a half left of the song, a guest that was due in the studio any moment and insistent phone lines. Old habits died hard and she snapped back into producer mode, scooping up the phone.

'Rural AM, can I put you on hold please?'

The first caller agreed, but the second interrupted.

'Lauren, it's just me,' said Gabrielle. 'What's happening? You were on a roll earlier this week and today you're flaking out.'

'Mum! This isn't helpful! I'm in the middle of the brekky show.'

Patrice chose that moment to return, studying her with another patronising smile.

'Just a minute, darling,' said Gabrielle over the phone. 'Before you knock off work, call me. I've heard from Bunny, who knows a TV news contact in Townsville. I need a copy of your Best in Show series—'

'Mum, I've got to go,' Lauren hissed, hanging up the call.

'Personal phone calls while you're working? Really?' Patrice said. 'I've got the mayor outside and you're on in forty-five seconds. Are you ready?'

Lauren nodded, quickly scanning her notes. 'Remind me of the mayor's main talking point today? The show?'

Patrice's smile was icy. 'Change of plans—haven't you checked your email? The Penwarra Show's old news. Jillian's talking about a petition, apparently there's a property in your neck of the woods that's an absolute eyesore.'

Lauren barely had time to gather her wits before Jillian Dangerfield was ushered in and miked up. She scrambled through her emails, frantic to find the revised information but the only thing from Patrice was a snarky all-staff email about labelling items in the staff fridge. *Bugger it, I'm going to have to wing it.*

'We're changing gears a little with our final guest of the day, as we welcome the mayor, Jillian Dangerfield, into the studio. Can you tell us about this petition?'

Jillian adjusted her glasses and settled into her chair. 'Thanks, Lauren, and let's face it, nobody likes these types of sticky issues, but as a councillor, we have to listen to residents' concerns. And I can tell you this, there's a lot of angst in the community about a particular unkempt property on the outskirts of Penwarra, as you can see from the long list of signatures on the petition.' Jillian flipped through the pages for good measure. 'For a small town, a lot of people are campaigning for action.'

While Lauren had heard grumbles about Victor Jenkins' property over the years, this was the first time she'd seen a petition. She stared at the number of signatures.

'This seems quite sudden. Are you sure this hasn't been blown out of proportion, Mayor Dangerfield?'

'Quite the opposite, Lauren. It's long overdue. Just last week, a resident was cycling past and counted ten cats plus kittens. Ten! The mess was one thing, but breeding pests is another. Word spread at the show last weekend, and somewhere between the fancy-dress pet contest and the sheaf tossing, someone started a petition. We simply can't ignore this issue any longer.'

A message came through from Patrice.

Phones are running hot, prepare to throw to callers.

Lauren thought of Jack's afternoons with Sebastian and Cohen, welding, painting, tree planting, culling the collection of car bodies in Victor's yard. Jack hadn't gone into specifics, but from what she'd gathered from Arthur, Victor's sentimental attachment had hamstrung his previous clean-up efforts.

Remember what they taught you in university: Your role is to remain impartial. And if you're about to be offered the job as brekky presenter, impartiality is more important than ever.

But as Jillian waved the petition around, Lauren couldn't help picturing the magnificent metal sculpture Jack had started welding from Victor's car parts; the way Victor had fixed the damaged sewing room window for Clem without accepting a cent; the tales Harriet had told about him rescuing the one-eyed goat. They were all aspects of the story she wanted to raise in support of Victor, but couldn't possibly mention on air.

'We'll take calls in a moment, but, Mayor Dangerfield, haven't there been recent efforts made to tidy the property?'

Jillian laughed. 'Cutting the grass and moving a few car bodies isn't what I'd call a clean-up. I live in Penwarra myself, but I'm not the only person who feels this way. And from the phone lines lighting up your studio at this very minute, it's clear my constituents are fed up.'

Another thought struck Lauren. Had Arthur said the radio was Victor's main source of company? Was he listening right now as Patrice patched through callers?

It was only when she looked at the board in front of her that she realised no one had hit the delay button.

The weak coffee curdled inside her stomach. The delay button was the radio equivalent of a life jacket or pilot's parachute, and she was supposed to push it before each interview. If a guest swore or a caller said something derogatory, the ten-second delay allowed them to dump the audio so listeners were spared the inappropriate comments.

Please don't say anything stupid, please don't say anything stupid, Lauren silently urged as Patrice connected a call.

'What about all those rabbits burrows, snake holes and cats?' the caller said. 'You can't drive down that road without spotting a feral kitten or skittling a snake. I'm all about giving a fella a fair go, but like it or not, he's breeding up three of the biggest pests and we're flaming sick of it.'

Patrice nodded emphatically from the production studio.

Jillian gave Lauren a resigned look and spoke into the microphone. 'As you can see, people are getting hot under the collar. I know it's only autumn now, but during summer it's a fire hazard, in spring the rabbit kits will come out of their burrows and even if the cats keep a few pests at bay, proper measures need to be put in place. I'm tired of waiting for councillors to make it a priority, while council staff handball the issue from one department to another. The weight of the community should make them sit up and pay attention.'

Lauren checked the screen, relieved to see one message that wasn't anti-Victor. 'We're going to have to come back to this another day, as we're almost out of time, but one last message from listeners, I've got an anonymous texter who suggests the property owner might be an election scapegoat, Jillian. Your thoughts before we finish up?'

'Election or not,' Jillian said, 'if there's a risk to property values and public safety, we can't afford to sit idle. There are zoning declarations against junkyards and if we need to use the full force of the law, then I'm prepared to investigate.'

'Thanks for your time on this difficult topic,' said Lauren. She looked up at the producer's studio but Petrice had vanished. Lauren hit 'play' on the string of promos scheduled to run at the end of the show, switched off the Mayor's microphone and turned to her guest.

'Tough topic,' Jillian said, removing her headphones. 'I've got as much sympathy as the next person, but who could possibly live in such squalor? Victor Jenkins must be nuttier than a fruitcake.'

'I know Vic, and he's not a bad guy,' Lauren said, not liking the way Jillian had rolled her eyes as soon as she'd mentioned Victor's name. 'I really feel for him, given his situation.'

'Some people hide behind the guise of ill health to shirk their civic duties.'

'Seriously?'

The mayor baulked at Lauren's sharp tone. 'Excuse me?'

Lauren was furious on Victor's behalf. 'Victor's obviously got hoarding issues, his son's a missing person, for God's sake, and from what Jack says, he's scratching to make ends meet. Can you not show some more empathy?'

'Lauren, you really don't know what you're talking about. These days everyone's on antidepressants or on the spectrum, right? It's convenient to play the mental-health card when someone wants an excuse or pity.'

'Are you kidding?' Lauren felt her hands tremor and while her words were hushed, her tone was steely. 'I know better than you might think, Jillian. Labelling and humiliating people isn't the answer and if you don't see that, then you're an ignorant cow.'

A knocking came at the studio door and she turned to see Patrice making a cutting throat gesture with one hand, furiously pointing to the microphone with the other.

Lauren gulped as she realised that not only had the promos just finished, but in her heated rush to defend Victor, she'd forgotten her own mike was still turned on.

Jack shaded his eyes, scanning the roadside for Logan's trio of roaming goats. It wasn't how he'd planned on spending his day off, but after storming around the house all morning, then welding and cutting metal until he'd exhausted his supply of welding rods and grinding discs, the diversion was welcome. Better than dwelling on Adam Dunkirk and the mess he'd leave in his wake.

'There,' Logan said, elbowing Jack. 'Reckon that's them.'

Jack followed his pointed finger to three stud billy goats grazing beside a stand of cypress pines.

'It's times like this I wish I had a kelpie or a border collie to help with the leg work,' Logan said. 'Thanks again for lending a hand. Sammi would put my nuts in a vice if I didn't bring them home.'

'Don't thank me yet,' Jack said, climbing out of the car. 'Wait until we've caught them.'

It didn't take long to create a set of portable stockyards, and once the panels were bolted together and Jack had made a makeshift fence across the road, Logan reversed the ute so the trailer lined up with the race. From there it was a straight-forward job of herding the wandering goats into the yards, pushing them up into the trailer and packing up.

'You're a ripper, Jack, thanks heaps. Would've taken me ages to catch them on my own. I owe you a coldie,' Logan said.

'Nah, all in a good day's work,' said Jack. 'I barely know my Merinos from my Dorpers, let alone goat breeds. They're fine fellas, what kind are they?'

'Anglo-Nubian, common as muck but good all-rounders,' Logan said. 'Gunther's the light one, Joey's the black one with white ears and this here's Chandler.' He scratched the brown goat between the ears. 'Sammi inherited them from her grandad in Victoria, and she's going to get a breeding program together when we have kids. Goat kids and human kids . . . Sounds like chaos to me, but that's her dream and you know what Sammi's like—'

'Well . . .' With a start, Jack realised he'd never thought much about his receptionist's life outside work. He eyed the closest goat, determined to file away that kernel of information about Sammi. That and the fact she was obviously a *Friends* fan. 'They're the same goats as the Moriartys, right?'

'Same but different.' Logan gave a wry grin. 'Depends who you're asking. These bucks are like teddy bears compared to Moriarty's monsters. He breeds for meat, so he's focused on size, but we'll be going for temperament, and producing goats that are happy to be handled. From what I've seen, his herd is three parts muscle, two parts mean. I don't want Sammi's breeders anywhere near his paddocks.'

They climbed back into the ute. Logan turned the engine over and rap music filled the cab.

Jack leaned forward. 'You mind if I change the channel?'

'Talkback radio?' Logan groaned. 'Anyone would think you're sixty-five years older than you actually are, man. Only people my dad's age listen to that station.'

'You're full of it,' Jack said, grinning at the gentle jibe. 'Any other time I'd put up with rap, but Lauren's filling in this week, so I don't want to miss when she's on air.'

'I forgot you were going out with the presenter chick.' Logan looked from Jack to the radio, noting Jack's hesitation. 'She's your girlfriend, yeah?'

Jack leaned against the window, a smile on his face, as Lauren laughed at a quip from the lady she was interviewing about a canned food fundraiser. He could hear the smile in her voice and it made him want to phone in and pledge as many cans as they needed. Jack had tried to kept his personal life and his work life separate, but maybe that was where he was going wrong.

What had Matilda said at her wedding? Him being closed off from the world was only isolating him? And while Logan was younger than him by a decade, the guy had made regular attempts to include him in social events. What was the harm in sharing?

'I'm a lucky man,' Jack said. 'Lauren's something else.'

Logan turned the radio up, listening intently. While they'd been talking, a new guest had come on and from the change in Lauren's tone, Jack picked up pretty quickly that she wasn't a fan of whoever she was sharing the airwaves with.

'Woah, someone's got the shits up,' said Logan. 'Hold on, is that the mayor?'

They listened closely. *There's a petition for action against Vic Jenkins' property?* And from the sounds of it, Mayor Dangerfield was jumping on the bandwagon.

They both listened to the end of the interview and the promos, then Lauren's voice came through the stereo again, loud and clear. It seemed she was just as unhappy about the insensitive comments as Jack was. He turned the radio up even louder, then heard Lauren mention Victor's name, and then his own.

'Victor's obviously got hoarding issues,' Lauren said on air, her voice crackly but strong. 'His son's a missing person, for God's sake, and from what Jack says, he's scratching to make ends meet.'

'What the actual hell?'

Whether it was intended for an audience or not, one thing was clear: Lauren had just revealed confidential information about Victor's personal details—and named Jack as the source.

☙

Lauren's mouth felt like the Simpson Desert and horror swelled as she stared at the flashing red light that confirmed she was still on air. The lights flashing on the switchboard told her the phone lines were filling up. She reached out to steady herself with a trembling hand.

Is the room moving around me? Breathe, breathe, breathe.

The urge to flee was suddenly all encompassing but the dizziness made breathing so difficult she couldn't imagine walking let alone running.

Lauren tugged at her neckline, trying to help the great gulps of air make their way into her lungs, but the harder she breathed, the worse it became.

'Did I just—? Tell me that wasn't—' Her gulps turned to quicker, shorter breaths as she struggled for oxygen. Her heart rate soared and her muscles tensed as she tried to recall what she'd said.

Oh my God. Did I really just slam the mayor on air! And Victor? And Jack?

Poor Victor, having his personal details flung across the airwaves in a frustrated rant. What would Jack say when he heard that she'd betrayed his trust?

Lauren swooned and it was like watching someone else from afar as she doubled over, gasping for breath and clutching her stomach. She squeezed her eyes shut, imagining the shock and hurt on Jack's face.

Am I dying? Never in her life had she felt the piercing fear of not being able to breathe, and the terror was all consuming.

Somehow a soft jacket appeared, smelling like Paul's aftershave.

Paul must have stepped past her to switch off the mike, because when Lauren opened her eyes, the editor was on the other side of the room. He spoke soothingly, and then Sarah was there, leading her into a chair.

Lauren found herself holding a mug of milky, lukewarm tea. It was sweet—someone had put both milk and sugar into it—and the effort of not spilling it all over herself proved enough of a distraction that she finally, *thankfully*, caught her breath.

'Take a deep breath, no hurry,' came Sarah's kind voice. 'That's right, and another.'

'My God, please tell me someone hit the dump button,' she squeaked, the words rasping and desperate, even though she had seen with her own eyes that it wasn't engaged. Not one but two gaping errors and she had no one to blame but herself.

She looked from Paul to Sarah, who shook their heads. Years and years of work undone in a horrid moment of stupidity. They'd never let her on air again, and if Patrice had her way, she probably wouldn't be allowed near the mixing board either.

'I'm so sorry,' Lauren eventually managed, panic giving way to acute embarrassment. Tears flowed. 'I have to call Jack. And Vic.' She forced herself to her feet and saw Patrice ushering Jillian outside, their heads bowed in hushed conversation.

'We're going to need to talk about this,' Paul said, wincing. 'There's a whole load to unpack, but the HR team will have to be involved.'

What exactly had she said? Lauren cringed as the conversation ran through her mind . . . A breach of privacy; discussing a listener's medical details on air without their approval; throwing the local police senior constable under the bus; calling the mayor an ignorant cow.

The human resources team might be the least of my problems.

22

Victor didn't answer his door, nor did he pick up the phone, although Jack could hear it ringing inside the house from where he stood on the front step.

Shit.

He knocked loudly again. 'Vic? It's Jack.'

He'd almost finished writing a note when the goat rounded the corner, tipped its head to the side quizzically and hopped on the spot. It was a move that never failed to crack Sebastian and Cohen up, but Jack ignored the bouncing animal until the notepad flew from his hands.

'Hey!' He shooed the goat away, but before he could retrieve the pad, the goat had started chewing it, as if it too realised a note wouldn't come close to repairing the damage Jack had done.

He had wrestled the notepad back and tried the door knocker again, his hands sticky with goat saliva, but there was still no answer.

I'll try again after I see Clem.

He went to Sunny Cross Farm next.

'Since when do you need to knock?' Clem looked up from a mixing bowl, a puff of flour falling onto the bench as she transferred lamb into a baking dish.

'I didn't want to intrude,' he said, noticing the Ray-Bans on the counter, an Android phone charger in the powerpoint Clem favoured for her Kenwood Chef and an Adelaide Crows mug on the coffee table.

His sister's eyes followed his gaze. 'Adam's back in the city, packing up his townhouse.'

Jack swallowed the urge to caution her, to ask if it was what she really wanted, what she thought was best for Harriet.

'And I'm prepping lamb chops with caramelised onions, sticky apricot glaze and a couscous salad for tea. Harriet would love to see you.'

Jack shook his head. 'I'll pass, thanks. You listen to the radio this morning?'

'Nope.' Clem replenished the breadcrumbs. 'By the time I'd got Harriet to school, Lauren's show was over. Did she mention the show cook-along again?'

Jack explained the situation.

Clem's eyebrows flew up. 'Oh, boy. What the hell was she thinking?'

Jack pinched the bridge of his nose. 'I wish I knew, but the damage is done now. I shouldn't have disclosed anything about Vic. It shouldn't have passed my lips, let alone Lauren's on air.'

Clem crossed her arms in front of her chest, leaving floury smears across her navy apron. 'We're all human, Jack. I mean, *your* mistakes are few and far between, but it happens. Don't crucify yourself or Lauren. I'm sure she wasn't being nasty.'

'The intent doesn't matter, Clem, that's the whole point. It wasn't my information to share, and it definitely wasn't Lauren's to broadcast on live radio. How can you of all people say it's okay?'

'Me of all people?' Her eyes flashed. 'What's that supposed to mean?'

'Clem.' Jack sighed. 'I don't want an argument, I just thought you'd be livid too.'

'No, no, no.' Clem pointed at him, sending breadcrumbs and flour across the bench. 'Go back a bit and tell me what you mean by me "of all people". I'm not a hoarder, I don't have a missing kid and while we have a tight budget, I wouldn't say we're scratching to make ends meet. Or do you think I'm the authority on being publicly humiliated after what happened with Adam? Or are you referring to my struggles after Harriet's birth?'

Jack pressed his temples, trying to quell the pounding in his head. 'That's not what I meant, Clem.'

'Are you sure?' She swore and looked away. 'I've gotta say, Jack, it's pretty hard living up to your ideals of perfection all the time.'

'Perfection?' Jack glanced at the trail of goat snot on his trousers, the limestone dust clinging to his shoes. They were nothing compared to the repercussions of his stuff-up. 'I meant you've been let down too, more than once, and you know what it feels like. My ideals are protecting the people I love and the community I serve, steering a steady ship. I thought that's what you wanted.'

'Maybe it's a good thing I'm a screw-up, because at least that way you get to be the strong, dependable one. Maybe Harriet and the baby and Adam and I will work out just beautifully.'

'I hope so, I really do, Clem. And I'm not perfect, I stuff up too.'

'Ha! Fat chance. This thing on the radio's the first stuff-up you've made in two decades. Tell me otherwise—' She crossed her arms again, smearing more food. 'Give me a solid example.'

Jack looked away, weighing up his options.

'There was a snake in the ute.' He looked up, meeting her eyes. *Too late to go back now.* 'With Harriet. I didn't know, and obviously she wasn't hurt but—'

'*What?*' Clem's voice was ice and Jack felt shame burning his cheeks. 'And you didn't think to tell me this tiny detail? When the hell was this?'

Jack barely got halfway through explaining before Clem yanked open the door.

'This is too much. I'm so mad I could throttle you. Maybe Adam's right, maybe I've been relying on you too much. Just go.'

'Clem—'

'Go!' Her shout startled a blue wren on the verandah and it flew full pelt into the window before flopping to the ground.

'Now look what you've done!' Clem wailed, and he could tell she was fighting back tears as she cupped the dazed bird in her hands.

Jack marched numbly to the fence that marked Victor's boundary, almost as stunned as the tiny blue wren. *Is that what she really thinks of me? That I like seeing her fail? That I get a kick out of her relying on me?*

His phone buzzed, again, and this time he answered.

'Jack,' Lauren gasped. 'I'm so sorry. I don't know if you heard the radio—'

'I heard it,' Jack said curtly. 'I'm on my way to check on Vic.'

'I'll come with you,' Lauren said. 'Just wait—'

'Lauren, no.' He held down the fence wire with one hand and scanned the long grass for snakes as he headed towards the pile of rusty scrap. 'I need to get my own head straight first,' he said. 'I don't know when I commented on Victor's income, or lack of it, but I should have known better. I shouldn't have—'

I shouldn't have let my guard down.

I shouldn't have forgotten that my job and my family come first.

I shouldn't have fallen for you.

The path between the Fords and the Valiants was clearer now the Holdens and the Volkswagens were gone, and Jack paused. What if the radio discussion had been slightly different, and Lauren had accidentally shared an anecdote about his father's suicide or Clem's post-natal breakdown on air?

The more ties you have, the more you can get hurt. Sooner or later, people will let you down.

'I shouldn't have trusted anyone with confidential information, especially someone in the media. This isn't going to work, Lauren.'

The line was silent. The fact that Lauren wasn't rushing to try to salvage the relationship wasn't lost on him, nor was the stark reminder that Clem had made her thoughts crystal clear. Jack tried Victor's front door again, nearly tripping over the goat as it hopped in front of him.

'Dammit.'

White hot pain seared his ankle as Jack veered off the path to dodge the goat. He took a sharp breath and hobbled the final steps to the gate, hoping the pain in his rolled ankle would override the ache in his heart and the implosion of the relationship he'd almost believed could work.

The next morning, Lauren woke with a racing mind and an aching heart, sitting bolt upright and scanning the room for potential threats as the phone alarm chimed and buzzed. But as she stood under the shower, she realised the biggest threat to her wellbeing and safety was staring right at her in the foggy shower screen reflection.

Tahnee had been good on the phone last night, calm as a cucumber as Lauren blurted out the whole sorry situation. It was the first time her sister had listened without interruption before doling out advice, and when Lauren reread her tear-smudged notes that morning, she could see why Tahnee's employers held her in such high esteem. She knew her stuff when it came to workplace screw-ups.

Lauren flicked through her wardrobe. The pink, yellow and aqua clothes felt like an assault on her senses, so she slipped a loose grey dress from its hanger. It was the type of dress she'd bought with good intentions of wearing, but had overlooked in favour of brighter, more cheerful colour combinations. Today, paired with black leggings and a grim ponytail, it felt like the exact outfit she needed. The type of outfit that would help her shrink into the background and avoid drawing attention to herself.

The streets of Penwarra were still dark when she drove towards Mount Gambier and only the log trucks and an occasional shift worker passed her on the road. Normally, she listened to music or a podcast to fire up her early-morning starts, but like the clothes, today she kept the stereo low and her eyes on the road. Paul had been calm yesterday, but would he be livid today? Would he ask her to pack her desk and toss in any idea of working in the media?

It was an effort to park outside the station when everything inside her screamed, *Reverse out now and save a thread of your dignity.*

She found Paul in the kitchen.

'You look knackered,' he said, sliding an armful of files, newspapers and hot cross buns onto the staffroom table. He poured himself a tea.

'I can't even begin to apologise for yesterday, Paul. I know I let you down,' Lauren said, chancing a look at her boss, who had pulled up a chair and was listening quietly. 'I shouldn't have lost my temper at Jillian or mouthed off like that. I definitely didn't intend for that to go on air and then I made things worse by having a meltdown. I'm so, so sorry.'

Paul nodded, blowing on the top of his tea. 'You're right, there's better ways that could have been handled, but I've seen worse.'

He had? Lauren joined him at the table. This wasn't how she thought this would pan out.

'So you're not firing me?'

'It's not clear cut.' Paul looked at his watch. 'I went out on a limb campaigning for you in the presenter's job, Lauren, and after yesterday and all the flack we've copped since, I'm questioning that decision. Legal might have to get involved, depending on how Victor and Jillian react. Our listeners have to trust you and we'll never get guests on if they think you're going to reveal their personal details on air . . .' He lifted his hands. 'I think we'll have to rethink the job offer or at least put it through an official review.'

So they were *going to offer me the job.*

Lauren gulped her tea, burning most of her tastebuds and scalding her throat as she gathered up the last of her courage.

'But Patrice should have—'

Paul held up a hand. 'Lauren, I'm going to stop you there. I know you and Patrice don't get along, but you have to own this vast lapse of judgement. You can't blame this on her.'

'I wish I could take it all back,' Lauren said, fighting against a wave of nausea.

'Don't we all,' he said, with a weary smile. 'Look, you've probably beaten yourself up enough for the both of us, so let's leave it there. I'll do the show today and then we'll find a fill-in. Go home, get yourself a doctor's certificate, we'll arrange some sick leave and you can regroup, work out where to go from here, okay?'

As Lauren drove home to Penwarra, a fresh wave of pain hit her as she imagined Jack on Victor's doorstep and in Clem's kitchen, discussing the incident. Jack had trusted her and she'd ruined it. And Paul had taken a leap of faith and this was how she had repaid him.

Tahnee's advice from last night ran through Lauren's mind: *Admit nothing, deny everything and keep your head down.*

Perhaps she'd got ahead of herself and this was the point where she admitted she wasn't going to make it in radio. Perhaps this job wasn't even worth the heartache.

Fifty laps didn't dull the pain in Jack's heart, nor had a week stewing on the radio incident, hours working on the sculpture and nights tossing and turning, but the shock of the cold water when he entered the pool each morning and the gruelling, monotonous laps freed up brain space like nothing else.

It hadn't been brave opening his heart to Lauren, it had been a kamikaze mission. It hadn't been a matter of *if* she let him down, but *when*. And the sad thing was, it had happened even sooner than he'd expected. He ploughed through the water until her golden hair and racer-back swimsuit were at the back of his mind.

He was tantalisingly close to reaching autopilot, where his brain blocked out everything but counting the laps and the number of strokes between breaths, when thoughts of the SAPOL internal investigations hijacked his flow.

There'd be repercussions for sure, but to what extent? Would he drop rank or get away with a slap on the wrist at the upcoming meeting? Jack swam harder, trying to outrun his worries.

When he got out of the pool, the lanky lifeguard looked impressed. 'You were charging through that water like a shark was on your tail. I've been watching you all week—pretty quick times. Are you training for the Masters Games? The local swimming team would have you in a flash if you want me to introduce you.'

Yeah, because that worked so well last time. Dunkirk had officially cured him of team training pursuits.

'Not my thing,' Jack said, thanking him for the offer and heading for the showers. He felt like he'd aged a decade in the last week and he noticed a few more grey hairs in his change-room reflection.

A pair of ladies jogged past the pool gates, their conversation as fast as their pace, and as he drove back to the station, Jack counted a handful of walkers, dog owners and even a pair of cyclists starting their day exercising and chatting. He'd kept his circle of friends small by choice, but now Clem wasn't talking to him, Harriet was probably besotted with her newly arrived father and Lauren had heeded his request for space, he felt untethered.

Stay or go? He turned the ute towards the police station and pulled up hard against the 'staff parking' sign in the car park. Negotiating a new post wouldn't be easy, not when he'd promised to serve the Penwarra community for two years, and Arthur would be devastated if Jack pulled the pin, but maybe him leaving would help everyone?

Jack straightened the collar of his uniform and marched into the station. Sammi looked up from her laptop, then looked down again, her fingers thundering across the keyboard.

'Morning,' he said, not breaking stride.

He turned his attention to the pile of paperwork in front of him, only leaving his desk a couple of hours later to smash out a furious 25-kilometre cycle, shower and reheat his lunch in the staff microwave.

He heard Sammi's shoes click-clack into the kitchenette.

'Microwave's yours in thirty seconds.' He grabbed a fork and set it on the table, looking up to see her watching him. 'What?'

'Are you sure you're not going to bite my head off for slurping my cup of soup or breathing too loudly?'

Jack shook his head, confused. 'Beg your pardon?'

'You've been like a bear with a sore head all week. Geraldine said you bit her head off yesterday when she reported a trailer with faulty lights, and you nearly ran Logan over when you roared out of the car park last night. Everyone's lying low, and I don't blame them.'

That was news to Jack.

'Have you noticed how many hours you've logged this week? Almost twenty per cent up on the previous week, according to my calculations. And don't get me started on the exercising. You come here straight from the pool, you're out at the gym or running or cycling in your lunch break.'

The microwave dinged, but neither Jack or Sammi moved. 'No laws against working hard and looking after myself.'

Now Sammi stepped closer, lowering her voice. 'That's the thing though, boss, this doesn't look like self-care—it looks more like punishment to me. Escapism at best. This isn't the same guy who rounds up stray goats on his days off and gives shoulder rides to little girls with pigtails. Speaking of which . . .' She opened the fridge, peered inside, then shut it again. 'Just as I thought. Usually by this time on a Friday there'd be vanilla slice in the fridge or funny-face biscuits in the bikkie jar. What's Miss Harriet going to think when she gets here this afternoon?'

Avoiding her eye, Jack took his lunch from the microwave. It felt like he'd lost everyone he cared about in the space of a week. Sammi knew he and Lauren had parted ways, and to his credit, Logan had continued reaching out even after Jack ignored his calls, but he didn't have the energy to explain it right now.

'Harriet's not coming today,' he said, swapping the scalding bowl to his other hand and piercing the plastic wrap with a fork. Focusing on work and exercise hadn't delivered quite the distraction he'd hoped, and he felt a lot like the gush of steam and deflating balloon of plastic on the bowl. He needed more time hammering old car bonnets into flat, usable sheets, more hours transforming twisted, rusty and pockmarked steel into birds and sunflowers.

'Nobody in Penwarra wants you burning out, neither do we want everyone's feathers ruffled because you're in a foul mood. If something's weighing on your mind, my door's always open.'

Jack dropped her gaze. The last thing he wanted to do was relive Lauren's on-air betrayal, dwell on the distance between him and Clem, or explain the difficulty of making amends to Vic when the bloke wasn't answering the door to him. 'There's nothing to talk about, but thanks anyway,' he said, looking out the window. He needed some space and fresh air, and fast.

Jack headed for the lemon-scented gum tree in the nearby park and sat with his back resting against the smooth, salmon-coloured trunk.

He was staring up at the canopy, trying to untangle the thoughts that were looping through his mind, when Logan ventured over.

'Mate?'

Jack pushed a piece of broccolini around his bowl. 'Sammi sent you?'

'She's worried, mate. Me too. You haven't returned any of my calls.'

'Busy week,' Jack said evenly.

To his surprise, Logan took a seat on the grass beside him and hooked an arm around his knee, like he had nothing better to do than lounge around on the grass. 'Hit me with it, then.'

Jack laughed.

Logan laughed too. 'Look, I know you think I'm only a young gun, and if we were both cops and we'd both joined the police force at the same time, I'd be the cop doing the bakery run and running regos through a computer, and you'd be the cop kicking down doors in a SWAT vest, but I've been through a bit of stuff in my time too. Technically, I'm just another public servant like you, but I'd like to think we're also friends, Jack. I'm serious, man. If you don't want to talk now, that's cool, but you've got my number and I want you to call me.'

Jack studied him, and he wasn't sure who was more surprised when he promised Logan he would.

The afternoon was a long one, and Jack's plans for a forty-kilometre post-work bike ride veered off track as he cycled past the retirement village. A quick look over his shoulder for traffic, and he wheeled around, keen for his grandfather's wisecracks and wisdom.

'What, no coffee and cake today?' Arthur joked, folding the newspaper he'd been reading and swiping a hand across his whiskers. 'Clementine's dropped the ball with food deliveries too. I'll fade away at this rate.'

Jack quirked an eyebrow. 'Not likely, Pop.'

'How are you holding up, Jacko? Vic get back in touch?'

Jack shook his head. He went to the edge of Arthur's bed, retucked the sheets and then sat down. 'No word, but I can understand why. I'd be livid too if my dirty laundry was aired like that. I've left him a message, and as long as the goat hasn't eaten through the phone lines, then he knows I'm keen to make it up to him, whatever it takes.'

'And how about Clem? Or are she and Harriet still orbiting around Dropkick Dunkirk?'

Jack shrugged, toying with his bicycle helmet. 'You'd know better than me. Harri was supposed to come round tonight, but apparently Dunkirk's taking her to the beach.'

'Jean saw them in the playground yesterday. Dunkirk was pushing the swings, fetching milkshakes, lifting Harriet onto the monkey bars. Sure, he's playing the game for now, lovebombing them or whatever it is the young people call it, but it's just a matter of time before he takes off like a rat up a drainpipe.'

'Great,' Jack said, rolling his eyes. If Jean had anything to do with it, most of Penwarra would know about Dunkirk's arrival now too.

Arthur tapped Jack's shoulder. 'You're a good bloke, Jacko, hang in there.'

'That's the thing, Pop, maybe it's better for everyone if I just leave them to it, request a transfer to a different station. Go bush to Arnhem Land or Alice Springs.'

Arthur's sharp gaze locked onto Jack. 'That's bullshit . . . A real man faces his problems, he doesn't run or take the easy way out. You don't just quit on your family.' He was silent then, and from the way his jaw flexed, Jack guessed his train of thought; Arthur had struggled to say his son's name after he took his life, let alone share details or memories of the man.

'You're the strong one, Jacko, always were and always will be. But that doesn't mean you don't feel the pain, it just means you're better at working through it. I give Dunkirk a few months at best. It's not just Clem and Harriet who'd miss your ugly mug if you buggered off to the bush. I'm quite partial to your pastry deliveries, those lads from Morley-Morley Road

look up to you and I bet the lovely Lauren would be disappointed as well.'

Jack shoved the helmet back on his head. If he left now, he
could still manage an hour of cycling before dusk.

'That's where you're wrong, Pop. It's over. Done. Finito.'

Lauren peeked through the front door and looked both ways.
She was sure Val's car hadn't returned after the school run,
but she'd been caught out earlier in the week and subjected to
an impromptu and oh so awkward over-the-fence counselling
session, full of empathy and good intentions. One moment
Val had been making sympathetic murmurs and handing a
basket of fresh eggs over the picket fence and the next she'd
been fishing a slightly wrinkled tissue from her pocket and
putting an arm around Lauren.

'Get it all out, atta girl,' Val had said, patting Lauren's back.
'We all need a good cry sometime or . . . or . . . another, don't
w . . . w . . . worry about that.'

Lauren had comforted her neighbour, and even though a
Napisan soaking had removed most of Val's mascara from
Lauren's softest cotton top, she wasn't keen to repeat the
embarrassing exchange.

On Wednesday, Val left a stack of DVDs and a family-sized
block of chocolate on Lauren's doorstep, with a post-it note
stuck to the top: *Perfect time to watch a few weepies*. And
from the shape of the bag at Lauren's feet this morning, Val
had delivered another lot of goodies.

Lauren leaned against the soft-pink weatherboards and
read the accompanying note.

Now that you've had a good cry, you'll need some laughs.

These are my favourite romcoms, hope you like them too.

She opened the tote to see a pile of books and more chocolate. Lauren was touched by the kind gesture.

Setting the books inside, Lauren took another glance up and down the street then hurried down the garden-lined path to see what the postie had delivered.

Two bills, a parcel slip and a huntsman spider were waiting for her in the mailbox.

Won't be collecting this in a hurry, she thought as she pulled out the bills and the parcel slip, then turned on her heel and marched back up the driveway. It wasn't just the idea of standing in line at the post office, or possibly running into someone who wanted to talk about her on-air stuff-up, the contents of the package were no longer required.

Had it really been a fortnight ago that she'd gone on that online shopping spree, making ridiculous Jack-inspired purchases like silky pyjamas, a *Triathlons for Beginners* book and new set of bathers? It felt like eons.

The flamingo-pink roses were still blooming their socks off, and as Lauren rushed past, her dressing gown caught on the Princess Alexandra of Kent rosebush she'd repotted by the door. As she went to yank the fabric free from its thorny trap, she realised the dressing gown's delicate lace edging would be ruined if she didn't untangle it carefully. For the first time all day, she felt her breathing slow down as she unhooked the rows of thorns.

Lauren spared a thought for the plant's namesake. Princess Alexandra herself had weathered a few storms in her past. She recalled the controversy surrounding the princess's daughter, who had supposedly shamed the family by announcing a pregnancy out of wedlock. Someone had shared the story on a David Austin Rose Lovers Facebook page the other month, and while it had been a major tabloid scandal in the late eighties, the story had been new to Lauren and most of the

Facebook group. A storm in a teacup, was how one of the green thumbs put it. Recalling the story, and comparing her own woes to someone else's worst moments, slightly eased the pain in Lauren's chest.

She retrieved her secateurs and snipped off a spray of roses. Maybe the blooms would remind her that everyone made bad decisions, whether they were country journalists or royal matriarchs. She put them into an empty jam jar and set the jar beside her coffee machine.

A knock came at the front door. Lauren paused, a bag of coffee beans in her hand, and peered out the kitchen window to see an enormous bunch of flowers. Her heart sped up then came to a grinding halt as April called out.

'Door's open,' Lauren said, kicking herself for thinking—even if only for a second—that the flowers may have been held by Jack. She was the one in the wrong, not him.

'Aren't you supposed to be in Margaret River?'

April kicked off her boots and plonked the bouquet on the table, waiting for Gary to stop his screeching before trying to speak.

'It wasn't much fun sunning myself on a beach and traipsing around fancy vineyards when I knew you were holed up here, hiding from the world. When we FaceTimed yesterday, and you were still wearing that darn dressing gown, I changed my flights. Con stayed behind, so we can have a proper debrief and come up with a plan of attack together.'

Lauren groaned. 'You shouldn't have come home—now I've got to add your ruined holiday to my list of stuff-ups. All we need is Mum and Tahnee to hotfoot it down the Riddoch Highway, hit a kangaroo on the way and I'll have a full scorecard.'

'Oh, come here, you idiot,' April said, pulling her into a fierce hug. 'I was getting tired of all that sun, those disgustingly productive vines and sickeningly good weather, anyway. Tell me everything.'

And even though it was only 10.30 am, and Lauren was still wearing her pyjamas, April opened the fridge and pulled out a bottle of sparkling wine and some cheese and found the stash of dark chocolate Lauren kept in the same compartment.

'Do we need wine, chocolate and cheese or coffee, chocolate and toast? No judgement—' April lifted an eyebrow. 'Actually those pyjamas have bird poo running down the shoulder, so maybe a *slight* bit of judgement, but I'm not going to make a big deal of it. Will you feel better knowing there's trouble in paradise for our favourite Scotsman and the delicate Clarissa? Word on the street is she's spending an awful lot of time with her pottery teacher, a hardcore vegan whose idea of fun is attending PETA rallies.'

'Poor Ferg,' Lauren said. 'He'll be gutted.'

'He will,' April agreed. 'But enough about him . . .' She piled chocolate and cheese onto a platter and shelved the wine.

Lauren shrugged. 'I don't even know where to start.' She wiped the white splodge below her collarbone. Yep, definitely bird poo.

'You,' April said, refilling the coffee grinder. 'We're starting with you. Are you okay?'

'Well, the entire town's talking about me, my face is on page three of the local newspaper and the mayor herself has sent me a strongly worded email suggesting I rethink my career in media.'

'All that stuff is just background noise, and it will blow over, I promise. You probably just said what everyone was thinking. Put a microphone or TV camera in front of her, and Jillian Dangerfield is Miss Congeniality. Talk to her off the record and you'll quickly learn she *is* small-minded and the only reason she's still mayor is because she's related to half the town. It's so unfair that nobody but you heard her comments. If only you'd accidentally left her microphone on instead of yours.'

'If only I'd remembered the number one rule of journalism, and kept my cool instead of seeing red the moment Jillian started slagging off Vic. And only a space cadet would forget the mike. I keep reliving that moment again and again and wishing I'd paused for five seconds before blurting everything out. A professional *and* personal lapse in judgement, to say the least. But that's only part of the problem,' Lauren said, sinking into the dining chair. 'After what I said, I'm not sure if I've even got a job to go back to. The switchboard had so many callers I thought it was going to blow up. And Victor told me exactly what I could do with my apple pie when I tried to deliver it last night.'

April filled a plunger with ground coffee and boiling water, then fished a loaf of sourdough from the freezer, letting her talk.

'I've ruined everything.' Lauren looked at her phone. 'Mum's pressing me to apply for a marketing role at her work, or at the very least do a few years in commercial radio and then circle back to telly. According to her doubles partner, Bunny, I should strike while the iron's hot and leak the story to *A Current Affair* or *Sixty Minutes*.' Lauren cleared her throat and tried to imitate a sensationalist newsreader. 'A town divided, a hoarder who won't leave the house, a mayor's politically incorrect views almost exposed on live radio and the idiot presenter who can't keep her mouth shut.'

April snorted, amused by Lauren's parody. 'You're a natural, and if I know Gabrielle Bickford, she won't rest until you're recording a demo tape and sending in a video pitch.'

Lauren let Gary out of his cage and stroked his rosy-pink chest feathers. 'She's probably on the phone to them as we speak, booking me an interview spot. You know her tennis buddies have connections all over the place.'

April rolled her eyes. 'Love her to death but I'd throttle her if she was my mother. And what about Tahnee? Is she on your case too?'

'Surprisingly sympathetic,' Lauren admitted, glancing at the flowers her sister had sent, along with a Haigh's chocolate frog that was bigger than her head. 'She thinks I should come up to the city for a spell, live with her until this mess blows over. And you won't bloody well believe it,' Lauren said, tearing a crust off the hot toast and handing it to Gary, 'but it's tempting. I hate that everyone here knows exactly how badly I stuffed up. People either give me dirty looks in the supermarket or pump me for more information—well, the ones that thrive on the gossip do anyway. And Jack—'

April watched her over the top of her coffee mug, a compassionate look at the ready.

'Jack doesn't want me to call,' Lauren said softly. 'And before I stuffed everything up royally, he told me he might be moving away anyway.'

'Ouch,' said April, listening as Lauren told her about Clem, the unexpected pregnancy and what Adam Dunkirk's return could mean for the Crossleys. 'That's a lot to take in. I bet he's feeling a bit at sea too.'

Lauren sighed, nodding. 'And I just made it all a hundred times worse, me and my big mouth.'

April laid a hand over hers. 'Hold that thought,' she said, rifling through Lauren's handbag and retrieving one of her battered notebooks. 'I've got this friend, you see, and she always told me there's nothing like a checklist to bring things into perspective. I've waited long and hard to be the scribe in this situation, so fire away and we'll rank the stuff-ups, examine them until we're blue in the face and draw up the worst-case scenario. Deal?'

For the first time all week, Lauren felt the tiniest smile creep onto her lips. 'Deal.'

23

23

'That's the last of the small stuff, Vic, I'll drop this off at the scrapyard on the way to town and you'll be able to see almost an acre of lawn in that yard again,' Jack said, angling the old go-cart onto the jam-packed trailer. It was a tight fit, given the rusty scrap and lawn mower chassis, but it did the trick.

Victor had avoided Jack's calls for over a week, but instead of the ear-bashing he expected when the older man finally answered his phone, Jack was surprised with a request for help.

'You can cart away the small engine machinery on the condition that you don't drone on about that bloody radio mess,' Victor had told him. 'I don't want to hear about it, I don't want to talk about it, got it?'

Jack had agreed and now, a week later, he and Victor surveyed the yard, which was down to half-a-dozen cars. The young goat had made a good dent on the grass now that there were fewer rusty obstacles in its way, but the result was patchier than a home haircut. And there were still cats lounging on cars and rabbit scratchings you could roll your ankle on if you weren't watching your step.

'Looking better,' Jack said.

'It'll get some of the haters off my back, at the very least,' Victor said, looping a hand through his overall strap.

Seb and Cohen rounded the corner, and without being asked, loaded the gardening equipment into the back of Jack's ute and brushed the grass clippings off their clothes. Their initiative and chatty manner as they recapped the day's work almost made Jack smile.

'It's looking pretty good, Vic,' Sebastian said, rocking back on his heels and sweeping the hair out of his eyes before replacing his cap. Somewhere along the way, the flat-brimmed baseball caps had disappeared and now both he and Cohen wore the Blue Light SA caps Jack had given them.

'We doing a final blitz this weekend?' Cohen asked.

They looked to Jack, who nodded.

'Only if you've got nothing better to do,' Victor huffed, using his steelcap boot to unearth a milk thistle. The goat rushed over, eager for the treat. 'You're alright for teenagers, I guess.'

Sebastian and Cohen exchanged a look, now well accustomed to the old man's mannerisms. They accepted the begrudging praise with a nod and headed to Jack's car.

'How's your sister?' Victor said, bending down to give the goat a scratch between the ears. 'Your curried sausages aren't half as good as hers, you know.'

Jack looked to the east, where the property boundaries met. 'You can tell her that next time you see her.'

He said goodbye to Victor and got into the ute. It was now two weeks since his blow-up with Clem, two uneasy weeks of treading on eggshells and straddling the line of watching out for her and giving her and Dunkirk their own space. Two weeks since he'd started driving straight past her driveway when Adam Dunkirk's Cruiser ute was parked out the front, fourteen days of missing Harriet—and 20,160 minutes of ignoring the ache in his chest whenever he thought of Lauren.

Which, he admitted, as the signpost for Petticoat Lane came into view, was often.

Just call her.

But no matter what his heart thought, Jack couldn't switch off the warning light that flashed every time he thought of her radio slip-up. And how could a relationship go anywhere without trust?

He dropped Victor's junk off at the scrapyard on the outskirts of town, returned Sebastian and Cohen to Morley-Morley Road and went back to the tiny police house that was yet to feel like home. Within five minutes he was back in the ute, this time wearing a fresh set of overalls.

There was no sign of Dunkirk's LandCruiser or Clem's Jeep at Sunny Cross Farm, and Jack sank another hour into the recycled metal sculpture, welding coils, cogs and checker plate together for the wedgie's torso. The life-sized eagle took up a large chunk of floorspace in the shed, and as he closed the door behind him on the way out, Jack took a moment to admire his work. Attaching the final feathers and dulling the last of the sharp edges would be a bittersweet moment, but the sculpture would look good standing guard over Victor's property.

Jean's car pulled into the driveway not long after Jack had returned home.

'I was going to invite you to join us at the golf club, but it looks like you've already started fixing a meal,' she said, setting her handbag down as Jack diced veggies for dinner.

Jack noticed she was dressed in her Sunday finest, and when he glanced out the window at the car, he saw Arthur was sitting in the passenger seat, waving.

'I'm good, thanks, Aunty Jean, can't let this produce go to waste. Tell Pop I'll visit soon.' He continued chopping, as if the action would cover his feeble excuse, and wasn't surprised when Jean made a 'pffft' noise.

'Jack Albert Crossley, do you really think that's going to work on me? I watched your grandparents dust themselves off and do a fine job of dragging you and Clem through your teenage years. Whatever you and your sister are going through now, don't let it blow what's left of your family apart. Art's ticker isn't going to take too much more heartache and if you're not coming to the golf club with us, then maybe we'll pull up a pew here and talk some sense into you.' Jean folded her arms across her generous chest and leaned on the kitchen bench. 'What'll it be?'

Jack looked at the soft swede and limp celery he'd been dicing, the bowl of almost-thawed mince sitting on the window-sill and the potatoes with eyes almost as sharp as his great aunt's. 'You're welcome to join me,' he said, putting the knife down. 'It's only potato and beef pie, nothing fancy.'

She nodded, tucked her handbag back under her arm and, with Jack's help, fetched Arthur from the car.

'Wasn't sure I'd ever get to see inside this humpy,' Arthur said, squeezing the brakes on his walking frame and squinting around the sparse house. 'A man could die waiting for his grandson to invite him round.'

'I thought you liked me taking you to the farm,' Jack said, shifting a pot plant so the walker could fit down the hallway. 'This place isn't anything special, just standard-issue cop housing.'

The no-frills decor didn't escape Jean's close attention either. 'No photos, no pictures on the walls, not a fluffy pillow or throw rug in sight. Dare say it'd be more homely in those cells next door,' she said and grinned, holding out a chair for Arthur.

'What about those beautiful patchwork quilts your gran sewed you? They'd add a little colour hanging over the back of the couches,' Arthur said.

'Perhaps remind you where you've come from too, lad,' Jean added.

'I'm never going to forget, Aunty Jean.'

'Your sister said you two have barely spoken in weeks.'

'Clem's all or nothing, and if Adam Dunkirk's back in her life, he's the centre of her world now. I'm with Pop on this one: I don't like him, I don't trust him, and I don't want to see the way she looks at him when I know darn well he's going to break her heart.'

Jack went back to the chopping board, adding carrot to the mixture before scraping the veggies into a bowl and flicking on the oven. The potatoes were bubbling away nicely, almost ready to mash, so he heated a frypan and watched the olive oil hiss and spit as he added the mince.

Jean left the room and returned with a bottle of Lacewing Estate red from the wine rack. 'So you're just going to avoid your sister until then?' she said, opening overhead cabinets until she found the wine glasses.

'That's the plan,' Jack said, peeling an onion. The acrid juices made his eyes water, but he kept dicing.

'A bit harsh for Harriet, isn't it? And what about Lauren Bickford?' Jean asked. 'How come I had to hear from Art that you've called things off?'

Jack added the onion to the pan and wiped his eyes with the sleeve of his shirt. 'This is an ambush, not a visit,' he said gruffly. He turned to see Jean and Arthur staring at him with the same dark-lashed Crossley frown that glared back at him in the mirror each day. Gesturing to the police station next door, Jack splayed his hands. 'Are you done? Any comments on my work, given you've already covered my home, family and love life?'

Jean nudged Arthur, a twinkle back in her eyes. 'I told you they were bonking?'

'Gah!' The spatula slipped out of Jack's hand, catapulting a wad of browned beef across the kitchen. The clump of meat landed with a splat on the bench, and Arthur picked it up gingerly, blew on it and popped it into his mouth.

'More salt,' he said with a wink at Jean, who barely managed to bite back a grin. 'Maybe some garlic too.'

Jack swore under his breath, took a sip of the wine Jean had poured, then added the veggies, plus the seasonings and sauce, to the frypan. And while he never understood why his mother had chosen the church over her children, he felt the kernel of resentment ease a little as he contemplated life without anyone sticking their nose into his business, helping themselves to his wine collection and offering unsolicited advice. The thought lasted no longer than the mouthful of wine.

'I'm giving Clem her space. I'll be here if she or Harriet need me, but far enough away that I don't have to deal with Dunkirk.' Jack drained the potatoes and grabbed the masher, channelling his frustration into making the lightest, fluffiest mash possible. He was itching to get back to his workshop, using real tools like the hammer and anvil, the angle grinder and welder.

'And I can't do anything about the situation with Lauren. I'm the idiot who should've kept my trap shut about Vic, and even though she didn't mean to broadcast it to the entire Limestone Coast, we can't put the genie back in the bottle. I'm lucky the internal investigations team let me off with a slap on the wrist.'

'Poor Lauren,' Jean said, opening and shutting drawers until she found a fluted pie dish. She placed it on the bench in front of Jack and returned to her seat. 'April said she's bunkered down in that sweet little cottage of hers, riding out the worst of the storm.'

'All alone,' Arthur added with a rueful sigh. 'Apart from that rowdy galah.'

Jack greased the pie dish, draped a sheet of puff pastry over it and trimmed the sides, refusing to meet their eyes. His initial anger had died down after speaking with Victor, but he couldn't forgive Lauren any more than he could safeguard his sister's heart from Adam Dunkirk.

All he could do was learn from his mistakes.

Lauren had arrived at the radio station in daylight plenty of times, and the sun was always up when she left after her shift, but there was something disconcerting about driving into the car park when the rest of the team was already there and working.

Folding the resignation letter into perfect thirds with shaking hands was near impossible, but eventually she slid it into the envelope and headed inside.

'Thought you were taking the month off,' Patrice said, raising her eyebrows when she spotted Lauren. 'Poor Nigel's downing pain killers at a rapid rate, you know.'

Lauren *had* noticed that Nigel had sounded a bit off this week.

'He's on crutches but you don't see him calling in sick,' Patrice continued. 'A team's only as good as its weakest link, I always say. Other employers might be happy to overlook laziness or bad habits, but these things don't go unnoticed in a high-pressure environment.'

'I'm not lazy,' Lauren said quietly, looking into the staff room to see if Paul was in. *Just like April said, get the hardest bit out of the way first.*

'Didn't say you were,' Patrice said, raising her eyebrows. 'We were just surprised Paul was going to offer you the job. I'd care more about what everyone else on the staff thought about me, if I were in your position.'

Is she right? Does everyone else at work think I'm the weakest link?

It was hard to think straight with Patrice's eagle eyes on her. Lauren looked down to the envelope in her hand, her resolve stiffening.

Why am I standing here, listening to this? Belittling comments had become a mainstay of Patrice's banter these last few months, but today, with her resignation in hand, Lauren didn't have to stand here and take it. After so many years of being scared to upset Patrice, being told that her way of doing things was incorrect or inept, she recalled Carli's words. Perhaps the older lady was only as powerful as she'd allowed her to become.

'You know what, Patrice? If I had been in the producer's chair that day, I would've hit the mute button the moment the promos rolled, or at least as soon as the presenter started talking. I made a mistake, but you did too. You should have been there.'

Lauren's voice shook but she lifted her chin and held her ground until Patrice turned on her heel and harrumphed away. It was the first time she'd stood up to Patrice and it was probably two years overdue.

She found Paul in the second studio, drafting a script for an upcoming series.

'You're supposed to be home with your feet up, aren't you?' His gaze dropped to the envelope in Lauren's hand. 'Tell me that's not what I think it is?' Removing his glasses, he sighed and polished the lenses on the end of his shirt. 'You don't need to do that, Lauren. Everyone stuffs up, you know. I could fill an entire show with the champagne radio moments.'

Some stations made a B-reel out of their 'champagne radio' moments, when their presenters went 'pop' all over the radio, or collected the audio from their on-air stuff-ups to play at the Christmas party. The thought of her mistake being replayed even once more made Lauren feel sick to her stomach.

Paul quirked an eyebrow and replaced his glasses. 'It's one hell of a drug, this live-radio gig, but every single person behind the mikes is imperfect. You, me, George, Nigel, even Patrice. Don't let this derail you.'

'I've already made up my mind,' Lauren said softly, handing the envelope over. She gulped down the lump in her throat and although her hands wouldn't quit trembling, she walked out with her head held high.

'How did you go?' Tahnee asked, answering her phone on the first ring.

Lauren backed out of the parking space as fast as she could. She'd held it together in front of her colleagues, but her composure was plummeting faster than a cray boat anchor. She filled Tahnee in as she headed for the highway.

'On a scale of joyous to rock bottom, I'd say it was about fair to middling,' she joked, hating the tell-tale squeak in her voice. *Don't you dare cry.*

'Well, at least it's behind you now,' Tahnee said, the *click-clack* of her heels on tiles echoing down the phone. 'You can put a line under it and move on.' She sounded so much like their mum, and Lauren wished she'd called April instead.

'Cool, yep,' Lauren said, feeling the heat rise across her cheeks. She was kidding herself if she'd thought Tahnee had softened in these last few weeks. *Maybe my judgement is completely up the creek.* 'You sound busy, I'll let you go.'

'Wait—'

Lauren heard the soft click of a door and a creak that sounded like their father's old leather chair. 'I've got a certain reputation to uphold at work,' Tahnee said, 'and I wouldn't hear the end of it if I started doling out fluffy life advice in the office.'

The traffic slowed and Lauren hesitated as the intersection loomed, making a last-minute decision to head west instead of north. 'Let me guess,' she said. 'If you were in my shoes, you'd book an appointment with the most expensive salon in town and pep yourself up with a spa day and a good hard look in the mirror? Or maybe I should buy another suit, one with bigger shoulder pads this time?'

Lauren knew it wasn't fair to take her anger out on Tahnee, but if she'd wanted a tough-love sermon, she would have called Gabrielle.

'No, Loz, I was going to tell you to do something for you. Maybe road-test a new hobby until you find something that sparks joy. Basket weaving, learning to play the tambourine, short story writing, pottery . . .'

Lauren thought of Fergus and Clarissa. '*Definitely* not pottery.'

'Well, something different,' Tahnee said. 'Could be hula hoop twirling, starting that podcast you talked about or blogging, for all I care. I'm not far off my forties, before I know it, I'll be the same age Dad was when he died, and as that birthday looms closer, I'm wondering what he'd make of all this.'

Lauren's breath caught as she passed a sign for the Southern Ports. 'He would've reminded us that we're Bickfords, and Bickford women always back themselves.'

Tahnee sighed. 'I'm not sure whether he really said that, or if Mum butchered a random remark and turned it into her own personal mantra.'

They were both silent for a moment, Lauren trying to recall when her sister had last uttered a word against their mother. High school, maybe? When the office phone trilled, Lauren expected Tahnee would end the call, but to her surprise, Tahnee let it ring out.

'Dad would have told us that everyone messes up, I think. And I've had an idea about the Mayor's petition. That list of signatures wouldn't hold any weight in court but if it's troubling Victor, or being used to threaten him, I can look into it if you like, make it disappear.'

'I can't ask that,' Lauren said, picking her jaw up off the floor. 'I've already got Mum offering assistance left, right and centre. I hate being needy.'

'You're not asking, I'm offering and you're not needy, you're *in need*. There's a clear difference. And sniffing out regulation breaches is my catnip. The mayor will pull her head in and be grovelling in no time.'

Tearing up, Lauren bit her lip and murmured her thanks.

'So what's this checklist you mentioned?'

Lauren looked at the notepad on the passenger seat. She and April had filled it with every idea that had popped into their heads. She could tick a few tasks off the shortlist, starting with *Make a clean break from the radio station* and *Tell Patrice to take a flying leap.*

'It's basically a road map for pulling up my socks and getting on with things. I don't know if it's batshit crazy or brilliant, but it's better than nothing.'

'You always did love a checklist.'

Lauren managed a laugh. 'I'll take any win I can at this stage. And if I have to write something on that list just for the satisfaction of crossing it off, then so be it.'

'Just promise me you'll add something fun to the list,' Tahnee said as they made their farewells. 'Something that's not about reparation or self-improvement or career progress. Something that makes you feel alive.'

Lauren scanned the horizon, thinking of the ocean awaiting her in Beachport and the long timber jetty she'd never been game enough to jump off. For the very first time in her life, Lauren felt one step ahead of her big sister.

'My bathers are already in the boot, jetty jumping's next on the list.'

'Oh,' Tahnee said, worry suffusing that one word. 'That's—'

Lauren braced for the sting of Tahnee's censure but instead, her sister sounded impressed.

'That's ballsy.'

24

Jack wasn't sure when winter had found its way to Penwarra, but as he drove through the quiet town after a late call-out, the radio on low and just his thoughts for company, the chimneys were crowned with smoke, the trees were bare and there were wheelbarrows of firewood tucked under verandahs. He turned onto Petticoat Lane.

The street was the oldest residential area in town, with nineteenth-century stone and timber cottages, immaculate gardens and lavender hedges, but it was the soft-pink weatherboard cottage that he was drawn to. He slowed as Lauren's white picket fence appeared in his headlights. While he hadn't intentionally set out to drive past Lauren's, the ute had somehow ended up here.

Shadows from the television flickered in the small lounge window and he saw the bathroom light flicker on. He hadn't heard her on the radio since the incident and judging by the odd hours she seemed to be keeping, she wasn't producing the breakfast show either. Was it because of him? Had his reaction to the on-air incident been the final straw? Jack wound down his window, regret creeping in with the icy night air.

Working was easier than dwelling on matters of the heart, but quiet nights sprinkled with minor call-outs were the prime time for Jack's mind to consider the 'what ifs'. He'd been so angry with himself for breaching workplace confidentiality and so cross with Lauren for highlighting it, he'd believed he had every reason to keep his distance from her.

Just get over yourself already, Jack told himself brusquely, making a U-turn and pulling up outside Lauren's cottage. He rummaged in the glove box and scribbled a note on the back of a rumpled envelope. Then he paused with his hand on the car door, nerves getting the better of him. The auto wipers kicked in as rain pelted down. Just as he was pulling the hood of his jacket over his head, the lights in Lauren's bathroom window went off. The lounge lights flickered off next and then the bedroom light, until it was black and still inside her cottage.

Sighing, Jack folded the note and pushed it back into his glove box. He knew from experience that her letterbox wasn't watertight. He could picture it now. Lauren would fish his soggy note from the bottom of the letterbox tomorrow morning, the writing indecipherable, and know for sure that he was too gutless to apologise in person.

Tomorrow, he told himself, but as he moved through the next day, and the one after that, the note stayed stashed in his glove box.

When he walked from the police station to the house later that week, Harriet was huddled on his doorstep, looking like a drowned cat with a school backpack.

'Harri!' He jogged across the driveway that divided the two buildings and gathered her in his arms. 'You're drenched. Where's Mum?'

Her shoulders shook and she hiccuped as she tried to speak through the tears. 'Mum's at work, so I'm coming to stay with you, Uncle Jack. Dad forgot to pick me up after school again.'

Again?

His jaw set, Jack unlocked the door and helped Harriet out of her sopping wet jacket. The sight of her in the oversized school jumper and mismatched socks warmed his heart. How had he managed so many weeks without her cheeky smile?

'I'll find you a towel and while you're in the shower, I'll see if there's anything in my wardrobe that might fit, okay? And I'd better let your mum know you're here, she'll be worried sick.'

Harriet stopped, her soggy socks squelching against the tiles as she spun around. 'You can't tell them. I don't want to go home when everyone's grumpy, Uncle Jack. I'll run away, I will.'

'Why's everyone grumpy?'

Her lip quivered and Jack knelt down so he could look into her eyes. It wasn't his place to meddle but he didn't like hearing things weren't peachy, especially if it was impacting Harriet.

'Mum's been cleaning everything, even when we've already done it, and her eyes are crinkly more often, but not because she's happy.'

Jack's breath caught in his throat.

'And Dad said we could get a puppy and it could sleep on my bed but it's been ages and ages and we haven't got one yet. Mum says if we do get a dog, it's not coming inside but Dad says it can. And he doesn't like pudding *or* doll's tea parties.' She said the last bit as if it were the most contentious issue of all.

'Maybe you can stay for a game of cards and a Milo, then?'

'And some baking?' she said, and when she smiled hopefully, Jack saw she'd lost another tooth. What else had he missed?

'We'll see,' he said, taking her tiny hand in his and giving it a squeeze.

Clem's reply came through when Harriet was perched at the kitchen bench, wearing one of Jack's black t-shirts and a hoodie that came down to her ankles, a pair of his socks pulled up to her knees and a leather belt looped almost twice around her middle.

'Mum says you can stay for a little bit, kiddo,' he said, taking the empty mug from his niece and washing the dregs of Milo down the sink. He handed her a bran muffin and took the last one for himself.

'Okay,' she said with a nod. 'These are yummy, Uncle Jack, is it one of Lauren's recipes?'

Jack paused mid-bite then slowly shook his head. 'They're from the Penwarra Show cookbook, but they're from a lady called Heather.'

'Oh, yeah, Mum and me made these ones too. Aunty Jean says Heather's one of the best cooks in the district. Did Lauren interview her on the radio too?'

Jack turned his attention to the phone, tapping back a response to Clem and trying to ignore the pain that came each time he thought of Harriet and Lauren chatting in the farmhouse kitchen; Harriet sitting on Lauren's sofa with the galah perched on her shoulder; Harriet begging Lauren to come rollerskating.

He looked up to see his niece at the bookcase, pulling a box from the board-games shelf.

'We don't have time for a game of Scrabble tonight, sorry, Harri.'

'Can we go see Gary? I've got some new words to teach him.'

Words she'd heard from Dunkirk or the Penwarra Primary School playground? He wasn't sure which would be a better answer.

Harriet's oversized socks came loose as she walked, tripping her, and Scrabble tiles burst out from the box, spilling across the kitchen floor.

'Oh no!' she gasped, her wide eyes filling with tears. 'I can't do anything right. I can't sleep in Mum's bed anymore, I can't watch my TV shows or bake biscuits after school. I can't do anything.'

'Hey, it's okay,' he said, brushing a teardrop from her cheek. 'In fact, you know what my nan used to do with Scrabble pieces when your mum and I were little?'

She shook her head. Remembering the gentle guidance of his grandparents, Jack crouched down beside her and pointed to the letter tiles, picking out the letters of their surname.

'That's my last name,' Harriet sniffled as he arranged the Scrabble tiles on the floor to spell Crossley.

'*Our* last name,' Jack corrected, passing her an H, T and two R tiles. 'See if you can find the rest of your tiles and I'll find mine.'

'I like this game,' Harriet said, digging through the tiles to find Clem's name next.

'Sometimes we had to add a few pets or filler words,' Jack said, 'to make all the names lock together, and other times we put Penwarra in, or Nan and Pop's full names, but they always made sure there was room for everyone,' he said, spelling out 'sister'.

Soon enough, they had seven words on the board.

'What's this word again?'

Jack looked where Harriet had pointed. 'That spells "family",' he said, and saw there was an opening off the letter 'a' where Lauren's name would fit right in.

It's too late now, he thought as he drove past Petticoat Lane on his way to drop Harriet home.

Arthur's gravelly voice echoed through his mind: *You miss all the shots you don't take.*

'Right, Harri, you'd better run inside before you get drenched again,' he said, pulling up next to the farmhouse's front door.

'And next time, let's work out a plan that doesn't involve running away from home or dodging the school pick-up line.'

'O-kay,' she said reluctantly, fumbling with her seatbelt.

Through the sheets of rain, Jack watched Clem open the front door. Even from twenty metres away, her pregnant belly was unmistakable. Jack tugged on the handbrake and was about to follow Harriet in when Adam Dunkirk stepped out beside Clem, one arm around her and the other outstretched to welcome Harriet home.

And despite her earlier tears, Harriet ran straight to him.

Jack put the ute into gear. There was no place for him here, not anymore.

25

'Good weather for ducks,' chortled the community radio station manager, Wayne, as Lauren dripped her way inside. 'You'll catch your death if you stand out in that August deluge much longer. Come in, I'll fix you a hot drink and bikkie.'

After shaking out her jacket, Lauren gratefully accepted the coffee. Waking up early for breakfast radio was one thing, staying awake for the evening slots was a whole other ball game, and she hadn't yet mastered the perfect ratio of caffeine and daytime naps.

Wayne offered the biscuit tin, crumbs still clinging to his straggly white beard. Lauren thought of Jack's grandfather, Arthur. For the last few months, she'd worked hard to push Jack to the back of her mind, just like the storm that had flared up over her on-air catastrophe. As the therapist she'd started seeing had predicted, the incident *had* died down the moment the next scandal came along, but the memory made Lauren cringe all the same.

'Maybe just one biscuit,' she conceded.

The community station had been like a second home during her uni school holidays, but now she felt too old for the Gen Z crew with their loose work ethic and large social lives, and about forty years too young to fit in with the older crew who treated their weekly programs like their life purpose.

Wayne opened the office door, moving a pile of faded newspapers off the chair so Lauren could sit. 'You mind filling in for Perry tonight? His hip replacement was brought forward a few days. He's put together a few running sheets, but I've seen you in action, and after the way you sailed through the heavy metal show last Friday night and then the gospel program on Sunday morning, I'm sure you can breeze through this one.'

Lauren grinned. 'I'll give it a crack.'

'And how's sponsorship for the spring advertising special?' Wayne looked at the spreadsheet she'd brought with her, nodding as he recognised the names of local businesses she'd approached. Presenting on the community radio station was completely voluntary of course, but between her mornings managing social media for the local organic farming collective and afternoons handling the station's sponsorship sales, she made enough money to get by.

Still a far cry from presenting breakfast for a national broadcaster or even producing, though . . . The recurring thought was like the tip of a rose thorn in her finger, easier to ignore when she wasn't poking and prodding it. Lauren gulped down the last of her coffee and set to work.

After three hours cold-calling small businesses to drum up advertising dollars, Lauren had earned enough in commission to keep Gary in almonds and Iced VoVos for another week or two. She donned the headphones and settled herself in the presenter's chair. The classical music was calm and soothing, with just a few callers to pass the time.

She headed home in the dark, leaving the twinkling lights of the state's largest regional city behind her as she drove back to Penwarra. It wasn't a big life, but she'd already tried that on for size, and look where it had got her: publicly humiliated and heartbroken.

She'd been right all along . . . It was much safer staying in her own lane.

Jack finished his morning laps in good time, washed off the chlorine with a quick shower and dressed for work. He detoured to the supermarket on his way home to collect the extra supplies he needed for Harriet's birthday party later in the week. And just as he was bagging up the groceries, April Lacey appeared at the checkout beside him, phone pressed against her ear. A birthday card and packet of candles sat atop a mountain of chocolate in April's basket.

Lauren's birthday?

He waited by the counter as April ended her call and purchased a tray of Lindt, an extra-large box of Roses, Ferreros and Favourites, plus a length of Toblerone.

'Oh, Jack! Hi,' April said. She swept her dark fringe from her eyes and eyed the icing sugar and wrapping paper in his hands. 'Are you doing some sneaky birthday shopping too?'

'For my niece,' he said, glancing at her basket. 'But am I right in guessing it's Lauren's birthday soon?'

'Sure is.'

'Is she—' Jack paused, choosing his words carefully. 'Is she doing okay?' He wasn't sure what would be worse, hearing that she was loving life and had moved on without a backwards glance or discovering she was as miserable as him.

April waved a hand. 'I'm not sure she's over the hump yet, but there's plenty to do at the community station and the team there have welcomed her back with open arms. I'm pretty sure she's doing an afternoon slot today and then backing it up with Classics Up Late tonight. Not exactly her niche, but after the disaster on air . . .'

Jack cringed, knowing his overreaction was partly to blame for this whole series of events. 'I wish it hadn't worked out that way,' he said. 'When you see her—' He stopped abruptly. It would be a cop-out to send her second-hand birthday wishes.

'I might be wrong, but I'm pretty sure she'd be happy to hear from you,' April said, glancing at her watch. 'I'd better get a wriggle on, we've got guests checking out of Kookaburra Cottage and an early check-in scheduled. The start of spring always brings the holiday-makers out in force.'

Jack thought about Lauren and last year's birthday dinner as he drove out of the Foodland parking lot. Sammi was already at the desk when he arrived at the police station.

'Who knew Tuesdays could be so busy?' she said, handing him three phone messages. 'Mrs Spencer called to say someone's cat-napped her beloved Tintin, so I promised you'd call in.'

Jack groaned. 'You didn't, did you? Remember how long she kept me last time, when she thought someone had stolen her dog Bonnie? Did she check the garden shed before calling this time, or ask Mr Spencer if he's taken the cat for a vet check-up?'

'Yes and yes,' Sammi said with a grin. 'But she insisted you investigate. You've also got a few documents that need serving today, and if you've got a moment before you finish your shift, you might want to have a word with the young couple that brought the Gregsons' property. Logan said they've got a loose approach to road-worthiness and the neighbour also called with a complaint about reckless driving. Says they're treating Finch Road like a rally track.'

Jack kitted up and headed out the door again.

Mrs Spencer met him at the gate with a plate of ginger biscuits and a framed watercolour of the missing tabby cat.

'An extraordinarily long tail, you see,' she said, tapping the glass. 'Very handsome fellow, our Tintin. Someone would've taken him, mark my words,' she said, swapping the painting for a handwritten list.

'And what's this?' Jack asked, politely declining the biscuits and the offer of tea in the sitting room, and taking the piece of paper she handed him.

'A list of suspects.' Mrs Spencer nodded. 'You can take it with you, I've made a copy for myself. And I'm going to call that lovely young lass at the community station too, see if she'll do a news article on it, or at the very least a classified. Someone out there must know what's happened to Tintin.'

Lauren. After eight weeks of ignoring the ache in his heart, there it was again, like a sucker punch to the chest for the second time in the same day.

'I'll do my best,' Jack promised, then left to make his way out to the hobby farms on the outskirts of town. He called Logan as he drove. 'So what am I looking at here, mate? Unsecured loads? An unroadworthy ute? A rusty trailer hanging together with baling twine?'

In the background, he heard dogs barking, the persistent sound of indignant cattle and the call of an auctioneer. Sale day at the cattle yards.

'All of the above,' Logan said, explaining how the couple had purchased a pen of sheep and loaded them into a dodgy trailer. 'Nice pair, but wait until you see their stock crate.'

The trailer was parked in the driveway when Jack arrived. Just like Logan had described, instead of a fixed stock crate, the couple had fashioned a makeshift crate from four farm gates held together with chunky cable ties and tied down with ropes. It had been years since he'd been on traffic detail, but he was pretty sure his former colleagues would have booked them for such a hodgepodge contraption.

'It did the trick,' the young bloke said cheerfully, tugging on the truckie's knots that secured the gates to the box trailer. 'Got the new sheep from A to B without a hiccup, and saved us a few bucks.'

Even at a glance, Jack could see the old Mazda ute was equally low on the priority list.

'We've only just bought the place,' the young woman added with a big grin. 'Starting small with sheep, but hopefully we'll have cattle before long.'

'We've just fixed the dodgiest fences on the new block and added a strand of barbed wire on top for good measure,' the bloke said, rolling up his sleeves to show the evidence of his fencing. 'That's just the start, though. We've troughs to repair, an old dairy to reroof, endless rocks and sticks that need clearing and we're halfway through building a new set of sheep yards. Should be cemented in by the end of the week.'

'I'm campaigning for some dairy bull calves,' the woman added, 'then we'll get the joy of bottle feeding too.'

'The joy?' Her husband chuckled, putting an arm around her. 'You'll be sick of it before long. Just wait until we have kids, then you'll be ditching all these plans for ducklings, orphaned lambs and bottle-reared calves.'

Jack couldn't help a twinge of loneliness. He could picture the Gregsons setting up their hobby farm, digging the footings for new sheep yards, dividing paddocks into smaller blocks, and building a house, a garden and a life together. From the look of their battered ute and unconventional trailer, they weren't rolling in cash, but there was something enviable about their giddy excitement and the future they could see in front of them.

'Well, you'd better fix your car first. I don't want to stick a canary on it, but that crack in the windscreen's a shocker, your tyres are bald and the exhaust looks like it's hanging on with fencing wire. And keep an eye on the speedo when you're on these backroads. Plenty of old farmers around here who like their roads quiet and aren't afraid to pipe up when there's a noisy ute thrashing around.'

Jack returned to the patrol car. 'I'll be back in a week to check the car. Good luck with those sheep yards. Neither will be a cheap exercise.'

'Worth it, though,' the woman said, squeezing her husband's hand.

Jack drove off their property, wondering when he'd last felt a similar rush of excitement for the future. He thought of the board games he and Lauren had played on quiet nights together, then the day he'd hiked the Woakwine Cutting with her. They'd worked so well as a team, removing ticks from the blue-tongue lizard and releasing the reptile back into the scrub, and although there was nothing astounding about the task they'd completed, he'd hoped it would be the first of many such rescues, with plenty more quiet evenings on the horizon—just him, Lauren and a game of Scrabble, Cluedo or Monopoly.

It had been weeks since he'd stopped writing text messages to Lauren and deleting them before he could hit send, and that handwritten note was still stashed in his glove box. Were the rush of romance and excitement for the future worth the risk or the fallout if—*not if, when*—things went pear-shaped?

He eased out a breath. Sparkly bright futures were for fairytales, not real life, and the sooner he remembered that, the sooner he could get back on track. Only a fool would keep making the same mistakes again and again.

Maybe Victor Jenkins was right. Maybe it was easier to live in a mess of your own creation and be a little lonely from time to time than live on other people's terms and risk your heart being shattered.

In a practical sense, it sounded like a tough but necessary decision, but in Jack's heart, the idea made him feel as empty as a woodshed at the end of a wet winter.

Lauren arrived home to find a little white BMW in the driveway and Tahnee dozing on the couch, a pair of three-inch stiletto heels peeking out from under the throw rug. She blinked sleepily as Lauren locked the door behind her.

'Hey,' Tahnee said, rubbing her eyes and stifling a yawn. She got off the couch, and Lauren's jaw dropped at the sight of her sister's outfit. As well as the sky-high heels, Tahnee was wearing a leather miniskirt and a sheer black blouse.

'Where the hell have you come from? The catwalk?'

A cloud of Dior perfume engulfed Lauren as Tahnee leaned in to kiss her. 'I was supposed to be going to a hen's night in Naracoorte, but the bride was sick and I was already halfway from Adelaide when it was cancelled. I thought you and I might hit the town instead? Early birthday celebrations?'

Lauren's shoulders shook as she laughed. 'Thanks, Tahns, I needed a laugh. What are you really doing here?' She grabbed a handful of kindling, coaxed the red coals into flames and warmed her hands by the wood fire.

'Seriously,' Tahnee said, looking hurt. 'I'm in the mood for dancing. We'll hit the old spots, remember what it was like to be footloose and fancy free!'

'Is this the same girl who turned her nose up at the selection of single men on show night? And I'm not sure if you noticed, but it's chilly out there. I'm cold just looking at you.'

'Lauren, please.' Tahnee was pouring them both a glass of wine, so she didn't see Lauren's double take.

Please? Who was this doppelgänger and what had she done with bossy, no-nonsense Tahnee?

'I've got hen's nights, baby showers and wedding invites coming out my ears. The Tinder landscape is dire in the city and if I get matched with another self-absorbed gym junkie investment banker, I'm going to scream.' She took a sip of wine and raised her eyes to meet Lauren's. 'And Mum is driving me up the wall. Now that she's not fixated on your career, she's homing in on me. I love her, but, Christ, that woman needs to take a chill pill.'

Lauren let out a snort of laughter. 'You've only just realised that now?'

Tahnee's heels clicked against the floor as she huddled close to show Lauren her phone. 'See this?'

Lauren watched as a search for 'egg freezing services near me' appeared on her sister's phone.

'It's terrifying stuff! And the worst bit?' Tahnee refilled her glass. 'Now it's all I can think about. And you know what else I can't get out of my head?'

Lauren was struggling to keep up. Her big sister, who had always been so sure of her place in the corporate world, was normally so focused and driven and career orientated.

'Those country blokes you had on your radio show when you were doing the show feature. The dairy farmer who makes a dairy-themed scarecrow year in, year out. The bloke repainting the horse jumps in his spare time; the guy who entered the home-brew competition with beer made from hops he'd grown on his back deck; the man in charge of the speed shears. I've even started watching *Farmer Wants a Wife*, Lauren, and I'm waking up in the middle of the night, not thinking about lawsuits, but about a bloke who can fix things, build things, grow things.'

Lauren snorted with laughter. Not so long ago, Tahnee had called that program complete rubbish and said it should be *Farmer Wants a Life*.

Tahnee set down her empty glass before marching Lauren to her bedroom. 'So my birthday present to you is me, at my most vulnerable, begging you to help me get this madness out of my system so I can go back to normal.'

'How about a nice, quiet game of Scrabble instead? I'll let you start first.'

'Pffft. Not happening, Lauren. You shower, I'll choose your clothes.'

In the bathroom, Lauren undressed, her mind going to Jack again. She'd kept her word about giving him space, and while she didn't owe him anything, she hadn't been out to the local pubs, and certainly not dancing. She didn't want another man in her life and she couldn't face running into him or Fergus.

But wasn't that what her therapist had encouraged her to do? Put herself in new situations and sit with the discomfort, and not try to live with no fear, but less fear. It was one of the reasons she'd put her hand up for fill-in roles at the community station. She didn't know her Beethoven from her Mozart, and the uncertainty about the future was at times debilitating, but she was leaning into the discomfort.

After her shower, Lauren swept her hair into a high bun and studied the pale-blue strapless dress Tahnee had found at the back of her wardrobe. 'Great for the night clubs in Adelaide, but definitely not right for Penwarra.'

Tahnee waved off her protests, dabbing a little glitter onto Lauren's cheekbones, but Lauren was firm.

'If we're going out tonight, I'm choosing the dresses. And your blouse is gorgeous, but I dare say it'll scare the pants off anyone within cooee of here.' She reached for a linen top and handed it to Tahnee.

Loud music was pumping out the doorways and windows of the Oak & Anchor when they arrived. It was a spot Lauren had snuck into as a seventeen-year-old, but somewhere along the way, it had lost the grungy pub vibe and been refreshed as a trendy live music venue.

'I'm going to need shots for this,' Lauren said, following Tahnee into the venue. She ordered tequila.

'So there's your sense of adventure!' Tahnee called, sprinkling salt onto the back of their hands.

The shots burned all the way down and Lauren slapped the bar with her hand, sucking the lemon wedge as Tahnee hooted with laughter.

'That's horrendous.'

Tahnee ordered them another round.

It didn't take long for the tequila to work its magic, taking the edge off Lauren's nerves, and soon her shoulders were swinging in time to the music. The glitter on her cheekbones shimmered in the periphery of her vision as the strobe lights started up.

'I told you this would be fun,' Tahnee said, scanning the dance floor. 'Who knew sleepy little Penwarra had such a strong social scene?'

The place was pumping now and a fresh wave of lads rolled in through the door, catching Tahnee's attention.

'Now here's a likely bunch,' she said, checking her reflection in her mirrored phone case. 'Nice shirts, R.M. boots and belts. You get the shots, I'll powder my nose.'

Lauren made for the bar and with April's warning in her ear—*too many tequilas and you'll be anyone's*—opted for something lighter.

She carried the sparkling shiraz across the room, surveying the crowd as she went. There was no sign of Jack Crossley, either in uniform or civvies, and she tried to bite back the one per cent of her that was disappointed.

A familiar face caught her eye across the room. 'Hey, I know you!'

Setting down her glass, Lauren joined Eamon from the Langhorne Creek wedding. Just like that night in the Fleurieu Peninsular, he was grooving with the music.

'The karaoke queen,' he said, kissing her cheek. 'So good to see you.' He glanced around, a question in his eyes. 'Where's Jack?'

Lauren took a gulp of the sparkling shiraz, trying to wash down the ache that arose at the mention of Jack, and spluttered when the bubbles went down the wrong way.

'Steady on there,' Eamon said, thumping her back.

Lauren stumbled, caught off guard by the gesture, and before she knew it, shiraz was splashed across Eamon's shirt, his tan slacks and R.M. Williams boots.

'I'm so sorry,' she said, sobering up fast.

'This takes me right back to my B & S days,' Eamon said, shaking the drips off his hand with a rueful laugh. 'I think I'm to blame for the spill anyway. Can I get you a fresh one?'

Lauren looked at the wine glass. 'I should probably quit while I'm ahead,' she said.

'Have you been dancing yet?'

She shook her head.

Eamon tipped his head to the bar. 'In that case, you really need another drink, then a dance. So where did you say Jack was?'

'I haven't seen him in months,' she said.

'Might head out to Sunny Cross Farm tomorrow before my mates drag me around the wineries. See how Clem's getting on, call into the cop shop and say g'day to Jack.'

Lauren allowed Eamon to steer her to the bar, his hand light against the small of her back, and tried not to picture Jack in the police station, Jack swimming laps at the pool, or Jack wishing her 'happy birthday' on her verandah last year, after crayfish, wine and lemon tart.

She closed her eyes a beat, forcing herself to focus on Eamon's story about the uni mates he was catching up with tomorrow. They'd almost finished their drinks when Tahnee returned.

'This is Jack and Clem's cousin, Eamon,' Lauren yelled over the music, which seemed to be getting louder as the night wore on. 'Absolute demon on the dance floor and you should hear him sing.'

Another round of tequila shots appeared in front of them. *Don't be a party pooper,* Lauren told herself, licking the salt off her hand and throwing back the fiery liquor. They moved as a group onto the dance floor, forming a circle and cheering as each person had a turn dancing in the middle.

Somewhere between Gloria Gaynor's 'I Will Survive' and Ed Sheeran's 'Shivers', Lauren realised the crowd had thinned out and there were only half-a-dozen of them left. The lights flickered on and the bar staff started stacking chairs onto tables.

'It's too early to call it a night yet,' Tahnee hiccuped indignantly. 'Come back to ours for a nightcap.'

A cheer went up from within the group.

'Ours?' Lauren groaned. 'I'm ready for bed.'

'The night is young! One drink,' said one of the girls— Kirsten? Kristen? Kristy? Lauren couldn't recall her name, but she allowed herself to be swept up in the enthusiastic campaign.

The wind stung Lauren's cheeks and rain lashed at her bare arms and legs as they dashed across the footpath towards a waiting taxi. Laughing and giggling, they piled into the cab, then tumbled out at Petticoat Lane, cheering when Tahnee accepted Eamon's offer of a piggyback ride down the driveway.

'One drink,' Lauren vowed, shushing them and glancing at Val's house next door.

Lauren's cottage felt much smaller with six people inside.

'So what'll it be? Bubbles?' Tahnee said, looking in the fridge. 'I bet Loz has vodka in the freezer too.'

Lauren blinked at the wine bottles as Tahnee popped the corks. While it had felt good to let loose at the pub, it seemed wasteful to be drinking top-shelf wine from her best friend's vineyard when she was halfway to being drunk.

'Say cheeeeeese,' called one of Tahnee's new friends, leaning in close and snapping a selfie of them. Eamon crammed into the photo, hamming it up by pretending to neck the sparkling wine.

The room spun as Lauren hurried to the loo, and she realised she was *more* than halfway to being drunk. She paused in the bathroom door, listening to the conversation. They were playing Seven Degrees of Separation and Lauren laughed as Tahnee and one of the other girls realised they'd been at uni at the same time.

'Remember share-house living?' said Tahnee's friend. 'Drinking out of jam jars, living on two-minute noodles. Hard to believe we had such low standards. I couldn't imagine sharing a house again, my sister was the worst housemate ever. Treated the place like a tip and thought I'd tidy up after her like our folks did.'

'Ugh, living with siblings is the worst!' someone else added.

'You obviously get along well with Lauren?' It was Eamon asking the question now and Lauren's breath caught in her throat as she waited for Tahnee's answer.

How long had she spent feeling like she'd never lived up to Tahnee's high standards and good grades? How many years had their mum pressed Tahnee's school dresses and starched the collar on her blazer as she accepted award after award, Dux of Year 12, university scholarships. Three months ago, she would have expected Tahnee's answer to be something ambivalent, the kind of compliment sandwich their mum gave: *Lauren's got so much potential, if only she'd try harder. She's my sister, of course I love her, despite her faults. Lauren needs someone to push her along, I hate to think what type of mess she'd make of things if I wasn't propping her up. You should see the work I had to do to help dig her out of the latest disaster.*

But now . . . Lauren wasn't sure whether it was the tequila or the tiredness that was rolling in like sets of waves, but Tahnee's answer came as a shock.

'She's amazing, and don't tell her I said this, because I think it's supposed to be the other way around, but I look up to her. Lauren's got a way with people, a way with words, the kind of warmth you can't find in textbooks. She sees the good in everyone else, though she's not so good at seeing it in herself.'

She's drunk, that's all, Lauren told herself. But she couldn't deny there was something affirming about hearing those words.

There hadn't been many idle moments in his workday, but whenever his phone wasn't ringing and he wasn't knee-deep in scrap steel, permits or paperwork, Jack couldn't stop his thoughts straying to Lauren. Would she be kicking up her heels with her friends this weekend, a raucous rendition of 'Happy Birthday' floating through a Mount Gambier restaurant? He could picture her cutting up the dance floor, dragging her friends to a karaoke bar.

It was easier to stomach than imagining her out for dinner, an intimate evening for two with someone new. Or perhaps there'd be slow dancing—

He blinked away the image.

'You coming, Jack, or shall I leave you to lock up?' Sammi called from the sliding door.

'I'm done here too,' Jack replied. 'Don't let me hold you up, Sammi. I'll sort it.'

'Good luck with Harriet's birthday cake, I want photos,' she called and then the door shut behind her.

The birthday cake . . . It had been months since he'd set foot inside the kitchen at Sunny Cross Farm, and while it had been tough keeping his distance from Clem and especially Harriet, it had been easy steering clear of Adam Dunkirk. So why on earth had he let Harriet convince him to break his vow this Sunday?

It was a stupid question; he'd scale a cliff for that kid.

They'd managed only three more catch-ups since the time Dunkirk had forgotten to pick her up, and from Harriet's chatty reports, the mood in the farmhouse hadn't improved.

Just two hours, he told himself. Surely he could put up with Adam Dropkick Dunkirk for two hours?

He locked the police station, walked to the house and changed into civvies.

He was halfway through sifting flour into a mixing bowl when his phone buzzed.

'Vic, is everything okay?'

Phone calls from Victor were only slightly more frequent than house visits and an uneasy feeling stirred in Jack's guts.

'You won't believe what's happened,' Victor said.

Jack sat the sieve on the bench, a cloud of powder going everywhere, and reached for his patrol keys. 'Why? What's up?'

But to Jack's confusion, instead of reporting a barrage of verbal abuse from an irate neighbour or another nasty note in his mailbox, Victor laughed, coughed and then sniffed.

Jack paused, one arm inside his kit vest and the other still holding the phone.

'Kev's been in touch,' Victor said. 'He just called me.'

Jack felt his shoulders easing as he sank into the leather armchair. 'You're joking? After all these years? Is he okay?'

'I'll find out soon enough. He's been overseas, in and out of work, even done a few years behind bars. But he's alive, Jack, and he called, and that's more than I thought I'd ever get.'

'You wouldn't bloody read about it,' Jack murmured, feeling both relieved for Victor and sad that he and his son had missed such a big chunk of one another's lives.

'Tread carefully, Vic. Make sure it's really Kev before you get too excited. Find out if he wants something from you. Some people get their kicks out of interfering with old missing persons cases. If he asks you for money, or tries to—'

'I didn't come down in the last shower, mate,' Victor said over the top of him. 'I'm not rolling out the red carpet just yet. But if he does come, and I hope he will, then I'll know him a mile away. Those wingnut ears won't have shrunk with age, and if there's still any doubt, I'll stand him in front of that massive sculpture you made me.'

Sebastian, Cohen and Jack had shifted the scrap metal eagle from the shed at Sunny Cross Farm to Victor's property, and their help had been invaluable as Jack fixed it in place—right by Victor's front gate on Wallaby Lane.

'If Kev doesn't say a thing about the Ford Falcon badge you've used,' Victor continued, 'I'll know it's not him. Oh, and by the way, the petition's been dropped. Not sure whether the mayor came to her senses or whether she grew a heart, but I ain't arguing.'

Jack smiled to himself as he ended the call. He took his arm out of the police vest and returned to the kitchen.

He creamed butter with sugar and swirled eggs through the cake batter, mixing them after each addition, and wondering whether Victor had shared the good news with Lauren. He knew that the gross breach of privacy would still weigh on her conscience, too, months later.

Jack swallowed hard, trying to quell the urge to send her a message. His head was telling him not to touch the topic with a ten-foot barge pole, but his heart, and all the parts of him that missed Lauren's laugh, missed the way she made him feel, were pushing him to press forward.

Jack dropped the spatula. He didn't have time to stand here idly, deliberating on love and loyalty. But as he looked out the kitchen window and saw the paddock behind the police station illuminated by an amazing sunset, he knew he couldn't leave things the way they were. Lauren deserved to know some good had come of the mistakes she'd made. The mistakes he'd made too.

Pulling his phone from his pocket, he stepped outside and snapped a photo of the sun lightening the clouds and casting a golden glow on the neighbourhood. What was it Lauren called those clouds? He remembered the sunrises and sunsets they'd shared, and how she'd likened the fluffy, cotton-wool ball clouds to computer-generated images found in movie backgrounds.

His fingers flew across the phone.

Found you some Pixar clouds.

He paused, deliberating over the next part of the message. He'd learned the hard way that he shouldn't share private information, but if Lauren called Victor for an update and Victor told her what had unfolded, then he wasn't officially breaking police protocol.

Not sure if you've heard from Vic but things are working out okay for him. PS happy birthday for tomorrow x

He hit send before he could change his mind.

26

Lauren dragged herself to the door on 16 September, regret as well as Gary's shrieking thumping in her ears.

'I'm coming, calm the farm,' she mumbled, answering the door to find April and Connor with an armful of chocolate.

'Happy birthday!' April sang, pulling a party blower from her pocket and putting it to her lips.

'For the love of God, please don't blow that,' Lauren said, squeezing her eyes shut and clamping her hands over her ears. 'Give me five minutes, I need to get dressed.'

When she returned to the lounge, Connor had confiscated the noisy toy, set out the mugs and located the tea bags. A double-tier cake had somehow appeared on the kitchen bench and April was holding her hands up in apology. 'Sorry,' she said in a stage whisper, reaching out for a hug. 'Did you have a big pre-birthday bash?'

'Tahnee staged a coup and there was tequila involved.'

They moved into the lounge room and the girls settled on the couch.

'Enough said,' Connor said with a grin. 'How about I make us a cuppa?'

'Tahnee?' April rolled her eyes. 'Don't tell me she was here for another career intervention? Is Gabrielle here too?'

Lauren had opened her mouth to reply when the toilet flushed and Eamon emerged from the bathroom wearing just boxer shorts.

Connor nodded at him. 'Alright, mate?'

'Pleased to meet you, I'm Eamon,' he said, the scent of alcohol and sleep rolling off him as stepped closer for a handshake.

April's mouth hung open. 'Who the hell's *that*?'

Eamon declined an offer of tea from Connor, but accepted April's shellshocked offer of a Ferrero Rocher from the brimming gift bag, before turning and walking down the corridor.

It wasn't until he disappeared behind the guestroom door that Lauren burst out laughing.

'I'm *never* going to let Tahnee live this one down,' Lauren said.

'I thought he was with *you*,' April said.

'It was a big night, but I'm bloody sure I'd have the good sense not to hook up with Jack's cousin. Tahnee on the other hand . . .'

April unwrapped another chocolate as Lauren explained, starting with Tahnee's revelation that her biological clock was ticking and ending with the conversation Lauren had overheard.

'I'm glad to hear that Tahnee really is supportive, but Lauren—' April laughed, shaking her head. 'I could have told you all that. I know the team at Rural AM miss you too. Paul traipsed into Lacewing Estate last weekend, trying to track down your favourite bottle of sparkling red, and I even bumped into Jack yesterday morning. He asked after you.'

Lauren reached for the bag of chocolates, busying herself with the Ferreros. She shook her head. 'Don't,' she said, wrestling a gold-foil-covered ball from the tray and silencing her friend's protests with a hand. 'Not today. It's my birthday and we are *not* going down the Jack Crossley path. He messaged me last night, you know.'

April sat bolt upright. 'And?'

'Not an apology, not a "miss you". Nothing. Nada!'

'But you still like him, I can tell.'

Lauren popped a chocolate in April's mouth before she got on a roll. 'My birthday, my rules. And I'm not starting the day dwelling on something I can't change. And before you say anything else, I'm happy at 106.6FM. It's not a bucket-list job but it's not high pressure either.'

But even as she said it, Lauren thought of the regulars that used to call her at the AM station several times a week, recalled the programs she'd presented without a single stumble or stutter and how she'd felt invincible afterwards. She missed getting to know her listeners, anticipating which songs and conversation topics would light up the switchboard, and receiving news tips from locals in the supermarket aisles.

'And Archie asked me to tell you his Instagram page for the giant pumpkins is going gangbusters. His page's got a thousand followers already, all thanks to your shout-out. The show committee's going to have a flood of entries in the giant pumpkin contest next year if these enthusiasts are anything to go by.'

Lauren sighed and buried her head in her hands. 'I can't bear the thought of looking like a loser, crawling back to the station with my tail between my legs, only to glitch on air again.'

'You're human, Lauren, like every single one of us,' April said, reaching into the gift bag and passing her another box of chocolates.

After they'd eaten their fill of chocolate, sampled a slice of April's cake for breakfast and teased a sheepish Tahnee when she emerged from the bedroom with mussed hair and burning cheeks, they pulled on their jackets and headed for the door.

'We're off to the markets, text me if you need anything,' Lauren called as they left.

Gary let out an ear-splitting squawk. 'Piss off, Curly!' the bird said, bobbing up and down on his perch.

Lauren backtracked into the kitchen, upended half-a-dozen almonds into his aviary and stroked the side of his cheek. 'Shush, you'll give the lovebirds a headache.'

The town square was a hive of activity and they barely made it past one stall before getting swept up in conversation. The locals seemed happy to see her; a laugh here, a smile there, little updates on town happenings. It felt like a weight was off her shoulders, and as they chose picnicky fare for her birthday lunch, Lauren couldn't help thinking that maybe she'd been wrong about a few things. Maybe it wasn't pride stopping her, it was fear of failing.

'I was dreading this,' Lauren told April as Connor stepped away to shop at a seafood stall.

'What, your re-entry to civilisation? Were you expecting people to shun you? Think they were sitting at home sharpening their pitch forks, ready for the moment you emerged from hiding?'

'Maybe not pitch forks, but I thought I'd get a few scathing looks,' Lauren admitted. 'I think I'd built it up in my head that I'd be walking out into the street with a target on my back. Months of shopping in Mount Gambier, months denying myself the best vanilla slice in all of South Australia, almost five months thinking I'd let the whole town down.'

'Penwarra loves you, Lauren.' April looped an arm through Lauren's, pulling her close. 'And you're thirty-four now, older and wiser than ever.'

'I think it's going to be a good year ahead,' Lauren said. 'I'm going to do better, starting right now. Did I tell you I've been seeing someone?'

'Like Mr Beefcake in the cottage this morning? I mean, I'm sure he's a nice guy but—'

Lauren juggled her bags of fresh produce. 'Not *seeing* seeing. I mean I've been talking to a counsellor. About my anxiety.'

April's joking evaporated and in her hesitation, Lauren's thoughts began that nervous whirr that prefaced the racing. She'd heard so many 'helpful' comments that she instinctively braced herself for whatever April was about to say. She switched the shopping bag to her other arm. It was full of olives, salami, baguettes and cheese, and getting heavier by the minute.

'That must be tough,' April said. 'I'd like to hear about it, if you ever want to share. No pressure, though.'

'Thanks.' Lauren nodded. 'I'm trying to get better at talking about it, especially after the panic attack at the station. Most of the time, I'm pretty good at masking it, but I'm working on being kinder to myself.'

'Has it always been like that?'

And as shoppers meandered through the markets with shopping bags and baskets, Lauren opened up about the tough times she'd kept close to her chest.

'I wish I'd known,' April said. 'I can't believe you'd ever want to go back on air after all that.'

Lauren gave her a wry smile and paused as a fishmonger shouted out a two-for-one deal on Coorong mullet. 'That's the funny thing, the radio stuff is addictive,' she said. 'It's probably as close to drugs as I want to get, and when it's going well, it's the best feeling ever. But that icky in-between, when you're about to go live, or you stuff-up on air, they're the polar opposite. And I was handling it pretty well, until Patrice started ramping up again and I made the mother of all stuff-ups.'

Connor walked back with not one but three different jars of pickled octopus, a bag of mullet and two types of dipping sauce.

'The salesman saw you coming a mile away,' Lauren joked.

'It was the British accent. He knew I couldn't resist the lure of fresh South Aussie seafood, especially if I don't have to catch it myself. So, what have I missed?' He smiled broadly, looking between the two of them.

'Way too much to recap,' April said and laughed, leading them through the markets. The spring sun was peeping through the clouds, and they found a spot on the grassy town green that was safe from the wind.

'But from what I can see, things are looking up?' Connor prompted, shaking out a picnic rug. 'Have we lost you to the community station for good, Lauren? There're so many stories yet to cover. I thought you were just hitting your stride.'

Lauren looked around at the familiar faces strolling in and out of the market tents, wondering how many untold tales there were within the crowd today. How many great stories that would be perfect for radio, or the podcast she'd been pondering. 'It's not my forever home,' she said, 'but I'm not sure I'm ready to go back to Rural AM just yet.'

She thought about the group fitness sessions she'd started, to improve her physical strength alongside her mental strength. A smart woman would focus on the healing, getting match fit again before attempting to steer her life back on track. As she soaked up the sunshine with her best friend by her side, Lauren felt determined to do just that.

Jack wiped the last of the icing sugar off the bench that night, opened his laptop and pulled up the website for Lauren's community station. It was easy enough to find, and although the website indicated a crusty old man with a bowtie and waistcoat was currently on air, Lauren's voice filled the room. *Just as April had predicted.*

'If you recognise that song, you're going to love the next one,' Lauren announced. 'We're all about film, television and advertising soundtracks on the show tonight, and this next track, by Chopin, is just beautiful, and if you've binge-watched seasons five and six of *Lost*, then you might recognise it. Thanks to Sandie in Redgum River for the request, and remember you can call or text me your suggestions. If I can find it, and it fits with tonight's theme, I'll play it for you.'

He could hear the smile in Lauren's voice, and though he didn't recognise the composer's name or the title, he instantly recognised the piano music.

Jack divided the icing into three. He folded purple food dye through the first bowl of icing, green through another and left the other untinted. He referred back to the glossy photograph in the recipe book underneath the step-by-step instructions. It was a cake Harriet had earmarked after getting into skating.

Jack sculpted the cake into the shape of rollerskates, then started icing it, his ears pricking up as the piece of music ended and Lauren returned to the airwaves. She hadn't replied to yesterday's text about the clouds.

'Such a quiet night tonight,' Lauren said. 'I'd have thought movies and classical music would be a hot topic, but perhaps you're happy letting me choose the songs? Or maybe,' she paused, and Jack could picture the corners of her lips twitching, 'maybe you're piecing together a jigsaw or studying. I like imagining you out there, tuning in from your kitchens and your cars. Perhaps you're writing a bestseller while the rest of your household sleeps. Or painting. Oh, here's a message coming through.'

Jack could hear rustling as Lauren moved around in the studio. He scooped a drip of icing off the benchtop and dunked the sticky purple bowl in the sink.

'A big hello to Kym, an ex-pat tuning in via the website, all the way from Uruguay. She's requested "Clair de Lune", and says it was played in the *Twilight* movies.' Lauren laughed, and now Jack imagined her in the studio, twirling the cord of her headphones around her finger. 'Vampires and piano, not really a traditional pairing, but I'll see if I can find it. And a lovely note to say she's crocheting tonight, and grateful for the music and a familiar voice from home.'

What would he say if he were to call in? Or would he just text? He twisted the platter around to better access the bottom of the cake and slathered white icing onto the wheels.

The theme from *The Lone Ranger* came over the speakers next. Jack looked at the cake he was making for his niece. What was he grateful for tonight? A few months ago, he'd have said he was grateful for his family, for the cheeky Harriet who never failed to surprise him, for the friendships he had with his sister, aunt and grandfather. Grateful that his cousin Eamon had dropped by to see him, and although they'd missed one another this time, he was touched that Eamon had left him a note and promised to return soon. A few months ago he would've been grateful for the blonde-haired radio producer who brought sunshine into his life.

But now . . .

He swallowed and returned to the cake.

Soon the icing was done and the workspace was clean. Jack stared at his phone. He had nothing to lose by messaging Lauren, and his number wouldn't come up on the station phone, so she wouldn't necessarily know it was him. He typed out the message he'd mentally composed, sent it and returned to the rollerskate-shaped cake. Would she know it was him? Was it lame messaging anonymously when she hadn't replied to his text from yesterday?

Jack sliced liquorice straps into fine strips, using them to outline the cake and fashion the laces.

'Ah, and we've got a message from a listener who's grateful for good health. I don't know what they're doing tonight while they're listening or even their name, but I do know the area they're tuning in from. Thank you for your text, Penwarra listener,' she said, her voice softening. 'And your sentiment about things not being black and white struck quite a chord, if you'll excuse the pun. It's something I'm getting better at dealing with too.'

Wiping his sticky hands on the dishcloth, Jack sent another text.

And in addition to good health, I'm also grateful for good cake.

He snapped a quick picture of Harriet's cake and sent it with his message. It didn't look half as good in the photograph and the minute he hit send, he wished he'd cleared away the drips and smoothed out the lumpy bit where a chunk of cake crumbs had broken through the icing. He scrolled through the internet for ways to unsend a text message, Clem's words echoing through his head. *It's not easy living up to your perfect standards, Jack . . .*

He caught sight of his reflection in the dark window, set the phone down and turned the radio up.

What had started as a quiet night working on her birthday had quickly became a busy one, and Lauren felt the old adrenaline buzz as she scoured the music catalogue for the requested songs and read the messages. Perhaps it was the thrill of being offered a producer's job in Western Australia, researching the online podcasting workshops or making contact with Miriam and contemplating an eventual return to Warrnambool, but she found herself opening up more on air than usual. And, as it turned out, opening up had prompted more listeners to text in. Her mobile phone buzzed on the desk.

How's my favourite radio gal holding up? Connor's putting in a request for Swan Lake by Tchaikovsky. xx April

Lauren looked at the name and groaned. How on earth was she supposed to pronounce Tchaikovsky?

I'll try to find it, but tell Connor he could've chosen a composer without a tongue twister of a name! 😊 Good night here, it was crickets for the first hour but requests flooding in now. Was so great to see you, I'm savouring your cake BTW x

Lauren scooped another forkful of the hummingbird birthday cake April had made. Only twenty minutes left of the show and she found her toes tapping along to the jaunty piano music.

'Almost time to wrap up the show tonight folks, it's been great having your company. And one of our listeners has written back to say they're grateful for good health *and* good cake. It's my birthday today, so I'm fully onboard that train of thought.' She announced the next song and started gathering her belongings.

Her phone buzzed again, and a photo of a wonky purple-and-green rollerskate cake appeared on her screen.

It *was* Jack.

It's 90 per cent sugar and looks only vaguely like the glossy cookbook photo, but it'll do. Hope your birthday's been good.

Lauren was so busy smiling at the screen that she nearly missed the cues for the song ending. 'That was close,' she gasped, rolling over to the next track. She finished the show, locked up the station and paused in the doorway to tap out a text.

> Stephanie Alexander, eat your heart out. Harriet will love it. You're up late, and thanks for the update re Vic. He hasn't returned my calls these last few months, so not sure he'll take them now, but good to know things are going well for him. Assuming it's about the petition? Did they dismiss it at the council meeting?

Satisfied the message struck a balance between eager and aloof, Lauren hit send and returned the phone to her jacket pocket. Driving towards Penwarra in the drizzly rain, she felt like maybe—finally—things were getting back on track.

'This is the bestest cake ever, Uncle Jack,' Harriet said, pushing the princess crown back onto her head. It had been decorated by her classmates, many of whom would be descending on Sunny Cross Farm for the party in a few hours. 'Can I taste it?'

'Not until all your friends are here.' Jack laughed, looking around again.

Clem had tidied the farmhouse to gleaming, but it wasn't just the clutter and chaos that were tidied away. Just like the khaki LandCruiser that was noticeably absent from the driveway, there was no sign of Adam Dunkirk.

'Where's your dad?'

Harriet's shoulders fell and she blinked quickly, her voice small. 'He was too busy.'

'Oh, Harri.' He looked up to find Clem's eyes on his, and didn't do more than lift his eyebrows before her brow darkened.

'He's at a conference in Melbourne,' his sister snapped. 'And everything's just fine, thanks for asking.'

A conference on a Sunday?

Clem's belly had popped since he'd last seen her, and judging from the dark circles under her eyes, prepping for a big birthday party had tuckered her out. He smiled lightly, relieved that he wouldn't have to sidestep around Dunkirk's forced attempts at small talk.

'Fair enough,' Jack said. 'What time's Aunty Jean bringing Pop?'

After spending months living together, it still felt weird that Arthur and Harriet remained the neutral territory of their conversation, but Clem looked too exhausted to maintain a prickly aloofness and as she updated him on the day's proceedings, he kicked himself for not jumping in to help earlier. Especially if Dunkirk was going to be away the whole time.

Harriet returned with her haul of birthday presents—an armful of stuffed toys, a new jigsaw puzzle and her very own pack of Monopoly Deal cards.

'I can bring them when I come stay at your place, Uncle Jack?'

Clem and Jack looked at one another and he felt the tendrils of a truce stretching between them. 'Sounds great, Harri. Though now you've got all those presents, you probably don't want this then?' He produced a small gift bag.

Harriet pounced upon it eagerly but her little brow furrowed as she studied the gift. 'But we've already got gardening tools.'

Jack laughed. 'Your *mum* has tools, but they're not as snazzy as these ones. If you're planting sunflowers in summer, it'll be all hands on deck, shorty. You'll get a few good years out of that set,' he said, helping her open the child-sized gardening tools.

Harriet snapped the purple tool belt around her waist, slipped the fork and hand trowel into it and did a little jig. 'I can keep my lollies in here,' she said, beaming and opening the pocket flap. 'Maybe some frogs too. They're always hiding in the dirt near the garden.'

'Perhaps not frogs and lollies at the same time though,' he said with a wink, offering her a piggyback outside. Harriet skipped off in search of unsuspecting frogs.

Jack turned to his sister. 'You sure you're right to host a heap of seven-year-olds this afternoon?'

'Too late to cancel now,' Clem said. 'Aunty Jean's bringing the finger food at two, Archie is arriving with his stereo and bag of party tricks to entertain the kids for the hour and I've asked the other mums to stay, so if anyone gets unruly, they're on hand to intervene. We'll be fine.'

'This is chaos,' Jack said, laughing, an hour later, covering his ears as a dozen little girls crash tackled the piñata to the ground, high on sugar and birthday excitement. Archie Winklin's magic tricks and party games had gone down a treat, but even the boy was flagging by the time the festivities wrapped up.

'You've more than earned your pocket money,' Clem said, handing Archie his fee.

Arthur ambled across with his walking frame. 'I could have made a motza selling these earmuffs to the adults.' He grinned, tapping the noise-cancelling headphones that were now draped around his neck. 'Still, little miss was in her element, wasn't she? Worth it to see her in seventh heaven.'

Jack was pleased Dunkirk's absence hadn't ruined the party for Harriet.

Archie stayed for another hour to help with the clean-up, scoring him Clem's undevoted loyalty, the promise of word-of-mouth recommendations from Jean in her coffee van and hero status in the eyes of the birthday girl.

'Look at my rollerskating, Archie! Come see my presents! Teach me that disappearing coin trick, Arch!'

Jean unhooked a bunch of balloons from the porch railing and handed them to Jack. 'Looks like she's got a new idol, doesn't it? If all the singletons in the district looked at their suitors with half as much adoration as that, I'd be out of a job.'

'Beats me why you bother,' Jack said. 'Surely after all these years playing Cupid, you'd be sick of the drama?'

Harriet skated past them, hot on Archie's tail, begging for 'just one more' balloon shape.

'Ah,' Jean sighed, a wistful smile on her face. 'Everyone wants to be loved, but sometimes they just need a helping hand. And when you've been part of the magic, when all the stars align and you've made a good match, then it's all worth it. Speaking of which, I've heard there's a new librarian moving back to town, Hazel, I think her name is. And the dear Clarissa is single again and looking for love. Tell me when you're ready to put yourself out there and I'll suss them out.'

Jack zipped his jacket up and backed away with his hands up. 'Thanks but no thanks, Aunty Jean. I think I'm all out of luck there.'

'Pfft, that's hogwash, Jack. Look at your nan and pop. Married for sixty years. Your parents were a bad match right from the start, everyone could see that, and your first marriage didn't work out either, but there's plenty of time for you and Clem to find the right fit.'

'It's a little more complex than searching for a pair of shoes. Anyway, Clem's sorted.'

Jean lifted an eyebrow. 'Is she, though? Where was Adam Dunkirk when the wave of seven-year-olds stormed the property? Where's his birthday cake masterpiece? Has he picked Harriet up from school in the last few weeks or driven her to netball training?'

Jack looked across the yard, where Clem was scraping a plate of fairy bread, half-eaten chocolate crackles and fruit scraps to the chickens.

'I always knew he was a scumbag,' Arthur said, joining their group. As they watched, Clem yawned, rubbed the small of her back and then massaged the underside of her pregnant belly. 'Has she said anything to you?'

'Apparently he's interstate for work.'

'I know I'm just an old lady with time on her hands,' Jean said, 'but my coffee van roves this town all week long and I've not seen hide nor hair of him in yonks.'

'Good riddance,' Arthur barked. 'I can't say I'm surprised. She gave him more than he deserved with a second chance.'

Jack nodded. 'Poor Harriet must be pretty cut up about it too. But why would Clem make up a cock-and-bull excuse about a Melbourne conference?'

Jean rolled her eyes at both of them. 'I wonder,' she said drily. 'I'm sorry, Arthur, but these two are more like you than you'd care to admit. Stubborn as mules when it comes to saying sorry or admitting you were wrong.'

Jack's splutter came in unison with Arthur's objection. 'Steady on.'

Jean held up a hand. 'She went out on a limb. Last thing she wants to do is have you two waving it in her face. How's everything going with you and Lauren, Jack? Have you patched things up there?'

Jack opened his mouth but Jean ploughed on.

'But you know what you *are* good at?' She looped an arm through each of their elbows and pulled them close to her.

'Letting nosy relatives bulldoze their way over conversations?' Arthur said.

Jean ignored him. 'You're both good at second chances,' she said. 'Those lads you recruited to help clean up Vic's yard, Jack. Everyone in town was giving them curry for those nuisance issues, just like Kev Jenkins all those years ago, but instead of hunting them down and humiliating them, you gave them jobs they could get behind.

'And how about you, Art?' Jean said. 'You took Clem and Jack under your wing each time they messed up, and you left the door open for your son every time he went downhill. Not your fault he did what he did, or that your daughter-in-law chose the church over her family.'

The men were silent for a long moment, watching Clem help Harriet tie her laces.

Jack gouged a line into the timber verandah railing with his thumbnail. *Was Aunty Jean right?* Partly; he *was* ready to crack out the party poppers over Adam Dunkirk's possible departure, but what would that mean for Clem? He was ashamed that she couldn't face telling him. Was he really that focused on being right all the time?

'The jonquils are all finished,' Lauren said, tossing the pile of weeds into the bucket beside her and dusting the dirt from her knees. She hadn't planned to spend her Friday gardening, but when April had called around with dahlia tubers that needed planting, the afternoon had turned into an impromptu working bee. Out with the jonquils, in with the dahlias.

'I can't believe how much we've got done, there's barely a weed left in the front yard,' she continued, proudly surveying her front garden. 'And did you see the black hellebores Fiona gave me?'

'Stunning,' April said, admiring the flowers that ran up and down the path. 'I'll have to grab a few babies when they start self-seeding next year.'

They had just delivered the last wheelbarrow load to the compost heap and were sitting at the kitchen bench with a cuppa when the doorbell rang. Lauren looked at April, wondering if her best friend could hear her heart pounding in her chest.

April grinned. 'Is that Jack?' Somewhere between eradicating the onion weeds and mulching the roses, she'd loosened Lauren's defences and learned about the texts they'd exchanged since her birthday. Maybe he was as keen as her to see where things were at . . .

'He said he was flat strap at work, but maybe things have eased off?' Lauren craned her neck, but instead of Jack's tall frame, a woman's figure was silhouetted in the leadlight door panels.

'I'm heading off anyway,' April said, following Lauren down the hallway. 'Hey, Tahnee. You're looking mighty fine.'

'Don't look too closely, I've slopped coffee on my dress thanks to those wretched potholes by Coonalpyn,' she said, waving April goodbye before giving Lauren a hug.

'I thought you'd go straight to Eamon's hotel, or is he visiting the Crossleys?'

'Maybe I wanted to see my favourite sister first,' Tahnee said, stepping inside and handing over a gift bag. 'I'm getting used to this charming little cottage.'

It was on the tip of Lauren's tongue to remind Tahnee of all the times she'd bemoaned the lengthy drive from Adelaide, and hurried back to the city the moment she could.

'It's good to have you back so soon,' Lauren said instead, opening the gift Tahnee had brought with her. She pulled out a coral-coloured blouse that she'd complimented her on during her last visit. 'What's this?'

'That's the one you liked, right?' Tahnee smiled and gave a shrug. 'I've got too many clothes anyway. I thought you'd look good in it, maybe something fresh for your hot date? Or—' Tahnee tried to look casual '—your big meeting at the station? No pressure either way.'

Lauren opened her mouth, then shut it again, and remembered the counsellor's words. *Acknowledge the emotion, give it a name, then put it back on its shelf.*

With the kookaburras calling in the backyard, and the sound of violin practice coming from next door, Lauren took a moment.

'I'm calling in to see Paul on Monday,' she said, giving Tahnee a grateful smile, 'and perhaps we'll go from there? Starting the podcast has been a good side project too.'

'And you're feeling better?'

Lauren broke into a bright smile and nodded vigorously. 'Yep, absolutely,' she said, the assurances falling from her lips as easily as all the other white lies she'd told. *Really? You're playing that old song again?*

Feeling her cheeks flush as she recognised herself masking, Lauren tucked her hair behind her ear and met Tahnee's eye. 'Actually, that *might* be overstating it. But I'm working on a few things, and I'm in a better place than I was in March.'

There. She'd said it. And to her relief, Tahnee didn't jump in with advice, nor did she head straight to her phone to report back to their mother. There was no pity flooding her face.

'Good to hear,' Tahnee said simply, unzipping her suitcase and changing into a charcoal knit dress. 'We're behind you whatever way you decide to go, Lauren. Did you hear from Mum?'

Lauren nodded. She'd been dreading the call with Gabrielle, wary that the time between her mum's calls signalled a deep and unshakable hurt, but Gabrielle had listened, and to Lauren's surprise, apologised.

'She's trying, Lauren,' Tahnee said, closing the suitcase, then reopening it and swapping her heels for a pair of scratch- and scuff-free R.M. Williams boots.

'Do you really think she's capable of easing off the pressure, though? I know she means well, but you know what she's like.

'If the radio station gives me back the producer's role, Mum will wonder when I'll get promoted to show host. If I make show host, she'll be asking when I'm an editor. I think she cried for a day when I told her I wasn't calling the media contacts Bunny had shared.'

'I think she's planning to *try*,' Tahnee said.

Lauren watched her sister drive off, wondering if Gabrielle was also doing her best to give Tahnee the space to make her own decisions too. She sure hoped so.

She loaded the fire with wood and settled back down on the couch. The podcasting platforms had been pretty easy to get the hang of, given her experience with the radio tech gear, but there was still plenty to learn about uploading episodes, transcripts and the multitude of listening platforms.

Pen and notepad in hand, she pressed play and Ruby McInnes's faint American accent came through the laptop speakers. It was the third episode to go to air, and judging from the ratings and downloads, the story had struck a chord with listeners.

27

Jack joined the queue of parents outside the school gates, jingling the change in his pocket as he waited for the teachers to shepherd each child to the relevant carer.

Harriet was past the gate supervisor's side in a jiffy, running headlong into Jack's arms.

'Did Mum have the baby? Is she cute? Is Dad meeting us there? What are we calling her, Uncle Jack?'

Jack slung her backpack over his shoulder and ruffled Harriet's curly hair. 'All I know is that your mum's up and at 'em and the baby's got almost as much hair as you, Harri. The rest we'll find out when we get there.'

They spent the drive to the hospital brainstorming baby names. Harriet exploded out of the car and raced across the car park, stopping only at the small kiosk to choose a bright purple teddy bear for her new sister.

There was no sign of Adam Dunkirk, and any lingering awkwardness between the siblings faded away when Jack saw Clem with the baby.

'She's so cuuuuu-te,' Harriet crooned, peering into the bundle of blankets. 'But she definitely doesn't look like she should be called Jackie, does she, Mum?'

Clem looked at Jack, a smile on her face. 'I'm guessing that was Uncle Jack's suggestion? I'm thinking Lily, or maybe Indi. What do you think?'

Jack took a closer look at the baby, with her thick mop of hair, the little nose that was one hundred per cent Crossley and the indignant red face that reminded him of both Clem and Harriet when they were upset. He touched her soft, warm skin, and at Clem's urging, carried the baby to her proud big sister. She was lighter than he remembered Harriet ever being, and smelled like Johnson & Johnson's baby wash.

'I think she looks like an Indi,' Harriet said, shuffling back on the vinyl armchair and gazing at the bundle in her arms. With her name settled, Harriet told her new little sister all about the size and colour of her rollerskates, the bedroom they'd be sharing and their home at Sunny Cross Farm.

'And Uncle Jack lives in town too, and him and Mum and me are going to plant a gazillion sunflowers next month. I don't think you'll be old enough to help but maybe Uncle Jack can carry you in his special backpack, like he used to do for me until I growed out of it. And we kind of have a dad but he lives in the city a lot of the time now. Don't worry, Indi, he wasn't very good at Scrabble or tea parties anyway and now we can sneak into Mum's bed all the time.'

Harriet kept chattering away to her little sister, oblivious to the look that her mother and her uncle exchanged. Jack felt his eyes watering as Harriet continued, detailing all the fun things they did as a family. It looked like the commentary was having an equally poignant impact on Clem. She wiped her eyes before reaching for his hand.

'Thanks for coming, Jack, and I'm sorry about what I said. I was angry, and you were bloody well right about Adam. I've been kicking myself ever since. I don't know what I'd do without you,' she said, quickly correcting herself. 'What *we'd* do, I mean. You've put your life on hold and I'll never stop appreciating that.'

He looked from his sister to his nieces, feeling choked up as he shook his head. 'I wouldn't trade it for the world, but you've gotta know, it doesn't give me any joy to be right about that bastard. I want you and Harriet to be happy, even if it meant watching you go out with a bloke like Dunkirk. I never want you to think my suggestions trump your choices.'

She shook her head, squeezing his arm. 'I can't believe I went to war on that topic. I've gone over it a million times in my head ever since. I won't—no, I can't—go back to Adam again. I called him last week when the doctor set the date for the C-section, and gave him one last chance, but—surprise, surprise—he's not here.'

Jack looked from his nieces to his sister. Dunkirk had no idea what he was missing out on.

'Pop said you thought about leaving,' Clem said softly.

Jack shook his head. 'For all of about two minutes. I want to support you, Clem. And Harri and Indi. Really, I do,' he said, knowing that finally, he really did.

'It's got to be a two-way street, Jack. You don't have to carry the weight of this family all on your own. And you have to promise me that you'll open yourself up to love. I know it sounds crazy, going back for seconds after I was so sick and then letting Adam back in only to have him ditch me all over again, but I don't regret it.'

Jack didn't know much about caesarians, but for someone who'd given birth just hours ago, Clem showed no sign of fatigue. 'Let's talk about this later,' he said. 'You must be knackered.'

Clem propped herself up on an elbow to look at her two girls, Indi swaddled in Harriet's arms, then turned back to Jack. She grinned. 'I am, but I'm not. This adrenaline won't wear off for hours. If Harriet's birth was anything to go by, I'll still be wide awake at 3 am.'

Again, Jack felt out of his depth. Clem's post-natal troubles had stemmed from lack of sleep, hadn't they? 'Isn't that a red flag? I should let you sleep.'

Clem laughed. 'My problem was weeks and months of poor sleep, plus the unknown of being a new mother. Don't worry, I've got the warning signs written down, and I know what I'm doing this time. I can make you a copy too, so you know what to look out for.'

A cart rolled down the hallway and stopped at the door. 'Cup of tea, love? Bikkie?'

Clem said yes to both, and the moment the tea lady left, she picked up the conversation where she'd left off.

'You know that Lauren's got her own troubles too?'

Jack was confused. 'What's that?'

'You're a daft twit, sometimes. After she blurted out Vic's issues, she explained why she was so offended by the mayor's glib comments, and how it wasn't her first panic attack. You didn't see the article she wrote about mental health?'

He shook his head. Could he really have missed something that crucial?

Clem pulled up an article on her phone, an opinion piece for the *Advertiser* that Lauren had written. And as he looked at his sister and his nieces, then back at the screen in front of him, he realised just how strong the women in his life really were. All these years he'd been so focused on avoiding hurt and thinking he didn't deserve love. But maybe true strength lay in handling what came your way, then dusting yourself off and trying again.

'I've sent Lauren a few texts,' Jack admitted.

'Messages?' Clem snorted out a laugh. 'If you're serious, just call her. Messages don't convey tone and you're pretty stiff and guarded at the best of times. I can only imagine how cold the texts are.' She held up her hands, her smile softening. 'But don't do it because someone else is telling you to. Do it because you want to, Jack. Because you can't go another week without her in your life.'

With the sound of beeping monitors and crying babies in the background, Jack stepped into the hallway and pulled out his phone.

Lauren felt her feet moving faster as the Penwarra oval came into view, and it took all of her self-control not to break into a run and launch herself into Jack's arms, like she'd seen Harriet do a dozen times before, the moment she spotted him.

Harriet caught up with her on the final stretch.

'Hi, Lauren! Did you bring Gary with you?'

Lauren laughed. 'He'd fly away if I took him outside, Harriet. And I can't imagine he'd survive long without his almonds and Iced VoVos, can you?'

Harriet giggled and put a finger to her lips. 'Don't tell all the other birds, or they'll be pecking at your windows and doors for their bikkies.'

There were plenty of puddles on the track around the football field, and judging by the splattered streaks running down the back of Harriet's jacket, she'd pedalled straight through each and every one of them.

'I thought you were ditching those training wheels?'

'In a minute,' puffed Harriet, her little legs pumping. She gritted her teeth in determination. 'This is just my warm-up.'

They were both puffing by the time they reached Jack, whose smile broadened as they got closer. Lauren stopped a few steps away, awkward now. She wanted to loop her arms around his neck, check that her body still moulded to his like it used to, but uncertainty held her back. As anxiety shimmered and stirred, Lauren took a deep breath, accepting the discomfort. *I see you, I feel you, but I'm sticking it out anyway.*

She shoved her hands into her pockets to stop them reaching for him. 'I've missed you, Jack.'

'Me too,' he said, folding his arms, then unfolding them. 'Do you know how many times I drove down Petticoat Lane, almost willing someone to push over your pot plants or throw rocks on your roof, just so I had a legitimate excuse to see you again?'

She took a step closer, then another, until they were nearly touching.

He smells just the same, he's as handsome as ever ... A shot of happiness surged through her body as she rested a hand on his chest, and from the steady beat of his heart, she realised he was just as nervous and every bit as happy to see her as she was him.

'Uncle Jack, I'm ready!'

They sprang apart as Harriet hurled herself between them, all bike helmet and elbow pads and possessing as much subtlety as a Labrador puppy.

'You're supposed to be taking the training wheels off, Uncle Jack. You promised, and you said a real man always keeps his promises.'

Jack put a hand on the little girl's shoulders. 'That's true,' he said. 'But a good bloke also knows when to apologise and

I've left it way too long to say sorry to Lauren in person. How about this?' He pulled two shifting spanners from the back pocket of his jeans and crouched in front of his niece. 'Remember how to use a shifting spanner?'

Harriet nodded.

'We need them the right size for loosening those nuts there.' He showed her where the training wheels were fastened to the bike. 'You get the spanners ready and I'll make amends with Lauren.'

Lauren felt the nervous fizzing again as Jack closed the gap and laced his fingers through hers, sharing his warmth. He'd phoned the radio show several more times this week, his voice low and sexy as hell while driving sleeping baby Indi across the countryside, but it was nothing compared to talking face to face.

His eyes searched hers. 'I really am sorry, Lauren. I should've cut you more slack. I overreacted.'

Lauren shook her head, squeezing his hand back and blinking furiously to contain the tears that threatened to spill. 'You're not the only one at fault,' she said, her voice cracking. *Hold it together. Don't cry.* 'I'm sorry too. Can we try again?'

His nod was the tipping point and Lauren covered her eyes before turning away. *Stop being a sooky-la-la. Chin up, buttercup.*

She felt Jack's warm hands on her waist as he gently turned her back to face him.

'I don't know why I'm crying,' she hiccupped, swiping her tears and ducking her head. 'I'm sorry.' *God, how embarrassing. Enough with the waterworks already.* But as much as she willed her sobs to stop, they kept coming.

'You have nothing to be sorry for, Lauren,' Jack whispered, ducking his head to hers and kissing away the tears before pulling her in closer.

Lauren pressed her face into the warmth of his embrace. Then she lifted her lips to his and brought her arms around his neck, her fingertips finding the velvety cropped hair at the nape of his neck.

The sounds of Harriet hopping from foot to foot, then rocking the bike back and forth, interrupted the moment and put a stop to the tears.

'Are you sad, Lauren?'

Lauren shrugged, eyes glistening. 'Kinda sad but also really happy to be here. And you know what would make me even happier?'

Harriet beamed up at her and Jack laced his fingers through hers again.

'Watching you ride that bike on two wheels.'

Together they removed the training wheels and, with Jack's guiding hand on her back, Harriet was off and riding.

Clapping wildly, Lauren turned at the sound of gravel crunching under a different set of wheels and found Clem with Indi in the pram beside her.

'Oh, Clem! Congratulations on little Indi. She'll have a mighty task keeping up with that little speedster over there,' Lauren said.

'This little sleep-thief hasn't quite worked out day and night,' Clem said, pulling Lauren into a one-armed hug. 'But when she does, we'll have to have you over for dinner.'

'I'd love that,' Lauren said, watching Clem shuffle things in the bottom of the pram until she eventually produced a milk-filled bottle. She unzipped the pram's rain cover.

Lauren's breath caught in her throat as Clem lifted the baby out of the pram and she saw Indi's milky skin and thick head of hair. 'She's even more divine than in the photos,' she murmured.

'Good genetics,' Clem said with a wink, nestling the baby into her arms. Indi drank greedily from the bottle, her mitten-covered hands scrambling around, while across the other side of the footy oval, Jack was helping Harriet off the ground. They both watched as he brushed off her knees, wiped her cheeks and patted her shoulder, before holding the bike steady for her to climb on again.

'I'm glad you're back, Lauren. And not just for Jack's sake. The radio's not the same without you and we need a journo with a good investigative eye around here. Did you read that report on the property stakeholders trying to fudge numbers in the annual cockatoo count?'

Lauren nodded, stroking Indi's hair. It was a cross between satin and velvet, and just as black as Clem's, Harriet's and Jack's. 'I'm just a producer, but I'll definitely look into it,' she said. She looked up to see Clem holding back a smile.

'For a producer, you've sure got a nose for news. And I love the podcast you made about the war bride. I never got to meet Ruby, but I feel I know her through your episodes.'

Lauren beamed. Of all the projects she'd ticked off her to-do list, launching the podcast was the one she was most proud of. 'Hearing someone speak so honestly about the challenges they've overcome, the highs and lows, the risks that paid off and those that didn't, really puts things in perspective. It's Ruby's story, I'm just the one lucky enough to help tell it.'

Clem adjusted her grip on baby Indi and lifted the bottle. 'I've been thinking about doing something similar.'

'Really? I didn't know you were into podcasts?'

'Well, not making one myself, more like sharing my story. I've listened to plenty of them, and they've helped me on topics I've found difficult. We don't know what we don't know, right?' Clem said. 'If just one new parent doesn't have to go through what I did, or it helps one family know what signs to look out for and saves the life of a new mum or a baby, then it's worth it.'

She's so darn brave. From Jack's updates, Lauren knew Clem had shown no signs of relapsing since Indi's arrival, but they would both be on high alert for at least another month or two, until the most dangerous post-natal period had passed.

'I'd love to be the one to tell that story, Clem, if and when you feel ready to share it. And you know what? Podcasting goes completely against the grain of what I've been taught to do on radio. Instead of shying away from delicate topics and watching the clock to ensure guests don't waffle on, podcasts dive deep, and conversations can be as long as you like. And the more we talk about the tough things, the less the stigma for the next person to walk those dark roads.'

'I've been trying to get Jack to listen to a few—there's a whole bunch of stuff he's avoided dealing with—but he's not quite there yet. Has he ever told you about our parents?'

Lauren shook her head. 'Not yet,' she said, but as she watched Jack jogging towards them, his smile just as wide as Harriet's, she felt confident the day would come when he'd feel comfortable enough to do so.

Jack swam the last of his laps at a burning pace, delighted to see Lauren's orange swimming cap as she set the pace. How had he ever thought their relationship wasn't worth trying to save? Why had he spent such a long time with his head in the sand, so certain that Lauren would let him down, or that she'd be unable to handle the skeletons in his closet?

The black line on the bottom of the pool finished. He glided, letting his momentum take him the final length, and turned to see Lauren's fingers graze the edge just moments before his.

He broke the surface of the water, gasping for breath, the silly smile on his face hindering his ability to get the oxygen he needed. *This*, he told himself, *this is what's important. Not the what ifs, not trying to write a spreadsheet of pros and cons or a formula to calculate the risks of getting hurt.*

All he could focus on was the here and now. And as he looked from Lauren's goggle-rimmed eyes, red cheeks and triumphant smile to the clouds of steam coming off the heated pool and the sunrise that was painting the town of Penwarra in pinks and oranges, he knew he was a bloody lucky guy.

'I don't know what you reckon, but I think I just whipped your butt,' Lauren said, folding her arms above her head and leaning back into a shoulder stretch. 'So it looks like you're cooking Sunday breakfast.'

He tossed his goggles onto the concrete edge, did a quick check to confirm the lifeguard was still concentrating on collecting water samples at the far end and ducked under the lane divider. Lauren threaded her hands behind his neck in the way that always felt so good and wrapped her legs around his waist.

'Remember that night in Langhorne Creek? We could always skip the shower here, take a quick stroll down memory lane when we get back to my place and *then* have scrambled eggs?'

Jack kissed her, nipping her bottom lip gently, then disentangled himself before the poor lifeguard got more than he'd bargained for. 'Lead the way, m'lady,' he said, hoisting himself from the water. He followed Lauren, wrapped in one of his beach towels, to the car park.

'You know, if you joined me at the triathlon event, you'd have your own triathlon towel,' he said. 'It's for a great cause.'

He smiled as he drove. He'd signed up for the Victor Harbor Triathlon on a whim, and while it had been easy to nominate

MAYA LINNELL

his fundraising charity, he hadn't had any luck convincing Lauren to join him. Yet.

'I'm still thinking about it,' she said, twisting in her seat to fix him with one of those gorgeous smiles. 'And that reminds me. Our support team t-shirts are at the post office. I ordered them in several sizes, so there're plenty for the crew and if the sizing runs small and makes me look like a sausage, then Harriet can wear mine as a dress.'

'You'd look good in a hessian sack,' Jack said, forcing his eyes off the damp hoodie that clung to her curves and back onto the road, thanking the universe once again for putting Lauren directly in his path.

His phone rang as they pulled up in the driveway.

'Hey, Pop, everything okay?'

Jack passed the house keys to Lauren and switched the phone to the other ear, keeping his answers short.

'Yep. Tell him we'll be there at ten,' Jack said, avoiding Lauren's curious smile.

'I thought we were having a slow Sunday morning?' she teased. 'Duty calls?'

'You'll see,' Jack grinned, as he led the way to the bathroom.

True to his word, when they eventually emerged from the shower clean, warm and sated, Jack pulled together the fixings for a breakfast, albeit a more streamlined affair than he'd originally planned. He sloshed a dash of vinegar into the pot of simmering water and cracked an egg into a soup ladle propped on the bench.

'Anything I can do?' Lauren asked as he carefully lowered the ladle into the water.

He nodded to the toaster. 'Once I've got all the eggs in the water, can you get the toast on? And do we have enough basil on the windowsill?' *We . . .* How easily it rolled off his tongue these days.

'Sure do,' Lauren said, carrying a pair of scissors to the self-watering pot she'd given him. The basil plant was only tiny, but it was otherwise a carbon copy of the windowsill box in her cottage.

As he watched Lauren harvesting the herbs, Jack felt a surge of love so ferocious it almost scared him.

Jack buttered the toast, then drained the poached eggs with a slotted spoon and sat one on top of each slice of toast. He topped them both with avocado, basil and tomato and sprinkled chilli flakes on his own before taking the plates to the tiny dining table.

'Divine,' Lauren said, tasting a mouthful. 'So, how's Art been? Did I tell you he ordered a triathlon support team t-shirt *and* two hats? Do you think he really wanted two or was it a typo?'

'You can ask him yourself,' Jack said. 'We're picking him up on the way.'

Jack had enjoyed keeping their destination a surprise but when he spotted Lauren's stricken look as he helped his grandfather out of the car at Victor's house, he wondered if maybe he'd made a big mistake.

Lauren gulped down her unease as she stared at the brick home. It had been months since she'd been down Wallaby Lane to Sunny Cross Farm, and even longer since she'd clapped eyes on Victor's property, but instead of marvelling at the cleared paddocks or the massive eagle sculpture Jack had made from scrap metal, all she could see was risk.

Jack opened her car door and leaned in close. 'You okay?'

Lauren nodded, then stopped and shook her head. 'Um, I know in theory that Vic accepted my apology and he's moved on, but all I can think of right now is him hanging up on me and refusing to accept the apple pie I baked him. What if he's still angry about the radio thing? What if—' *I see you, fear. I feel you, I'm going ahead anyway.*

Arthur turned his walking frame around and sat down, and instead of chipping in with advice or reassuring her, Jack squeezed her hand, walked to the other side of the car and slid into the back seat beside her.

She wasn't sure how long it was until the fight or flight instinct died down, but when she'd got her breathing under control and run through a dozen scenarios of how this meeting could go, she fixed her attention on Jack.

'What if Vic only accepted my apology to make me feel better, but really he hates my guts?'

'I think he's over all that, and there's this wallaby, you see,' Jack said, his voice uncharacteristically uncertain. 'But if you don't feel up to it, I can go in with just Pop and Harriet. No pressure at all, only if you're up for it. Or we can stay here a little longer.'

Arthur leaned in towards the car, pulling his beanie lower over his ears. 'Ready when you are, love, or I can go in with the girls.'

Lauren looked at the man she loved and his family, who had somehow slipped into the yard without Lauren noticing. She nodded, her mind made up. *Worst-case scenario, Vic will slam the door in my face and tell me to nick off.*

'Best-case scenario,' Jack murmured, more attuned to her mental checklist than she'd given him credit for, 'you get to meet Vic's son, Kev, and receive a queen's welcome for inadvertently bringing them back together while Harri falls in love with a joey.'

Victor was waiting for them on his front porch by the time they all traipsed down the driveway, a small joey nestled in the crook of his arm. 'He's just had his supper,' he said, removing the teat from its mouth. The animal promptly replaced the teat with a clawed paw.

'It's sucking its thumb,' Harriet gasped, peering in for a closer look.

'They have forepaws, not thumbs,' said Victor. 'Lucky we'll have you around to teach him some better habits.'

Harriet reeled around, her eyes dancing with delight. 'Is it for me? Do I get to keep it?'

Lauren looked at Jack, who lifted a shoulder. 'Maybe "keep" isn't the right word, but we can help raise him until he's old enough to fend for himself at the wildlife sanctuary. I've got the permits sorted and it just so happens that Sebastian and his folks needed some extra carers. Think we can manage that?'

Harriet nodded emphatically, her little hand latching onto Lauren's. 'Yep!'

'Good to hear, otherwise we were going to be looking after two,' said Victor, handing Harriet the wallaby. He gave Lauren a wink as he did so and she finally felt her shoulders relax.

A tall man appeared in the doorway with an even smaller joey in his arms. He didn't look a thing like Victor, and was tall and lean where Victor was short and heavy-set, but there was no mistaking the trademark ears that Arthur had mentioned on the car ride over.

'Kev's just put in for a job at the sawmill, so you'll be seeing more of him over the next few months,' Victor said after the introductions. 'And it's all thanks to you, Lauren. If you hadn't gone ballistic on air, and your sister hadn't looked through his records and tracked him down, then he mightn't have found his way home again. And I've heard you Bickford girls had a role in getting that community petition dropped too.'

A lump formed in Lauren's throat as Victor stood next to his son. Tahnee had been a sounding board for her frustrations over the last few months, and while she'd mentioned looking into Victor's situation, she hadn't given Lauren any specifics. She certainly hadn't mentioned playing a starring role in Kev's return.

Had Tahnee really done that for Victor? For her?

'It's true,' Kev said, smoothing his hair behind his generous ears.

'Now this wallaby needs a bit more attention,' Victor said. 'And given you've got a newborn on your side of the fence, I figured we'd keep the neediest one. This here's Marvin.' He revealed an almost furless little face. 'He was a hungry bugger when they found him on the roadside. Seb named him Starvin' Marvin but I think Marvin's a bit more dignified. What about your one?'

Harriet rocked the joey from side to side, the same way Clem did with Indi, studying the joey. 'Maybe we could call him Jigsaw, because Mum loves jigsaws.'

Lauren was impressed with Harriet's suggestion. She'd expected something like Fluffy or Princess Sunshine. 'Or Scrabble,' Lauren offered quietly, thinking of the games she'd played with Jack over the year, and the many games ahead she hoped to play with Clem and Harriet.

Harriet nodded. 'Scrabble is a fantabulous name!'

Lauren wasn't sure what the future held for her career wise, but watching the Crossleys with the wallaby, and the reunited father and son on the front porch of a property that had nearly been condemned, she knew she was right where she was supposed to be.

Acknowledgements

Every time I get to the end of a book, and start writing acknowledgements, I'm humbled by the generosity of the people who helped create the story you're reading today.

The first thanks must always go to you, my readers, for picking up this novel, spreading the word, celebrating the characters and immersing yourself in their fictional world. I love that you get super excited about these stories. Your photos, messages and enthusiasm always make me smile. I also love seeing you at events and appreciate you coming out (often in the middle of winter) to my author talks.

Thanks to the dream team at Allen & Unwin, especially Annette, Samantha, Bella, Isabelle, Jenn, Shannon, Rosie, Sandra, Tom, Odette, Matt and Andrew, and freelancers Nada, Kylie and Megan. It's a pleasure working with you.

To the booksellers, reviewers, bloggers, librarians, Q&A hosts, Instagrammers, newsletter and Facebook communities—mwah! Your support in sharing my novels and flying the Maya Linnell flag is brilliant.

I couldn't do this writing gig without the blessing of my family, so big thanks again to Jase, Charlie, Amelia and

Elizabeth for brainstorming ideas, book names, character dilemmas, subplots, joining me on book tours, cheering me on when I'm in the drafting trenches and propping me up when the words don't flow. I couldn't be prouder or luckier to have you in my corner. Ditto for team Linnell. I'm so grateful to have unfailing support, excitement and enthusiasm from my parents, siblings and their families every step of the way.

Friends play a big role in dragging me away from the keyboard. My weekly ocean swimming group deserve a big shout out, plus Karena for all the early-morning walking and talking and brainstorming, and the lovely librarians from the Portland Library for letting me squirrel myself and my laptop away in the sunniest corner of the library on deadline. Many thanks to Kaneana May, Fiona Lowe and the Not So Solitary Scribes writing group, legal superstar Penelope Janu, plus one of my oldest friends, Kym, for helping me get the story straight in my head.

While this story is a figment of my imagination, and all mistakes are totally my own, many aspects of this story are richer because they're rooted in fact or sprinkled with snippets of reality.

You'll notice mental health plays a key role in this story. I called on my experience with post-natal psychosis to form Clem's back story. If, like me pre-2008, you've never heard of post-natal psychosis (or post-partum psychosis as it's called internationally), please look it up. Knowing what this illness looks like might just save the life of your daughter, sister, neighbour, daughter-in-law, granddaughter, niece or friend. I'm one of the lucky ones who survived this devastating and completely unexpected illness, with a wonderful husband and family by my side.

Sixteen years later, PNP is still the scariest and most dangerous thing I've ever experienced. It affects 1 in 1000 new mums every year and can have horrific consequences if it's not picked up and managed early.

Hearing about a friend of a friend who didn't survive this illness last year made me determined to shed a light on it in *Wallaby Lane*. If any of these issues raise warning bells, please know Lifeline, Beyond Blue and PANDA are only a phone call away.

Thanks to Narelle and Allan from Duck-A-Roo Wildlife Sanctuary for explaining some of the pressures, joys and predicaments in caring for orphaned and injured native animals; Lisa and Sarah from GSC and NGSC for local laws information; Jarrod and Ashlee Anderson for always answering my calls about police-related questions; superstar Kate Jackson, for reading one of the last drafts with an eye for policing protocol; Alissa Callen for the beautiful cover endorsement; my dad, Bruce, for the greasy pig and pickled hydatids cyst show day memories; the readers who suggested show day dramas; Rebekah Lowe for teaching me the radio ropes back in 2001, and helping me finesse Lauren's workdays.

A huge thanks to Sarah Walker for being the spreadsheet whiz and character tracker I've always dreamed of, for putting every character I've ever written into the one document. Mind! Blown!

My American war bride Ruby McInnes is fictional, but she was inspired by real-life Aussie war bride Ruth Frost. I was fascinated by the war-bride movement as a young cadet journalist, back in the early 2000s, when I read excerpts from Ruth's memoir, 'From Pavlova to Popcorn', which were serialised in a small SA country newspaper. I also borrowed the title and used it for Ruth's memoir to honour the plucky young lady I read about twenty years ago, who has since passed away.

The recycled metal sculpture subplot was inspired by WA artist Jordan Sprigg. If you're on social media, check out his amazing sculptures @jordanspriggsculptures and think of Jack in his grandfather's shed, channelling his frustrations into beautiful artwork.

Thanks also to the Coonawarra Vignerons Association. This story may be set in the fictional town of Penwarra, but if you like my fictional setting, then you must go to Penola and Coonawarra, where the wine is wonderful and the welcome is always warm.

Despite all these fabulous helpers, I take complete responsibility for all errors and admit to fudging some timelines and scenarios to better suit my story. I know solo police stations rarely have admin support, different police stations have different approaches to community service parameters and radio stations don't operate exactly the way I've depicted in Lauren's workplace.

Thank you for stretching your imagination to accommodate my storytelling, I hope you've enjoyed Lauren and Jack's story. If so, please tell a friend and watch out for the next story in winter 2025.

Love,

Maya

Fiction
with heart

Craving more heartwarming tales from the countryside? Join our online rural fiction community, **FICTION** *with* **HEART**, where you'll discover a treasure trove of similar books that will capture your imagination and warm your soul.

Visit **fictionwithheart.com.au** or scan the QR code below to access exclusive content from our authors, stay updated on upcoming events, participate in exciting competitions and much more.

See you there!

A&U